W

It's on a quiet street in the charming _____ of Cape May, New Jersey. Built in the late 1850s as a rooming house by the enigmatic Nicholas Abbadon, the Inn has been used over the years as a brothel, a restaurant, a speakeasy . . . and more.

SETTLE IN.

It has withstood war, fire, and flood. It has survived the suspicions about the guests who died there and owners who disappeared, the rumors about what went on behind the closed doors of the third floor, and the whispers about Abbadon and his mysterious female companion.

Abandoned and vacant for years, it's ready for renovation. But as a new generation is about to discover, the Abbadon Inn has never really been empty at all. . . .

ENJOY YOUR STAY.

TWISTED BRANCH

A Novel of the Abbadon Inn

Chris Blaine

BERKLEY BOOKS, NEW YORK

THE BERKLEY PUBLISHING GROUP
Published by the Penguin Group
Penguin Group (USA) Inc.
375 Hudson Street, New York, New York 10014, USA

Penguin Group (Canada), 90 Eglinton Avenue East, Suite 700, Toronto, Ontario M4P 2Y3, Canada
(a division of Pearson Penguin Canada Inc.)
Penguin Books Ltd., 80 Strand, London WC2R 0RL, England
Penguin Group Ireland, 25 St. Stephen's Green, Dublin 2, Ireland (a division of Penguin Books Ltd.)
Penguin Group (Australia), 250 Camberwell Road, Camberwell, Victoria 3124, Australia
(a division of Pearson Australia Group Pty. Ltd.)
Penguin Books India Pvt. Ltd., 11 Community Centre, Panchsheel Park, New Delhi—110 017, India
Penguin Group (NZ), Cnr. Airborne and Rosedale Roads, Albany, Auckland 1310, New Zealand
(a division of Pearson New Zealand Ltd.)
Penguin Books (South Africa) (Pty.) Ltd., 24 Sturdee Avenue, Rosebank, Johannesburg 2196,
South Africa

Penguin Books Ltd., Registered Offices: 80 Strand, London WC2R 0RL, England

This is a work of fiction. Names, characters, places, and incidents either are the product of the author's
imagination or are used fictitiously, and any resemblance to actual persons, living or dead, business
establishments, events, or locales is entirely coincidental. The publisher does not have any control over
and does not assume any responsibility for author or third-party websites or their content.

TWISTED BRANCH

A Berkley Book / published by arrangement with the author

PRINTING HISTORY
Berkley mass-market edition / September 2005

Copyright © 2005 by The Berkley Publishing Group.
Cover design by Steven Ferlauto.
Interior art by Cortney Skinner.
Interior text design by Kristin del Rosario.

ISBN: 0-425-20524-X

BERKLEY®
Berkley Books are published by The Berkley Publishing Group,
a division of Penguin Group (USA) Inc.,
375 Hudson Street, New York, New York 10014.
BERKLEY is a registered trademark of Penguin Group (USA) Inc.
The "B" design is a trademark belonging to Penguin Group (USA) Inc.

PRINTED IN THE UNITED STATES OF AMERICA

10 9 8 7 6 5 4 3 2 1

Many thanks to Susan Crossan, teacher and fellow writer, for her willingness to answer a lot of my pesky Cape May questions, to Brian McEwing and J. Fred Coldren of the Cape May–Lewes Ferry for help with 1978 details, to Ginjer Buchanan for coming up with such a great idea for a haunted series, to Cortney Skinner for his constant encouragement, and to Elizabeth Massie for her behind-the-scenes assistance.

ONE

MARCH 1978

Carl Morrison dragged the shard of glass across his skinny forearm, pressing down hard, watching as the flesh parted in a pulpy pout then released a thick drool of bright blood. The warm fluid rolled across his skin toward his elbow, plipped onto the windowsill and fell to the floor. It hurt, but in a grand way: powerful, unrelenting. Carl was strong. He was in charge.

Three floors below him, just beyond the newly shingled first-floor porch roof, two workmen in heavy coats were busy in the yard. Carl's breath fogged the gritty glass as he looked down at them. His temples pounded in rapid, electric pulses.

"Nnnnnnnn," Carl intoned softly through his teeth as he glared at the workmen. "Nnnnnnn." One of the men looked up and about, then slapped at his neck as if something had stung him there. There was no fly, no bee. It was Carl.

Nnnnnnnnn.

Carl tied one of his father's socks around his arm to stop the bleeding. He rolled his sweater sleeve down over the sock. The blood oozed through the sweater, leaving a near-black spot, but then stopped flowing. He would wash the sweater and sock out in the sink later; his mother would never know. Carl picked up the block of wood he'd brought upstairs with him, a splintery piece about a foot long, one of a gazillion discarded in the backyard by the men who had renovated the kitchen. Carl had driven countless nails most of the way in on all four of the block's sides. It looked like a porcupine with short, silvery, flat-headed quills.

Nnnnnnnnn . . .

He hated this place, this enormous, ancient inn. His parents had brought him here against his will. They didn't care that he was away from everything he had ever known. Not that he'd liked Connecticut much. Not that he'd had any friends there. It didn't matter. He'd grown up in his Danbury home. He'd had a bedroom that he'd made his own with posters, models, games he played by himself, and the secret stash of books he had stolen from the magic shop. The posters, models, comics, and games were gone now, charred chunks in the Danbury landfill.

"Honey, you're thirteen," his mother had said nervously when Carl had caught her hauling a box load from his bedroom to the garage. "You've outgrown these things. What is this here, a *Voyage to the Bottom of the Sea* game? We gave that to you two years ago. Speed Burners? A bunch of, what are these, Hot Wheels?" Her fingernail flicked at items in the box. "These are a child's toys."

Carl had eyed her, hands in his jeans pockets, unblinking. It was clear his mother felt the rage behind the blank expression.

She continued, speaking a bit faster now, "Moving to Cape May is a new start for all of us. Maybe you'd want to try to go to school there? A new school, with new students and new teachers?" Each of his mother's sentences came across as a question; her voice rose and twisted nervously on each final word. "You can do things teenagers do. Hang out on the shore when the weather is good. Play Frisbee, volleyball. Maybe we can get you a dog. I know you miss Tippy."

Carl said nothing. He took his hands from his pockets and crossed his arms over his chest. He stared at his mother. For the last few months she had been shapeshifting into the hippie she'd never been allowed to be ten years earlier. Her hair, which she had started to grow ever since Mitchell declared himself retired, had become a fuzzy, brown, shoulder-length mop. Instead of the tailored suits and proper white blouses that had been the staples of her wardrobe the entire thirteen years of Carl's life, she had recently taken to long, loose skirts and crinkly tops, necklaces and earrings made of nuts and beads.

"Carl, did you hear me?" She tossed her brown mop and

tried to smile, though her lips only hitched. "It will be a wonderful new start for us all."

Carl continued to stare at her. He knew she hated his stare. She pushed a knot of hair behind her ear and said, "You just might make some friends." Her jaw clicked on the last word. Carl hadn't had any friends since kindergarten. Then she said, "So."

So.

That was his mother's closing comment for every conversation she didn't want to continue. She went then and took the box of Carl's treasures to the garage, and then another box and another box. "These will go to Goodwill," she'd said. "There are children who will be thrilled to have these. Children, not teenagers like you." Carl knew he could have challenged her. She often backed down when he pitched a fit. But this time, he knew that with or without his Hot Wheels, Speed Burners, and his collection of *UFO Outer Space* comics, he was going to Cape May, New Jersey. And so he said nothing more, but burned the boxes in the garage when his mother had gone to the basement to find the family's suitcases. His father had caught the fire and put it out before the camping gear went up, too. His mother had cried, and that was good.

The workmen outside were putting in a new walkway from the porch to the front gate that opened onto the street. The chipped, concrete walk had been dug up last week and was being replaced with flat marbled stones his mother had handpicked at some garden center north of town. The workmen had put up string to delineate the line of the new walk, to give it the "casual curve" his mother had requested. They were prissy-looking men, these two, compared to the guys working on the porch and the ones reflooring the inn's north-side guest wing. Throughout the inn, there was the whack-thump of hammers, the whining of sanders, the low, gravelly voices of workers renovating Rebecca Morrison's newest and grandest hobby. It was cold today, nearly freezing, but Rebecca had promised the workers time and a half for any day they worked outdoors at temperatures thirty-five degrees or lower. Carl's father, Mitchell, hadn't argued. He was just satisfied that she was

busy, engaged, and seemingly happy. It was Rebecca's
hope that the Abbadon Inn would be ready for the height of
tourist season come late spring.

Carl shoved the window up a few inches. The window
men hadn't replaced the third-floor windows yet, and this
one was a bitch to open. There was no screen yet, and a
brain-damaged, early-season fly immediately flew in and
buzzed around Carl's nose.

The prissy stone-layers were talking, though Carl
couldn't catch what they were saying. One stood with his
hands on his hips; the other adjusted one large, flat rock in
the sand bed that had been poured for the occasion. He
shook his head, picked up the rock, and put it down again.

"What's the big deal about rocks?" Carl whispered.
"You're stupid as a couple damn dogs!" He put the wood
block on the sill, took a deep breath then shoved it as hard
as he could. The block of wood flew from the window,
bounced off the center of the first-floor porch roof, and
turned end over end as it hurtled toward the ground.

Chad hummed. A long, single note that burred the back
of his throat. He'd learned it in one of his secret books, a
concentrated sound to carry his desire to its destination.
Make it happen make it happen make it happen . . .

Nnnnnnnnn . . . !

The block struck the standing workman on the shoulder,
driving him to his knees in the damp grass with a loud
"Umph! Whoa!" He grasped his shoulder with his right
hand. The other workman stood from the sand and glared
up at the porch roof.

"What the fuck?" This, Carl heard and understood.

Carl drew himself up beneath the window. It hadn't
worked as it was supposed to. It was supposed to hit the
man's head, cut him in a hundred little places at once, and
knock him senseless. Then Rebecca would have to pay
workmen's compensation or bribe him not to sue her,
something fun like that. Carl had willed it, using what he'd
learned from a book called *And You Shall Make it So*. He
had envisioned it just like the author said he needed to do,
he had seen it striking home, the center of the workman's
head. He had imagined the dismayed shouts from one

worker as the other lay dazed and bleeding. He'd heard the squeals of his mother as she rushed out in her hippie skirt and tried to pat the man back to consciousness. And he had heard the wail of the sirens as the Cape May rescue squad had pulled up to the curb to take the man to the hospital.

But now all he heard was the one prissy workman shouting, "Where'd that come from? Damn, is the inn falling down around us? David, are you all right?"

"Fuck," hissed Carl. He crossed his arms and drew them tightly into his ribs. *Stupid stupid stupid!* he thought, his teeth clenched. *You didn't concentrate enough. You didn't hum right!*

Then Carl touched the bloody spot on his sweater, counted backward from ten, and said, "No, no, it's okay. We've only been here since January. I don't know this place too good yet. I got to know the place like I know myself, the book says so. I'll get it right, I just need time. And when I do, I feel sorry for anybody who gets in my way."

He clasped his hands together and grinned. It felt as though something large and unseen in the room was smiling with him. Then he went to the bathroom to rinse out his sweater, slipped into a clean sweatshirt, and hurried downstairs to reward himself with chocolate chip cookies from the inn's blindingly white, renovated kitchen.

TWO

"Nice town," said Dani as she snapped her compact shut and stuffed it into her purse. "I love beach towns. They've got a whole different spirit from inland places. They have their own rhythms, smells, and tastes. Don't you?"

"Don't I what?"

"Love the beach?"

"It's fine," said Sam. He glanced out the window at the rain-slicked street of the resort town. On either side of the street two- and three-story Victorian houses held sentinel behind wrought-iron fences like elegant, nosy grandmothers. Nice? He didn't know nice right now. He was trying to listen to the car. It had been making odd noises for the past two hundred or so miles. The sounds had gotten worse. Clanking. Whining. The transmission seemed to be slipping when the car picked up speed. Even the steering felt a little off, a little loose. Of course, a screwed-up car would be just the thing his life needed. That, and a good whack to the head with a two-by-four. At this point in the game, neither would have been a surprise or shock.

Dani pulled down the visor to check herself in the mirror clipped there. She rolled her lips around, evening out the dark copper color she'd just applied, worked the tip of a pick through her modified Angela Davis 'fro, then pushed the visor back up. She looked gorgeous, as usual.

"Did you see the sign when we got to town?" she chirped. " 'Cape May, the Nation's Oldest Seashore Resort.' There's some old, white-bread money here, you can bet your life on it. I bet they support artists, real artists, with that kind of money. I could make a mark here, Sam, shake the place up with my oils. Don't you think?"

"Uh-huh."

Whine, clank.

Shit . . .

Dani clutched his arm. He could feel her long, mani-cured nails through the sleeves of his jacket. She smelled of sandalwood oil. "May Mist Studios. See that little brown shop? It's closed, but it looks like an art gallery. Yes, yes, see? Paintings in the windows. Lighthouses, seashells. Tourist crap. But they'd love my stuff if they got a look at it. If I lived here I could sit on the pier—they must have a pier somewhere—and paint my passion of the sea. An ab-stract in blues and sage and white. I can feel those colors rolling in me already, begging to be thrown onto the can-vas. I could become the new art sensation, the toast of the town. Keep going straight, Sam. I want to see the ocean. It's been years since I've seen the ocean."

Sam steered the car down Madison Avenue, heading to-ward the patches of green-gray sea that winked at the far end of the street. Other cars—nice cars—shared the road with him, heading to and from wherever the people who lived here worked, to whatever the people who lived here did. A few early-season tourists clustered together at inter-vals on the walkways, bundled beneath winter coats and faux-fur hats, gazing at maps. Sam's car hesitated and groaned, then picked up speed as Sam eased his foot on the accelerator.

Get to me a mechanic, God. Let it be something simple, a fifty-dollar fix, max. I don't want to get stranded in this place. I'm not ready to stay anywhere for more than a night. I gotta keep going . . .

Dani leaned against his right shoulder, her arm still en-twined with his. "I'm having a great time with you, hon. I needed to be gone from Virginia as much as you did. Bless their closed-minded little hearts, but those Jefferson Junior High teachers didn't give a shit about creativity. I was drowning there. I was trying to twist myself into something I'm not, and that hurts."

"I know, babe."

"You were, too."

I was more than drowning, Dani, if you only knew.

"I'm glad we stumbled on this place, Sam."
"Yeah."

They had hardly stumbled upon Cape May. The town wasn't exactly a metropolis along a major highway. It had taken them three days, countless back roads, and a ferry to get there. They had left Virginia on Tuesday and had meandered aimlessly along two-lane highways through small towns and down long stretches of open countryside. They'd stopped at cheap motels when the sun had gone down, and they had eaten at diners and boxy little slop shops with greasy burgers and scratchy-record jukeboxes that played Donna Summer's "Last Dance" and the bouncily irritating tunes from the new movie *Grease*. Sam had not even used a map. For the time being, maps pissed him off. Maps told you where to go, and the last thing Sam wanted was for anything, anyone, to tell him where to go or how to get there. He had felt a certain angry satisfaction in telling Dani that he was leaving Virginia, his house, and his job, that he had no idea where he was going, but if she wanted to join him, she was welcome.

He knew she would take him up on it, as surprised as she would be at his offer. She'd been making noise about her dissatisfaction at Jefferson since November. When they'd had New Year's Eve dinner together at his house, she'd said, "You've been teaching, what, ten years?"

"This is my tenth," Sam answered.

"How do you do it? Day after day, the same problems over and over?"

"I'm good at my job. I like it. I actually believe I make a difference." He took a bite of turkey, chewed it. It tasted slightly underdone, but in all these years living alone he'd never turned into much of a cook except for pancakes and hamburgers. He just hoped he and Dani wouldn't get worms.

"Well, I'm not sure I've picked the right career," said Dani. She put her fork down and placed her hands on either side of her plate.

"Are you saying you're quitting?"

"I might," she said, one brow up. "I feel constrained. The artist in me is suffering. I've painted precious little since September, and what I've done has been only marginal. You've seen my earlier stuff. Damn good, great actually. But even though I think I'm doing an adequate job teaching, I'm losing the creative me in the process."

"This age kid is a major headache." Sam took a bite of buttered roll. "It takes time to figure out how to balance your work with your out-of-school life."

"Maybe I'm not a teacher after all. Maybe I should stick with painting. Become famous, earn enough to take trips and paint places I've never been to and have always wanted to go. Chicago. New Orleans. The Nile River." She grinned and reached across the table for Sam's hand. He obliged.

"That'd be great," said Sam. "I'd love to drink some champagne at your Chicago opening and watch you paint the Zambezi Falls. But for me, for now, teaching is what I do. It's what I am. It doesn't just pay the bills."

"So what is it? A calling? Like your father, the preacher?"

Sam grinned. "Sounds sort of unintentionally pompous, but yeah, in a way."

"You have to be the most responsible person I know," Dani conceded, linking her long, elegant fingers beneath her chin. "I haven't known you that long, but I can't imagine you ever letting something slide, something that you felt you should take care of. How many days have you given up your planning period to help kids with their homework when they were stuck, or to talk to them when they didn't feel comfortable talking with the counselor?"

Sam shrugged. "I don't know. I do feel that's part of the whole package. If I'm going to teach, I want to do it the best way possible."

"Have you ever taken a sick day when you weren't sick?"

"Um . . . once?" He grinned sheepishly. "I had a dentist appointment."

"There you go, Sam. No surprises with you."

"Maybe not," he said. "Except for the dressing in the turkey. I dropped in a few water beetles from the cellar. Adds to the texture and the protein level."

"Mmm, good," said Dani. "I can always appreciate a surprise." She smiled, and he smiled back. She pretty much had him pegged, though, and the way she described Sam made him feel kind of, well, boring and old, even at thirty-two. He had always tried to be the responsible one, the take-care-of-it son. His parents had married late, and had gone through numerous miscarriages until Robert, Jr., and then Sam were born. In 1964, Robert, Jr., had shipped out to Southeast Asia and just over a year later was home in a body bag, leaving Sam an only child. Sam, who had been active in the Civil Rights movement as best he could from his rural community took it on himself to not only get a good education and teaching certificate, but to come back to the old home place, find a job nearby, and help out with his aging parents. It was a good thing, he was glad to have done it. Though, clearly, Dani didn't rate that trait up there at the top of her list, and she thought of him as a stick-in-the-mud.

"Well," she said, picking through her dressing with her knife tip, looking for beetle legs, "I don't think I can take teaching much longer."

"How will you make a living?" *Shit, not the best choice of questions.*

Her lips tightened. "With my painting, of course. Haven't you been listening?"

"You're not selling a lot at that Charlottesville co-op art studio, unfortunately."

"Hey, watch what you're saying, teacher man!" She leaned over the table and slapped his arm.

Sam held up his hands in defense and offered an apologetic smile. "It's not your work, Dani. Lord knows it's gorgeous, just like you. But who can figure what art patrons want from one year to the next? They're fickle. It's a crap-shoot, and you know it."

Dani tossed a roll at Sam. He caught it and threw it back. It bounced off her nose, and she laughed.

"Come on," she said, drawing her words out low, seductively, leaning forward and wrinkling her nose. "Don't tell me you wouldn't prefer to do something besides teaching? You're a history buff. You're into all that old stuff.

Wouldn't you just love to take off to some foreign land? Start digging around for ruins? Egyptian mummies? I can see you out there, sweating, your shirt on the ground at your feet, your muscles rippling in the sunlight, digging with a shovel for some valuable something or other." She shook her head and whistled low. "Mmm, that would be fine."

"And you'd be digging beside me, your shirt on the ground at your feet . . . Mmmm, that would be fine, too."

"Now you're talking."

"Maybe someday, who can say?" Sam conceded. "But not yet, babe. You know my dad wanted me to be a preacher like he was. Well, as you also know, I'm about as far from pious as, well, as you are, you scary heathen."

Dani stuck out her tongue, pleased.

"But," he took a chance to get serious. "I do want to do something valuable, something that'll last. Isn't that what an artist does, too, make paintings that will last, will carry an impression into the future? Kids are so receptive. Don't you remember the feelings, the loves, the hates, and the jealousies from your early teens? If there was ever a time to impress things on people, good things, it's at that age. Plus, the kids seem to genuinely like my classes. We make models of historic buildings. We go to cemeteries and do stone rubbings. We write songs based on different, important events in American history. We act out some of the WPA journals written by former slaves, and writings by European and Asian immigrants. People, kids especially, need to understand what came before them so they can understand where they are now and where they are going."

"Yes, I know all that." Dani waved her hand like she was waving at a fly. "But where are *you* going, Samuel Russell Ford? I understand your desire to share knowledge, but does it have to be in the very same county where you were born and grew up? Maybe you're stuck in the past and don't know how to get out of it."

A twinge of anger poked at Sam's gut. He speared some green beans with his fork. "I don't think so."

"I think you're more interested in what went before than what could be waiting for you in the future. Seriously,

Sam, look around your house. Everything is old. Jesus Christ, it's like living in a halfhearted museum. Some of the stuff is really great antique-old, I'll give you that. But other stuff is just cheap trash-old. I mean, look, here's your grandmother's oak dining table. Gorgeous. And on the wall there, Bible verses your mother cross-stitched. Beautiful. Next to it, the framed photo of you and Robert when you were little. That's precious. But these dishes are, what, the old Melamine your mom bought when you were a kid? Your television is a *console*, Sam! It's older than your car."

"I don't watch television much." He felt he needed to defend himself, and he knew he shouldn't feel that way. That was the one thing about Dani that irritated him. She liked to push people's buttons, and she was a master.

She continued, "Even the rug in the living room is some old, ratty woven rag thing you found in your cellar. One Saturday you and I need to drive into Charlottesville and check out the carpet and furniture stores. It could be fun. I have a good sense of color, you know."

Sam put the beans in his mouth and said nothing. It was true; there was some pretty trashy shit in his house. But it was his trashy shit. It wasn't her place to . . .

"It's not my place to say any of that, Sam," she said, her expression softening into an apology. "I know, I'm sorry. But I sense you may want something besides living here in the house your great grandparents built. Think about it, Sam. There has to be something in you just kicking to get out and away to something different."

"I like where I live. I like this house, this county."

"You're used to it is more like the truth."

"Yes, I'm used to it, but I like it, too. I know this land like the back of my hand. I have friends here. Most of the people know me and respect me. I am trying to make a good peace right here. Make a difference now."

"That's your father talking. The good Reverend Robert Ford."

"He had some good things to say, Dani."

Dani spun a topaz ring around her finger. "But think of the world as your home, not just one little corner of it. Let's skip out, Sam, find a new place where you can study and I can paint. Doesn't that sound like heaven?"

"You're such a dreamer."

"And you aren't?" She winked. "That's one reason I like you so much. I can see it in your eyes. Dreamin' man. You're all work on the outside, but there are some wild dreams on the inside, itching to get out."

Sam smiled, shook his head. "Dani . . ."

"You're a peace-loving man, oooh, yeah, but I bet there's a rebel hiding somewhere in there. Show me." Dani got up and came around the table. She knelt beside him and put her chin on his arm. Her eyes were beautiful, her skin tempting. She kissed his hand. She rubbed his thigh. "Come on, show me the rebel."

Sam bent down and kissed her full lips. He caught her tongue gently between his teeth, and she giggled. Then he slipped one hand behind her neck, kissed her eyelids, and found her left breast with confident fingers.

"Show me the rebel," she whispered.

They had embraced, caressed each other, and then unveiled their inner rebels and made the best love they'd made in weeks on his squeaky, antique four-poster bed.

Little did Sam know that it would be his own unforeseen, unfortunate circumstance that would offer Dani an escape from Jefferson Junior High School just two months after that dinner. On the afternoon of Monday, March 6th, he slipped his resignation letter into the principal's letterbox and walked away with just a crystal paperweight, a handful of Bic pens, and his prized, framed, original 1829 Virginia map. He was no longer a teacher. It had not been his plan, but it had become his decision. Sam didn't tell his best friend Geary, the Jefferson Junior High shop teacher, what had happened. He hadn't told Dani what had happened; he just let her assume he'd been bitten by the freedom bug after a long winter like she had. She also didn't know that he was now $10,000 poorer and a man hiding from himself.

* * *

Cape May's Madison Avenue ended at a T-intersection at the shoreline. A concrete walkway traveled beside the road, separating tarmac from sand. Choppy, silvered waves dashed themselves against the white sand. An old couple in slickers and hoods strolled the uneven lay of the beach, waving metal detectors back and forth. Herring gulls spun just above their heads, watching for any crabs that they might dig up with their beaks. Sandpipers darted up and back, chasing and chased by the line of waves, their little spindly legs a blur. Far out on the horizon sat a long, gray ship, its features softened by distance, heading somewhere from somewhere else.

Dani rolled the window down, letting in a swirl of chilly air. "Mmm, smell that! It's wonderful. See there, another art gallery! The paintings in the window look like oil originals. That's good. Cape May has a clientele that wants originals, not just prints."

Sam steered right onto Beach Avenue, hoping there was—but knowing there wasn't—a mechanic shop along this main stretch amid the restaurants, gift shops, and hotels that seemed right out of the nineteenth century.

The steering column screeched.

Dani glanced over. "What's wrong with this car?"

"I don't know."

"But something."

"Yep. Something."

"What are you going to do?"

"I've been watching for a service station, something with a garage."

"There has to be a garage in Cape May. People who live here have to get their cars fixed, you know."

"I know, Dani." He knew he sounded exasperated, but he was. With the car, with himself, with everything that had transpired over the last week. "We'll go around this block and then head back inland to see what we can find. Can you hold off on your enthusiasm for the briny air and sandy shore until I can get this damned thing looked at?"

Dani's eyes narrowed. He glanced away, back to the street. A well-dressed woman with squinty-eyed pug in tow trotted across in front of him, dodging a puddle.

"Why are you taking an attitude?"

"Sorry. I don't know . . ." He gritted his teeth. "I just better not talk for a few minutes, okay? I feel like this car is getting ready to . . ."

He was going to say "fall apart on me." But before he could say it, it did just that. Something underneath clanked so loudly the woman with the pug spun about to have a look. The steering column began to vibrate, and the tires seemed to take on lives of their own, feeling as if they were moving in four different directions at once.

"Shit!" This was Sam and Dani, both. Sam battled the car to the right side of the street, next to a red line and fire hydrant, of course, and turned off the ignition. He stared at the pug-steering lady who shook her head, adjusted her sunglasses, and went on her merry way on the beachside promenade.

Dani let out a long, low whistle. "Well, thank goodness you have Triple A."

"I did."

"What? No, you have it. There's a sticker on your car, on the bumper, I saw it."

"It expired in January. I didn't take the sticker off."

"You what?" Hesitation. "Shit."

They sat without speaking for a long minute, and then Sam got out and slammed the car door. Buicks, BMWs, Cadillacs hummed by on the wet tarmac. Children's faces pressed to the glass on passengers' sides and in backseats, wondering who the strangers with the bum car might be.

"Want me to go call for a tow?" Dani asked. "I'm sure the art gallery will let me use their phone. I could mention I'm an artist, introduce myself."

Sam shoved his hands into the pockets his denim jacket and stared at the car. *Fucking piece of worn-out trash! Now what the hell am I supposed to do?*

"Sam, do you want me to call for a tow?"

Sam moved to the sidewalk, purposefully stepping in a puddle and letting his sneakers get soaked. "I'm not sure what good that will do."

"How else are we going to get it to a fix-it place? We certainly can't push it."

Tension burned in Sam's shoulders like a branding iron. No use lying at this point of the game. She would either think he was an idiot or she wouldn't. "I don't have the money for a tow, Dani."

"You have a credit card."

"Yes, but I have very little room left on it. And my cash is gone except for," he pulled out his scratched leather wallet and thumbed through the bills inside, "twenty-three dollars. I spent most of what I had on the motels the last two nights. I bought the gas. I paid the ten dollars for the ride over here on the Cape May–Lewes Ferry."

Dani's brow furrowed. "You paid the eight for you and the car. But I did pay the extra two for me."

"Yes, okay, fine. You paid your two dollars. Thanks for the financial assistance."

"Damn it, Sam, what's wrong with you? You're acting like a complete asshole."

Deep breath. Don't take it out on her. She has nothing to do with the mess you're in. "I'm sorry. Really. But I'm being honest with you. I don't have money for a tow. I might as well just leave this heap here and let the street cleaners or cops or animal control officers scoop its carcass off the road. I'm pretty certain I can't afford to get it fixed, as much noise as it was making."

Dani sputtered, "But you can write a check. You have ID. You look trustworthy. You've got that noble teacher face."

"My checking account is almost as low as the cash in my pocket."

Dani put her hands on her hips. "What the hell? You hit the road with only enough cash to make it three days and without enough for emergencies in your checking account or on your card?"

"You have no idea, Dani."

"Obviously, I don't."

They stood on the sidewalk, neither looking at the other. Small drips began to fall from the sky. In a few minutes, Sam knew there would be a downpour. Cape May citizens continued their parade up and down the street in their automobiles. Off-season tourists with out-of-state license plates cruised by. A panel truck stenciled "Cape May Office and Business Supplies" stopped on the other side of the street and the window rolled down. The driver called out, "You two need some help?"

Dani said, "Yes!" Sam said, "No!" The truck driver rolled up the window and went on his way. Dani grabbed Sam's arm and shook it, hard. "What the hell is wrong with you? There was our help right there!"

"Dani, I don't know what help I even need! Was he offering a phone call? A ride? He surely wasn't going to offer to pay for a tow or for car repairs."

"You want to handle this alone? I'll be happy to go on for a while and let you stand here in the rain and stew."

"No, don't go." Sam looked at her again. Beneath the agitation was a look of genuine concern on her face. "Please, stay."

Dani let go of his arm. She leaned against his shoulder. "I don't know what it is about you and this money crisis all of a sudden, but I do have enough for a tow. Can't be more than fifteen, you think? Twenty? And I can spare some to help you with the repairs if they aren't too bad. Would a hundred and fifty help? With what you have left on the credit card?"

Sam shrugged. He truly didn't know. His brain was buzzing. He needed to sit down, get a beer, and think things out.

"Let's get the car towed. Get a room. Then talk," said Dani. "We'll stay at one of these inns. Or maybe there's a cheaper motel somewhere."

Sam shrugged.

"Okay?"

"Okay."

They did just that. The car was towed twenty miles north to a Chevy dealership in a town called Woodbine. The mechanic on duty said he'd give it a going-over the following morning. One of the salesmen who lived in Cape May gave Dani and Sam a ride back to the seaside resort, and dropped them off on Lafayette Street at the Surf 'n' Sand Motor Hotel, an inexpensive, one-story, 1950's-era motel wedged between a grocery store and a Burger King.

Dani paid for the room. Sam got a cold six-pack of Buds at
the grocery store, then he picked up two cheeseburgers and
fries from the burger joint. They ate in their room as *Welcome Back, Kotter* sputtered and jumped on the set. When
supper was done, Dani wanted to talk. Sam didn't; he said
they could talk in the morning when he felt better. He
wasn't ready to tell her what had gone down at the school.
Hell, *he* wasn't even ready to think about what had gone
down in the school. Dani didn't push it, thankfully, and
drifted off in Sam's arms after the eleven o'clock newscast.

Sam stared at the glowing nightstand clock for a long
time before he was able to sleep. Each time he closed his
eyes he saw Joy Spradlin's grinning, taunting face. Joy
Spradlin, seventh grader on his team, bleached blonde hair,
ass-high dresses that constantly got her sent home from
school. Sneaking cheater. Consummate liar. She and her
mother, Diana, were often seen at the local food mart and
Dollar General dressed like twins with matching hair clips,
heels, and blue eye shadow.

Joy constantly coaxed boys into the girls' bathroom to
feel them down or get felt up. She'd been in in-school suspension more days than not, and never once lost that shit-
eating grin and too-bright gleam in her eyes.

She hated Sam from the first day of school. She'd come
rolling into homeroom in a tight blue sweater and short
flouncy skirt, slammed her book bag down on a desk in the
rear of the class, and cracked her gum. She slowly looked
around the room to see who her classmates would be.
When she spotted Sam at the front of the room, she
coughed her gum out onto the floor.

"What the hell?" she demanded. "They give us an old
black boy for a teacher?"

Thus began the challenges, the whispers to friends, the
outright confrontations, the sneers and the rolling eyes, the
nasty notes left on his desk chair. "Black ass goes here,"
one read. "What smells so bad?" said another.

Sam conferred with the principal and the district superintendent. While they said they sympathized with the problem, they encouraged Sam to work with the girl as best as
he could. Joy was put into in-school suspension for her

comments and actions, but the powers that be didn't want to see Joy or any other student suspended out of school. They said it made the school personnel "look like they couldn't handle their own business." High school students could be suspended out of school, but junior high kids? They couldn't be that bad yet, they were too young.

Diana Spradlin never admitted to any of her daughter's faults. It was the school's problem, she said, for making her daughter anxious and upset. It was Sam's fault, in particular, for playing favorites with black students. Sam met with Diana Spradlin in the principal's office at least twice a month about the woman's complaints. Sam was failing Joy because he didn't like her. Sam had called Joy a bitch, which he never had and never would, at least not aloud. Sam had belittled her in front of other students to the point of tears, although Sam had never seen the girl cry once. Sam had ogled her legs, her breasts, and made lewd faces at her.

During the first few meetings, Sam had come to his own defense in the most professional manner, countering every charge with the truth. He treated every student fairly, he explained. Sometimes students had a hard time accepting a male teacher after having female teachers in the elementary school. Joy was an energetic girl who sometimes let her imagination run away with her, and who needed to learn to control her temper and her words. And so on and so on and so on.

By November, Sam just sat back with his arms crossed, listened to the most recent slew of accusations, and said little or nothing. There was no use wasting his breath. Nothing would change short of the girl getting suspended, expelled, dying of some disease, or moving the hell away. The first two were unlikely because of the superintendent's fear of looking bad. The third was unlikely because the girl and her mother seemed the pictures of redneck health. The fourth was unlikely because, like Sam's family, Joy's had lived in Albemarle County for going on one hundred fifty years. She had as many cousins and uncles and aunts in the county as an ant colony had workers. He considered getting the NAACP in on it; they could find a lawyer to fight this mess, but Sam decided to wait it out a little longer. Up until the final moment, he'd held on to the hope that he might, somehow, be able to get the girl and her mother to ease up just a little, to realize Sam was a forthright, honest man who did not let slings and arrows pierce his soul. To make it through the last semester and watch Joy move on to eighth grade.

In retrospect, Sam knew he shouldn't have been so completely blindsided by what happened on March second. But he was.

"Fucking bitches," he whispered in the dark. It felt good to say it out loud at last. "Fucking, lying whores."

"What's that?" mumbled Dani, flopping over to face him, her eyes still closed. "What did you say?"

"Nothing."

"Hmmm. Hey, Sam?"

"Yeah?"

"I like Cape May, in spite of the Nova and the rain. I'd like to stay here a while."

"No matter where we land, hon, I'll need to get a job."

"Well sure, me, too. Could be fun. Stay through the summer if it works out? Maybe longer?"

"Let's think about it again in the morning."

"Okay. But I really like this place. Really, really. Mmmmm."

Sam wrapped his arm around Dani's waist, drew his knees up behind hers, and counted her breaths until the darkness was complete, and he slept.

THREE

Sam showered, dressed in jeans, a faded blue Norfolk State University sweatshirt, boots, and fleece-lined jacket, and left the motel just after eight in the morning as Dani snored softly on her side of the bed. He wrote a short note and stuck it on the sink, "Checking out the territory. Back around noon. Stay warm." He used a motel lobby pay phone to call the garage, only to find out that the mechanic had just started looking it over, and the estimate was already seven hundred fifty dollars, give or take. Sam said, "Don't waste any more of your time. Strip what you can use off the Nova, if anything, and haul the rest away. I'm done with it." He hung up before the guy could tell Sam that it was his responsibility to get rid of the heap, not the dealership's.

Sam walked southeast along damp streets that were slowly evaporating in cold morning sunlight. Cape May seemed to be a town straight out of the last century, save for the occasional modern shop, school, and streetlight. Old homes with tiled roofs, quatrefoil windows, lace curtains, and cupolas sat in yards brimming with boxwoods and winter-naked trees. Signs in front of the homes offered tidbits of history.

"The Duke of Windsor Bed and Breakfast, circa 1896."

"The Washington Inn, circa 1840."

"The Southern Mansion, circa 1863–1864."

Any other circumstance, Sam would have stopped to have a look, would have talked to owners to learn the pasts of these homes, of the people who lived there, and especially of the people who worked and served there. But at the moment he couldn't have cared less. Overhead, a row of slate-gray pelicans headed southeast toward the sea. Atop several houses, pigeons watched him with steely eyes. Dead leaves spun in circles at Sam's feet, and he sighed. He had never felt so out of place, or so alone. There was a rock in his chest, and sand in the pit of his stomach.

It was Friday; bright yellow school buses competed for street space with cars, and Sam could see kids bouncing up and down on the seats, fumbling with the bus windows and laughing. One little girl pressed her nose to the glass and waved at him; she reminded Sam of his little cousin Rose when she was nine years old, petite with big eyes and a wide smile. Sam waved back. A boy stuck out his tongue then grinned. Sam nodded.

Kids. He'd miss them. They were energetic, curious. Most of them had a sense of immortality and wonder. Yeah, they could be brats, they could be slow, they could be smart-asses and big-mouths, but in the ten years he'd taught, he'd liked every single one of them for one reason or another. He'd heard other teachers grumbling over their coffees, swearing they couldn't wait until little so-and-so was out of their classes and on to the next grade. Sam complained about bad behavior as much as the next teacher, but he was never able to say with honesty, "I hate that kid," as did some teachers.

Until Joy Spradlin.

Bitch.

A brisk, wet wind picked up along Washington Street. Sam pulled his chin far down into his collar. He had a knit hat somewhere, back in his suitcase. He had leather gloves, too, for all the good they were doing him now. He walked on, having no idea where he was going or what he was looking for. But he had to move. He couldn't sit in that damned motel room and face Dani's unanswerable questions.

Several Victorian homes he passed were under renovation. Trucks in front, sawhorses and rotted boards and new, plastic-wrapped sheetrock in the yards. More inns and restaurants to offer nineteenth-century-like elegance to guests. He wondered how much an evening in such a place would cost. One hundred dollars? More? He'd never been truly poor before, but he felt so now. It depressed the hell out of him, the thought of people spending so much on a night away from home.

He took Franklin Street to Columbia Avenue. The wind shifted, as if determined to keep up with him. The air smelled of frozen earthworms and salt. A yellow cat beside a horse-headed hitching post blinked at him as he passed. More Victorian homes and mature trees lined Columbia, most dormant, each waiting for warmer weather and the rush of tourists.

Sam paused at a dented newspaper box carrying the weekly *Cape May Star and Wave* and stared through the glass at the stack, wondering what jobs might be listed in the classifieds. What employers would want to hire a teacher who had left his previous position because he'd been accused of raping a thirteen year old and had as good as confessed by paying the girl's mother to keep her fat, orange-lipsticked mouth shut?

Probably not many.

Sam plugged in a dime and snatched out a paper. He folded it, stuck it in his jacket, and walked on to the next intersection. He'd go grab a cup of coffee down by the waterfront and look the paper over. There had to be something someone would pay him to do.

Something . . . someone . . .

Someone squealed on the other side of the street. Sam stopped to look. A red-haired boy of about twelve was bounding down the front steps of an enormous Victorian house, clenching his fists and swearing, "Go to hell!" He slammed through the iron gate that opened to the street and dashed up the sidewalk. A woman in a floor-length, paisley print skirt and bright blue knitted shawl came out on the porch, watched after the boy, then put her hand to her forehead and went back inside. In the yard beside the front steps, a man and woman in caps, heavy coats, and work gloves wrestled a barberry bush into a hole. Several newly planted shrubs sat side by side along the base of the porch. A second later, the woman in the long skirt came back out, called, "Carl? Carl!" then said something to the bush planters and went inside again.

Sam crossed the intersection and stared at the house

from the walk. It had to be one of the largest residences in
Cape May, surprisingly intricate in its enormity, like an
elephant dressed in lace and tatting. It was three-storied,
L-shaped, and covered in white clapboard that looked almost blue. The sloping, black-tiled mansard roof was
topped in delicate iron cresting and punctuated by dormer
windows. At the peak and very center of the inn's roof sat
an elegant art nouveau–styled cupola with glass sides.
Carved spandrel arches accentuated the small, outset porch
that fronted the main entrance. A separate wraparound
porch clung to the front of the house to the right of the
main entrance, then turned to span the northern wing of the
house, which was nearly a half-block long. Ornamental
brick chimneys poked out from the top of the house in random places, with bits of grass and twigs hanging from their
tops like Christmas tinsel. Immediately behind the small
entrance porch, embedded into the building and covered in
clapboarding that seemed a shade darker than the rest, was
a five-story tower that was tall enough, Sam guessed, to offer an ocean view from the tiny room at the top. The left
side of the house was almost obliterated by two large, vine-
wrapped oaks and stands of lilac and boxwoods, but behind them Sam was able to make out a porte cochere
topped by a two-storied, windowed compartment. A grav-
eled carriage drive, which at one point in time had run
through the porte cochere to allow visitors to stay out of
rain and snow, was almost totally consumed by grass.
Stone walks had been laid from each set of porch steps to
the wrought-iron fence that defined the property along the
public sidewalks. The second-floor windows were new.
Third-floor windows were in need of repair. Carpenters
were on the porch of the long, northern wing, putting in
new floorboards.

According to the wooden sign wired to the front gate,
this place was the "Abbadon Inn and Orchid Restaurant,
est. 1856" and it would be "Opening Soon!"

The place had an odd, unsettling sense of familiarity to
it. Sam gazed at the mansion for several long minutes, his
mind grappling for the connection. He felt as if he'd been
here before, that he'd seen this inn somewhere, someway.

It was a bad feeling. It made his stomach flutter as if trying to get away.

And then he knew what it was.

Back home at his house in Virginia, Sam had a collection of old family photos. Some of them were framed; others were wrapped in tissue paper and stored in boxes in a closet. Most were black-and-white. They showed Ford family members from more than a hundred years back all the way up through Sam's own young adulthood in the 1960s.

Amid the pictures of brides and babies, anniversaries and wakes, birthday parties and cover-dish suppers at the Pine Grove Baptist Church, were photos that had always intrigued Sam. They were portraits of what he called his "waiter uncles."

Several generations of Ford men had worked at elegant Virginia hotels in the late 1800s and early 1900s. The was a photo of Great-Great-Uncle Andrew at the Homestead Hotel in Hot Springs, dressed in long jacket and top hat, bowing as he opened the hotel door for President and Mrs. Grover Cleveland in 1896. The picture had been taken by a newspaper reporter who'd been following the president's summer jaunts, and the president's aide had, surprisingly, arranged for a copy to be mailed to Andrew. There was another photo, cracked and slightly blurry, of Great-Uncle Robert beside the Chamberlain Hotel pool in 1912, a crisp white uniform, white gloves, black bow tie, tray in hand. He was not smiling, but there was a hint of pride in his face. Another photo showed Uncle Josiah on the grounds of Virginia Beach's Cavalier Hotel in 1938, standing shoulder to shoulder with other waiters, bellmen, and attendants. Behind them, on its well-manicured, landscaped hill, the hotel stood like a towering and vicious bird of prey.

As a child, the photos had intrigued Sam. He stared at them for long stretches of time, looking at faces that were unknown yet familiar. Did these men sometimes play baseball with their kids in the backyard or go fishing with them, like Sam's father had? Did these men get to eat some of the fancy food and swim in the fancy pools when no one else was around? Did they preach on Sundays like his father did, and sometimes cry late at night when they thought no one was listening, because they didn't know what God wanted of their lives?

Then, as a teen, Sam found the photos infuriating, almost unbearable to witness. How could his relatives, those strong, bright black men have demeaned themselves as to be servants to people who just a generation or two before had enslaved their families? Rich white people who, at the very time the photos were taken, justified the sins of Jim Crow, refused to share bus seats or park benches or school buildings, and who could have lynched, flayed, or burned any of his uncles alive for daring to look a white person in the eye? People who had built those towering hotels for the sole intention of remaining separate, for the express purpose of flaunting their wealth and their status, giving them exclusive getaways where they could dine and swim and ride and dance with their feet just a few feet above the stench of the real world.

Sam's young cousins Frank and Rose were denied an education when, in 1959, Prince Edward County closed its schools rather than desegregate them. While a foundation was set up to provide schooling for the white students, there was nothing provided for the black students. Some attended makeshift schools in church basements. Others went out of state. Six-year-old Frank and nine-year-old Rose came to live with the Fords in Albemarle County in August of '59. Two months later, on a bright orange October morning when Sam invited Rose to walk with him up the road to buy some groceries, the two were surrounded by trucks filled with stick-wielding white teens who said they'd had enough "niggers cryin' for civil rights" in their own county and didn't take to no extras coming in. Sam was overpowered, beaten down, and by the time he was able to stand the trucks were gone and so was Rose. She was found a week later a couple miles down the river, raped and dead. Since Sam didn't witness her attack, and no one was talking, only two boys went to juvenile detention for assaulting Sam. Frank stayed on with the Fords until Prince Edward County was forced to reopen and integrate its schools. Sam had read newspaper accounts of the Little Rock Nine, of the brave teenagers challenging the system for nearly six months by sitting at the white's-only lunch counters day after day in a Greensboro Woolworth Store, about the firebombing of a Freedom Riders' bus and the beatings of some of the riders by infuriated Alabamans. He found himself nearly out of his skin at reports of the bombings of African-American churches, homes, and businesses throughout the South. He wrote passionate, carefully scripted letters to his local newspaper to explain how prejudice harmed society as a whole, all of which were rejected for publication without explanation. He had ridden with his best friend, Geary, to Richmond to join a peaceful protest of Virginia high school students, both black and white, against the racist "Student Placement Board" that continued to keep the many of the state's schools segregated. There, Sam barely missed a clubbing by police who arrested ten of the crowd for assembling without a permit. He used some of the money he earned working at his father's grocery store to buy a bus ticket to D.C. in August 1963 to take part in the March on Washington, but his father's heart attack four days prior kept him home to help his mother care for him.

Would his waiter uncles have joined Sam in the struggle? Or would they have just tipped their hats to the offenders, muttered, "Yessuh," and continued to open doors with nods and smiles? He had wished he could wake the men from their graves, dust them off, and walk them around so he would know for sure. So he could see their reactions and demand to know what they were thinking.

By the time Sam reached thirty, his attitude toward his uncles had shifted once more. He'd graduated from Norfolk State University with a double major in education and history. In the fall of 1967 he accepted a teaching position in a county high school just five miles from his parents' house, the same high school where, six years earlier, no black student or teacher were allowed to set foot. The struggle for equality and acceptance still had long way to go, and there were pockets of resentment at Jefferson High School from white students, parents, and some teachers alike. But Sam had decided this was his battlefront. Education. It was his way to make a difference. To make some wrong things right.

With a cool head and sense of humor, he made it through the first year and into the second, even though there were nights when he lay awake in cold sweats, riddled with anxieties, many of them shapeless and nameless but real nonetheless. In time Sam won over many students by turning his history classes into havens for free speech and open discussions, as long as there was an atmosphere of respect. When King was assassinated in April 1968, several of white students from his sophomore American history class left a vase of flowers on Sam's desk with a note, "We know you really liked him . . ."

Sam stayed at Jefferson when the new high school was built and his school became a junior high. He found he enjoyed the younger kids as much as the older ones. He started a school newspaper, and each monthly edition had an article about the history of Albemarle County, researched and written by the students. The students' enthusiasm was incredible, and what they learned about their homes and their families was eye-opening. They learned that grandparents had suffered under the Great Depression. They learned that their great grandmothers did not have the right to vote, and that some marched and were even arrested in an attempt to gain that right. Students learned they had relatives who fought and died during the World Wars, and even further back there were those who fought and died during the Civil War. Some had ancestors who had been enslaved. Others' ancestors owned slaves. Some bore up under Jim Crow. Others enforced those unjust and dreadful laws. It was during that time that Sam came to truly appreciate his uncles. They had done what they felt they had to do to make it through the times in which they lived. They had been incredibly strong. They had survived and had passed on a sense of familial pride to the subsequent generation.

The Abbadon Inn reminded Sam of the old hotels in the "waiter uncle" photos. It was stately, looming and dark, though not from paint but from something within, something ancient and haughty that seemed to emanate from the windows, the tower, the cupola. It looked like a man-eating shark made of shingles, shutters, and railings.

"My uncles put up with those places," Sam said to himself. "They made do."

He walked through the open iron gate and up the short, curving stone walkway. The bush-planters cast him a disinterested glance and continued shoveling topsoil in around the barberry bush. Sam could hear workers inside upstairs, banging around. He took the steps to the porch. There were double front doors, set with beveled, smoky glass and matching brass doorknobs. Sam turned the doorbell key and could hear a soft tinkling inside. He realized he was hardly dressed to interview for a job, and for a moment considered leaving and changing into one of his sports jackets and ties. But before he could, the door was yanked open and the paisley-skirted woman was looking at him. She squinted as if she needed glasses but didn't want to wear them.

"Ah, yes?"

Just jump in, both feet, ready, go. "Hi. My name is Sam Ford. I just moved here from Virginia. I noticed the 'Opening Soon' sign on your gate. I was wondering if you also might be hiring at this time?"

"Hmmm," the woman looked past him, watching, Sam guessed, for the boy who had run off. "It's cold out there. Won't you come in, Mr. . . . . ?"

"Ford, Sam Ford."

"Yes, Mr. Ford. Please come in. We're letting out the heat, letting in the cold."

Sam stepped inside the small, enclosed foyer and through another set of open double doors to a dark-paneled, high-ceilinged front hallway. He was immediately struck by mingled scents of sawdust, furniture polish, and something else . . . rich, putrid mud, a smell he knew well having grown up in the country, near the woods, where animals crawled away to die. He ran his knuckles under his nose and took a breath through his mouth. He could taste the mud on his tongue and swallowed back a cough. Was something dead in here? The woman didn't seem to notice, or if she did, she didn't care. The smell faded quickly then, and was gone.

To the right a set of glass-paneled French doors were closed. Behind the doors Sam could see a bar/restaurant with peeling floral wallpaper and near-black tables with cushioned chairs. Little white cloths covered the tables even as the bar itself was loose from the wall and lying in sections on the floor. A wide main flight of stairs clung to the left side of the hallway. To the right of the stairs the hall narrowed. It ended twenty or so feet back at a closed door. Several small doors punctuated the solid wall beneath the stairs—one rather rustic, likely to a cellar, and the other two clearly marked with hand-carved signs: LADIES. GENTLEMEN. Oil portraits hung on the wall across from the rest rooms. Were these paintings of previous owners of the inn? Or random paintings scavenged from an antique shop to give the place a sense of time?

On the left was an open reception room, bare except for a desk, a wooden cubby on the wall behind the desk, and a compact brick fireplace. Empty built-in bookshelves lined two walls. A blue ceramic inkwell sat on the desk, with a quill pen poking up proudly from it. Double doors opened from the rear of the reception room into an office. Sam could see the edge of a metal file box, a wheeled wooden chair, and towers of cardboard boxes with accordioned sides.

"We aren't ready for guests yet," the woman said with a sweep of an arm and a slightly flustered expression. She was short, perhaps five-foot-two, mid-thirties, slender and pretty, with curly auburn hair secured on both sides with rainbow-painted wooden hairclips. She had on very little makeup except for eyeliner worked carefully around her light blue eyes and a dab of pink lip gloss. "I've been doing all sorts of things, but it has a ways to go. It's taken more work than I'd expected. My main concern is the guest wing. We have three floors of rooms we're refinishing as quickly as possible. Hopefully, we'll have those bedrooms, the restaurant, and this sitting room ready by early May."

"Oh."

"I'm sorry, you said you were interested in working?"

"Yes, I am, Ms. . . . ?"

"*Mrs.* Morrison. Mrs. Rebecca Morrison. My husband is Mitchell Morrison, the attorney. You've heard of him?"

"No, I haven't."

"Well, he's retired now, but he was quite the name up in Connecticut."

"I see."

Rebecca Morrison rubbed the corners of her mouth and then put her hands in her skirt pockets. Her could see her fingers strumming there. "So, are you a handyman? A couple of our workers have been injured recently, and they haven't all been replaced yet. We still have windows to finish in the main part and the guest wing, a small staircase to repair, some painting, some plumbing, some electric work on the third floor, oh, so much. I don't think I planned it out as well as I should have, but I just figured it couldn't hurt to try to do it all at once instead of a step at a time, since I have . . ."

"I'm sorry, I don't do handiwork," said Sam.

Rebecca stopped talking, but her mouth hung open for a second too long. Then it snapped shut. She said, "Oh."

Sam heard footsteps on the stairs and looked up to see a tall, chubby, white-haired man in a cardigan and tie descending, his arms wrapped about a splintery wooden trunk. His face was flushed with the effort, but as Sam made a move to help, the man shook his head. "No, no, I've got it, thanks." He reached the bottom and put the trunk down on its end. He straightened, blowing like bellows. "Becky, this one's full of old clothes," he said, clearing his throat. "Found it in the closet in the second-story room over the porte cochere. Looks like trash from a decade ago, some old jeans and shirts. They're stiff with old sweat and, well, God knows what else. There are also some silky gowns and scarves that might have been nice last century, but they're pocked with moth holes and dry rot. You can go through it. See if there is anything you'd care to save, but my vote is that we toss the whole thing into the Dumpster along with the rest of the trash." He rubbed his hands together, delicately. Then he looked at Sam again. "Who's this?"

"Sam Ford," said Rebecca. "He's here to apply for a job."

"Handyman?"

Sam shook his head. "No, I'm not good with that sort of

thing. But I thought you might be hiring waiters or perhaps a bartender. I see you have a restaurant here, and a bar. Or perhaps you'll need a concierge?"

"Well, yes," said Rebecca. "We'll be needing those in time, I just didn't . . ."

"You didn't think it would take this much work, did you, this much time?" her husband said, his cheeks tightening. "You've done everything so haphazardly. When we bought this place in December and the first thing you did was to get the plumbing replaced, I thought, good, we're on the right track. Next step was checking and rewiring the electric. Good move, I'll hand you that. But we move in here in February, and the next thing you do is hire men to polyurethane all the floors. We hadn't even gotten the windows replaced when those men were up and down with their buckets of polish, making our floors nice and shiny, for who? More workmen?"

Rebecca said, "Mitchell . . ."

"Then you bought tablecloths for the restaurant before we even got the wallpaper torn down, the walls refinished, painted, and the bar repaired? Not exactly the way I'd have done it. I'd have sat down with renovators, talked out a plan that made some sense, instead of hiring willy-nilly and ending up with people tripping over each other when there was no—"

"Well," Rebecca interrupted through pursed lips. "Now, Mitchell, can we talk about this later?"

"As long as this is taking, I think we'll have quite a few 'laters' for discussion. We won't have the place finished, and you certainly won't be ready for guests. They'll call the Cape May tourism board and end up booking elsewhere because, my, my, that Abbadon Inn isn't ready to accept reservations, I'm so sorry."

Sam crammed his hands into his pockets and looked through the French doors, pretending to be interested in something inside the bar, even though there wasn't much to see. Tidy little tables. Flopped-over bar. Wallpaper that looked like a skin disease.

"You're right, Becky," said Mitchell. He lifted his hands

in resignation. "My objection is overruled. This is your inn, your project. I should keep my mouth closed."

"Yes, that would work just fine. Mr. Ford?"

Sam looked back at her.

"You said you didn't do carpentry or the like?"

"No. I'd like to apply for a waiter, bartender, receptionist, though, if you haven't already filled those positions."

"I'm afraid we won't be needing anyone for at least a month or two."

"Or more," said Mitchell.

"I thought you were going to . . ."

"Keep my mouth closed," said Mitchell. "Certainly, your honor."

To Sam, Rebecca said, "If you would like to leave your name, number, and references, we could get in touch with you closer to opening?"

"I'm sorry, I can't wait that long. I'll look elsewhere."

"Oh, well, all right."

Sam turned to the door.

"Are you from Cape May, Mr. Ford? You don't sound like a New Jersey native."

Sam looked back. Mitchell went into the bar, tugging a cigar from his shirt pocket as he went. "I'm from Virginia."

"We've just moved here, too, well, four weeks ago. From Danbury."

"Yes, I've just moved here." *Moved here. So that's what I've up and done. I thought I was just passing through, but I guess not.*

"I hope you like the town as much as we do, and again, if you want to leave your references . . ."

"That won't be necessary, Mrs. Morrison," said Sam. *Back to the newspaper, check out the classifieds. I wonder how much coffee costs in Cape May?* "I'll find something else. Best of luck with your venture here. This is an extraordinary house. It must have an extraordinary history. I'm sure you'll be very successful."

Rebecca Morrison beamed.

Sam went outside and down the front steps. The bush-putter-inners were gone from the front yard and were now around the side where Sam could hear them yammering about fungus on a root bag. Men on the long side porch were on break, leaning against the new section of railing and smoking cigarettes. They watched him from beneath floppy winter caps.

A bit of hard sky had cracked open, letting through a pattering of sunlight. The red-haired boy who had run off earlier stood by the open gate, his arms crossed. One of his legs was sticking out across the stone walkway. He stared at Sam, his cheeks pulsing.

Oh great, this is exactly what I don't need.

Sam strolled down the short stone walk and stopped at the boy's leg. He looked the boy in the eyes and kept his voice pleasant. "Yes? Did you want to speak to me?"

The boy's head wiggled a little on his neck, like a little rooster posturing for a fight. "Why would I want to talk to an old pickaninny?"

Shit, a little red-haired New Jersey redneck. But Sam used his teacher training. "Interesting and crude term. Do you know what that word means?"

The boy hesitated. "Yeah, it means you."

"Can you spell it for me?"

The boy's eyes narrowed. They were light blue, like his mother's. "Spell what?"

The word tasted nasty, but he said, "Pickaninny."

"Why?"

"Well," said Sam, rubbing his chin pensively as he had when he had a class full of kids who were trying to get his goat. "As I'm sure you must know, bright people who use what they assume are large and complex words, especially words meant to shock or to show disrespect, should be able to spell those words or not use them at all."

"Huh? That's the stupidest thing I've ever heard."

"Can you spell that for me?"

"What?"

"Stupidest."

"No, but I'll use it in another sentence, though. You're the stupidest pickaninny I ever met."

"That would be, 'I have ever met,' not 'I ever met.' "

"What?" The boy's fists clenched at his sides.

"If you use language correctly, you'll make a much bigger impression on other people."

"Why would I want to impress you?"

"It's clear you do."

"Why? You famous? You one of the Commodores or something?"

"Are you John Travolta's kid brother or something?"

The boy scratched his neck and looked around as if hoping there was someone nearby to whom he could roll his eyes. There was no one, only cars passing on the street, glinting bits of dim sunlight off chrome.

"That's the stupidest question I ever heard. Why did you ask me that?"

"Why did you ask if I'm one of the Commodores?"

"Because," the boy intoned, "you're *black*, if you haven't looked in a mirror recently."

"And you're *white*, if you haven't looked in a mirror recently."

The boy shook his head and let out a long breath. He glanced up at the front porch of the inn and then back at Sam. "You're having me on, aren't you."

"Absolutely."

"Huh." The boy almost smiled, and then he pulled it back together. "I thought so."

"What grade are you in?" asked Sam.

"I'm not in any grade. I don't go to school. I don't have to."

"No?" It wasn't the answer Sam expected. But he gave the boy some wiggle room. "Why is that, did you graduate early?"

"Maybe I did, and maybe I didn't." The boy squinted again, shifted his shoulders, and flared his nose, like a little fox trying to look big. Sam had seen that expression a hundred times, maybe a thousand.

"School was boring, so your parents let you quit?"

"I . . ." the kid faltered a moment. "Maybe it was, maybe it wasn't."

Sam nodded knowingly. "Play it carefully, that's the

way to do it. Never give a direct answer, because you don't know who's trying to take advantage of you, right? You don't know me from Adam. Or Lionel Ritchie."

The boy frowned. "Yeah, uh-huh, that's right."

"Well, it was nice to meet you," said Sam. He held out his hand. The boy's leg drew back, and he moved against the gate, as if a torch had been waved in his face. He stared at Sam's hand, then, as if taking a major dare, shook it. The boy's hand was clammy and soft.

Sam strode through the gate and to the intersection. From behind, the boy called out, "Tell Lionel, hi!"

Sam looked over his shoulder. "Tell John, hi!"

The weird kid was actually grinning.

Four

~≈⊙≈~

He found a small coffee shop called Salty Eddie's on Beach Avenue, and took a booth by the window where he could look out at the foamy breakers. He ordered coffee and a slice of pecan pie, hold the ice cream. It came to $2.06 with tax. He could do this five more times before he would be flat broke. He'd never been flat broke before. Financially strapped at times, but never completely, totally without money.

I could sell my house. I could get $60,000 for it, I bet, with the two acres. Geary would put it on the market for me. He moonlights as a real estate agent; he knows that shit. He'd get a percent so it would be worth his while.

Sam looked at the rhythmic crashing of the waves, at the relentless, stiff-legged sandpipers running up and back as the waves washed up then retreated, at a circle of gulls clustered in the air like chattery teenagers, watching the sand for dead crabs or chunks of bloated fish. Then his vision shifted to his own reflection in the glass. For a moment, he looked like he remembered his father looking before he died in 1973—hunched over the grocery-store books on a Saturday afternoon or his Bible on a Saturday night. Preparing for both the practical and the spiritual of the coming week. Sam had his father's near-black eyes and prominent cheeks. He had the same strong jaw and broad shoulders. Women in their church were constantly telling a young Sam that he was as good-looking as his daddy, and the girls his age were always trying to catch get his attention, much to the flustered consternation of Sam's mother.

But now, all Sam could see in the window glass was the sense of defeat his father fell prey to in his last years. The death of Sam's mother in 1970 had drained much of the spark from his father's bright eyes. The heart attack and stroke took the rest.

I can't sell the house. It's the only thing of any value left from my family. It's the only connection I have to who I am. I have to keep it.

A couple with a baby settled in the booth next to Sam. The mother plunked the child down in a high chair, and the little girl immediately gave Sam a wide and toothless grin. Sam looked away.

Maybe I can rent the house. That might be better. Make a few hundred dollars a month? But I'd have to maintain it somehow. Arrange for yard care, for upkeep. I can't do that from New Jersey. There's always Geary. Should I ask him to do that for me? What if the pipes break, should he have to deal with that?

The baby girl banged a spoon her father gave her on the chair's plastic tray. Sam glanced over. The child giggled at him and offered the spoon. Sam gave her a smile he didn't feel, then turned his gaze back to the window.

Regardless, I can't go back. Not now. Maybe never. I don't know. Could things be any fucking worse? Could I have ended up in any deeper shit than this mess?

" 'But you're alive,' Dad would say," he whispered into the coffee cup. "I can hear him now, that voice of pure confidence and commitment. 'You're still breathing and you still have your wits. Things can change. Things will change. When you're at your lowest, God'll lift you to your feet.' He always said that, from his pulpit, from the kitchen table. 'Sam, the Lord will lift you up, if you'll only reach out.' "

Well, Dad, I don't feel the heavenly arms pulling me up. I'm reaching out, I'm ready for my rescue, but I don't hear a glorious rustling of angel wings. All I'm hearing is a squealing baby, a guy at the table nearby chewing with his mouth open, and Barry Manilow on the jukebox singing that he ready to take a chance again. Good for Barry. I'm happy for the man.

The waitress, a young Hispanic girl with heavy brows and a bent nose, stopped by his booth to offer more coffee. He looked into his cup to find he still had more than a half-cup left. "No, thanks," he said. The menu had not stated free refills. Either he wasn't as in need of caffeine as he'd thought, or something inside him was starting to make him conserve. When the ability to afford anything was coming to a rapid end, you had to make what you had in hand last.

Sam sipped the coffee, and it tasted like nothing.

Sixty grand would go a hell of a long way.

The baby squealed and threw the spoon on the floor.

Shut up on that, Sam. You won't sell the house. You can't fail the family in that way. You're the only one of us left. There's no more Dad, no more Mom, no more Robbie. It's up to you to hang on to what we have. It's your responsibility.

"Mr. Ford?"

Sam looked up from the cup and swallowed the mouthful he'd been swilling. At first he didn't recognize the white-haired man in the wool trench coat and gray Ontario hat who stood beside his booth. A guy from the car dealership, maybe, who'd hunted him down to threaten him to get his shitty car off their premises? An insurance salesman, thinking he might be a good target? A Jehovah's Witness, hoping to save another soul to help assure himself a spot in heaven with the 144,000 Elite? Nah, Sam knew Witnesses from way back. This guy didn't have the right clothes, the right stance, and there was no *Watchtower* in his hands.

A deep, silent sigh. "Yes?"

"Mr. Ford, excuse me, I don't mean to bother you."

But that didn't stop you.

"We spoke briefly back at the Abbadon Inn. I'm Mitchell Morrison, owner, I mean co-owner, of the inn."

Oh, yeah. The lawyer. What the hell does this guy want with me?

"May I sit down?"

I'd rather you not. "Certainly."

The man slid into the seat across from Sam and took off his hat. He put it on the seat beside him. He looked older without it. His brow was furrowed with deep creases. Puffy bags of skin hung beneath his eyes. But the man's brown eyes were keen and sharp. "My wife and I were watching you talk with our son out by the gate," he said.

Sam's stomach flipped, and his breath locked. The blood in his arms ran cold. *Oh fucking shit do they think I did something to that clammy-handed little kid? Dear God, no, not this again!*

Sam managed, "Yes?"

"Our son, Carl, has difficulties." The man let out a breath, picked up the saltshaker and put it back down. It was clear what he was saying embarrassed him, though the voice kept an even, cool calm. "He doesn't relate well to other children. He doesn't relate well to anyone, as a matter of fact. I've not seen the child smile in, I don't know, years, perhaps? I don't know exactly what went wrong, but there he is, in his miserable little closed-off life."

So you aren't saying you think I molested your son? Sam let out the breath he'd been holding. It tasted sour as it passed his tongue. "I'm sorry to hear that, Mr. Morrison. Some children have a more difficult time during adolescence than others."

"Becky and I saw Carl talking to you. He actually smiled at you. He actually shook your hand. Becky was stunned. Frankly, so was I." Mitchell Morrison looked back at Sam. His gray eyebrows were raised slightly, in some sort of expectation that Sam couldn't figure.

"Carl and I just chewed the fat some," said Sam. It was impossible to say, "You have a nice son," because Mitchell Morrison didn't have a nice son. He had a creepy son.

"Have you ever done any teaching, Mr. Ford? Counseling, any kind of work with youths?"

Sure, and I was accused of raping a student. Paid her mom $10,000 so she wouldn't tell her police cousins and judge uncle and have me sent to prison for fifteen years. He wasn't sure he would tell Mitchell Morrison the truth until he heard himself say, "Yes."

One side of Mitchell's mouth went up, a triumphant smile. "You were a teacher, then?"

"Yes. Back in Virginia."

"What is your experience, exactly?"

Dig that hole deep, Sam, dig it deep. "Seventh grade, primarily history. Ten years' experience."

"And you quit?"

Sam nodded.

"Why?"

None of your fucking business. "I was looking for a change of pace. Ten-year itch, perhaps?"

"How much of a change do you really need?"

God, this guy talked like a lawyer. Probing, picking, never getting quite to the point. "I'm not sure I know what you mean." Sam drained the remaining puddle from his coffee. He picked a pecan from the top of the pie and stuck it in his mouth.

"I mean would you be interested in teaching again? A classroom of one, so to speak. Our boy doesn't go to school. Well, he used to, but not for the last few years. He doesn't fit in well with others, as I mentioned. If you have a good reference or two, and I could make it worth your while, perhaps you'd be willing to work for us? To tutor Carl?"

It was all Sam could do to keep from laughing out loud, a bitter, sarcastic laugh. "I'm sorry, Mitchell, but I'm really looking for something different. Both my girlfriend and I decided it was time to move on."

Mitchell placed his hands, flat, on the tabletop. "Carl is very bright. You might find your time together mutually instructive."

Sam chewed the pecan. "That could be, but no, thank you."

"Four hundred dollars a week."

Sam shook his head. "I'm sorry. I just don't think it'll work out."

"Becky and I need a teacher for Carl. Someone who can really get along with him, teach him some damn thing. He won't pay attention to us. And we won't have our son grow up like some . . . some uneducated street urchin. Four-fifty a week."

"Mr. Mitchell . . ."

"Five hundred a week. That's as high as I can go."

That's $2,000 a month. That's more than I made as a teacher with ten years' experience.

"Do you have a place to stay yet? Have you rented an apartment? A house?"

"We only got to Cape May yesterday. We haven't looked yet."

"I'll offer five hundred dollars a week plus room and board at the Abbadon Inn. No rent, Mr. Ford. You can join us for meals, if you are so inclined. Or fix your own meals in the inn's kitchen, though you'll have to get your own groceries."

That's $2,000 a week with the major expenses taken care of. Sam pretended to take a long sip of coffee, though there was none left, to hide the conflicting emotions he knew were rattling across his face. With that kind of money, he could get a new car in a matter of months. Dani could relax and paint without having to sling hash or ring up souvenir sales part-time at some bitchy, beachy gift shop. But it would mean dealing with this Carl kid, what . . . not all the time, the Morrisons couldn't expect . . .

"Your hours would be school hours," said Mitchell. "Nine to four should be a reasonable day. The rest of the time would be your own. Is it a deal?"

Sam swallowed air. He lowered the cup. "I don't know. I'm going to have to think it over. I'm going to have to talk with Dani."

"Dani?"

"My girlfriend, Danielle Payne. She came to Cape May with me."

"She's welcome to stay at the Abbadon, too. Just tell Becky you're married. She's particular that way. And," Mitchell Morrison leaned over the booth and lowered his voice. "We can do this under the table. Nothing taxable. What do you say?"

"Isn't that illegal?"

Mitchell Morrison smiled as if he'd just played a great hand of poker. His fingers linked together. "I'm a lawyer, Mr. Ford. Newly retired but still in the swing. I can make it work out."

I could do it for a while. I could manage. But I need a reference. I need to get hold of Geary right away.

"Mr. Ford? What do you think?"

The waitress returned with her coffeepot, and Sam let

her pour another round. Mitchell shook his head when the girl asked if he needed anything. When she was gone Sam said, "Yes, all right, that sounds fine." Fine? It sounded great. Well, except for the kid part of it.

Mitchell nodded, pleased, and shook Sam's hand across the remaining chunk of pecan pie. And suddenly, Sam felt famished. When the man left, he ordered a late breakfast of eggs, sausage, and hash browns. Leaving a whopping $6.79 in his pocket.

FIVE

Dani had bought Sam a carpetbag. She'd found it at an antique shop, having gone hiking herself when she found Sam's note by the sink in the motel bathroom. The bag was circa 1866, made in Worcester, Massachusetts, used, according to the shop owner, by a man who had gone south from New Jersey as an official with the Freedman's Bureau after the Civil War. Sam doubted the specific pedigree, but he did recognize the age of the bag at being mid-nineteenth century. It was the size of a small suitcase, covered in faded, threadbare floral brocade and secured with brass clasps and a tiny lock. The bone handle was polished with the sweat of many hands, over many, many years.

Sam knew had he not talked to Mitchell Morrison in the seaside coffee shop, he would have cringed at the purchase, in spite of his love of antiques, especially antiques that had a connection to African-American history. But he gave Dani a big hug, thanked her for her thoughtfulness, and broke the news about moving to Abbadon Inn.

They took a cab from the motel to the Abbadon Inn Saturday morning, having spent one last night together, alone. Dani was hesitant about the move, but Sam assured her they would take it one day at a time, he wasn't signing any contracts with the Morrisons. "Hon," he said in the cab as it pulled up to the curb in front of the inn, "at two thousand dollars a month with room and board, I'm going to try my best to make it work. There are too many benefits at stake."

"I suppose," said Dani. "I've never liked living under someone else's roof, though. I spent two years with my mom after college, and no matter how much she promised she would let me be, she just couldn't do it. Oh, my God,

but did she ever stick her nose in my business. I couldn't
talk on the phone without her listening. I couldn't brew a
cup of tea without her telling me how to do it. Ugh."

"It won't be that way here. You'll get to paint all you
want. The boy is my responsibility. And the parents are
too busy with their own interests to care how you brew
your tea."

"I'll hold you to it," she said.

Sam climbed from the taxi and waited as the driver
popped the trunk and placed his suitcases, box of books,
and carpetbag, and Dani's suitcases, portfolio, and easel on
the sidewalk. Sam paid the driver and gave him a five-
dollar tip. He thought that was a good tip, but the driver
didn't seem impressed.

The day was pleasant, with a clear blue sky, puffs of
foam-white clouds, and an almost-warm sunlight despite
sporadic, chilly breezes. The yard workers had finished
with the barberry bushes and were gone. Other workers
were on the far end of the porch that sided on Ocean Street,
replacing floorboards and putting in a wide wooden swing
with a cheerful, red seat cushion.

Carl was nowhere to be seen. Sam wondered if he were
off playing with friends as it was a Saturday, but then reminded himself that according to Mitchell, the boy had no
friends. Most likely, then, Carl was probably hiding. Sam
could only imagine the Morrisons' dinner conversation the
night before. Mitchell calmly pointing out the inevitable,
Rebecca patting at her hair and fuming, Carl throwing a
plate across the room and storming away.

No pickaninny's gonna to teach me nothin'!

And Rebecca Morrison's weak protest, *Honey, don't say
pickaninny. That's not nice.*

After several turns of the doorbell key, Rebecca Morrison opened the door. She was dressed in a calf-length
denim skirt and black peasant blouse. Her hair was back in
a leather headband. She smiled cordially and stepped back
to let Dani and Sam inside. The hardwood floor squeaked
beneath them. Sunlight flickered on the polished paneled
walls and off the well-buffed staircase.

Before Sam could even put his cases and box down in

the front hall, Rebecca said, "First, though, the references, Mr. Ford. Mitchell assures me everything is in order. But I need to make sure."

Sam handed her Geary's phone number and address, hoping one would be enough. He'd called Geary the night before while Dani was in the shower. He apologized for leaving without saying anything and asked his friend to give a good reference, regardless of how weird it was that he'd run off to New Jersey to take one teaching job after abandoning another. He also asked if he might be willing to look after his house while he was gone, and forward his mail when he had an actual address. Geary had answered in a very Geary-like manner, "Sure, man, I'll do whatever you need, you know me. But this is one big-ass surprise. I never took you for such as free spirit. I'll miss you and that shitty car of yours." The tone of voice had been affectionate, and for a moment Sam had to clamp his teeth together to keep from tearing up. Sam had promised to explain someday what had gone down, but Geary only said, "You don't have to explain anything. You do what you have to do. Love you, man. Take care, brother."

"Thank you, Mr. Ford," said Rebecca Morrison. "I'll call . . ." she looked at the paper Sam had given her, ". . . Mr. LeVarge right away. I'm sure you understand that I have to be careful. I'm a mother, and you know how mothers are."

"I do, indeed," said Dani.

Rebecca glanced at Dani, her eyes locking on the younger woman, noticing her in the hall for the first time. She studied Dani for a long moment as if trying to figure her out—a tall, slender black woman with a 'fro, a bright African patterned cape, bell-bottomed jeans, and black, high-heeled boots.

Dani grinned and extended her hand. "Mrs. Morrison, *Jambo,* and *astante!* I'm Dani, Sam's wife. *Anasa* to meet you, a pleasure."

It was all Sam could do to keep from rolling his eyes. Dani knew all of, maybe, thirty words in Swahili, picked up from a friend when she was in college. But the words were already working their charm on the owner of the Abbadon Inn. Rebecca suddenly thought she had an exotic visitor.

"Oh, it's nice to meet you, too, Dani. Welcome." Rebecca glanced at the leather portfolio under Dani's arm. "You are an artist?"

Dani nodded, giving her widest smile. "Yes, yes. I look forward to painting *bahari*—the sea—here in your lovely town. Do you think you could introduce me to the owners of your Cape May galleries?"

"Are you from Africa?"

Dani lowered her voice, and her face clouded over. "My family is, yes, but I don't care to speak of the pain they have endured. I care only to think of the future. I'm sure you understand."

Rebecca nodded vigorously and apologetically. "Indeed, well, I understand. I'll make sure you meet some of the gallery owners and have a chance to show your work." Dani looked at Sam and grinned in triumph. Rebecca had been wooed. The curly-haired woman clearly imagined Dani in a recent flight from some warring tribal conflict, happy to have made it to the civilized safety of American shores. She probably never thought further back than her own life experience except when it came to replacing eighty-year-old plumbing or electrical wiring.

Rebecca, Sam, and Dani walked up the steep stairs to the second floor, Rebecca carrying Dani's small suitcase and Sam's carpetbag, though at first he resisted giving it to her. "Oh, you don't think I'll drop it?" she smiled. "This old thing?" The rest of the baggage was left in the reception room.

At the landing they turned into a wide sitting area that Rebecca had decorated with a bench, more framed portraits in rectangular frames, several silhouettes in small oval frames, and an antique spinning wheel nestled in the left corner. "The wheel was my mother's," said Rebecca. "She gave it to me for my wedding present. I asked her if she wanted me to prick my thumb and go to sleep for a hundred years, but she only laughed. Oh, and that door,"

Rebecca pointed to the closed door in the wall to the left of the spinning wheel, "opens to the guest wing. I keep that shut for now. Helps with heating."

Off the sitting area was the long, main hallway. The hall floor was polished oak. A plush Oriental runner traveled from one end to the other. Brass, dragon-headed sconces bearing electric lightbulbs and crystal globes clung to the walls between each of the bedroom doors. Sam caught a trace of the rancid mud again, thick, nauseating. The hairs in his nose recoiled; his stomach turned uneasily. Had something died up here? Sam nudged Dani, made a face to see if she smelled it, too. She shrugged, shook her head.

"Mitchell and I use the room down the hall there," Rebecca said, pointing to the last room on the right. "It's very nice, and we've put in a small water closet for our own personal use. A shower, too! Each floor does have a communal bathroom, however. You won't have to go too far in the middle of the night if the need arises."

Dani gave Sam a desperate look. Sam shrugged.

Rebecca continued, "I'd thought about the room across from the stairs, there, but Mitchell said, 'Lord, no, Rebecca, you think I want to wake with sun in my face? I'm retired now, I don't want the sun or anything else telling me when to get up.' Hmmm."

The door to the room was open, and Sam took a quick peek inside. It was large and empty, extending forward into what was the tower portion of the house. The walls had been patched and plastered but not painted. A new light fixture was in place. In the ceiling portion of the tower section was a trapdoor with a cord dangling from it. Sam could smell the foul odor in here, laced with a scent of something oddly sweet.

"Come on," said Rebecca, like a kindergarten teacher. She steered them up a slightly more narrow set of stairs to the third floor. The wall along the stairs was in need of sanding and painting. The hand railing was wobbly. Mitchell had been right that Rebecca seemed to be making improvements on the building in odd bits and pieces, with no real clear plan. Not that it mattered to Sam. As long as the Morrisons paid him weekly, as long as they gave him and Dani the space they needed, as long as Carl was manageable, things would be okay. He would be able to breathe again.

The third floor had the same layout as the second, though the open sitting area was not decorated with framed portraits or spinning wheels. Instead, plastic containers and cardboard boxes, stacked one upon another, made irregular and precarious sculptures. There was a panel in the ceiling right off the stairs; Sam guessed at one time there were steps into the cupola from the sitting area, but at some point they'd been removed and the cupola sealed off. The ceilings were a bit lower on this floor. The floors were polished, but there was no Oriental carpeting in the main hall. Cardboard boxes lined the walls, stuffed with old rags, broken lightbulbs, old curtain rods and tangled Venetian blinds. There were several rusted iron sconces on the walls, but others had been ripped out, leaving exposed wiring.

"I thought the electric had been fixed," said Sam, nodding at the wires.

"The wiring, yes, all good as new," said Rebecca, "but I haven't decided what I want in the halls up here yet. So much to do! But some of the sconces work. You won't be in the dark."

"How nice," said Dani. She was pissed.

"The bathroom is off the hall, next to the sitting area, see here?" She went around the corner, pushed open the door, and flicked the light switch. Sam and Dani looked in over her shoulders. "The little white tiles haven't been replaced. Aren't they nice? Neither have the tub and the sink, they were the ones here when we bought the place. I love claw-foot tubs. No shower on this floor, sorry. Now, the pot . . . the toilet . . . is a brand-new one. The toilet that was in here when we came, oh, all I can say is that it looked like some mold, fungi, and creeping crud had got together to throw themselves a party. And there is plenty of hot water."

Sam could read Dani's mind. *What the fuck? No shower?*

Rebecca opened the door across the hall from the bathroom. "And this is for you. It should give you the most privacy, I would think." She went in; Sam and Dani followed.

The bedroom was about fifteen feet square and freezing cold. Pools of dust-tainted sunlight from the front and side windows lay across each other on the floor. A once-white radiator, looking like the bleached skeleton of a large dog, stood near the front window. The floor had been buffed and polished, but there was still a dark water stain in the center. The walls were painted a ghastly lime green with large white, blue, and yellow daisies and lopsided peace signs dabbled here and there, making Sam wonder if a decade ago the room hadn't been a hot spot for a little bit of free love. A single straight-backed chair sat by the door. Lighting was a cheap round ball of glass over a bulb in the ceiling. The door to the closet had been painted with a yellow latex, and the paint looked as though it was in the middle of a desperate escape attempt with flakes popping up here and there and loose strips hanging free.

Carl could feel Dani's displeasure from across the room. He put the suitcase and box of books on the floor. Dani followed suit. Rebecca handed Dani's suitcase to her and Sam's carpetbag to him, as if it wasn't her job to put them down.

"Someday we'll be fixing these top-floor rooms for guests," said Rebecca, tipping her head and making a little *tsking* sound. "We plan on making the Abbadon Inn the most popular establishment in Cape May. But for now, we're going to use only the rooms on the L-extension of the inn, what I call the guest wing. That's where most of the work is being done at the moment. I want to get at least that part ready before spring. These third-floor rooms will be left until later in the season. And so until then you'll have the upper part of the inn to yourselves. Well, except for Carl."

"Carl?" asked Sam.

"We want him to feel at home and to feel he's got some freedom, since he wasn't very happy about moving here. So, we let him sleep pretty much anywhere in the inn that catches his fancy. He likes that. He takes his sleeping bag here and there. His most recent hidey-hole is the fifth-floor tower room."

"I see," said Dani.

"So," said Rebecca. She held her folded hands to her breast.

"So I think we're going to need some furniture," said Sam.

"Oh! Ah! Yes, I see your trouble," said Rebecca with a slight giggle, touching her lip as if just noticing there was no bed, no dresser. "I'll have that taken care of before dinner. We have some extra pieces about the place. And you'll join us for dinner?"

"I think we'll just explore the town the rest of the day," said Sam. "Get a feel for the area. That way, come Monday morning when I'm with Carl, I'll know good places to take him, educational spots, as part of his schooling."

Sam knew what Dani was thinking. *Lay it on thick there, babe.*

"All right," said Rebecca, her voice dropping in disappointment. Perhaps she wanted to talk art with the Kenyan princess from Virginia. "I'll leave you alone, then."

After Rebecca left, Dani and Sam looked at each other. Then Dani burst out in pained laughter, holding her hand to her mouth to keep the sound down. "What is with this place? It's hideous! And that woman? Spacey as a damn Martian. No, she's worse than that, she's farther out, she like a damn Plutonian! Bringing us up here like everything's fine and dandy, and all we have is a chair?"

"I think she's just a bit scattered," said Sam.

"God, don't you just hate 'scattered'?"

"Hey, Dani, I've been scattered lately."

"You? No, babe, you're not scattered." Dani squeezed his arm. "You've just been . . . preoccupied. Needing a getaway. I totally understand that. But Rebecca Morrison. She's dopey, probably been dopey her whole life. I just hope we don't have to spend much time with her."

"She's not all that bad."

Dani tilted her head. "Damn, Sam, you like her?"

"I feel sorry for her. Her husband is a bit of an arrogant ass."

"She raised a messed-up kid, you said so yourself."

"She sure did that." Sam went to the radiator, turned the valve, and listened for the hissing sound that indicated they would have a little heat shortly. Then he leaned on the windowsill and looked out. Down past the slight slope of the mansard roof and the roof of the first-floor porch, he could see the narrow slice of front yard, the stone walkway, the iron fence, and Columbia Avenue. As he watched, an old-fashioned trolley drawn by two mules ambled past the Abbadon Inn. A sign on the side boldly proclaimed that it belonged to the "Victorian Village Transit Company." The roof of the trolley hid those inside, though Sam couldn't imagine there would be very many riders this time of year. An old couple, maybe, on an anniversary ride, huddled together, arms linked. A young family with children, coming in early March so they could better afford the trip. People wanting to enjoy this historic resort town, to pretend to be back in time when things were slower-paced, simpler, happier.

Simpler. Happier, Sam thought. *I guess that all depends on whom you ask.*

His fingers scratched mindlessly at the rough wooden sill and came away with something cold and thick beneath his nails. He held up his hands. Dull, red flakes caked his fingertips. He looked at the windowsill. There was blood on the wood. It was dried, but there was a fair amount of it pooled on the sill, then trailing down along the dingy green wall to the floor.

"Ugh," said Sam.

"What?" Dani had moved up beside him.

"There's blood."

Dani frowned. "Nasty."

"Yeah." Sam pulled a Bic pen from his inside jacket pocket and popped off the cap. He worked the plastic clip beneath his nails, scraping out the dried blood. He felt his gorge rise as the red curled up and out. Whose blood? What happened here? He dug as hard as he could but wasn't able to get all of it out. He'd have to wash his hands in hot water. "Rebecca said some workers had been injured recently. I wonder if one of them got cut?"

"She said they hadn't done any work up here yet."

"Hmm. Yeah, she did say that."

"I really don't care whose it is. I just think Little Miss Sunshine needs to get someone up here to clean this crap up and get us some furniture. You don't bring someone into your place without taking care of the simplest amenities. Even if we, you, are just seen as hired help."

"We'll tell her about it on our way out."

"You bet we will." Dani crossed her arms. "I hope this isn't an omen of things to come. I'm okay with a few bumps and starts, but I can't get much painting done if my creature comforts aren't at least satisfied to a minimum. Not that this room even constitutes a minimum."

She was right. The room was dreadful. But all Sam could think of saying at the moment was, "Uh-huh."

Dani moved behind Sam, spread her hands, and ran them up the back of Sam's thighs. One hand came around and gently cupped his balls. Sam let out a long breath and leaned back into her. He put his hands behind him, around her, to draw her in closer. He closed his eyes, loving the sensations, though he was still aware of the bits of blood beneath his nails. They made his fingers feel cold.

"But with you, babe," Dani said, "there are at least some creature comforts I can count on. Mmm-hmmm."

Heat moved through Sam's groin as Dani moved her thumbs up and down his shaft through the thick denim fabric. His thoughts began to soften. He was glad Dani was with him, even though she had no clue of the reason he'd left Virginia. They were away from the mess now, and they would start over. His body felt as if it was drawing downward, falling happily away, ready to spring up again if things continued as they were. "Let's count on each other," he muttered, pacing his words with the increased speed of his breathing. "We'll manage. You'll paint. I'll teach. We'll see how it goes. I think it'll be . . . just fine . . ."

There was a loud thump upstairs. Dani let go of Sam's balls, and they both stared at the ceiling. There were more thumps, then the sound of rapid footsteps coming down an unseen flight of stairs above and beyond the wall.

"What the hell's that?" asked Dani.

"Carl," said Sam.

"Shit, yeah," Dani groaned. "Rebecca said he'd laid claim to the top tower room."

There was another whacking sound, then more footsteps, continuing downward. The whole room rocked with the pounding of the footfalls.

"Think we'll have to listen to that all the time?"

"Until he decides to haul his sleeping bag elsewhere, I guess," said Sam.

"That's just great."

They went downstairs after Sam took a quick side trip to the bathroom—"Can you believe this, only one bathroom on a floor?" Dani complained. "I hope your little charge doesn't decide to start sleeping on our floor. I will *not* share such a private space with a hoodlum"—so he could scour the rest of the blood from beneath his fingernails. It took a good three minutes and his toothbrush, which he promptly tossed in the trash.

Rebecca caught them in the front hall. She was all smiles and dimples.

"I spoke with Mr. LeVarge just a moment ago. What a pleasant man. He says you and he have taught together for many years. He couldn't say enough good things about you, and that he was sorry you decided it was time to move on from Virginia. He said Virginia's loss is New Jersey's gain."

Dani linked her arm through Sam's, and Sam could feel her straighten up, preparing for more of the Kenyan princess.

"So, then!" said Rebecca. "I suppose that's done. Please come in and sign our guest register. To make everything official."

"*Asante,* Rebecca," said Dani, sarcasm just under the surface of her words.

Rebecca walked behind the desk in the reception room and pulled out an enormous, thick leather-bound volume. It hit the desktop with a muffled thwack. The cover was dark and cracked, the creases still bearing minute traces of dust and cobwebs. Rebecca opened it slowly, almost reverently, her fingers pinching the first page and peeling it open.

"I found this myself," she said. "In the old kitchen pantry behind some loose shelves that had been turned on end. Isn't it just fabulous?"

Sam moved to the desk to have a close look at the signatures. They were inscribed in beautiful script, an elegant, controlled style used by all literate people of the nineteenth century. Rebecca turned the book to make it easier for Sam to see. He could smell the age, lifting from the page like steam, burning his nostrils. "Nicholas Abbadon," said Sam. "He signed first. I'm assuming he's the man who built the inn?"

"Yes," said Rebecca. "No one in the Preservation Society knows exactly when he came to Cape May, or where he came from exactly, but he arrived sometime in the 1850s."

The inn builder's signature was larger than the others on the page, the ink seemingly blacker even after all the years. Beside his name was the date, October 3, 1856. Beneath his name was one that bore no surname at all. Lillith. Same date. Next to the date was a small yet intricately drawn design that appeared to be some sort of Celtic knot or hex symbol.

"Who was Lillith?" Sam asked. "A daughter?"

Rebecca shrugged.

"A servant? Certainly not a slave in New Jersey, not in 1856."

"Oh, no. Some have speculated that Lillith was Nicholas's common-law wife, though no one is sure about that, either. Back in those days," Rebecca lowered her voice, "there were certain people who lived in sin, much the way some people do today."

Dani, who had taken hold of Sam's hand, squeezed it so hard it stung. She wanted out of there. Immediately. Sam gave her a quick squeeze back to say, *Give me a minute*.

"See the marking beside Lillith's name?" asked Rebecca, tapping the page. "I found the same on the headboard of a bed in one of the third-floor rooms. I moved it to Mitchell's and my room. I'm sure it was Lillith's bed. I had it refinished, though not so much as to ruin the value. It's a beautiful piece of handiwork. Mitchell suggested we sell it because he thinks it is rather ugly, but I said, 'Oh, no, we won't!' "

Sam flipped carefully through the book. Many signatures filled the lined pages, month after month, year after year. Most of the names seemed to be those of men, some were women, and only a few married couples had signed in as husband and wife. He reached the center of the book and the signatures stopped, the last historic name signed in September of 1880. The final three signatures were those of Mitchell and Rebecca, signed in contemporary cursive, and then Carl's, a scribbled mess that took up three lines, all dated January 30, 1978.

"Please, sign in as our first guests," said Rebecca. "With so much space still left in the book, Mitchell and I thought it would be charming to have guests sign the very same book that folks did when the inn first opened."

"A nice idea," said Dani evenly.

A small piece of yellowed cloth protruded from the pages near the back of the book; a tattered bookmark. Sam slid his finger behind the marker to open the book at the marked spot. Rebecca dropped the pen and yanked the book back from under Sam's hand. Her face had gone red in an instant. "Oh," she blustered, "let's see. If you'll sign right after our names, not there in the back, it would be perfect." She dabbed the quill pen in the inkwell, a bit too hard, then handed the pen to Sam. Sam passed the pen to Dani.

"Ladies first," he said.

She gave him a cool smile. "*Asante*," she said, and signed her name. Then Sam took the pen and put it to the paper. He thought of signing his whole name—what the hell, it was rare he went by Samuel Russell Ford—but he wrote only, "Sam . . ."

The pen began to tremble slightly in his hand. It grew instantly warm in his grasp. *What the hell?*

". . . Ford."

And then the pen went scaldingly hot, searing itself to the web of skin between his thumb and forefinger, shooting a spiraling, electrical current up his arm to his spine and to the base of his skull. Sam groaned and shook his hand violently, sending the pen flying against the wooden cubbies on the wall behind Rebecca. He could feel the top layer of singed skin go with it.

Dani grabbed Sam's arm.

"Jesus, Sam, what's the matter?" she demanded, her Kenyan accent gone.

Sam couldn't speak, his lips were sealed shut with the current, buzzing as if he was kissing a high wire. He tried to take a breath and nothing came. *Oh, my God, what is this?*

Dani shook Sam by the arm. Her eyes were huge. Sam could not see Rebecca; his vision was swirling, fading. "Sam, what's wrong?"

And then the current prickled, went cold, and drained from his body. Sam leaned both hands on the counter and drew in air through his teeth. His heart hammered madly.

"Are you having a heart attack?" wailed Rebecca.

"No," Sam managed. "I don't know what happened, but I think . . ." *What the hell was that? Shit, my hand hurts.* ". . . I think I'm all right now."

"This wasn't my fault," said Rebecca, picking up the pen from the floor and holding it as if it were a wounded infant. Her mouth was contorted, dragged down at the corners as if fishhooks were tugging on them. She didn't seem to notice the small patch of skin attached to the pen. "I didn't do anything to you."

Sam rubbed beads of sweat from his face and said, "Mrs. Morrison, I know you didn't. It was just a reaction to something. Maybe something I ate, or maybe some of the chemicals the workmen are using in and around the house." *You've never had an allergic reaction like that, Sam, don't kid yourself. And allergies don't make your hand blaze up like that.* "I'm fine. And now," he said pointing to the guest book, "you have your first two official guest signatures. The book has been christened."

"Hmm," said Rebecca, still not smiling. "Well, I suppose."

Dani and Sam excused themselves and left the inn. They walked the short distance to the shore and toured up and down Beach Avenue, going in and out every open shop and browsing tediously and extensively through the art galleries. They dined on hamburgers and hush puppies at

Salty Eddie's. Dani, having believed Sam's statement that
he was all right, chatted on about the shifting colors of the
fading sky and sea and how she couldn't wait to get out
here with her paints.

Sam glanced at his hand off and on, and at the small,
tender spot that remained from where the quill pen had
torn away the bit of his flesh. It was as though writing his
name had been a bad thing, as if the pen, or the book, had
been furious at his inclusion. He knew that was impossible.
Completely and totally crazy.

But if, by some insane stretch of the imagination, it
wasn't impossible, what the fuck was that all about?

SIX

The furniture supplied by the Morrisons was a curious, mismatched collection; a 1920s' bed with a gauche headboard and footboard carved in ribbons and flowers. The dresser was huge and made of ebony, a good fifty years older than the bed, with a large beveled-edged mirror attached to the back. The chair had been replaced with an overstuffed Victorian settee, recently re-covered in gold velvet. Sam thought it was great. Dani hated the "old shit" and complained that the Morrisons could have done better at a damned Helig-Myers. Rebecca offered to let Sam and Dani decorate with some of the old paintings they'd found in various closets. Dani declined with an *"asante*, no," and assured Rebecca that she had enough of her own paintings to fill a gallery and would put some of them on their bedroom wall. Rebecca understood, then *ooooed* and *ahhhed* over the abstract landscapes and still lifes Dani showed her but didn't offer to buy anything, which pissed Dani off no end.

The first week stumbled along, a cold, yet clear, stretch of days. Dani left each morning clutching canvas, easel, and paints. She was gone most of each day but returned with very little done. "It will come," she explained before Sam could ask. "I need to get in touch with my beach soul." However, it was clear she was not especially happy at the Abbadon Inn and was only biding her time until Sam noticed she was unhappy, or became unhappy himself. At night, she was reluctant to make love. She didn't even want to be held. She would clutch her pillow to her chest and pretend to sleep so as to be left alone.

Without the dreary chore of tending her son, Rebecca was now free to do her own thing—isometric stretches in the reception room each morning, lunching with the "Bed-and-Breakfast Brigade"—a group of female inn owners who liked to gather at each others' inns and discuss the finer points of the business—and sipping afternoon tea in one of the new rockers on the almost-finished side porch in spite of the chill and beneath a heavy patchwork quilt. Mitchell Morrison, as far as Sam could tell, spent his days and a great deal of his evenings at some men's club north of town, with other wealthy old men, doing whatever wealthy old men did.

While Dani and Mitchell were out in the world and Rebecca was playing leisurely hippie, Sam was spending half his time trying to find Carl and the other half in the small, fourth-floor tower room trying to "relate" through the closed trapdoor to the fifth-floor room. Sam attempted to pull the door down but it was obvious that Carl kept cramming things through the folding steps so they would not open.

In addition to the aggravating Carl-games and the increasing aloofness from Dani, Sam found the inn itself to be less than welcoming. The lighting on the third floor was unpredictable; some mornings the light over the bathroom sink wouldn't come on at all. Other times, it flickered and sputtered before holding its own. The fixtures themselves had unseen, ragged edges—he bore several small cuts from the side of the sink and the tub from careless grabbing of the sides. The heating was inefficient and unreliable. Some nights Sam woke up sweating, the room hot as a sauna. Other times he found himself passing through pockets of frigid air that seemed to hang in the rooms and hallways like invisible curtains of ice. Yet when he touched the radiators throughout the inn, he found them in working condition. Dani didn't seem aware of the temperature extremes; neither did Rebecca, nor Mitchell when he was around. And so Sam chalked it up to tension. His body and mind had become supersensitive because of all the troubles and changes he'd experienced over the past ten days. And the most recent trouble was Carl and his infuriating, childish power play up in the fifth-floor tower room.

Come Thursday morning, Sam had had enough of the

cat-and-mouse. He hunted Rebecca down in the Orchid Restaurant, where she was preparing to host a luncheon for the Bed-and-Breakfast Brigade. The restaurant, like the bar, was far from being ready for company, with its pocked brick fireplace, its replaced but untreated windows, and the plaster-patched walls. Yet the tables not only bore the same white tablecloths as the bar, but little crystal vases holding dried flower arrangements as well. Rebecca had set out a silver tray of finger sandwiches and veggie sticks on one of the tables, and at another table she and three ladies—none of them hippie types but who seemed to enjoy Rebecca's free-spiritedness—flipped through clunky wallpaper books in search of a pattern that would, Sam heard Rebecca say as he entered the restaurant from the bar, "best pick up the natural light and the tone of the floor."

"Excuse me," said Sam. Rebecca looked up from the book and blinked, as if for a moment she didn't remember who he was. "I need your help."

"What is it?" she asked.

"I've got a question."

The other ladies looked at Sam but said nothing. Rebecca didn't make a move to introduce him, so he put out his hand to them. "Good morning, I'm Sam Ford." The ladies, both quite a few years older than Rebecca, glanced at each other, then each gave him a quick handshake. "Nice to meet you," one said, but the other two remained quiet. They turned their attention back to the wallpaper book. Sam grit his teeth, feeling for a moment that he was regarded no more than a white-gloved, black-tied doorman. Smiling for the camera, slaving for the bucks. *Just let it go, Sam*, he told himself.

"What's your question?" asked Rebecca.

"This is a private matter, unless you'd rather . . ."

"Oh, well, all right." She shrugged slightly at her guests, then ushered Sam into the kitchen. It was a large room with white walls, white cabinets, blue granite countertops, blue-and-white tiled floor, two new white refrigerators, two new white stoves, a walk-in pantry, and a huge butcher-block island in the center. A small round table with three chairs sat by the corner. A windowed door led out to the backyard.

When Rebecca turned to Sam, he could see immediately that she was put out with the interruption. "What is it, Sam? You saw I had company."

"It's your son," said Sam. Her exasperated expression heightened his own exasperation; he could taste it at the back of his mouth, bitter, cold. *She really doesn't care, does she?* "Carl."

"Yes," said Rebecca. "And?"

"And I spent all Monday working up an initial curriculum for him; history, math, science, even a touch of art and music history. I spoke on the phone to the guidance counselor at the middle school here to see what they cover in seventh grade and to find out where I might be able to get a few materials for Carl. I thought it was a good idea to work alongside the curriculum already in place in the public schools so when Carl is ready for that, he could step right in."

"Yes?" Rebecca's mind was back out in the restaurant with the wallpaper book. Sam felt like shaking her.

"The counselor was very helpful. She directed me to a teacher supply store. I bought some books, notebooks, pens, a calculator, compass and protractor, everything he needs but didn't seem to have."

"You want to be reimbursed? Give me the receipts, and I'll see to it."

"Yes, I do. But that's not my major problem, Rebecca. I've not been able to work with Carl at all. He won't come out of his room. He fixes it so I can't get in. When he does come out, he hides from me."

"So what can I do about it?"

"I was hoping you would give me a hint. You know him much better than I do. What *do* you want me to do, short of blowing the trapdoor off its hinges?"

Rebecca's brows furrowed. "You don't have to be so . . . so graphic."

"There's not much he can learn through the floor. You and Mitchell need to have a serious talk with him, to let him know I'm not here just to entertain myself. I need to get off on the right foot with the boy, and we haven't even seen each other face-to-face since I moved in on Saturday."

Rebecca turned away to the counter and fumbled with the plastic wrap over a platter of ham she had sliced for the luncheon. Sam could see her shoulders rise and fall. "Mr. Ford . . ." she began.

"Sam."

"Sam. Yes, I am his mother, but Carl is just . . ." She paused, took a breath. "He . . . I don't know."

"Help me out here."

"You're the teacher. I don't know what to suggest you do. You're supposed to know what to do."

"He's your son."

"We hired you because you seemed to have a rapport with him."

"One conversation isn't rapport. That has to be built with time."

"We're paying you to tutor him."

"I can't do my job this way."

A loud, long sigh. "He worries me. I don't know how to talk to him. I don't know what to say or do with him. So you just do what you have to do. All right?" She turned back, and it looked as if she were trying not to cry.

Sam didn't want to lose this gig. He needed the cash, the roof over his head. And he really felt he was up to the challenge of Carl, if he could ever get hold of the boy. Sam tried to hide the anger in his voice. "All right, then. I will." Rebecca went back into the restaurant.

Furious, Sam slammed through the back door and into the yard. It was cold, but his anger kept him warm. *Fucking detached parents! Fucking psycho kid!*

Sam crossed his arms, his hands clenched. Blood rushed through his temples; his head throbbed. This whole thing was ridiculous. It was as if the Morrisons didn't care if Carl ever learned anything, only that he was out of their hair and under the care of someone else. No wonder the kid was so screwed up. Carl was in need of at least one adult who was on his side.

But how could Sam be on Carl's side when Carl was never around?

Maybe I should just quit, if that's the way it's going to be.

Sam closed his eyes. Frosty air batted his eyelashes and

tugged at his ears. Crows called to each other from tree-tops in this yard and the next, sounding like messengers of despair.

"Uh-oh, uh-oh, uh-oh."

Sam opened his eyes and looked about the yard. It was larger than most Cape May yards, delineated by a tall wooden privacy fence on the south side and along the back. A short stone walk, newly laid, led to a gate and the alley beyond. A dead garden bearing teetering grapevine trellises and broken morning-glory stakes stood near the kitchen. In the left corner of the yard, choked in an impenetrable tangle of untrimmed holly, scrubby cedars, and dried thistles, was a splintery, peak-roofed wooden shed with a stone chimney. It looked as if Rebecca's yard workers had been back here long enough to lay the stone walk, run the mower over most of the yard, and trim the tall weeds along the exterior wall of the inn itself. The rest of the trim work along the fence line and, in particular, the mess around the shed, was left untouched. Sam picked up a scrap of stray paper that had blown into the yard. He stuck it in his jeans pocket. The Morrisons might as well have hired him as a janitor for all the work he was doing with Carl.

Enough, man. Pull it together. You can't quit. Carl needs a good teacher. And if nothing else, you need the money. Go back inside, borrow a saw from one of the guys putting in the new bathroom on the second floor, and cut a damn hole in the trapdoor. Rebecca said do whatever I had to do.

Sam let out a breath that hung before him for a moment like filmy cotton. *Then what, pull the kid out by his feet? Yeah, I can just see that rodeo now.*

He stretched his neck to work out the tension and turned toward the kitchen door.

Then he whipped back around, the hairs on his arms standing up, his heart clenching.

Something dark and shapeless had skittered across the yard to the shed, had run impossibly fast like something in a film clip cranked to an unnatural speed. The figure had darted into the cover of holly and cedars and disappeared. It could have been a large dog. It could have been a child, or a small adult, bent over so as not to be seen, and who was now hunched down, hiding amid the weeds and the thorny branches, waiting for . . .

Waiting for what?

It can't be human. I've never seen anyone, or anything, move like that!

A chill climbed Sam's spine and thrummed the base of his neck. The throbbing of his heart intensified.

He snatched a large and muddy rock from the edge of the dead garden and walked slowly to the shed, squinting, trying to see inside the tall, thick growth. If he found a dog, he would chase it out. If it were a trespassing bum, he'd threaten the guy with the police. If it were Carl, he'd grab the kid up and they'd have a most major confrontation.

"Who's in there?" he said.

There was no answer.

"I saw you go in there. Come out now!"

Silence.

Then a single branch shivered and went still. There was a short and barely audible groan.

"Carl, that's you, isn't it?" said Sam, his voice less authoritative than he'd hoped. "Come out, now, do you hear me?"

Sam pulled back several holly branches and peered in. All he could see were shadows crisscrossed with even darker shadows.

Don't get too close, Sam. It might not be Carl. It moved so fast, it was unreal.

Careful. Careful.

"Carl, it'll be easier on you if you'd come out now and not drag this out any longer. I know you know I mean what I say."

Silence. Sam worked his shoulder through the bushes and tipped his head, trying to see. Through the twisted branches and sharp, ragged leaves he could see the edge of the shed's door. It was cracked open a foot, a slice of blackness beyond. He caught a scent of heavy mud and dead things.

"Carl, come out of there. Now!" *There have to be black widows in there, brown recluse spiders, rusted nails, loose floorboards. Can the Morrisons sue me if their son gets seriously hurt while trying to avoid me? Damn well better not.*

"Carl!"

But is it Carl?

There was another groan, raspier, even softer than the first. Sam wedged his body into the bushes, tucking his head so as not to get a thorn to the eye. *How the hell did the kid get in there? I can hardly move.*

"Carl, now!"

Sam tried to touch the door but could move no farther. The woven branches were too heavy to be bent any more. He tried to kneel down, but the shrubs held him too tightly. *Fuck it, that's enough.* "You're on your own, little boy," said Sam. "Come out whenever you're ready, I'm not going to get chewed up by these bushes on your account. And when you're out, and you will come out at some point, we'll have a serious, big-time come-to-Jesus meeting."

Sam dropped the rock and wormed his way back out of the brush. He could hear the fabric of his shirt catching, ripping. *You'll pay for this out of your allowance, if you get any.*

Out in the sunlight he took stock of the battle scars. There were pinpricks along his sleeves, several short tears near the elbow. His jeans bore a few major snags. The backs of his hands were raked and raw. Sam touched one of the small, bloody spots on his knuckles. Then he looked up at the inn.

There was a high-pitched whoosh to his right, and a large, thorny branch caught him across the face. Sam cried out in pain, stumbled, and knocked the branch away. He whirled around to confront the wielder of the branch, but no one was there. He felt his face and the angry welts already springing up.

"Damn!"

Holding his cheek and nose, he quickly walked the rim of the shrub line, batting at the branches, looking for evidence of someone having just dashed back into them to hide—a noise, a movement—but there was nothing. A trickle of blood coursed Sam's nose.

"Who did that?"

There was no one.

Sam looked at the culprit branch on the ground, a single

snapped-off, barren stem covered in long, sharp barbs. Not holly or boxwood, but a branch from a quince bush. Was there a quince in this yard? Not that he could see. Did people in Cape May even raise quinces?

"Carl!" *You little ass!*

It had to have been the kid. The boy had lived at the Abbadon long enough to scout out the place and know its ins and outs. He knew how to attack and withdraw like a little Swamp Fox.

But where the hell is he hiding now?

Sam wiped his forehead with his thumb and looked at the blood. He debated on going back into the inn by way of the porte cochere on the other side so he wouldn't have to pass Rebecca and her gang with a damaged face, but then thought, no. The woman needed to see exactly what Sam was dealing with. Then he would insist that she and Mitchell sit the kid down, tie him down if necessary, and put the fear of God in him. Or Sam would sue for damages.

Right. And lose this job.

Tell me just what job that is, Sammy boy.

Sam strode to the kitchen door, went inside, and wet a paper towel to wipe his forehead. He then joined the ladies at their luncheon. Rebecca hopped up immediately. The other ladies, who were through with the wallpaper samples and had just begun their salads, peered at Sam from behind white linen napkins.

"Oh, dear, but you've gotten yourself scratched up," Rebecca said.

"No," said Sam. "I haven't gotten myself scratched up. It was done to me."

"It was? Oh, dear! I've got a first-aid kit out here, if you'll follow me." Her hair bouncing, and her long floral skirt whipping around her legs, Rebecca hurried from the restaurant, though the bar, and across the front hall to the reception room. She tugged open the closet door and removed a plastic box from the top shelf. But when she popped it open and held out the Band-Aids and tube of Neosporin, Sam shook his head. "No, thanks."

"Why not? You don't think you need to go to the hospital, do you? It's not bad enough for stitches. And it wasn't

our fault, that happening. We haven't gotten all the trees
and bushes trimmed out back, but you should have watched
where you were going."

"Rebecca, Carl did this. He hit me with a quince
branch, hard enough for this."

"We don't have quince bushes."

"Did you hear what I said? Carl whacked me in the
face!"

Rebecca shook her head. "No, he didn't."

"Yes."

"No, no, he couldn't have. He was in here, with me."

"Rebecca, he is outside, hiding in the bushes beside the
shed or maybe even inside the shed."

Rebecca put her hands on her hips. Her skirt hiked up
on one side, revealing a slouched wool sock. "No, he was
here with me. Carl came into the restaurant right after you
went outside. He visited with us for a minute or two, actually talked politely to the other ladies, and then I gave him
a couple of ham biscuits. He went back upstairs. I heard
him go, right up the stairs. Ask any of my guests."

That's impossible. "Are you sure?"

"I don't lie, Sam. I'm surprised you would even suggest
that."

"I don't think you lie, I think . . ." *What do I think? If it
wasn't Carl, then who wielded that branch? What ran
across the yard so quickly?* "I guess I made a mistake, Rebecca. I'm sorry."

Rebecca put the plastic kit on the registration desk and
peeled open a Band-Aid. Again Sam said, "No, that's okay.
The bleeding's stopped."

What is hiding in the shed?

"All right," said Rebecca. She tossed the peeled bandage into the trash can behind the counter, packed the kit
up, and shoved it back into the closet. As she returned to
the restaurant, Sam went upstairs to the second floor.

Two men were hammering in the communal bathroom
at the end of the hall, putting in a new wall to separate the
toilet and bathtub from the sink, so bathroom visitors
wouldn't have to either wait to brush their teeth or do so
while another bathroom visitor took a dump in plain view.

"Excuse me," Sam called through the door. "You seen the kid around?"

One nodded. "The redhead? Yeah, he stopped by just a minute ago. Backed his little ass inside here and cut loose with a major fart."

The other man rubbed his arm under his nose. "A really nasty one. We told him to get out of here, that we had work to do, but he got snotty and said a bathroom's for farting, didn't we know that?"

"Little turd," said the first man.

Sam nodded. Then he said, "Got a saw and extension cord I can borrow?"

The tower rooms were something Sam would have loved as a kid but that he found particularly unpleasant as an adult. The first floor of the tower was the small, enclosed entrance porch that led to the main front hallway of the inn. The second floor of the tower was just a bay off a bedroom. However, for some reason known only to some past owner, the other three floors could only be reached from the room below it by sets of cheap steps that folded up into trapdoors. Sam wondered if at an earlier time there had been narrow stationary steps, but that someone in the 1950s had thought folding, space-saving steps was the way to go. The steps to the third and fourth floors were down, and Sam wrangled the electric saber saw up through the openings. On the fourth floor, he stopped to look out the front window, feeling, once again, a little claustrophobic. The room was about seven feet square, and the realization that the only way out was back through the trapdoors or straight out a window added to the feeling of oppression. There was no furniture in the room, only a small stepladder Carl used so he could reach the string to the door in the ceiling. Candy wrappers and gum wrappers lay along the walls, and dust balls seemed to hover just above the floor. The door and folding steps to the fifth-floor room were closed up against the ceiling.

Get ready, Carl. I hope you aren't sitting on the trapdoor or you might not be able to cut good, juicy farts for the rest of your life.

Sam plugged the saw into the only outlet in the wall, centered the stepladder beneath the trapdoor, and then stood on the top on the ladder. He held the base of the saw against the plywood overhead. He thumbed the switch and nothing happened. Sam got off the ladder, pulled the plug from the outlet and several sparks came with it, shocking his hand. "Damn. Rebecca swore the whole place has been rewired."

He hesitated, then plugged it back into the outlet and pushed the ON button. The saw whirled into life. He switched it off, climbed back on the ladder, and held the saw against the ceiling. He turned the saw on. With a loud grinding, it bit into the wood. Sawdust blew into Sam's face.

There was a loud shout behind him.

Sam leapt from the ladder and held the saw up like a weapon. There, head poking up through the trapdoor in the floor like a fucking prairie dog, was Carl. The boy's wide grin froze on his face when he saw Sam's saw. "Whoa, man!" the boy shouted, his hands coming up through the hole beside his head. "Who you think you are? Leatherface?"

Sam flicked off the saw; he shook sawdust from his face. It was all he could do to keep from pushing the boy down the hole with his foot. He spoke slowly, evenly. "What was that you just said?"

Carl laughed. "I said, who do you think you are? Leatherface?"

Sam slowly put the saw on the ladder top. He narrowed his eyes at the boy. "Just because I put up with your disrespectful slur when we first met doesn't mean I'll give you a pass every time you decide to throw an insult my way. You will show respect, do you understand me? I will not tolerate any less than that."

Carl's face fell. "What? Ho, wait a minute."

"I'll repeat—do you understand me?"

"Hey, no, no!" Carl was flustered. He shook his head vigorously. "Don't you know about the *Texas Chainsaw Massacre*?"

"About what?"

"*The Texas Chainsaw Massacre*. The movie. That guy

chasing girls through the woods with a chainsaw. The family that ate people and stuff. Where have you been? Came out a couple years ago. Jeez, man, didn't you see it?"

"No. Did you?"

Carl's face squirmed a little, as if he were deciding to lie or not. Then he said, "Well, no, but I saw the poster. And I read all about it in my monster magazines. I'm going to see it as soon as I can, when it comes back to the theaters."

Sam thought for a moment. It did sound familiar. "All right. I think I remember something like that. But what's a leatherface?"

"It's not a what, it's a *who*. The guy in the mask that chased people with a saw. He wore a mask made of human skin, so they called him Leatherface. Don't you get it? You were holding a saw up like you wanted to kill me. Like the guy in the movie."

Sam stared at the boy.

"It's a joke, okay? A damn joke." Carl scratched his cheek nervously. "Don't you get it?"

Sam said, "Yeah, I get it."

"Okay, then?" Carl spread his fingers out and scrunched his lips.

"Okay, then."

"So what were you doing with the saw?"

"Cutting a hole in your trapdoor. How long did you think I'd stand in here and try to talk to you up there?"

Carl grinned, his sneaky expression back. "Forever, maybe. Guess I'll just move to another room if you cut a hole in my door. I'll go to some place I can lock the door."

"I can do more than wield a saw. I can take any door in this place off its hinges. Your mom's given me the right to do what I need to do. You're stuck with me."

Carl rolled his eyes and said, "Fuck that shit."

Sam squatted down, crossed his arms over his knees, and said sternly, "And I won't tolerate that kind of talk."

"What are you going to do? Wash my mouth out with soap?"

"What brand do you prefer, Ivory or Dial? I've got both. I even have a sliver of Lava. That would do some good."

"Ha," said Carl. "Yeah, right." His gaze shifted up to Sam's forehead. He jabbed his finger in that direction. "And just what happened to you?"

"I walked into a quince bush," said Sam. "Now let's get out of this blasted tower and make out a study plan that works for us both."

"You think I'm going to do that with you?"

"Yes, I do."

Carl's tongue came out, worked at the corner of his mouth and then went back in. He chuckled, once. " 'Cause you got the saw, right?"

"Like your mom said, whatever it takes." Though he didn't feel like it, he winked at the boy.

Carl dropped through the opening to the floor below. He stared up at Sam. Sam, surprised Carl was actually waiting for him, unplugged the saw, wrapped up the cord, and tucked it under his arm. He climbed down the stairs and joined his irritating charge.

SEVEN

Carl dragged his sleeping bag into the new room, flopped it open on the floor, and tossed his pillow and blanket on top. He scratched his ass and looked around. He'd been getting tired of the top tower room, anyway, all that pulling of trapdoors up and down and unfolding of stairs each time he wanted to go anywhere. Sam coming at the trapdoor with a saw a week and a half ago didn't really make the call, though; it was just time for Carl to be on the move again. He was a ramblin' man, like that song by the Allman Brothers, even though his father hadn't gotten shot, and Carl hadn't been born on the backseat of a Greyhound bus.

His new room was on the third floor, sitting directly over the porte cochere and the second-floor "sunroom," as his mother called it. Carl liked that; at first he didn't want to be hanging anywhere near Sam Ford, but now he liked the idea of being just down the hall from his tutor and the girlfriend. This way, Carl would be in a better position to try out his spells on them.

The room was pretty damned nifty. The walls were sloped, the ceiling just high enough to clear Carl's five-foot frame by about a foot, and there was a spiral staircase enclosed in a tight little corner closet. He knew that the staircase led down to the sunroom—his mom had told him—though he'd not tried to get into it before. He yanked on the door to the staircase; it was painted shut. He tugged harder, then found a loose nail on the floor and dug around the crack. At last, the door came open. Carl looked inside the stairwell. It was dark and musty inside. The steel rack of stairs wobbled a bit on its center pole when he shook them. There were spray-painted peace symbols on the walls, and someone had used a permanent marker to draw a crude naked woman with long hair bending over and a man with long hair and a bloated, erect penis poised at her butt. Both figures wore vague line smiles.

Carl had watched his mother talking to a friend on the kitchen phone a couple days after the Morrisons had moved to Cape May. She said that the Abbadon Inn had been owned by a lot of people over the last one hundred twenty-some years. In the 1960s it had been abandoned ("left, unloved, and forgotten," was how his mother had put it) and the flower children had discovered it. They held their parties, smoked their pot, and dropped their acid in just about every room in the place from the cellar to the bathrooms to the guest rooms and the kitchen. The police raided the inn frequently, but the hippies kept coming back. Carl had been aware that as his mother told the story, she had a funny curl to her lip, as if she wished she'd been free back then, free to party in the Abbadon Inn with a bunch of longhaired, guitar-strumming teenagers instead of chasing after a three-year-old.

Amid all of his mother's sporadic renovations of the place, it was clear she had not taken a good look inside the spiral stairwell and found the naked marker-people on the wall. If Rebecca had, she would have slapped paint on it first thing. Rebecca didn't like the idea of Carl seeing naked women. When Rebecca had caught Carl with his father's *Penthouse* two years back, she'd gone into a major hissy fit, stomping around, swearing the women in those pictures were nothing more than cheap tramps.

"Nice women respect their bodies!" she'd insisted.

"Respect them for what?" Carl had asked her in all honesty.

But Rebecca had only hemmed and hawed and then asked him if he was interested in taking golf lessons at the Danbury Country Club next month, wouldn't that be fun with all those other boys and girls?

But Carl was older now. He knew a bit more about things. Hadn't hippies been into love, peace, and getting naked? Weren't they into fucking each other? Love the one you're with, like that? Sure looked like it from the picture on the stairwell wall. Carl smiled, touched himself, and wondered what a hippie girl's ass would look like and what it would feel like. He wondered if the girl would smile back at him and say that, like in the song, she was just waiting for something to do.

He shut the staircase door and turned the latch. Then he locked the door to the hallway and balanced a large piece of scrap wood against it. If Sam took the door off the hinges even while Carl was sleeping, the falling board would wake him up. So there, Leatherface.

It was a Sunday night, raining steadily, with rivulets coursing down the window glass. The room, with only one side unprotected from the wind, rattled like an old man's dentures. Dani and Sam had gone out to dinner somewhere, taking a taxi since they did not have a car. Carl's mother and father were downstairs in the bar, fussing about something, most likely the still-unfinished restaurant walls, the poor job the workers had done on the second-floor bathroom, or Carl.

Carl sat cross-legged on his sleeping bag and pulled open the canvas laundry bag. Inside were all his clothes, well, all those he would wear, wrinkled and in need of a wash fairly soon. The rest of his clothes, ones his mother thought were nice and he thought were stupid, were in suitcases and garment bags down in his parents' bedroom, still packed from the trip from Connecticut. Carl clawed out a pair of socks and put them over the ones he already had on. His feet were cold.

He dug deeper in the bag. He pulled out the books he'd smuggled from Danbury, the books his parents didn't know he had. He'd gotten them last June at a store several miles from his house, a dark little shop called *Magisch en Macht*. The place was run by an old guy and his wife who'd come from somewhere that wasn't America. The shop specialized in magic. Real magic.

When Carl was a little kid, magic was Mickey Mouse directing dancing mops and the Wicked Witch making poppies grow in a field so Dorothy would fall asleep and never reach Oz. Magic was a kit you bought from the back of a comic book—card tricks and disappearing coins and scarves that rose up out of a black, plastic box. But at *Magisch en Macht*, magic was contained in ancient, dried-up books, bottles of oily liquids, jars of powders, straw figures with beaded eyes, and a back room draped in a black velvet curtain.

Carl discovered the shop the day after his thirteenth birthday. He had been running away from home for the fourth time, this time for good, this time for keeps. The place was near the railroad tracks south of town, tucked between an abandoned gas station and a mechanic shop boasting dead cars, piles of rusted engines, and a sign reading LAST CHANCE AUTO REPAIR.

The skulls and feathers in the shop window caught Carl's attention, and he pushed open the jingly door and went inside. The only light in the front room was provided by red shaded lamps and smoky candles; all the windows were covered in heavy, dark drapes. A skeletally thin young woman and her bearded boyfriend were buying a bagful of things Carl tried to see but couldn't, and they passed by him on their way out with only a cursory glance. The old couple was cordial to Carl but distant, as if they thought he couldn't possibly appreciate what real magic was all about. And of course, as if they thought he had no money.

"Here," said the old woman after Carl browsed for a few minutes. She directed him toward items she felt he might be able to buy with whatever means he had in his pockets, things contained in little plastic tubs beside the door. "You're on a trip, yes?" said the woman, and Carl was impressed that she knew, because he had left his pack outside behind a bush. "You might want a charm for safety. Here, look and see. These are not expensive." In one orange plastic bin were cheap metal tokens on chains, on the backs of which were inscribed, "safety," "peace," "adventure," "love," "money," "happiness," "revenge," "health."

Carl picked through the tokens, and selected "adventure" and "money." He paid the two dollars and slipped them around his neck. Immediately, he could feel something inside his gut, something stirring around, rearranging itself. He liked the feel. Carl flipped through a rack of magazines on the occult and then through a box of turtle heads and claws. He moved toward the black velvet curtain, but the old man, faster than any old man Carl had ever seen, thrust out his hand to block the way.

"No, son," said the man. "That's for experienced practitioners, only."

"I got more money," Carl said.

The man only shook his head.

Carl stamped his foot. "Customer's always right, my mom says."

"I'm not your mom."

This pissed Carl off enough to postpone his running away. He hid in the slimy bathroom of the old gas station next door until nightfall, playing with the Matchbox cars he'd put in his duffle bag and munching from the box of Frosted Flakes he'd taken from his kitchen. Late afternoon, the old couple came out of the shop, locked the door, climbed into their station wagon and drove off. Carl waited another few hours until it was completely dark outside. Then he grabbed a brick from the gas station parking lot, hurled it through a side window in the magic shop, and hoisted himself up and in.

He didn't have much time to rummage; he thought he heard sirens several blocks away the moment his feet hit the floor inside the store. But he made it through the velvet curtain and snatched what he could. He collected several small, corked vials, some wrinkled pamphlets, a little skull of some sort, and as many of the dusty, leather-bound books as he could hold in his arms. He stuck the vials, pamphlets, and skull into his pocket then tossed the books out through the window and climbed after them. He hid in the gas station bathroom and flipped through the books with the beam from his flashlight.

The books convinced him he didn't need to run away. Though he didn't understand much of what was written inside, he immediately realized he was holding a real, potential power in his hands. He had a book on Asian magic, one on the life and teachings of Aleister Crowley, and a third on about different types of kinesis. There was one on cooking and magic and two others written in a foreign language, all three of which he tossed aside. The seventh book, entitled *And You Shall Make It So* by Rowan Margaret Ponsonby, so intrigued Carl that he stayed up all night, reading bits and pieces, feeling a latent power in himself rise and demand satisfaction and release.

When the sky was torn open by fingers of orange and scarlet the following morning, Carl went home instead of hopping the westbound freight train. His mother was ecstatic he was back and begged him to promise he would never run off again. His father threatened to lock him up for life. But Carl only stared at them, and in his mind, dared them to try anything against him. Because now he held the key to power. The key to his own freedom.

Over the next months he read as much as he could of the books, his favorite remaining *And You Shall Make It So*. He kept the books beneath his mattress and read them when his mother was napping and his father was at the firm. He stumbled over the text, but put together what he could, and began testing small spells and curses.

His mother's dog, Tippy, had been a bane to Carl's existence ever since it had bounded into the house as a puppy. It was a snippy, yappy thing that wore blue bows between his ears and was constantly drooling out the corners of his sticky little mouth. Tippy had grown old, but was more energetic than Carl felt most of the time. The dog liked to trot up and down the steps endlessly, nails clicking on the hardwood, checking out the positions and activities of the family. Tippy liked to chew on things that belonged to Carl. Tippy liked to sit in Rebecca's lap in the evenings when she and Mitchell watched the news before dinner. Carl hated Tippy.

Carl composed a simple spell in October, his first, combining a chant from the *You Shall* book and a posture from the Asian magic book. He sat straight on the sofa, his back as erect as possible, and stared at the dog from across the room during the *NBC Nightly News with David Brinkley*. Mitchell alternated between reading the *New York Times* and watching the show. Rebecca drank her tea, nibbled on some Pepperidge Farm cookies, and rubbed the dog's bow-bedecked head. *Nnnnnn*, thought Carl, squinting his eyes at the pooch. *Nnnnnnnnnnnn. Die, you sloppy ball of crap. Die, you worthless old flea-sack.*

The dog looked up several times and stared at Carl. Carl kept up his mental humming. *Nnnnnnnn. Die, Tippy. Croak already.*

Tippy didn't die during the news. And when it was over, and Rebecca got up to take her evening bath, Tippy tapped after her into the bathroom as he always did, to watch her draw the water. Mitchell went into his office to make his nightly phone calls. Carl went to his room and pulled a large hunk of hair from his scalp as punishment, thinking, *You're a stupid idiot. You can't even do the easy spells!* He sucked the blood from his fingers, read a comic book, then tore it up in anger and went to sleep.

The next morning, Tippy was dead. Lying by his bowl at six thirty in the morning as if he'd fallen asleep waiting for Rebecca to offer up a scoop of dog chow. He was cold and stiff, the little blue bow still clipped to his hair, the drool on the corners of his mouth, for the first time since Carl had known the dog, dried.

The spell had worked, though Carl's mother and the vet said it was old age and inevitable, a case of heart failure. Yes, the dog was old, and that might have helped push through the spell he'd put on the damn drooly thing, but Carl had been thrilled. He had wielded the final push. He also knew it would just be a matter of time before he could master more magic and have more control over the things and the people around him.

During the month of November he had been able to make his mother break out in hives, a case big enough that she was sent scurrying to see a dermatologist. By intoning silently in the back of the family's Buick LeSabre, Carl was able to make his father clip the side of a parked automobile the night his family had gone Christmas shopping in Hartford. Ha! The men even had to exchange insurance company numbers, a circumstance that made Mitchell look angry and degraded. Sure, there were lots of times, most of the time, really, that nothing happened when Carl sat in his positions, hummed his chants, and made his spells, but he knew that magicians had to work at their craft. Some practitioners spent their whole lives getting good at it. And hell, Carl figured, there wasn't much else going on in his life. He might as well take his time and get it right.

The move to the southern New Jersey shore shook things up. While Carl's parents packed up most of his stuff, Carl packed his own laundry bag with stuff he didn't want them to see. Carl had wrapped the vials and the skull—which by now he'd figured was either a raccoon or skunk—in his *Mork and Mindy* T-shirt. The vials had cracked in transit, leaking oily fluid all over the skull, the shirt, and a pair of shorts. The pamphlets were likewise ruined. The books, however, were on the opposite end of the bag and suffered no damage. Carl had never figured out what the vials had been for, and hadn't gotten much out of the pamphlets, which were introductions to exorcisms, channeling, and UFOs, so their loss wasn't major. He mainly cared that the books had made it safely.

Yet when he stepped foot inside the Abbadon Inn, Carl felt eaten alive by the place. He could feel the inn swallowing up all the supernatural energy he'd been collecting, draining him, making him feel weak and stupid all over again. He knew he'd have to start over from scratch.

And, literally, scratch it was, because in January he discovered cutting.

At first, it wasn't much, just a picked scab, but when he spoke a chant and released his own blood, he knew he was back on track. The heat and the pain assured him that his power was returning. It had worked, sort of, with the workman laying the stone walk. It had worked, sort of, when he made one of Rebecca's girlfriends trip on the curb outside the inn's gate and split her lip open against the sidewalk, and when one of the carpenters in the second-floor bathroom drove the hammer into his index finger instead of a nail head. All Carl needed to do was to keep on practicing.

Sam Ford and his stuck-up wife Dani were good new subjects for his experiments in magic. Carl had whispered a small spell a couple days ago while he and Sam sat in the bar, reading through the first pages of an American history book. He'd silently spoken another as they ate pumpkin pie and worked out an algebra problem in the kitchen. Yet, even as Carl hummed in his mind and pinched the thin flesh on his wrist hard enough for it to weep red, Sam seemed oblivious to it all. He hadn't broken anything, he hadn't spilled boiling water from the tea kettle on himself, or gone into coughing fits like he was supposed to. Carl wondered if people whose ancestors came from Africa would be less susceptible to magic than the basic white person.

Or maybe he was just aiming spells at the wrong person for the time being.

Carl couldn't stand Dani. She smiled a lot and talked all that prissy African talk, but Carl could tell she hated him, his parents, and the Abbadon Inn. He'd listened through Sam and Dani's door a couple times late at night, and she was always griping about Carl's mother, how she was scatterbrained and clueless. She hated the furniture, she didn't like sharing a kitchen, and she especially didn't like Carl's attitude. Sam talked in a very low voice, and it was hard for Carl to catch what he was saying, but he did hear snippets of the man's replies. Sam wanted to stay at the inn. He'd been working with "the kid" for only two weeks but felt he was doing some good, making some strides.

Strides, thought Carl. *Screw that. I'm just playing along with him for now. Stupid old Leatherface. He has no idea what's really going on.*

Carl didn't hang around their door long because he never knew when Dani would get in a huff and storm out, or decide she needed to mosey across to the communal bathroom to do whatever it was women did in bathrooms. But all her bitching was enough to convince Carl that she should be his next victim.

From his pocket, Carl pulled out some strands of curly black hair. He'd picked them out of the shower drain with tweezers. They were longer than Sam's by two inches, so Carl knew he had the right ones.

He had stolen several pillows from his mother and father's bedroom. He pulled one out of the laundry bag. It was too damn cute, this pillow, made of yellow dotted

Swiss and surrounded with white lace. With a pair of pinking shears he'd taken from his mother's bureau, Carl cut a five-inch-wide chunk from the pillow in a shape that resembled a human form. He stapled the gaping side together to keep the stuffing from coming out. It was hard to see clearly in the light from the grimy overhead fixture, so he had to squint as he worked. Yet this was a chore best done in darkness. Light would take away some of the power. Outside, the rain shifted direction and hit the front window, sounding like a bag of BBs dropped on a floor, spilling open, and rolling on forever.

Carl used a Magic Marker and drew big round eyes, a slit mouth, and round breasts with black nipples. He took a bottle of Elmer's Glue from his collection of things in the laundry bag and mounted the hair on the stuffed doll's flat-topped head, then some down on the crotch area like he'd seen in *Penthouse*. He had to blow on it a long time until it was tacky enough to hold the hair in place.

He didn't have a needle or a pin but didn't want to use the nail he'd found in the room because he didn't want to kill her, just hurt her and make her leave. He could only imagine that nails in a voodoo doll would be like driving a railroad spike through a living person. So he used the stapler.

First he stapled his own ankle several times, to bring on the blood. It wasn't much, just little dots, but it hurt well enough as it scraped the bone. Then he got up on his knees and placed the opened stapler against the doll's grim face. He pushed down quickly and hard, hearing the little metallic snap. *Nnnnnnnnn*, he hummed. He lifted the stapler and smiled. One was embedded nicely right beside the nose. He leaned over again and stapled the doll's neck and chest. *Nnnnnnnnnnn*. He closed the stapler to put it back in the laundry bag then slammed a staple in the leg area for good measure.

"Yep, that'll do it. That'll mess her up. That'll get her gone."

Carl smiled. He wished he was a fly on the wall at whatever restaurant Dani and Sam had gone to so he could see the wide-eyed terror in that prissy woman's eyes as she felt the pain stabbing through her body. He could see her, fork

in hand, smiling at something Sam had said, then dropping
the fork to the table and crying out. Carl stood and went to
the front window, his ankle stinging nicely, clutching the
doll to his chest. He couldn't see past his own reflection
and the rain against the pane, but he could imagine Dani
jumping up from the table in fear and agony, screaming
that something was wrong, she needed a doctor, something
was cutting her, hurting her!

The thought of that scene tasted good on Carl's tongue,
like pepper and vinegar.

He licked his lips, flicked off the light, curled up in his
sleeping bag, and slept well.

EIGHT

Dani sat up straight in bed. She wiped her eyes, held her breath, and listened.

There had been something, somewhere close by. A scuffling, scratching sound.

The night was sitting heavy and dark in the bedroom. The digital clock on the nightstand read 2:42 A.M. The rain had stopped at some point, but the wind was still whistling outside through the streets like a lonely banshee.

Dani's vision was fuzzy; her contact lenses sat in their plastic container on the nightstand. She grappled for the scratchy pair of wire-rimmed glasses she wore when her contacts were out, nearly whacking the digital clock onto the floor, and jammed the glasses on her face. Her mouth was dry, and her body ached from sleeping on the lumpy, too-soft mattress. She tipped her head, trying to hear above the wind.

The sound came again. A rustling and soft scratching at the door.

"Sam," she hissed. He did not move. She whacked him in the shoulder. "Sam!"

Sam mumbled something, coughed, then rolled over. "Wha . . . ?" he managed.

"Someone's outside our door."

"What? What time is it?" He still hadn't opened his eyes; even in the dark she could see his features vaguely. His lids were closed.

There was another fluttering rustle. Dani's heart kicked into double-time. Her bare feet hit the floor, and she stared at the door, clutching one end of the bedspread. Then she saw a flickering of bright orange beneath the crack.

Fire?

Fire!

"Sam!" Dani shouted, and ran for the door. Behind her, Sam was awake at last.

"What's wrong?" he shouted.

"There's a fire!" screamed Dani. She threw herself against the door, her heart pounding, thinking, *There are no fire escapes to this room! We can only jump out onto the roof and then fall to the ground. Oh, my God! We'll break our legs! I'll lose my paintings!*

She pressed her hands and the side of her face to the wood. Her glasses were knocked askew on her nose. Feel for the heat, she'd been taught. Then you'll know if it's safe to open the door during a fire.

If it's safe, we can run downstairs and get out. I'll take everything I can carry in one trip! I knew this place was a tinderbox!

"No!" cried Sam. He jumped from the bed, tripping through the fallen covers on the floor, and raced to Dani's side. "We have to warn the others, we have to get out!"

"Wait," said Dani.

The door was cold.

She pulled her face away. Sam was beside her now, feeling the door, too. "Wait a minute."

Dani walked her hands up and down the surface of the door. There was no heat, only the cool of the unpainted wood.

"Did you smell fire?" Sam asked, breathing heavily.

Dani adjusted her glasses and then knelt by the door. She peered beneath the crack. It was almost black out in the hallway. "No, no. I saw it. I saw something bright under the door. It looked just like flames."

Sam let out a breath. "Maybe you were dreaming."

"No! I saw it!" She stood quickly, turned the key in the lock, and slowly pulled the door open. She peered out, and in the heavy shadows saw nothing but the barren floor, closed doors to the other rooms, and the iron sconces hanging at their odd angles along the wall.

"Dani?" Sam was beside her, his head pushing hers out of the way. "I don't see anything, or smell any smoke."

"I did see something. You don't know what I saw."

Sam shut the door and put his hands on her shoulders. She felt herself trembling under his touch.

"No, I don't," he said. "Are you mad at me for some reason?"

"No." She took a deep breath. "Yes, because you're acting so damned calm. I saw something, all right? Maybe it was a flashlight? A match? I think that brat of yours is trying to spook us."

Sam rubbed his neck beneath the collar of the ratty T-shirt in which he always slept, and he sighed. That pissed Dani off even more. She twisted free of his grasp. "You think I'm kidding? Ever since he moved out of the tower room down to our floor, I've had a feeling he's been listening in through our door and otherwise just being a creep to see how we react."

"You could be right. I wouldn't put it past him."

"Yeah? Okay? And you think that's fine?"

"No, it's awful, Dani." Sam's voice was terse now. That was good. At least he was on her wavelength for the moment. "I have my work cut out for me with him."

Dani felt heat behind her eyes, anger flushing her skin. "Is that all you have to say? Here we are, living in a creaking, ancient inn with a screwed-up family, and you have your 'work cut out for you'? You want to keep dealing with that psycho kid?"

"Yes. I . . . you, we both need the money and the roof."

"Yeah? And I need privacy. I need to not be harassed in the middle of the night by a sniveling little fuck. I need to not have to put up with that ridiculous woman every time I go out to paint. She wants to know where I'm going, what I'm painting, when I'll be back, blah, blah, blah. Not that she cares. She's so goddamned nosy! I need a bed that doesn't leave me in agony every morning. You might think the thing is some great antique, but the mattress is a worthless, thirty-year-old piece of crap. My head and neck ache, my chest hurts. The muscles of my legs even hurt, Sam, like pins are jabbing me. I think I'd rather take my chances on the floor than sleep on that thing anymore."

Sam was silent for a moment. She hated when he was

silent. It made her want to yell. Then he said, "What do you want to do?"

"I want to move out of here. We've given it a two full weeks. That's plenty of time to realize this isn't right for us. Don't tell me you like it any more than I do. I've heard you complain about the cold air in this place, and about the shower that seems to want to give you cold water instead of hot."

"Yes, I have . . ."

"You've complained about things you put down in one place only to have them move to somewhere else. That kid's doing it, you know he is. He has nothing better to do in his free time than screw with us. Why doesn't the family at least buy a goddamned television so Carl can become a normal couch potato? He's not much good for anything else except trouble."

"I'll talk to Carl. I make him to lay the hell off and stay away from our room."

"You aren't listening to me!" Dani stamped her foot, feeling like a child for a moment but anxious to make her case.

"I am. We need the money, Dani. I need to get a car. I need to send a chunk back to Geary regularly so he can maintain my house. I need to build up some sort of damn bank account. I don't like being without, I don't like teetering on the brink of poverty."

Dani shoved her hands onto her hips. "Yeah? And just what did happen with you and money? Didn't you used to have quite a bit in savings? I remember you talking about saving up for an addition to your house. Where'd all that go?"

Sam went to the front window, put his hands against the sides, and looked out. A streetlight cut across his features. His face was stony, and his cheeks pulsed in and out like angry bellows.

"Sam?"

"I'm doing a pretty good job here, Dani. I can get this kid turned around. I'm not a quitter."

"No? You quit Jefferson Junior High."

"That was different."

"How? Why?"

"I don't want to talk about it."

"Oh, that's open of you."

"I'm sorry, Dani. I just can't get into that right now."

"Sam, you can work somewhere else, you can do something else."

"What else can I do, Dani? I'm not trained for shit."

"You said you'd thought about being a waiter or bartender. You could do that."

"I've been glancing at the newspapers off and on. They aren't hiring. Those jobs are already locked in for the season."

"There has to be *something*."

"Wishing won't make it happen."

"God!" Dani waved her fists in the air. "You make me so fucking mad!"

"Okay, say I left the Abbadon Inn. Found some shitty minimum wage job. Tell me, what would you do? You wouldn't expect me to support you."

"Of course not! I'd paint. I've finally got a good composition started. I'll show it to you in the morning if you really want to see it, if you really care enough to take a look. I know the galleries will pick me up soon. I'll make some money, hell, several hundred a painting, easy. And I paint fast once I'm in the right mood."

Sam turned from the window. He looked like a warrior, all painted up in stripes of light and dark. "Have you shown any of the galleries the work you've already done, the paintings you brought with you from Virginia?"

"Yes . . . but . . . well, but they said their clients prefer beach-themed works. That's what sells at the beach."

"No one has wanted anything from your portfolio?"

"No, and so what? Are you trying to rub it in?" Dani stalked back to the bed and sat, hard. "Are you trying to say people don't like what I've done? That I won't sell anything?"

"Not at all. I'm just trying to be practical. I have work here, and I'm doing pretty good with it now. I had a rough start, but Carl is actually learning some things. As unpleasant as he can be, I think he likes learning. I'm giving him some nutrition for his brain, something his parents haven't done in a long time. There have been few students I've not liked for one reason or other, Dani. Carl's got potential, and I know I can help him out."

"Ah! Enough!"

"And the Morrisons have paid me on time each Friday. Five hundred a week. That's nothing to spit at."

"Five hundred a week for being their little slave, if you ask me. You're like that boy's boy. Running around with him, trying to be his little buddy, all smiles and patience, all yessuh, Massa Carl, yessuh, Missus Rebecca."

Sam took two decided steps toward Dani. The streaks of streetlight shifted with him and reflected in his eyes, making them instantly cold and white.

"Don't you *ever* say that to me," he said evenly. "Don't you *dare* talk to me like that. You have no idea what I'm doing, how hard I'm working, how I think I may have an opportunity to turn a kid around, a kid who needs it as much if not more than any kid with whom I've ever worked. You're never here, Dani, you wouldn't know. You're always out on your jaunts, gone all day. I am a teacher. It's what I do."

"Then get a job at a Cape May school! There are a couple just down the road from here, I've passed them on my walks. You could substitute now and apply for next fall."

"I can't do that."

"Why not?"

"I just can't."

"I don't understand!" Dani jumped to her feet.

"I know you don't, but I do, and that should be enough."

Dani drew her arms across her chest and clutched her elbows. She knew she'd said the wrong thing to Sam, one of the worst things. But fuck it, she wanted out. She couldn't tolerate the Abbadon Inn any more. "I want out," she said simply.

Sam glared at her.

"Did you hear me? One way or another. With or without you."

"In spite of what you told Rebecca Morrison, we aren't married. There's nothing to hold you here."

Dani's breath caught and then came in rapid gasps. She

couldn't believe Sam was making this so easy. He was supposed to fight to keep her, to make concessions so they could stay together. "You mean that?"

"You're miserable here. I want you to be happy."

"That's such total bullshit. You're dumping me, plain and simple."

Sam stared at her for a long time. Then he came to her and put his arms around her. She pulled free. He came forward again and held out his arms. She moved into them slowly, unsure she wanted to be held, but not knowing what else to do.

"I'm sorry," he whispered into her hair. "Maybe this isn't the kind of decision we should make at three in the morning. Let's go back to sleep and talk in the morning."

"We can't talk in the morning, Sam. It's Monday. You're on duty with that kid at nine, don't forget."

"Then before I'm on duty. The light of day will help clear our heads."

Dani thought about that. She felt Sam's warm, strong arms around her waist and his warm face against her own. She wanted it to be all right, she wanted the coming dawn to wipe away her anger and her frustration, her sense of cloying imprisonment and feeling of helplessness. But she knew it wouldn't.

Backing away from Sam, Dani reached under the bed and took out one of her suitcases. She dropped it onto the mattress and flipped the latches open. The pain in her face, neck, chest, and legs kicked back in with the force of a freight train. She grit her teeth against it. "No, Sam," she said simply. "Daylight won't make a bit of difference. I'm thinking as clearly now as I will then."

"Then you're going to leave?"

"What does it look like?"

Sam watched as Dani yanked sweaters, jeans, and underwear from the dresser and stuffed them randomly into the open case. "If you get your own place, it will really be no different from Virginia, when you lived in your apartment, and I lived in my house. We can still be together. Still get together. It could be that we moved in together too soon. That all we need is time."

"Maybe. Maybe not. I've got a couple new friends already, other painters who sell at the galleries. I won't be lonely. You've got the kid. You won't be lonely. But just watch your back with him."

"Dani . . ."

"I don't want to talk anymore. I have to go. You need to stay."

Sam stood by the bed as Dani finished packing the first suitcase, and then the second suitcase. He said nothing more. By 3:52 A.M., she was on the front walkway, having called a cab from the phone in the bar. She could feel Sam at the third-floor bedroom window, watching her, but she did not turn around. It felt right, leaving, though terribly sad. She might call him at some point, but she doubted she would. Something had broken last night between them. Maybe it was a good thing. She had never thought they were meant to be life partners. But her going away was sad, nonetheless.

As the cab slowed at the curb, she glanced back over to wave good-bye. But Sam was no longer at the window.

NINE

Sam sat on the bed, leaning forward with his forearms on his knees, staring at the rumpled rug. It felt as if ground glass had settled at the base of his neck. He realized he was grinding his teeth and forced himself stop.

So, that's that. She's gone.

He looked up at the ridiculous flowers on the wall and wondered, vaguely, who had painted them there. Someone feeling cheerful, or at least hopeful. Someone with few troubles, or with many troubles left behind.

Dani left her troubles behind. She had dragged her precious possessions off in a Cape May taxicab and gone. Rose thought she had left her troubles behind when she and Frank moved in with the Fords. Robbie thought he'd left his troubles behind, too, when he joined the army. Against his father's insistence that Robbie go to school and study something that would be of value, and flying in the face of his mother's fear of war, Robbie had hitched to Washington, D.C., and enlisted. In July of '64 he went to Vietnam. On November 2, 1965, he arrived back in the States in a casket, the very same day Norman Morrison burned himself to death outside the Pentagon to protest the same war. One little girl. Two desperate men. All three leaving their troubles behind.

And leaving those behind with more troubles. More angst and pointless wonderings.

Sam rubbed his eyes. His chest hurt. He wondered what the teachers back at Jefferson were saying now. Would they still be talking in the teachers' lounge about Sam's mysterious up-and-going? The fact that he and Dani had gone off together? "Oh, maybe they've eloped!"

some of the more romantic of the staff would croon. "I hope they at least send a postcard!" Others might have seen Sam and Dani's escape as something more desperate than love. They would have suspected Dani was unhappy; and they would have begun to pick apart recollections of Sam's patient persona to see what might have been below the surface. Had there been something brewing inside for a long time? They would have cornered Geary at teachers' meetings or would have stopped by his shop room to say, "What do you hear from your buddy?" Geary would answer, "Oh, he's just out there being Sam." Someone might ask, "But what does that mean?" But Geary would say no more.

Or, most likely, a few days after Sam was gone, people had turned their attention to the new seventh grade social studies teacher and had pretty much forgotten that Sam had even been there.

Except Joy Spradlin. She wouldn't have forgotten. Just about now she would be prancing around the halls in her new skirts and shoes and bragging about her mama's new car. And, suitably rewarded, she and her mama would be looking for another opportunity to cash in on their familial connections to the county cops and legal system.

"I may have left behind my troubles in more ways than one," he said to the flowers on the wall.

There was a song by some country music group, a song about counting flowers on the wall. It was played over and over on the radio his junior year in college to the point where he learned the chorus whether he wanted to know it or not. Sam looked at the flowers, counting not the painted blooms but the heartbeats at his temples. Sleep swam before his eyes, but something inside him refused to give in to it. He picked at the little scar where he'd been burned by the pen, thinking that whole incident still carried an air of "oh, yeah, sure, you were burned by a *pen*, Sam?"

He sang in his night-raspy voice, " 'Countin' flowers on the wall, that don't bother me at all.' "

Outside, a dog barked loud and long. A distant car engine started up, someone going to work in the wee hours.

" 'Playing solitaire till dawn with a deck of fifty-one. Smokin' cigarettes and—' "

One of the flowers on the wall moved.

Sam's song locked in his throat.

It was just a small flower, the size of a large spider, wriggling its azure petals and shifting sluggishly from one spot to another.

He stared at the flower. His breath was dry through his mouth.

So don't tell me . . .

It stopped and moved no more. Maybe it hadn't moved at all. Of course it hadn't moved at all.

. . . I've nothing to do.

It wasn't a flower, it was a spider. Sam stood and forced his feet across the floor to the spot on the wall. He looked closely, and there was no spider, only the small, dark blue flower, now settled in a place a foot from its origin. He reached out to touch the flower but then pulled his hand back and retreated to the bed. It was all in his mind, of course. Shadows and light playing charades with weariness and anxiety.

No, don't tell me I've nothing to do.

The room went suddenly, mightily cold. Sam pulled a blanket from the foot of the bed and drew it around his shoulders. What was with this place? What was with the heat, or lack of it, in odd little pockets throughout the various floors, the various rooms?

He shivered. His head ached.

I hope Dani is warm, wherever she's gone off to. She'll be okay. We'll be okay. She needs to do her thing. I need to do mine.

He took a book from the nightstand drawer, a paperback he'd bought at a Cape May bookstore, on New Jersey shipwrecks, their legends and ghosts. His cardboard box of books still sat beneath the window. He would buy a bookshelf soon.

Sam flipped through the shipwreck book then put it back; he couldn't focus enough to read. He pulled the blanket around his body more tightly and stared at the wall again. One particularly tall shadow looked like a tree with gangly branches. A black, burned tree, naked of leaves, scratching out messages with sharp fingertips.

Jesus, I'm tired.

He closed his eyes.

No don't tell me . . . I've nothing to do.

He slept.

He dreamed.

He was in the woods, naked. No, not totally naked; he looked down to see that he had on a pair of ragged trousers that were torn off just below the knees. His feet were cut from the stones on the trail on which he was running. His hands were pricked open and bleeding from spiny shrubs along the path's edge. The moon was visible through the bare branches of the trees, a sickly yellow spot in the sky, hanging as if it had been left there to die. Sam could smell the breath of the moon; it was rancid like rotting meat and spoiled milk. He put his bloodied hand over his nose so not to smell it, but it did no good. The smell made him dizzy and beneath him his legs and wounded feet struggled to keep him upright.

Up the narrow trail he ran, heading somewhere he knew he had to be, though with no idea of where that might be. A frigid wind cut his flesh as surely as the briars, the stones. The trees by the path creaked and groaned in the wind; their leafless branches drooped and swayed under the weight of many large, heavy things tied there. Sam could not turn to see what hung in the trees, and he did not want to. He was deathly afraid to look. His heart hammered like an ancient drum, and his bones rattled within his skin.

Sam reached the top of a rise. In the distance, illuminated only by the pale moon, was the Abbadon Inn. Its great walls pulsed in and out as if breathing. Tiny, dark faces peered out of the many windows, watching Sam. He could hear them whisper, the voices burring into his brain, tremulous, terrified.

There he is!

He's come again!

Go away.
Go away.
GO AWAY!

Sam tried to cry out to them, to ask them why they were afraid of him, but he had no voice. His silent words fell out of his mouth in colorful and foul-tasting swirls, drifted to the ground, and lay still.

Just ahead, in the center of the pathway, stood a line of six men, shoulder to shoulder, dressed in identical long black coats and wide, floppy hats. Sam could not see their faces, as they were looking down, but he could see what they held. A long heavy chain. Each man clutched part of its length in his fat hands. At the end of the chain, lying on the ground with his legs curled up, was a black man, long dead, the iron at the end of the chain embedded in his neck. His mouth was cracked open and filled with spiders. They sauntered in and out, making merry with their draglines, slowly enshrouding the man's nose and ears and chin with their instinctive chore.

Then Sam felt someone beside him. He turned to see a man with ghostly white skin and a black beard. His eyes were bright silver chips in his head. He spoke, though his lips did not move. "You know me, Sam. I'm Nicholas. Don't stand there like a jackanapes, come on with me. Come up to the inn." The man put his arm around Sam's shoulder, and the embrace was as cold as the grave.

Sam did not want to go. He tried to say no, but he could not. The man drew him forward on the trail, closer to the line of men with the chain.

The dead black man on the ground suddenly threw back his withered head and wailed, the sound terrified, piercing. Then his head turned toward Sam slowly and mechanically, like the plastic top of a Crazy Ike swiveling round. His eyes opened and blinked. There were no eyeballs in the socket. Tears the color of tar poured down his cheeks.

Something thick and nauseous twisted in Sam's gut then wriggled up his throat. He felt at his lips and was at last able to scream as fat-bodied spiders crawled across his tongue and out between his swollen lips.

He awoke with his mouth open and his hands clawing at it to be rid of the spiders. Sam rolled over, spitting over and over to be rid of the dream-taste of them. Then he stared at the lamp on the stand for a long time, his heart thumping irregularly. When he slept again, it was free of dreams.

TEN

"Good morning, Sam, and such a nice Monday it is!" chirped Rebecca as she swept into the kitchen. It was 7:14 according to the stove clock, and Sam wasn't on duty for almost two hours. The last thing he wanted to do was talk to Rebecca Morrison.

He'd had little sleep after the terrible dream and had awakened after only an hour to lay in bed and stare at the walls until they were illuminated with faint daylight. It was still hard to believe that Dani was gone. He felt guilty for staying while she went, though he did not want to leave. Like she had said to him in the heat of the argument, they'd never made any promises to each other, they'd never talked marriage. But now he felt very much alone. He had no connection to the Morrisons other than teaching their son and living under their mammoth roof. He hoped Dani would call him from wherever she ended up. Even if they had fallen apart, he wanted to have a few pieces to cling to. Sam scratched at his cheek. He hadn't shaved yet and there was an uneven, sandpaper growth, but he thought that was appropriate. Looking scraggly on the outside would match how he felt on the inside.

"How are you, Sam?" Rebecca obviously didn't notice Sam's scraggliness, or if she had, she wasn't interested or didn't care.

"I'm awake," said Sam. Rebecca took that as a good answer. "Happy to hear! I had a wonderful stretching session this morning. You should try it. Not only does it awaken the body, but the mind and spirit as well." As if in a needed demonstration, she snaked her arms up over her head, pressed her palms together, and let her head roll around a few times. "Mmmm." She put her arms down. "Is Dani up and gone already?"

"She's up and gone already."

Painfully bright morning sun washed across the floor from the sheer-curtained windows and the glass in the door. Dust specs twirled in the air like minute insects.

Sam sat at the small table in the corner, his elbows secured to the tabletop, holding a teacup of overly strong instant tea. It was his second cup. It was his hope that the caffeine would drag him back up among the living long enough to survive the full day he had planned. He and Carl were going to work on math most of the morning, then take their first field trip to the Cape May library after lunch. They had been studying American history, beginning with the Native-American nations and tribes. Sam was going to assign Carl his first major project—an illustrated report on a tribe of his choice. Not only was the boy going to have to use reference books beyond those Sam himself had checked out and brought to the inn, but Carl was going to select a still-existing tribe, look in cataloged magazines for contact information, then write to the current chief or tribal leader to find out about the tribe in contemporary times. He would compose a report, complete with interview, illustrations, and a chart comparing his life to that of an Indian long ago. Sam knew it could be a delicate matter, tricking or coercing the boy into doing the work. But as curious and nosy as Carl was, Sam guessed that once involved with the research, Carl would enjoy it.

And speaking of nosy . . .

Along with giving Carl the Native-American assignment, Sam was going to give him the bottom line about listening in at other people's rooms and conversations uninvited, and about running around at night in an attempt to scare people. Carl seemed to have at least a bit of respect for Sam, and at times he even seemed to like his tutor, so Sam planned on using that to his advantage. If Carl wouldn't agree to stop the after-dark shenanigans, then Sam would refuse to play chess with Carl until he did. A late-afternoon go at the black-and-white board had become a fairly pleasant after-school tradition. Sam would flat out

refuse to play with Carl if the boy didn't promise to stay in
his room at night and stop sniffing around in the halls. Carl
liked the game enough that Sam thought the threat might
work. If not, well, he'd cross that bridge when he got to it.
He'd only throw in the teaching towel if he had to. And so
far, Carl was no worse than some of the other kids who'd
trooped through his classroom since 1967. Well, except for
Joy Spradlin.

Rebecca dumped a scoopful of coffee into the maker
and turned it on. "A morning like this makes me wish I had
a cat. They're so charming. Independent and sweet, both at
once. If I had a cat, I'd name it Boo. In college my friend
had a cat named Boo. Precious!"

Please go somewhere else, Sam thought into his teacup.

"In Connecticut I had a dog, but a bed-and-breakfast
needs a cat. Something to sleep in the windows and to lay
on guests' laps, if they'd like." Rebecca pulled a coffee cup
from the cabinet, wiped her hands, then turned toward
Sam. Her smile was a bit too bright, too wide. She looked
and sounded liked she'd had a nip of something before
coming downstairs. And from Sam's chair at the table, he
could smell something faint but unpleasant emanating
from the woman, a sweet and pungent scent like that of old
lavender perfume over sweat.

"The new chairs for the reception room are being delivered at ten," she purred, "along with two new cushioned
cobbler benches for the front hall. Guests can come in, sign
the registry, then sit and chat and relax. I also want them to
feel at home enough to stay downstairs with the other
guests, to select a book from the reception room, find a
cozy spot to read. Will you help me with something?"

Sam picked up the buttered toast he'd hoped to enjoy
alone. "What's that?"

"Victorian people loved to read. Here at the Abbadon, I
want to emphasize that fact. Bring it to the forefront. We
can be the literate bed-and-breakfast, one you think of
when you think of books!"

Sam took a bite of toast. It tasted peculiar, like the smell
drifting from Rebecca Morrison. He put the toast down and
picked at a crumb in a molar.

"Yet you may have noticed that downstairs there is not a single volume set out to peruse," Rebecca went on. "In the bedroom Mitchell and I share, in the closet, I've found boxes and boxes of old books. They're in good shape. I want to fill the bookshelves in the reception room with them. The rest will go in the bar and restaurant. Yes, I know, who's ever heard of books in a bar or restaurant? Well, I have. I thought that up myself. Rum, martinis, and poetry. Sloe gin fizzes, brandies, and novels. Sounds dignified and a little quirky, yes? I'm going to order custom bookshelves for the bar. The restaurant will continue to be the Orchid, but I am going to name the bar the 'Letters Lounge.'"

Sam sniffed the toast but it smelled okay. He took another bite. It still tasted off. He spit it out into his paper napkin and then balled the whole piece of toast in it. He tossed the wad toward the trashcan, and it dropped in without touching the sides.

Two points.

"I need help hauling the boxes of books downstairs. Mitchell is off already as usual, meeting with friends for breakfast. They hope the weather holds; they plan a morning game of golf at the club. Golf in March, can you see that? What a diehard! Will you help me?"

"Sure. And let's get Carl up, too. A little extra exercise will do him good."

Rebecca shook her head and pulled a plastic-wrapped muffin from one of the refrigerators. She peeled back the wrapping. "No, I'd rather him sleep. Wouldn't you?"

"He should only get the sleep he needs." *Good Lord, lady, you're his mother, aren't you at all interested in spending even fifteen minutes with him?*

"But he's a teenager." Rebecca chewed a piece of muffin and patted her lips with a napkin. "Teenagers have those weird bodies. Bodies that make them stay up late and then sleep late. You were a teenager. You must remember. I sure do."

Sam finished his tea, ignoring Rebecca's renewed chatter about bookshelves and guests. He knew it would do Carl some good to get up early for once and not sleep until eight forty-five like he usually did. Carting a few heavy boxes downstairs would work a few muscles the boy didn't know he had, and it was time for that. Sam planned on introducing physical education into the daily routine. They were beginning their third week together. A little running and weight training were in order. Hauling books could have been a little warm-up appetizer, but he knew he couldn't count on Rebecca to have a hand in much of Carl's care and instruction, mental or physical.

"You finished?"

Sam looked at Rebecca. She was done with her muffin.

"Sure," said Sam.

The Morrisons' bedroom was an impressive bit of renovation compared to the as-of-yet untouched rooms on the third floor. Obviously, it had been the first thing Rebecca tackled after moving from Danbury. The room was in the back of the inn overlooking the small grassy courtyard formed by the restaurant and the protruding kitchen, as well as the yard beyond that. It was quite a large bedroom, almost twice the size of Sam's third-floor fiasco, with three windows and private bath. The floors were polished to a glassy shine and covered with expensive area rugs. The walls had 1930s-style wallpaper—Art Deco–inspired lines and angles. The furniture was museum quality, the bed especially. It could have been as old as three hundred years, olivewood with heavy, spiral posts and a footboard set with alternating slatted wood and steel bars. There were carved cherubs on the headboard. Engraved on a sheet of hammered metal between the cherubs was the Celtic design Sam had seen in the guest registry. The mattress was covered with a Williamsburg-designed spread, and several dotted Swiss throw pillows that looked out of place but seemed very Rebecca.

As Rebecca yammered on about the drapes and the rugs, Sam stared out the window at the brush-ensnared shed. From the second-floor vantage point, the little building seemed to be drowning in a sea of green and black shrubbery, its roof gasping for breath, its chimney reaching to the sky for help. What had that place been used for?

And what was it that ran into those shadows?

"Any idea what the little building in the back of the house is, Rebecca?"

Rebecca blinked. "That old thing? I think the Preservation Society lady said it was a kitchen, then who knows, a smokehouse? Toolshed? Maybe kids used it as a playhouse. I hate to admit it, but I haven't done much research on the history of the inn. I should, because the guests are going to want to know all about it, I'm sure."

Sam turned back toward Rebecca. The movement stirred the air, and with the stirring came the overpowering stench of putrid mud and ripe decay. His stomach roiled with the odor, and he felt lightheaded. "If you were to hire someone to chop all the brush down around the shed, I'd be happy to look around and see if there is anything of value. Even little artifacts, little tidbits, can speak volumes. Nails, buttons, keys." The smell grew even stronger, licking at his eyes and burning his throat. "Don't you smell that?"

Rebecca's eyes narrowed. "Smell what?"

"Like something dead, dead and putrefying. I've smelled it in the inn before. Surely you have, too."

"It's probably just mice. We've got poison all over to get rid of them. Don't tell me you haven't heard mice scurrying around at night?"

Was that what Dani heard last night? Was it something as simple as mice that drove the final nail into our relationship's coffin? But no, she said there was a flicker light beneath the door. Mice don't glow, at least not in Virginia they don't. "This smell's much stronger. Have you ever gone hiking in the woods and run across a dead deer that's been out in the sun a couple days?"

She frowned, defensively. "I don't smell anything."

Sam waved his hand before his nose and as he did, the smell began to break apart, dissipate, and then it was gone. He took several deep breaths to clear his head, though particles of the smell still clung inside his nostrils and on the ridges of his tongue. Could it have really been dead mice, the odor kicked up by the radiator?

Sam said, "Let's get those boxes of books out of the closet."

But Rebecca spun back toward the bed, grinning, her

long patchwork skirt flouncing. "No, no, wait! You didn't let me tell you about *this* piece of furniture. As I told you, we bought the dresser and washstand at a local antique store. But I found this gem right here in the Abbadon. On the third floor, crammed in one of the smaller rooms, in pieces, forgotten for who knows how long, and . . ."

"And you think it belonged to the woman named Lillith, who signed the registry downstairs beneath Nicholas Abbadon's signature. The symbol on the headboard matches the one she drew beside her name."

"Oh." Rebecca blinked. "Yes, I did tell you that." She sat on the edge of the bed. She placed her palms down beside her and rubbed them back and forth, caressing the coverlet. "Have you ever slept on such a nice bed, Sam?"

"Can't say I have."

"This has a really special feel to it, like you're in a whole other time, a whole other place. It feels so good. Come, sit next to me and see."

Sam hitched his thumb at the closet door. "I think we should just take those books downstairs."

"Oh, we have a little time, Sam. Come, sit." Rebecca patted the mattress. Then she slipped out of her black slippers and lay down. She reached her arms over her head and touched the etched metal pattern in the headboard. She stretched her legs out until the tips of her toes almost came in contact with the slats of the footboard. The fabric of her skirt hiked up enough to reveal her shapely thighs. "This feels so good! It's a Yoga move, doing this. Come try it with me. We're friends by now, right? You'll like it, Sam. It feels so nice."

"I trust you on that."

Rebecca laughed and then rolled off the bed. She stood motionless for a moment, her smile teasing, her face flushing. Then she undid the top two buttons on her orange gauzy blouse and parted the cloth to reveal her cleavage. She rubbed the exposed flesh, bringing on a flush there, as well. Sam stared, not believing what she was suggesting.

"Mitchell is gone golfing," she said, her voice now deep and hoarse, as if someone else entirely was speaking. The backs of Sam's hands went cold. He swallowed and felt the painful tick at the back of his throat. "Carl's sleeping, and we can let him keep on sleeping. You know those teenagers and their silly, silly bodies." She took a step closer. "He could be out until lunch if we let him alone. Come sit with me."

"Rebecca, let it go. I am here to help with the books, nothing more."

"Aren't we friends?" she growled, smiling.

"Not if you try to push me in a direction I don't want to go."

"Oh, goodness, don't be such a jackanapes, Sam." *Nicholas Abbadon used that word in my dream! What is this?* Then Rebecca looked down for a moment, as if being coy, but when she looked back up, Sam gasped and stumbled backward. Her eyes were solid red, wide, blood-colored globes.

"Sam, try the bed with me. Come, come." Her voice was a low hiss, the teeth behind the smiling lips bright and silvery. The scarlet orbs were fixed on him. "You don't know what you're missing, standing there like a statue. So much pleasure to be had. So much pleasure to be shared."

Oh my God!

Sam struck out with his hands and pushed her away. She stumbled, gasped, hit the bed and collapsed there, folding down over her lap. When she looked up again, she was no longer red-eyed and threatening. Her blue eyes were drawn in anguish. Her body shook violently. "I . . . I . . ." she stammered.

"What was that?" Sam managed. His breath came in gulps; his chest hurt. "What just happened?"

"I'm sorry," wailed Rebecca, putting her hands over her mouth. "Oh, dear, no, I've offended you! I didn't mean to come across like that, like some kind of common . . . whore!"

"No, no," said Sam, shaking his head as much to clear her head as his. The air around him was warm again. "I mean, what did I just see? What happened to you? To your . . . Jesus Christ . . . your eyes?" He stepped back another step.

"I know what you just saw! You saw me behaving terribly, that's what you saw." Rebecca quickly buttoned up her blouse. She hung her head and began to sob. When she looked up again, Sam was afraid he might see the red globes, but all her eyes bore were red traces of angst along puffy lids. Her cheeks were wet. "I can't believe I acted that way. I've never, never acted like that before. You have to forgive me."

Sam stared at her, at the pretty, thirty-something hippie wanna-be, at her quivering lips and rolling tears. Had she truly been a hissing, red-eyed seductress a moment ago? Or had the odd smell in the room caused him to hallucinate? He'd dropped acid in college; he knew how reality could be altered in a heartbeat. Was this a flashback, or a combination of chemical-mental short circuits created by the inn's dead-smell?

"Can you ever forgive me? I will never come on to you again. I just felt . . ."

But, dear God, it seemed so real.

". . . lonely for a moment. Mitchell is gone so much . . ."

When my father learned about my drug experimentation at the university, he had been appalled. He had said, "Your sins will visit you again and again until you repent of them." I could never convince him that it hadn't been a sin; hurting someone would be a sin, having sex with a woman I didn't care about would have been a sin. But here in broad daylight, in a Victorian bed-and-breakfast on the shore of New Jersey, eleven years after Geary and I took our hits on the football field under a full moon, I've had a short but major freak-out. Have I just been revisited? Holy shit. Is something wrong with me?

". . . that I just . . . no, there's no excuse. It will never happen again. Please forgive me, Sam."

Sam scratched his stubbly cheek.

"Please, Sam, forgive me."

Sam imagined his father behind the pulpit of Pine Grove Baptist Church, his dark face filled with passion, his arms raised above the congregation, and his robe spread wide like a great bird's wing, admonishing his hesitant flock with words from the Scriptures:

"Lord, how often shall my brother sin against me, and I forgive him? Seventy times seven."

Sam shoved his hands into his jeans pockets and looked at Rebecca Morrison. *Yeah, okay, Dad, you're right. But I'd love to know what you'd have said had you been here yourself.*

"I swear to God . . ." she said, her voice almost hoarse now with pleading.

Sam shook his head. "You don't need to swear. I forgive you."

She sniffed and ran her hand under her nose. "Really?"

Sam nodded.

"Thank you. And please stay. Don't leave. Carl needs you so. We do, too."

"I think it best we don't mention it again. I'll just get the books. And I won't come up here to your room again."

"That's a good idea." Sniff. Another sniff. Then, a faint smile.

Sam told Rebecca to go on downstairs. Then he took five trips with the heavy cardboard boxes, wrapping his arms about them so they didn't pop apart at the seams, and left Rebecca to dusting, sorting, and shelving in the reception room.

He returned to his third-floor room to wait for nine o'clock and the beginning of his official day. He thought briefly of taking a walk, but he didn't have the energy to go anywhere. Picking up the shipwreck book, Sam flipped through the pages, but his gaze kept sliding off the words. Little registered except for a phrase here and there. "The specter rushed the unsuspecting seaman . . ." "Ghastly white faces with red eyes drifted in the foam . . ." "The spirits were angry and determined to take revenge on the most likely suspect . . ."

Yeah, this is just what I need to read right now.

Sam put the book down. He went to the window and watched a free-roaming dog take a dump on the sidewalk in front of the inn. The dog sniffed it as if the shit was something surprising and new, then trotted off across the street. Sam's head swam; images and sensations tossed back and forth like clothes in an agitator.

The skin-searing current that burned his hand when he signed the antique register. Rebecca's wild-eyed come-on.

The cold spots in the Abbadon Inn, and the smells he detected that no one else seemed to. The flower-that-wasn't-a-spider that had crawled—or not—across the wall. Dani, chased away.

What is all this? What is happening to me?

Reaching beneath the bed, Sam pulled out the carpetbag Dani had bought him. He pressed his hand against the cloth and felt a sudden sense of grief. For the person who had made this so very long ago and was now long dead, for the person who had bought it and had supposedly carried it to the South after the tragedy of the Civil War to help with Reconstruction. For the Southern blacks the carpetbag owner had helped, and for those he had not been able to. For the twisted, tangled mess that was the lives of slaves before the war and the lives of emancipated people after the war.

Sam opened the latch and thumbed through the letters and papers he now kept hidden inside the bag, and he felt a huge rush of grief for himself and the twisted tangle of his own life.

You're just falling apart, man.

In a few short weeks, the world had become difficult and bizarre. Sam found himself wondering what the hell he'd done to deserve it all.

ELEVEN

"You like math?"

Sam looked up from the papers he was grading, his vision blurring a little at first from the lack of sleep and from the headache he'd been fighting since Rebecca's early-morning freak-out. Across the kitchen table from him, Carl was dragging a length of Hubba Bubba through his teeth and examining it as if it were something profound. He let it snap back, and it whacked him on the chin. "Do you?" he repeated.

"Not especially."

"Least you're honest," said Carl. "Mitchell says math is the key to the universe."

"Why do you call your father Mitchell?"

"It's his name. Anyway, I think Mitchell's laying a heaping pile of bullshit on me about math."

Sam raised a brow.

"Crap, then. Is crap better than bullshit?"

"It's tolerable."

"I'm good at it, though."

"What, crap?"

"No, math. I'm good, don't you think?"

Sam nodded. "I think you're very good at it. You have a real grasp of concepts a lot of other students your age struggle with."

"How am I doin' on the stuff you're grading?"

Sam tapped Carl's open spiral notebook with his pen. "We need to get this finished, grab some lunch, then head out to the library."

"I don't want to go to the library. Libraries are for old ladies and little kids."

"I think you'll find it more interesting than you're imagining."

Carl chewed the gum then stretched it back out again. "Think I could make a lot of money, being good in math?"

"I'll just say that if you aren't good at math, people could take advantage of you, cheat you."

"Why'd you leave Virginia?"

Sam shook his head. "Not now, Carl. Work."

"It's not like you have family up here or anything. It's not like you wanted to buy a place and fix it up like my mom did, or retire like my dad did."

"I just moved. No reason."

"There's a reason for everything. Mitchell says so."

"Good for him."

"Mitchell's growing a mustache, you see that? He looks like an old beatnik. Beatnik for a dad and a hippie for a mom. Shit. I mean crap."

Sam then held up his finger. "Shh."

"Tell me why you came to Cape May."

Sam's head flared. God, if the kid would just *work*. "It's none of your business."

"How much do you make as a teacher?"

"Work."

"Maybe I don't want to."

Sam ran his thoughts over the next problem on the paper, scanned the equation and the conclusion. Perfect. This kid was good. Now if Sam could only get the boy to improve his atrocious handwriting a bit.

"How much do you make?"

Sam didn't look up.

"How much do painters make?"

"What?" Sam did look up then. One side of Carl's mouth was hitched, and his eyes were crinkled slightly, an expression Sam had come to know as a challenge.

"A painter," said the boy. "Not a housepainter, a painter painter. Like Dani."

"Why do you care? You said you hate art."

"Yeah, art is pussy stuff," said Carl. "But how much can

you make? How much does Dani make when she sells a big painting?"

"Why do you care?"

"If you don't tell me, I'll just ask her myself. Tonight." There. Sam saw it in Carl's eyes and heard it in the way Carl dragged out the word *tonight*. The boy knew Dani was gone. He was hoping to hear the why and the wherefore from Dani's boyfriend. "When will she be back?" A slight jiggle of the head. "Sam?"

Sam put his pen down and put an elbow on the table. "You don't care about painting or about how much painters make. You're trying to get out of your work, but it's not going to happen."

"Just tell me when she'll be back. Then I'll do the rest of my math like a good boy and not say another word until lunch." Carl's grin was cold.

"Okay, this is fine," Sam said, sitting back and crossing his arms. "You want to get into all this now? I was going to wait until lunch so we could get a clean run at the lessons this morning, but now's all right with me."

"Talk about what?" The kid's teeth worked in and out on his lip. He was loving it.

"Talk about your little late-night wanderings. Your little tiptoeing around the inn at night, listening in to other people's rooms, making noises to try to scare them."

Carl put his hands to his chest, raised his eyebrows, and stuck out a pouting lip. "Who, me?"

"That kind of behavior is inexcusable. It's what a bored five-year-old does, Carl."

"But I am bored."

"You're too smart to be bored. And unless your mother and you were lying, you're thirteen. You should be acting more like a man than a baby."

"So you think I've been listening in to your room?"

"I know you have. And you won't ever do it again. Last night was the last straw."

"Okay, okay," said Carl, waving Sam off. "I admit to snooping around. But it's my house, I can do what I want and go where I want."

"Not if it comes to invading other people's privacy."

"Whatever you say, boss. But I did not do anything last night. I stayed in my room. I was putting together a . . . project."

"Dani saw light beneath the door," said Sam, hearing the intensity in his voice growing. His headache and Carl's lie stoked the coals of anger. Would the kid ever learn to trust someone enough to tell the whole truth? Was he that hardened? "She heard you scratching around. You've done it before, and you did it last night."

"Nope!" Carl's voice had risen, too. "I sure as hell didn't."

"The best thing for you to do right now is to come clean. I can work with the truth even if it's not a good truth. I can't work with a lie."

"You don't have to work with shit!" Carl jumped up, knocking his chair against the wall. "I didn't shine a light under your fucking door last night. I didn't scratch on your fucking door, either. You can believe me or go to hell."

Sam stared at the boy. He'd taught for ten years and had come to know kids pretty well. He'd seen them steal, and he'd seen them cheat. He'd seen them punch each other, hug each other, and he'd seen them act like everything was cool when things were terrible. He'd run across a few pathological liars in his time, like Joy Spradlin. Yet Carl Morrison, for all his faults, was not a perfect liar.

Sam was certain as he studied the boy's face and posture. *Damn,* Sam thought, *he is telling the truth about last night.*

"Sit down, Carl."

"No, I'm done with this. You don't trust me. Fine! I don't care. Nobody trusts me, it's just the way it is. I trust myself is all I need!"

"You do things that aren't trustworthy. What do you expect? Sit down."

"No!"

"All right, stand there. But hear me out. I think you are telling the truth."

"What?"

"I think you're telling the truth about last night."

"You do?"

"Yeah. Okay? Now sit down."

Carl yanked the chair back into position and sat as hard as he could to make a statement. It wasn't much of one. He weighed maybe one hundred pounds. "I didn't come to your stupid room last night. Yeah, I did some other nights, but not then. As my mom says, 'give credit where credit is due.'"

Sam rubbed his chin, still stubbly from lack of a morning shave. "Did you see Dani leave this morning, then? Did you see her get into the cab? Is that why you were suddenly all interested in talking to her about her paintings?"

"Yeah, sure, I saw her leave from my window. No big surprise. I knew she . . ." Carl stopped, his jaws snapping shut.

"You knew she what?"

"That she wouldn't stay."

"How did you know?"

"I just did, okay? She hated it here."

"And you're glad? You wanted her gone?"

"She hated it here and I hated her."

Sam got up and poured a cup of coffee. It was lukewarm, but he didn't care.

"You didn't like her all that much, either," said Carl. "You never seemed all lovey with her. I never saw you two kissing or hugging."

"Our relationship is none of your business. And even if you didn't do anything last night . . ." *Dani swore she saw a light and heard scratching . . .* "you have been an eavesdropper other times. You owe me a major apology. And you owe Dani one, too."

"She said my mother was a scatterbrain! She talked bad about me, too."

Fuck it, Carl. "Not to you, she didn't. And you wouldn't have heard it if you hadn't been where you weren't supposed to be. Now, I want an apology."

"Sorry, okay? Sorry I listened in on your stupid talks at night. Oh, big deal, right? But I won't apologize to Dani. You can't make me. Besides, she isn't coming back, so I can't so there."

You're right about that, Carl.

Sam drank his coffee and looked past Carl out the window. The sky was heavy with swirling pewter clouds threatening yet more rain. The walk to the library, though not far, would be a hassle if there were a downpour. He could imagine Carl refusing to go, refusing to get his feet wet.

"You finished that problem?" Sam asked.

"You finished grading those papers?" Carl asked.

Sam sat. He did his work, and Carl did his. At noon, each made a sandwich—Carl, peanut butter and jelly; Sam, turkey and lettuce and tomato—and ate in the restaurant after removing one of the white tablecloths. Rebecca came in and out, speaking to them briefly but focused mainly on a greasy, disheveled carpenter she'd hired to put bookshelves in the Orchid. The man had bad teeth and bad skin. Sam caught a whiff of the dead-smell for a moment, but he chalked it up to the carpenter's lack of personal hygiene. When he went back into the kitchen for a glass of water, he felt almost normal again. Or whatever passed for normal these days.

After lunch the clouds dumped their soggy contents onto Cape May. And so armed with umbrellas and notebooks covered in plastic wrap, teacher and student made their way to the library, Carl bitching, Sam ignoring.

TWELVE

Sam explained the illustrated-report concept to Carl on the way. Carl said he hated the idea, but there wasn't a lot of fire behind the complaint. Natural busybody that he was, Carl seemed especially intrigued with the idea of corresponding with a real live Indian chief.

"Maybe I can get him to teach me some tribal chants," said Carl as he and Sam pushed their way through the front doors of the Cape May Public Library. "I bet Indians got a lot of magical stuff, don't you think? Spells against their enemies, potions to drink that give you visions. Think so? I'm sure so."

"You'll have to find that out on your own," said Sam, shaking out his umbrella and dropping it into the courtesy stand.

"I like Mohawks and Apaches," Carl said. He followed suit with his umbrella and readjusted his notebook under his arm. "Maybe I'll do one of them. They were so cool. Bloodthirsty! I bet they still are, but they just don't talk about it because other people wouldn't understand now that it's modern times and all. I'm going to get my hair cut like a Mohawk, too." The boy patted his head. "Yep, get some eagle feathers and wear them down the side of my head."

"Hey, talk quietly in here."

Carl glanced around at the tables and shelves then lowered his voice. "Hair and feathers and bird claws and shit . . . I mean stuff . . . like that gives Indians power."

"You think so?"

"I know so."

"Your parents will love the hair," said Sam. "But you can't wear eagle feathers. It's against the law."

"No, it's not."

"Then wear one, and I'll see you behind bars."

"Really they are?"

"Eagles are protected, and that means their feathers, too."

"How about crow feathers?"

Sam shrugged. "Look it up and find out."

"I want to go to one of those powwows. Smoke a peace pipe!"

"I don't think you can just go smoke a peace pipe."

"They'd let me. They'd see I'm one of them, see I'm something special."

"The Lenni-Lanape of New Jersey hold powwows in the summer, up in Salem. Maybe if I'm still around then we can go."

Carl tipped his head and frowned. "You might not be around?"

"As far as I can tell I plan on staying on."

"Well, okay, we'll go to the powwow. Maybe I'll do my report on the Lenni-Lanape. They had to have some good magic, too.

It took twenty minutes for Sam to orient Carl to the library—to the card catalog, the magazines, and the reference section. It was as though the boy hadn't been in a library for years, if ever. But he actually paid attention. He seemed enthralled with the place, with the possibilities it held. He trotted after Sam, taking scribbled little notes, asking questions. When Carl at last said, "Okay, I got enough. I get it. You don't have to tell me anymore, I'm not a baby," and then trudged off and disappeared between the 205.05 and the 310.666 shelves, Sam felt good. Like he'd done something worthwhile. His mind felt lighter and his head clearer.

Sam had given Carl two hours to research. He told the boy he would be wandering around himself, but that they were to meet at the front door at three P.M. Sam went to the librarian to apply for a card and one for Carl as well. The librarian said a parent had to sign for a juvenile, so Sam just applied for his own. If he could get Rebecca to focus long enough on something other than herself, Sam would send her down here as soon as possible to get a library card for her son.

"Is there a local history section?" Sam asked the librarian.

The librarian, an attractive African-American woman in her late twenties with round, horn-rimmed glasses and close-cropped hair, said, "Yes. You need to be signed in and out of the room. We keep it locked because it houses our most valuable books. Sometimes kids get to playing around, and that's the last place we need a game of hide and seek."

"I'd like to go in and have a look, please."

The librarian nodded, gave Sam a spiral notebook in which to sign his name, then took a key from her desk drawer and led him back through the maze of shelves to a small room with no windows. She put the key into the lock but before opening the door, looked at Sam and said, "I'm curious, if you don't mind. You're new to Cape May, aren't you?"

"How can you tell?"

She smiled, dimples showing on her cheeks. "Oh, come on. I'm a librarian. I know everything."

Sam smiled. "You're right, I'm the new kid in town. Just over two weeks in Cape May."

"Are you a historian?"

"Sort of. No, not really. I'm a teacher, history primarily but recently of science, math, and literature as well."

"Interesting."

"I'm Sam Ford."

"I know. I gave you your library card. I'm Jeanette Harris." She smiled and held out her hand. "Nice to meet you, Sam Ford."

Sam liked the way her hand felt. It was warm, strong, and not too soft. Jeanette let go and opened the door. The fluorescent lights flickered on, revealing a small table in the center of the room with two chairs, shelves covered with books in protective coverings, and several file cabinets.

"The Preservation Society has its own collection," said Jeanette "If you're truly interested in the history of the town, you might check with them, too."

"I'm mainly interested in the Abbadon Inn, the old bed-and-breakfast."

"Really?" asked Jeanette. "I know that place. It's been in disrepair for a long time, ever since I was a child. I didn't like going by there with my parents when I was little. It spooked me, all those broken windows staring out at us. Gave me nightmares. Even today, when I drive by on my way to work, I don't like looking at it. It just seems so big, so creepy. May I be nosy and ask why you are interested in that old place? You going to write one of those books that sell so well to tourists, like the ones on spooky lighthouses and mysterious shipwrecks?"

"As a matter of fact, I'm living there now. I just want to learn more about the place."

Jeanette cringed but then forced a smile. "Oh. Wow. How on earth did you choose the Abbadon as a new home?"

"I'm the live-in tutor for the son of the new owners, the Morrisons."

"Yeah? Well, I'm impressed. You are a brave soul."

"You don't think the place is haunted?"

"I don't know."

Sam raised a brow.

"Probably not. Well, not really." She wrinkled her nose. Damn, but she was cute. "Childhood fears are the strongest. They're the hardest to shake. Clowns. Dogs. Marionettes."

"Creepy old inns," offered Sam.

"Creepy old inns."

Sam smiled. "I thought it might be good to know the history of the place, to teach the Morrison boy something about his new home. And I'm a bit curious, too."

"I can understand that," said Jeanette. She touched her lip. "You know, I've been trying to figure out where you came from by your accent. You are from the South, but not the Deep South. Virginia?"

"Now it's me that's impressed," said Sam.

"I can't tell you what city, though. I have an interest in accents, but that doesn't mean I'm much good with them."

"I'm not from a city. I've never lived in a city in my life, until now. I was born and raised in the country, farmland far and wide."

"You're a little old farm boy!"

"Farmland, not farm boy. I never grew anything except sea monkeys that lived about four days. My mother always kept a garden of tomatoes, peppers, and squash, but that was about it. She worked as a nurse's aid. My father was a minister."

Jeanette smiled; pointed to the shelves. "We've got journals, newspapers going back almost one hundred fifty years. There are books about the area, published across the years. I don't know how much there is on the Abbadon Inn, but I'll leave you to it."

"Thanks so much."

"You're welcome. And please let me know what you find out. I'm curious now, too. Maybe what you learn will put my childish fears to bed once and for all." She winked both eyes at the same time.

"I will."

Jeanette left the room and closed the door.

Sam didn't know exactly what he was looking for other than a bit more information than Rebecca Morrison had been able to supply. Who was Nicholas Abbadon, really, and Lillith? Certainly, they were just a normal nineteenth-century couple out to make the best living possible, as were most other nineteenth-century couples. Just because Sam had had a nightmare showing Nicholas with flinty eyes and a cruel voice meant nothing. Sam had studied a little Jungian philosophy back at Norfolk State. He knew that dreams were most often compensatory offerings from the subconscious, mangled stories that tried to teach you what was wrong with yourself so you might, one day, get it right. Characters in dreams were usually just facets of your own self bebopping around, acting like nice folks or like assholes or worse, demanding you look them in the eye and acknowledge their presence. Sam had things to feel guilty about, things to mourn, things to regret. Things about which he was still furious.

Fucking bitch Joy Spradlin.

They had all come to a festering head in his dream last night.

Rebecca's red eyes were a dream. The flower-spider wasn't a dream. The dark figure running into the shed wasn't a dream.

Sam moved to the shelves and stared at the countless volumes.

They were waking dreams. They were my imagination running on edge. End of story.

He selected several stacks of written memorabilia, then sat with them at the table. Preserved in plastic covers were delicate letters written by Dutch settlers to their family and friends in Europe in the early 1700s, discussing trade with the Lanapes and the growing whaling industry offshore. Some missives praised God for bringing them to a rich land that allowed them to worship God as Quakers or as Baptists.

Dad would say, "Hallelujah" to that. Long live the Baptists.

Journals and letters from the later 1700s chatted on about the rich peninsular land and the buying and selling of African and Indian slaves to work the plantations, about the timber and grain industries powered by the rise and fall of the tides through small waterways, about the popularity of the region for people seeking time on the pleasant shore, and of the increasing tensions with King George III. According to one letter, written February 12, 1779, and addressed to a Captain Henry Alexander from a Mr. Randolph Blue, the Quakers were not willing to turn their backs on their vows of nonviolence in order to fight a war for independence, but were willing to help their fellows with the cause.

It read, "We of the Society of Friends find it within our brotherly duties to help our fellow countrymen as best we can during this time of great peril. Find with this letter a substantial shipment of salts extracted from the sea, clothing made by our women, and food we have gleaned from our own pantries and smokehouses. I hope it finds you and your men safe and that the scoundrel king's men do not intercept this correspondence. God be with you."

Sam found Trenton and Newark newspapers from the early 1800s, with advertisements boasting transportation to Cape May's casinos and fine restaurants. Amid the common business of shipbuilding and fishing, glassmaking and millinery, town meetings, shipwrecks, and farming, tourism was planting its firm and permanent foothold in the southern part of the state. Little square notices up and down the edges of the newspapers' pages boasted of Cape May's new hotels as "Healthful and Elegant," highly recommended places for "rest, relaxation, and a renovation of the body and spirit."

Sam put a spool of microfilm on the projector, and quickly perused the first years' editions of the resort town's own *Cape May Star and Wave.* A small paper, the issue focused in a pleasant yet formal manner on the lives of the residents, the good news and the bad, the welcome influx of wealthy visitors from the South who sought relief on the beautiful Jersey cape far from the heat and humidity of their own states. Many of the pages were dark and spotty, with chunks missing here and there.

Sam saw nothing on the Abbadon Inn.

He put in a new spool containing the contents of the *Illustrated East Coast Regional Directory, 1856,* and cranked it slowly, watching as half- and full-page advertisements for stores, publishers, manufacturers, hotels, and resorts throughout the eastern U.S.A. rolled by. He paused on a large advertisement for the Homestead in Hot Springs, Virginia, in which owner Thomas Goode claimed the benefits of their renowned "Spout Baths" as well as the graceful dining rooms, extensive ballroom, and unexcelled cuisine for the discriminating guest.

"Discriminating," said Sam. "Couldn't have put that more accurately."

He cranked the spool again.

And then he found it. He had turned the reel a bit too far and a bit too fast, but the wood engraving that whizzed past caught his attention, and he carefully rewound the spool until he found it again. It was a quarter-page ad for the Abbadon Inn.

Sam stared at the detailed engraving. It was blurred at

the top and pocked with water damage. But even without reading the caption or the blurb beneath the drawing, it was obvious this was the Abbadon Inn. The artist's rendering showed a building very much as it stood today. There were three stories, a mansard roof, no porte cochere, but a three-floored outset on the right that later would have its first floor opened for the arrivals of carriages and riders. A five-story tower clung to the front. There was no cupola or "guest wing" yet. The notice beneath the artwork was short, but to the point:

"Mr. Nicholas Abbadon of Cape May announces that his new rooming house, the Abbadon Inn, is ready to receive guests. The Abbadon Inn offers reasonably priced comforts and conveniences to its guests."

The advertisement was dated October 2, 1856.

There was no description of Nicholas Abbadon, of course, and no mention of Lillith. Sam wondered if the proprietor resembled in any way the dark-bearded man of his dream, of if it had merely been Sam's projection. He took the spool off and put on another—1866–1870. The Civil War had come and gone.

Only sixteen papers from that time period had survived well enough to be put on film. Most were missing pages, and the available pages had chips and corners gone. But Sam was able to determine that there was now a railroad reaching Cape May from the west. This brought even more tourists. Advertisements for visitors had doubled, and in addition to more hotels and gambling facilities for men, there were notices promoting summer cottages, ice cream parlors, bathhouses, cafés, concerts, cotillions, and lectures. Sam kept his eyes peeled for mention of the Abbadon Inn or of its owner. It came near the end of the spool. August 19, 1869.

"Mr. Nicholas Abbadon, administrator of the Abbadon Inn, has acquired the services of architect Stephen Decatur Button to design an expansion of his establishment. Plans are for a new wing that will allow the inn to accommodate upward of one hundred guests. The Orchid Restaurant will be expanded. The Abbadon Gambling Club for Gentlemen will offer recreation and entertainment for inn guests as well as local residents. When Mr. Abbadon was asked to give a statement as to the courted clientele, he would not reply directly, but sent, instead, this statement: 'The Abbadon Inn will continue to serve our clients without interruption, offering what they have come to expect. We shall not tolerate the ill-bred nor the jackanapes, for they have no place on our property. Those we will serve, as those who we have served in the past, will be satisfied."

Jackanapes. There is that word again.

The hairs on Sam's arms stood up. He leaned forward and stared at the screen. He knew the word, a term long out of popular usage that meant "monkey" or "ape." He'd never known anyone to use it in conversation. Yet within twenty-four hours, he had encountered it three times. Twice from Nicholas Abbadon. Once from Rebecca Morrison.

It was too odd to be a coincidence. Too unsettling to be happenstance. But if it wasn't coincidence or happenstance, what was it? Sam's heart beat heavily in his ears.

There was a knock on the door. Sam began to rewind the spool with the crank. His headache was back with a vengeance. "Who is it?"

"How long are you going to be in there, anyway?" It was Carl.

"I'm done."

"It's been more than two hours," came the voice through the door. "It's been almost three! By the time we get home it will be past chess time."

"If you want to play, we'll play," said Sam. He pulled the spool from the machine, stuffed it into its little protective box, tossed the box into the metal drawer from where it came, then joined Carl outside the room. "If you've done a good job with your research, I'm willing to give you extra time."

"Oh, I sure did," said Carl, holding up his notebook and several thick volumes. "Can't wait to tell you what I found."

Sam could wait, but he let Carl talk on the way back to the inn through the rain. But he didn't hear a word the boy said. He just kept thinking. Thinking.

Who was Nicholas Abbadon, really? If his dream was more than a dream, what the hell was it? And why did Jeanette Harris, as a reasonable adult, still feel the Abbadon Inn was a particularly unpleasant structure in an otherwise pleasant town?

THIRTEEN

"Geary?"

"Sam?"

"Yeah, it's me."

"Hey, man, how're you doing?" Geary sounded pleased to hear his old friend's voice. Sam couldn't begin to express how good it was to hear Geary's.

"Okay, I guess."

"Where are you now, New York? Maine?"

"Still in New Jersey. Didn't you get the letter and money I sent last week?"

"No. You send cash in the mail? That's not safe."

"Yeah, well, I know that. But I sent you seven hundred anyway."

"Seven hundred dollars? You owe me from one of our February poker games?"

"No, no bet. It's money for my house. I explained all this in the letter. It should be enough to top off the oil tank for the rest of the cold season, though I turned the heat down when I left. The money should also cover the electric bill for a few months, which shouldn't amount to much since I'm not there using anything. I called the phone company to have service disconnected. I don't think I want to rent it out at this point. That's too much to deal with long distance, and I wouldn't ask you to act as a landlord on my behalf. I thought for sure you'd have the letter by now."

"You want me to set up a bank account for all this?"

"You mind just putting it in yours?"

"No."

"And as as I said in the letter, three hundred of that is for you for helping me out."

"Hey, whatever you need. I'm just glad to hear you're still among the living. I thought maybe you'd gone off and joined the circus or the Marines."

"Nope. Still in Cape May. Still at the Abbadon Inn."

"Still teaching that kid I gave you a reference for?"

"Yep."

"How's that going?"

A sigh. "It's got its ups and downs. The kid's got big problems. But I've handled problems before." Sam switched the phone receiver from one hand to another. He was at a payphone at Salty Eddie's. The fish-shaped clock on the wall stated that it was 8:00 P.M., though Sam's watch read 8:12. Not that it made much difference.

"You have." There was a long pause. Then, "So what kind of problem are you handling now besides the kid?"

"What do you mean?"

Geary spoke evenly. "I've known you since you were a nappy-headed little peanut in Keds and overalls. I can hear it in your voice . . ."

"Dani's gone."

"Not dead I hope."

"No, just gone."

"Didn't like Cape May?"

"Didn't like the place we're living in, or what I was doing. Or maybe me. But it's probably better this way."

"What else is wrong? I'm listening, man."

Sam knew Geary was listening. If there was ever a trustful ear, it was his buddy's. If there was ever someone to count on, it was Geary. Sam had met Geary when they were in second grade. Geary was the new kid at school, having moved to Albemarle County all the way from Baltimore, Maryland, a foreign country as far as most Jackson Primary School kids were concerned. The other students avoided Geary because he was tall, quiet, and his mother made him wear a man's tie to school, and he didn't seem to care.

Sam and Geary became best friends on the warm November afternoon when Sam got into a fight on the playground with Joey Johnson, a flat-headed, jug-eared kid who was always pissed off about something. Joey swore Sam had peed on the swing and then Joey had sat in it. Sam had shouted, "Joey, if you'll just open your stupid baby eyes, you'll see I don't have wet pants!" That didn't matter. Joey had sat on a pee-wet swing, got wet pants himself, and it was Sam's fault. He came at Sam, his face scrunched into something that looked like one of Sam's grandma's apple-head dolls, and pounded his fists against Sam's chest. Sam's arms had pinwheeled, but he couldn't keep his balance. He dropped into a puddle. "Now!" yelled Joey, hands on his hips and his flat head shaking. "You got wet pants *and* muddy pants! Ha ha ha!" Sam leapt up, grabbed Joey by the shirt and whirled him around and let go. Joey, screeching, knocked into a little girl, who stared crying. Joey regained his balance, ran up to Sam, and popped him in the chin. Sam swung back but missed. It was then that Geary ambled over from the side of the school, where he'd been leaning against the wall, chewing on a grass blade, watching.

"That's enough of that," he said. Sam blinked at Geary. He'd never seen a kid try to break up a fight before. Usually kids either cheered it on or just stared in fascination. Joey didn't hear Geary, or didn't want to hear him. He struck out with his foot to catch Sam in the shin, but Sam jumped up and away in time. Joey cussed, and Sam smacked him soundly on the cheek with his fist.

"I'm telling the teacher!" wailed Joey, his last line of defense. "I'm going inside and get Mrs. Brown, and you'll be sorry!"

"And I'll tell Mrs. Brown, too," said Geary, as matter-of-factly as if he was reciting the times tables. "I'll tell her what I saw. She'll believe me because I'm the new kid. I'm teacher's pet until another new kid comes to school."

Joey blinked in disbelief, then spun with raised fists toward Geary. Geary just crossed his arms over the blue-and-black striped tie, rolled his lips between his teeth, and waited. Joey waved his arms at Geary but didn't actually hit him. It was as if he knew Geary was telling the truth. The teacher *would* believe the teacher's pet. The teacher *would* believe the new kid over him. Joey huffed and puffed and stormed away, pushing past the crying girl who stopped crying, clasped her hands, and looked at Geary as if she suddenly had a new boyfriend.

"You aren't teacher's pet," said Sam to Geary.

"Maybe. Maybe not," said Geary.

"Why'd you do that, say you'd tattle on Joey?"

"I don't like bullies."

"Me, neither. And I don't like tattlers."

"Me, neither. But I didn't tattle, did I?"

"No."

"All right, then," said Geary. That became the phrase Sam knew his best friend by. Geary, rarely flustered, rarely rattled, punctuating most events in his life with the simplest of observations.

All right, then.

"Yeah," said Sam into the phone at Salty Eddie's. "I do want to talk."

"All right, then," said Geary.

"You remember when we dropped some stuff back in college? Out on the football field? We lay around all night that first time, blown out of our minds. Me, watching stars turn into cats and goats that chased each other around the moon; you, watching, well, I don't know what you were watching. You remember doing that?"

"Yep. Wild days. But we got through our classes with flying colors, didn't we?"

"True. But back to the acid. We dropped it a couple times. I don't remember how much, but it wasn't as much as some of the students. We weren't druggies or anything."

"Nope. Not like Brewster Washington, that's for sure." There was a pause. "Why?"

"Did you ever have flashbacks after that?"

"Flashbacks?"

"Yeah."

"You mean like driving along in my car and suddenly I can see bushes dancing with fence posts outside my windshield or think my hands have turned into Jell-O Pudding Pops, that sort of thing?"

"I guess."

"Can't say that I have. How about you?"

"I don't know. Could be. I've experienced some really weird shit since coming to Cape May."

"And maybe some weird shit before you left Virginia for New Jersey, I'm guessing."

A thin middle-aged man in a coffee-colored leisure suit pushed by Sam to get to the rest room, casting a disinterested glance Sam's way. Sam noticed that the sign on the door said "Merman." Beneath the word was a lopsided, cartoon Neptune holding a triton. Sam glanced at the ladies' rest room door. "Mermaid." The illustration showed a top-heavy, fish-bottomed creature with brittle stars clinging to her nipples, her head tossing back a mound of golden curls. Dani would have loved the artwork's depth.

"Sam?"

"I can't talk about what happened back home, Geary. Not yet. And one has nothing to do with the other."

"Okay." A pause. "So, why the flashback question?"

"I think I might have had one. Damn, but it was bad."

"Yeah?"

"The woman who owns the inn came on to me this morning."

A mild chuckle on the other end of the line. "Hate to tell you, man, but there are a lot of women who wish they had the nerve to come on to you. You've been fighting babes all your life."

"Shut up, Geary. And that's not true."

"It is, too, but go on."

Sam lowered his voice. He could barely hear his own words over the clinking of the silverware, the clanking of glasses, and the conversation of the folks who were in the café for a late-night bite. "She came on to me, but it wasn't a normal come-on. She unbuttoned her blouse, hiked up her skirt, kicked off her shoes and then . . . looked at me. Geary, she had these fucking solid-red eyes. It makes my skin crawl just saying the words, just remembering it. She looked like someone had stripped the pupils and the whites from her eyes, leaving nothing but bloody balls in the sockets."

Geary let out a low whistle. "Are you sure?"

"Yeah, I'm sure. Thanks for believing me."

"No, I mean that's far out."

"Exactly. And I was wondering, does that happen to people? Flashbacks, this far removed from taking drugs? So many years later?"

"I don't think so. Never heard of it happening, what, twelve years after the fact? But that's why I teach shop and I'm not a doctor."

Sam closed his eyes. He heard the man come out of the rest room, and he turned away to the wall. "I didn't think so, either."

"Were you . . . had you been drinking this morning before all this happened?"

Sam opened his eyes and looked out at the crowd in the diner. The waitress who had served him coffee the first time he'd been there gave him a quick nod of recognition as she whipped past with a tray of dinner plates. "I'm not much of a drinker. You know that. A beer or two a couple times a week, or a glass of wine. And never in the morning. So, no. I was as sober as God."

"You never were much of a drinker, Sam. And you were also never one to run away from your problems. You were always the responsible guy, solid as a rock. Yet there you are, my friend, hiding in New Jersey, hiding from something. Things change. We do, too, sometimes."

"I'm not . . ." Sam stopped. Could he tell Geary what had happened? Geary would understand. But here, in this diner where he was within earshot of a good cross-section of Cape May, he couldn't do it. "Yeah, you're right. I never did run away from shit. Until now. But sometimes you have no choice. I had absolutely no choice."

There was a long, silent pause between the friends, punctuated by many, many miles and an unanswered question. Sam wished he was at Geary's house, sipping a beer, kicking back on the old vinyl sofa, the Redskins on the tube, and shop talk during commercials. *Things change. We do, too, sometimes.*

All right, then.

Geary broke the silence. "But back to the woman and

her red eyes. You didn't have a flashback, Sam. And I know you weren't drunk."

"Right."

"That leaves only two other possibilities."

"What's that?"

"Either you're suffering from severe stress."

"Yes?"

"Or you've got the devil on your tail."

Fourteen

The remainder of the week offered up no red eyes, no nightmares, and no dark, darting figures in the yard or elsewhere. Yet the inn's long halls and Sam's bedroom continued to throw cold pockets of air at him. The foul stench came and went, sometimes laced with traces of ash and other times the smell of cheap perfume. And still other times there was scratching and scraping inside the walls, which Sam chalked up to mice. Or squirrels. Though he noticed that sometimes the sounds were rhythmic, like someone tapping out a code.

Sam would not consider Geary's final conclusion.

Come Wednesday, Rebecca noticed that Dani was no longer around. "Where's your wife these days?" she asked. Sam explained that she needed to be gone for a while; an art trip. That satisfied the mistress of the inn's curiosity.

Sam and Carl studied from texts of literature, science, social studies, and math in the restaurant in the mornings, and after lunch they took field trips. One afternoon they perused the Fireman's Museum, though the docents were about as unhappy having Carl there, poking and picking at the exhibits, as Carl was being there. Sam and Carl took a bus to the Cape May Lighthouse, and climbed the 199 stairs to the top to look out across the Delaware Bay and Atlantic Ocean. Carl enjoyed this trip, though all he could say at the top was "I wonder what you'd look like if you jumped off this thing and landed on the ground?" Sam assigned Carl a short story about life in a lighthouse in the 1920s, and the following morning the boy turned in a surprisingly tame narrative about a boy keeper who tended the light during a storm and rowed out to rescue another small boat in distress. When he handed the paper in, he rolled his eyes and said, "I would have let the boy die, but I knew you'd give me a bad grade if I did."

"That's not true," said Sam.

"Oh, yes, it is," said Carl. Sam let it go.

Friday Carl got a large envelope in the mail. The return address was from the Nanticoke Lenni-Lanape Tribal Council. Carl stood on the front porch and ripped it open.

"I got a phone number from one of those magazines at the library and called 'em up Monday afternoon!" Carl explained to Sam, who stood beside him. "I told them I was doing this report for school, well, I said it was for school so they didn't think I was some retard, and told them to send me stuff about them. Like about their spirits and magic and all that stuff. This was fast! Cool!" Carl yanked his letter from the tattered envelope and let the envelope drift to the porch step. He read it, his lower lip curled between his teeth.

Sam looked at his own mail, his first letter from Geary since moving. He stuck his thumb beneath the envelope's flap and worked it open. "Got your letter and the cash," the letter began. "Way too much for watching your house, but I'm not going to complain."

"Hey! This is no good!" squawked Carl.

Sam looked up from his own letter. "What's wrong?"

Carl smacked the paper with his forefinger. "This guy's telling me about their crafts and clothes and stuff. There's something about where they live and a stinkin' map. He sent a couple photos of him in his Indian clothes." Carl threw the letter and photos down beside the envelope. "Big deal!"

"That is a big deal," said Sam. "This will be a lot of help for your illustrated report. Seems like he sent you quite a bit of current information."

"But it's not what I wanted!" Carl glared at Sam. "I wanted to know about their rituals and tortures!"

"I wasn't looking for rituals and torture, Carl."

"I was!" Carl stormed inside and left the letter on the steps.

Sam let out a long breath, then continued with Geary's short note.

"I'm close to asking Vasha to marry me, so every bit helps. If you're free come June, want to be my best man? You'll have a new car by then, no doubt."

Good for you, Geary. She's a great woman.

"Your house is fine. Nothing falling off yet. One of your old students stopped by my classroom at school a few days ago, asked how you were doing. Joy Spradlin. Said she missed you. Funny, since I thought she always hated you. Later. Geary."

I can see her now, playing that game. Geary, I'm going to tell you the truth next time we're on the phone. You might as well know the truth. Someone besides me and the Spradlins need to.

Sam went in to the Letters Lounge and sat at the table where Carl was spinning his science book around under his thumb. Workers were hammering and sanding in the rooms above the restaurant, so Sam had moved the classroom into the bar. Sam said, "Carl, you can leave the letters and pictures outside. It's your property. They can blow away, get rained on, that's fine. But I'll have no choice but to give you an F on your illustrated report, since you neglected an important part of the process." If Carl got an F or D on any of his schoolwork, Carl's mother said she would take away everything in his room except his sleeping bag and pillow, and he would be grounded inside the inn for a week. Sam had topped that off with "no chess for a week, either." Sam was sure Carl didn't believe his mother, but he knew Carl believed him. Carl retrieved the letter and the photos, slapped them on the tabletop, and grumblingly agreed to finish his report. "But it'll be really, really boring," he threatened.

"Boring's in the eye of the beholder," said Sam.

Carl flipped the science book open to the lesson on cell structure. "And just what was *your* letter about?"

"It was from a friend back home."

"Not who was it from, what was it about?"

"It's private."

"You're so hung up on private!"

Sam opened his own teacher text to the second chapter.

"Spinning like a top in the water is a single-celled organism called *Trichodina*," he read. "It skims over the slippery surface of a fish and then lands. The underside of *Trichodina*—see photo—is a complex, circular clamp made of toothlike spines and hooks. This makes it possible for the tiny creature to grip the skin of the fish."

"That's sick," said Carl.

"Now you read," said Sam.

"I hate to read."

Sam waited. Carl read.

By midweek Sam had started to suspect he was coming down with a virus. His nose prickled, and his eyes itched. His throat felt like someone had plumbed it with a razor. He complained to Rebecca several times about the irregular heating and how it was making him sick, but she only gave vague promises that the "heating man has been notified." And so, Sam went to Mitchell when the man arrived home late Friday evening.

Mitchell smelled strongly of whiskey when Sam met him in the front hallway and insisted he either be given another room or that the heating get repaired.

Mitchell shrugged out of his coat, hung it on the coat tree, and waved Sam into the Letters Lounge—Rebecca had put up a handcrafted, commissioned brass sign beside the French doors in the front hallway that read to that effect—where he dug in a cardboard box behind the still-collapsed bar. He pulled out a bottle of champagne and held it up. "Want some?" Sam noticed that Carl was right; the man was growing a mustache. It was bushy and gray, turned down at the ends. Maybe he hoped he would look like Barney Miller when all was said and done. Of course it would take a little dark shoe polish to make that happen.

"Why not?" said Sam. He sat at one of the white-clothed tables. Mitchell pointed a finger at the cloth.

"I feel like I'm living with Alice in Wonderland. Things just get curiouser and curiouser around here with her sense of organization." Mitchell snatched two glasses from the overhead rack and brought them and the champagne bottle to the table. He nudged a chair back with his foot and sat across from Sam. "I've decided to just let her run with it. See where it goes. I can make it a tax write-off if it goes belly up, and then we can move somewhere else to try something else. I'd rather it not, though. I hope some miracle happens, and Rebecca pulls it together. I'm doing my damndest to make sure we get our liquor license. There's a limited number of them based on the town's permanent population count. But, luck will have it, a small bar east of here looks to me like it's got quite a few safety and other violations. I've been scouting around, and this one, well, I'm guessing complaints from the right people, to the right people, and it'll close down. That leaves an available license, and who is next in line? You got it. The Abbadon Inn."

Mitchell popped the cork from the bottle, waved his hand over the top for a moment, and then poured the bubbly liquid into the glasses. "Cape May is a wonderful little place. I can't wait to see it in the springtime, and the summer, when tourists are buzzing and businesses are hopping. I plan on offering my services to folks on a freelance basis. I'll be a consultant to other businessmen . . . and businesswomen. I'll take on a case here and there to keep things interesting. The rest of the time I hope to be at the Cape May National Golf Club, teeing up and making the drives."

Mitchell lifted his glass and held it out toward Sam. Sam lifted his.

"Here's to good weather, good balls, and a good swing. Of course, that could apply to more than just golf!"

Sam took a sip. The stuff was wonderful.

"So what was it you asked me when I came in?" said Mitchell, putting his glass down. "I had my mind on something else and didn't quite catch it."

Sam rolled his glass in his fingers. "The heating in the inn needs overhauling. If you and Rebecca can tolerate the cold spots throughout the inn, that's fine, but my room should be tolerable. As it is, it's miserable. The radiator seems to work, but the room goes from hot to cold in a second. It might be insulation irregularity? I don't know. I'm not into that stuff. But it's very uncomfortable."

Mitchell took another drink, then put his elbows on the table and looked at his glass. "I knew this place had a lot of problems before we plunked down the big bucks on it. Rebecca didn't care. She fell in love with it the moment we first stepped inside with the realtor. I'd told her for years that when I retired I'd get her a bed-and-breakfast or some damn thing. She was a good lawyer's wife, Sam, I have to tell you that. She deserves a little something special. I do love her. I couldn't live without her, regardless."

Sam wasn't able to smell the booze on Mitchell, but it sure was making itself clear through the man's easy and open dialogue. Had this been midday, and Mitchell hadn't had a long evening of drinking under his belt already, Sam doubted the man would have opened up so much to his son's tutor. Still, Sam was enjoying the champagne.

"Great, great wife," said Mitchell. He took another sip and looked at the rim of the glass as if it held the answers to life's big questions. "She was twenty-two when we got married back in 1961. I was forty-eight. Old enough to be her father, that is what her father said to me, but what the hell, she was an adult. She looked just like Jackie Kennedy except for that red hair. Jesus Christ, but she was a beautiful girl. Dressed to kill. My associates were jealous as hell. Me, twice divorced, approaching middle age, snagging this little goddess. I treated her right, too, don't think I didn't. She gave me dinners, parties, and blowjobs to die for. Always ready and willing for me to stick it to her. Goddamn, but those were the good days. Then she got pregnant. I didn't want kids. I have two grown kids already with the first wife. But she wanted to be a mother." Mitchell took a drink. So did Sam. "And so there came Carl. God bless him, if you're into God. God bless *us*. I think Becky liked the idea of having a child but not raising one. She started feeling like she was missing something. She hinted at moving to San Francisco in the late 'sixties, can you believe that? I put my foot down, and she said no more about it, but I knew she was tiring of the way things were. So, honestly, she deserves to have a go at the bed-and-breakfast thing. I don't begrudge her that."

"Mitchell, hang on a second. Let's talk about the heating . . ."

"I just wish I understood her thinking processes." The

man loosened the knot in his tie and unbuttoned the top button of his shirt. He blew a noisy breath through his lips. "No, maybe I don't wish I knew. Men don't know squat when it comes to their women, and it might be better that way." Mitchell rubbed his chin, then tugged at his mustache. "I've noticed Dani isn't here anymore. She move out on you?"

Fuck this. "She decided this wasn't the best place for her, creatively. But I need to know you're going to fix the heating right away."

"Yes, well, I could have told you she'd go. Nice girl, and pretty, but I could see the edge on her from the get-go. Living here cramped her style. You, on the other hand, are much more practical."

You don't know shit about me, man. "Mitchell, did you hear . . ."

Mitchell drained his glass. "Yes, yes, I heard you the first time, well not the first, but the second time." He poured another glass. "Before I leave in the morning I'll get the heating and cooling company on the honk. Good enough?"

"Tell them it's a priority."

"Will do. We don't want Carl's teacher getting sick. And you do sound raspy."

"Speaking of Carl," said Sam. "You and Rebecca need to sit down and lay out the rules of the house to him. I caught him rummaging through my things this afternoon."

"Was your door locked?"

"Should it matter?"

"You have to keep things locked up with that boy."

"He's old enough to learn that a closed door represents a locked door."

"Well, certainly, we'll have a talk with him if you think that's what's needed." Mitchell cleared his throat. "Rebecca upstairs in bed?"

Lord, man, why ask me? "I suppose." Sam downed the rest of his champagne so fast he didn't taste a thing.

"I'll take the glasses," said Mitchell, standing. "It wouldn't do for the dear wife to come down in the morning and find someone had left a mess." He nodded at the bar sprawled on the floor and winked. "There's more where this came from if you want it. Might keep you warm if your room goes cold one last night."

Mitchell waddled through the restaurant and into the kitchen while Sam sat at the table, running his finger up and down the champagne bottle. He hadn't heard from Dani since she'd left. He wondered where she was staying and if she was happy. He was also pissed that she was leaving him hanging like this. She knew he'd be worried, but she was remaining silent. To punish him.

Outside the inn, the wind picked up. The walls of the bar creaked and whistled. Sam thought of the walls of his own little house, how the creaks and whistles were like friends speaking. Here, it was like enemies screaming. He took a swig from the bottle and put it down, his hand still wrapped around the label. His ears buzzed with the coming of a bad cold, his throat hurt, and his nose tickled.

I don't deserve to be punished, Dani, he thought. *I didn't do anything wrong.*

The bottle on the table began to shake.

Sam let go. He drew back in his chair.

The bottle rattled as if in a paint mixer, side to side, bang-bang-banging on Rebecca's white cloth. Down in the kitchen, Mitchell sang to himself in an off-key tenor. " 'It's not for me to say you love me, it's not for me to say you'll always care . . .' "

The bottle shook more fiercely and began to spin on its base. Sam thought, *Get up, Sam, move your ass!* but his muscles clamped on his bones and would not let him go. Droplets flew from the bottle like spittle. In its spinning madness, it began to creep across the table toward Sam.

Down in the kitchen, " 'As far as I can see, this is he-eeh-eeh-ven . . .' "

The bottle reached the edge of the table. Sam watched it, his teeth clamped down on the insides of his cheeks. And then the bottle exploded. Glass flew outward and skyward in glistening fragments. Small pieces pierced the backs of Sam's hands, his neck, and face. He cried out, and at that moment his body obeyed. He jumped to his feet and clawed at the shards embedded in his flesh. They flaked away, as if they were nothing more than melting snow. The pinpricks of pain remained, hot little spots all over his exposed flesh.

"Whoa, buddy, mind your grip." It was Mitchell, standing in the doorway between the restaurant and bar, a dishtowel over his arm, staring at the shattered remains of the bottle. He'd untied his tie; it hung down on either side of his shirt. He was very clearly drunk now. He dug in his ear with a pinkie. "When I was a young man, I used to be able to crush a tin can—not an aluminum one mind you—but a tin can in my grip. You wouldn't have wanted to arm wrestle me back then. But what's with smashing bottles with your bare hand? Trying to prove something? That has to hurt."

"I'll clean it up," said Sam, looking back at the remains of the champagne bottle on the tabletop and floor.

"No, no, I'll do it. I'm in the mood for cleaning." He began singing, " 'I'm in the mood to clean . . . simply because you're near me. Funny but when you're near me, I'm in the mood to clean.' " He laughed. Sam did not.

Could there have been a tremor? Or the old floor of the bar settling unevenly, making the bottle spin and break?

Mitchell waved a dismissive hand. "You go on upstairs to your room. Get a good night's sleep. Get over whatever you're coming down with. If the heat's a problem, hell, just move to the room next door. I'll get help to move the furniture over tomorrow if that's the case. As long as it's after my get-together uptown."

Or was it something else? Geary said the devil was on my tail.

"Sam, did you hear me? Go to bed. My kid's wearing you out. We want you to take care of yourself so you can do your job."

"Yeah, whatever," Sam said, and he knew it sounded either frightened or irritable, but he didn't care, and Mitchell didn't seem to care, either.

Sam left the bar and climbed the stairs. His hand shook on the railing, and he wondered if it was his hand or the railing. He reached the second floor and paused in the main hall, looking down the dark stretch at the closed door to

Rebecca and Mitchell's bedroom. No lights were on in the hall, but a faint light was visible beneath the door; Rebecca was either up or sleeping with a light on. Did this place spook her, too?

From somewhere on the floor, Sam heard chittering sounds, chewing sounds. He looked both ways, squinting as his eyes adjusted to the dimness, but saw nothing move, only the swirling dots on his eyes produced by champagne, weariness, illness.

He took hold of the wobbly banister to continue to the third floor, but then stopped and looked back around. There was something wrong on this floor, something that made his skin prickle. All along the wall, the brass, dragon-headed sconces seemed to have shifted, to have turned in on themselves like lizards trying to eat their own tails. One light at the far end of the hall by the sunroom's closed door began to sputter, a mindless and meaningless Morse code.

Blink. Blink. Bli-blink. Blink. Bli-blink.

Doors to the vacant bedrooms, which had been partially closed when he'd reached the second floor, were now completely open, revealing blackened maws. An icy river of air blew past Sam's face.

The scrabbling and scratching stopped; and for a moment there was total silence. Sam held his breath, listening. There was nothing but the hissing of blood behind his ears.

Then the pounding began. It was soft but definite. Like a heavy, padded hammer slowly driving spikes into soft wood.

Boom. Boom.

It was hard to pinpoint where the sound was coming from. Sam let go of the banister. His fists clenched instinctively. He glanced behind him, over the railing, down the steps to the first floor below. The stairs seemed to stretch and pull like Carl's gum, taking the first floor down with it until it seemed miles away.

The pounding grew slowly louder. Sam looked down the hall at Rebecca's door. The light had gone out. Was she asleep? Did she hear this?

I don't want to see what it is. I don't want to know what the hell it is.

Sam shook his head and whispered, "Fuck this." He had

to know. He had to clear his head of all the weird shit from the past weeks. He had to step up to it and know it so he could . . .

So you can what?

"Jesus, I don't know," he said, the words glass in his throat.

Sam moved quietly down the hall to Rebecca's closed door and pressed his ear to the wood. The only thing audible on the other side of the door was Rebecca's irregular snoring. The pounding was not there.

Boom. Boom. Boom.

Sam turned and looked back up the hall. The pounding continued, somewhere in one of the murky rooms with the open doors.

Go back to the stairs, Sam. Go up to bed. Leave this alone. You don't need this shit.

He drew in three long, deep breaths, flexed his freezing fists.

Boom.

Sam crossed the hall to the first open doorway. Beneath him, the thick nap of the Oriental runner began to squirm and ripple. He glanced down, but no, it was not moving at all; it lay still like any rug, its intricate patterns bled out in the dark. Another wisp of cool air caressed his cheek and moved on. In it, Sam caught the putrid reek of dying animals and rotted forests. He thought he heard his name called faintly, in a high-pitched, female's voice— "Saaaaaaaam"—but then the sound was gone, absorbed in the pounding and a new sound, a metallic sound, like chains dragging across a floor.

Boom. Boom.

Clink-clink-clink-clink.

Sam reached the doorway. The jamb was damp and slick as cold sweat. Sam leaned over far enough to look inside. Through the darkness, he could pick out only a ragged piece of rug rolled up along the wall, a drop cloth, and cans of paint in a neat little pyramid near the door. The window on the far wall was covered in heavy drapery, blocking out any light from beyond. Specks of black and gray swirled in the void. The pounding was not in this room; it was farther on. Sam pushed away from the door. He caught himself breathing in rhythm with the sounds.

Boom. Boom. Clink. Clank.

He moved to the next room, swallowed around the pain in his throat, and looked inside. There was nothing there but an overturned ladder. The window here was also enshrouded with drapery. Hot air drifted past him through the door, then cold, heavy with the ripe death-smell. Sam gagged and pulled the collar of his sweatshirt over his nose. The pounding and clanking continued. But it was somewhere else. The sounds echoed off his muscles and bones. The door to the third room was shut; locked. The knob was ice, and the door hot to the touch.

Saaaaaammmmmmm . . . Came a whisper on the air, but no, it was not his name but his own breath, forced through clenched teeth.

At the end of the hall was the communal bathroom. Its door, too, was open. The sounds seemed to originate in there. Sam slipped into the bathroom, his feet scuffing on sawdust.

BOOM BOOM CLINK CLINK CLINK

The porcelain sink and white tiled floor caught vague moonlight from the untreated window through the opening in the unfinished drywall divider. He looked at himself in the mirror above the sink, and the reflection was blurred, as though the glass were coated in grease. He held his breath, counted to—

One one one one

—and went through the divider door. The noises were louder here, slow, steady, though it didn't sound like it was so much in the room as inside the walls, behind the walls, pressed against the plaster from the inside, trying to get out. The dead-smell was here, too, sitting in the bathroom like a fat and foul-bodied ghost. Sam tucked his nose again into his shirt collar, but the stench stung his eyes. His stomach clamped on itself, and he thought he would throw up. Sweat broke out on his face.

To the right, beneath the window, was an old-fashioned toilet with a flush chain hanging from the ceiling. On the left was a claw-footed bathtub, the lace-covered white vinyl curtain drawn all the way round on its steel rings.

BOOM . . . BOOM . . . CLANK.
BOOM.
The sound's not in the walls, it's in there.

He stepped to the side of the tub. It was there, behind the drawn curtains.

Shit.

His heart stopped. His lungs froze.

Can't the fuck anyone else in this house hear this noise? Why aren't they here with me, trying to find out what the hell is going on?

He reached for the curtain.

Don't you hear it? Don't you smell it? God help me.

His fingers wrapped around the lace and the vinyl. He drew the curtain back.

Several yellow rubber duckies with their heads sliced off lay upside down in a cluster at the drain hole. Remnants of one of Carl's extra-curricular activities. There was nothing else in the tub.

And the noises were suddenly softer. The smell had faded. It was as if the sound and stench were moving away, traveling back through the inn. Leading him on.

Leading me on like Rebecca and her damned red eyes.

His heart picked up its beat again.

He left the bathroom for the hallway. The sounds of hammering and dragging chains again seemed to originate from the far end of the hall, up past Rebecca's room. It seemed to come from the small sunroom over the porte cochere, the room beneath which Carl was now residing.

Boom. Boom. Boom.

Downstairs, punctuating the eerie sounds, were high-pitched lyrics belted out by a besotted Mitchell Morrison. " 'The nightingale . . . tells her fairytale . . . of paradise where roses boom . . . boom . . . I mean bloom . . . !"

Boom. Boom.

The hammer continued to swing up and over and down, slamming into the soft wood . . .

. . . the soft flesh . . .

. . . and the chains continued to drag across the rough ground . . .

Wait . . . why did I think that? Why did I think flesh?
Fuck," he growled. "It's running me in circles!"
Boom.
Clank.
Clink.
Beneath the fear, an anger rose up in Sam. What the hell
was playing with him? His own mind? Sickness? The Abbadon Inn? Some fucking, ass-wiping, dick-sucking devil
that he didn't really believe in? He was going to face it.
To take it on.
Fuck you!
He ran down the hall, his teeth bared, his breath hissing
through them like the steam from a train. He slid to a stop
at the sunroom, his legs nearly buckling beneath him, and
put his hands on the rough surface of the closed door. It
pulsed with the throbbing; the sickening smell pouring out
from beneath, engulfing Sam in an eye-searing cloud. He
threw himself against the door and twisted the doorknob. It
was locked. He pounded the door in time with the pounding beyond the door.
Open up, damn you!
Was Carl hearing this from upstairs? How could he not,
if it was real?
Boom-boom boom-boom boom-boom!
Little pig little pig let me come in . . . !
The sound and smell welled up around him like swamp
water. He gulped in the stinking air, and he threw back his
head to drink in the thunderous pounding.
BOOM CLINK BOOM CLANK!
It came from everywhere then, from the walls, the ceiling, caressing and crushing him like invisible, dreadful
lovers; he felt he was falling.
Slipping. Drowning.
Then it moved into him.
Sam clutched his chest, and the pounding was in his
heart, it *was* his heart, hammering the flesh inside. The rattling chains slithered through his veins like a cold and
probing snake. Not painful, but terrifyingly awesome. The
dead-smell rose from him like steam, seeping through his

pores, saturating his clothing, his hair. Sam counted the
hammer falls within, his eyes open, his putrid sweat tracing
the lines of his face and catching on the corners of his
mouth. He stared at the ceiling. In one corner, a small
brown spider was being dragged into a cottony lair by a
larger, spotted spider. The brown spider struggled, but the
effort was worthless. The larger spider bit it over and over;
the thrashing stopped, and the spotted spider moved on
into its nest.

Nausea swept Sam like a tsunami. He groaned, doubled
over, and grabbed his knees. Sweat fell to the Oriental runner. He heaved.

God, what is this . . . will it stop? . . . I'm . . . I'm . . .

But then his heartbeats began to slow. He held his
knees, bore his chin down to his chest, and waited. The
beats, the pounding, eased, quieted. As his heart slowed, so
did his breathing, though his chest ached like he'd been
thrown on a train track and run over by a coal car.

The booming softened to a whisper and stopped.

Once again, he could hear Mitchell down in the Letters
Lounge, having moved on to another selection in his eclec-
tic repertoire.

" '. . . Move 'em on, head 'em up, head 'em up, move
'em out, move 'em on, head 'em out, Rawhide. Set 'em
out, ride 'em in, ride 'em in, let 'em out, cut 'em out, ride
'em in Rawhide . . .' "

I'm so sick . . .

Sam stood up, his legs trembling. He lifted his arm to
his nose and sniffed. He reeked like a cadaver that had sat
in the sun, ripened, and split open. His clothes and his skin,
rancid. He recoiled at his own stench. His head spun.

"I'm sick," he panted. "That's all this is. That's what
this has been about. I was getting sick, and now I am. No
fucking flashback. No fucking stress or devil. Just a virus
playing havoc with my body and my mind. I'll get over
this. That will be that."

Geary said the devil was . . .

"Fuck Geary. He was grabbing at straws."

The dead-smell remained. Sam dragged himself up the

final flight of stairs and stood in the scalding shower until the water went lukewarm. He leaned against the tiled wall, scrubbing himself raw with a sliver of Lava soap one of the workmen had left on the sink, and letting his thoughts and the misery drain away with the suds.

FIFTEEN

Carl was curled up inside his sleeping bag, his body drawn down into the lumpy sack as far as he could go, his pillow pulled inside with him. He had a flashlight on, and he was studying his penis. He wondered if it was small or regular or big. He guessed it wasn't so big based on what he'd seen. Not that he'd seen a lot. He'd only caught a few glimpses of naked men in books his mother had kept on the high shelf back in Danbury. He'd also read a book called *When a Boy Grows Up*, an "educational guide" Mitchell had left on Carl's dresser on his eleventh birthday. It was really no more than a stupid coloring book filled with cartoonish artwork. Each page showed, step by step, the hair growth, chest expansion, and dick changes of one particularly goofy character with bright white teeth and cocked eyes. And, of course, there was the illustration on the wall inside the spiral staircase stairwell.

Some cultures believed there was power in the male body. Carl remembered reading a short passage about that in one of his mother's top-shelf books. Both the Greeks and Romans had penis gods. The Romans even made penis bracelets to wear for magical protection and strength. The Egyptians put up obelisks as symbols of penis power all over the place. Carl's book on Asian magic talked about the yang, which was just another name for penis power. Carl didn't know if the Mohawks believed in penis power, but he thought they probably did since they were all into warriors and bravery and all that shit. Carl had already shaved the sides of his head, leaving a strip of hair from the nape of his neck to his forehead. It looked good, and it felt good, too.

Nnnnnnnnnn. Carl took a razor blade and cut three

small nicks in the base of his penis. He sucked air through his teeth. Blood welled, and he touched the blood with his thumb, then his thumb to his tongue. He took a sock and began rubbing his shaft. *Nnnnnnnnnn.* Male power. Blood power. Indian power. Yang power. Focus on the task at hand, the task in his hand.

"Nnnnnnnnn."

Carl's member hardened beneath the sock, and he panted with the motion. His groin grew fat and hot with pleasure. Blood streaked the sock. He picked up the pace, shutting his eyes and picturing Sam down in the communal bathroom (he could hear the water running), taking a shower, then stepping out of the tub, drying off. Opening the door to the hallway, and the door slamming shut—*Wham!*—on his right hand.

"Nnnnnnnnnn."

The hand would be crushed from the impact, with at least several fingers shattered. Sam would go to the emergency room and get it set in a cast. He would not be able to grade papers or write letters or do much else while he learned to use his left hand.

Ha!

Nnnnnnnnnnn . . .

One day soon, Carl would let Sam know that *he* had made it happen. He had willed the door to shut at the very second Sam had his hand there. At first Sam would think he was just telling a lie like he always did. But then he would cast another spell on him to show him how stupid he was to disbelieve him, to show how his blood power, his man power, had evolved. Then he would tell his mother and father what he'd been up to. He would make his mother fall down the steps, crush her legs, put her in a fucking wheelchair. That way, she couldn't do those stupid Yoga stretches in the morning anymore and prance around in those hippie skirts. He would make his father have a car wreck and break both his arms and his legs, or maybe fall asleep in a chair in the bar and burn himself with one of his expensive cigars. Burn himself so badly he couldn't play golf for a long, long time, if ever.

But for now, it was Sam's turn to hurt. The man pretended to be his friend. And at times Carl had thought it might be true. But late that afternoon, after their hour-long chess installment in the bar, Carl found out otherwise. Sam had gone out for a walk, so Carl had gone into Sam's room to have a little look around. The room wasn't locked or anything, so what did the man expect?

Then Sam had come back upstairs because he was tired and had changed his mind about the walk, and had caught Carl red-handed.

Jesus, it wasn't like Carl was pissing in the man's bed or taking a crap in his shoes, he was just looking through Sam's suitcases and dresser, trying to learn a little bit more about his mysterious tutor. Like that English lady sang in the movie about the Chinaman and all his gazillion kids, Carl was just "getting to know you, getting to know all about you." Sam had continued to be vague in his answers about his teaching back in Virginia, and so Carl decided to find the answers, himself.

At first he'd found little of interest. A couple paperback history books in the nightstand drawer. Some dirty clothes in a basket in the closet. Then, beneath the bed, he'd discovered an old bag made out of what looked like pieces of a rug. He sat on the bed to open it, and at that moment Sam appeared at the door, his face twisted and shiny. He had roared, "You put that down this minute!"

Carl held onto the rug-bag and glowered.

"What are you doing in here?"

"Don't yell at me!" Carl hurled the rug-bag across the room where it hit the window and drove a spider-crack into the glass.

"What are you doing in here?" Sam repeated.

"Nothing! Just looking. Goddamn, don't get your panties in a twist over it!"

Sam picked up the rug-bag and put it on top of the dresser. His fists were clenched. Carl had never seen the man so angry. It was exciting. It was scary. "You have no right to come in here and rifle through my things."

"Why not?"

"Oh, don't play stupid!"

"You said you were my friend."

"I said I was your teacher. I said we should treat each other kindly, like friends, if we were to work together."

"Well, friends let each other come in their rooms and look around."

"Not without asking, they don't."

"What do you know about it?"

"I have friends, so I should know. You don't have a single one, and at the rate you're going, you won't be making any in the foreseeable future."

As soon as Sam said those words, Carl could tell he regretted it. Carl didn't care, he didn't have friends, and it was no big secret. But he played with it. He screwed up his face and let his mouth fall open.

"That's a mean thing to say!"

"You're right, Carl. That was uncalled for."

"Say you're sorry!"

"No, because you still have no right to be in here. I don't sneak through things in your room. I demand the same consideration."

"You shouldn't have left your stupid door open!" Carl bit his lip to work out a few tears.

"It wasn't open."

"I mean unlocked!" The tears welled, but there weren't enough to fall. Carl bit his lip harder and felt the skin part and bleed. Good.

"I guess I'll have to lock it from now on. I can't trust you as much as I wanted to." Sam wiped sweat from his forehead. He leaned against the dresser, and Carl could see he wasn't feeling well. Who cared? Carl hoped he was big-time sick.

"You're so mean!"

"It's clear you have no notion of respect for privacy. I will not have this happen again. I'm going to arrange a meeting with you, me, and your parents to . . ."

"I'm going to tell my parents what you said about me not having friends and how you think it's funny!" There, a tear fell down his cheek. Good.

"I never said it was funny."

"You look like you think it's funny! And I'm going to tell them what you said and how you looked saying it! Then I'm . . . I'm going to tell them you hit me!"

"What? Why?"

"Because I hate you!"

Then Sam shoved his hands in his pockets. He shook his head and closed his eyes. When he opened them again, he said simply, "Do what you have to do, Carl. And I'll do what I have to do."

"Fuck you!" screamed Carl as loudly as he could, so hard that the words scraped his throat, and he dashed out into the hall. He ran down to his own room, his socked feet slipping on the bare wood of the floor, slammed the door and locked it. He kicked his sleeping bag and punched a dent in the door to the spiral staircase.

What the hell was Sam doing, getting mad over something like Carl snooping in his room? If he didn't have anything to hide, then he didn't have any reason to get so pissed off. Rebecca always said, "Wear clean underwear in case we're in a car crash and you have to go to the hospital." This was the same damn thing. This wasn't Sam's home, it was Carl's. Sam shouldn't have anything to be ashamed of in his room. His room should be like that clean underwear, ready to be shown at any time. Sam knew all about Carl's crappy life, but he never told Carl a damn thing about his own. Why wouldn't Carl be curious? Carl needed to know who his teacher was. Fuck, the man might have been really dangerous. Maybe he and Dani were like the bank robbers Bonnie and Clyde, running from the law, only Dani got tired of living a life of crime and left Sam to go paint pictures of boats. Maybe Sam was a crazy murderer like one of Charles Manson's gang, come to New Jersey to find a nice rich family to get in good with and then stab a million times over and write "Die Pigs" on their walls in their blood. Well, okay, Carl didn't really think he was, but, hell, maybe he was. Rebecca had called a teacher where Sam used to work, and he said Sam was okay, but why did Sam really leave Virginia? Why did he refuse to talk about it?

Sam thought he was a big shit with power. Well, Carl was a bigger shit. He was going to make Sam hurt.

Nnnnnnnnn. Carl bent over and worked hard at his dick. *Nnnnnnnnnn!*

He could imagine the door at just the moment Sam reached out for it. He could see the wood creak, and before Sam had a chance to think or move, the door whipped closed with the force of a hurricane behind it.

Crushing the hand. Making Sam scream out in pain.

Nnnnnnnnnnn! . . .

There was an explosion of raw ecstasy, and then Carl's hand was wet. He opened his eyes and trained the flashlight on the mess inside his sleeping bag. No matter. He'd turn it inside out to sleep; it was reversible. He crawled out of the bag and went to the door. Opening it slowly, he squinted through the darkness at the bathroom at the far end of the hall. There was still a light on in there, but the shower had been shut off. Just a matter of minutes now.

Carl closed his door and leaned against it. He hummed. "Nnnnnnnnnnn."

Then he heard the door open. There were several seconds of silence, and then a bang. Carl put his hand to his mouth to stifle a victorious laugh. He didn't hear a yell, but that was okay. He didn't think Sam was much of a yeller. But he was a bleeder, yes, sir, just like everybody else. And his bones could break, all righty. Carl counted to ten and looked out again, keeping the door crack small in case Sam was in the hallway. The bathroom door was partially open, and the bathroom was dark. Sam was nowhere to be seen. Carl tiptoed to Sam's closed bedroom door, making sure not to step on the squeaky boards.

The light was on in Sam's room. Carl could see shadows moving back and forth beneath the door. He tipped his head, listening as close as he could without touching the door or the frame. Sam had ears like a freakin' owl. The man was muttering to himself, breathing heavily, and stomping around. It sounded like the man was, indeed, hurting.

Good!

Carl hurried back to his room. He propped his wooden alarm stick up against his door then crawled into his sleeping bag, his bare toes coming in contact with the little cold wet clot at the bottom. Instead of turning the bag inside out, Carl just drew his knees up. He punched his pillow a

few times and then tucked it under his head. Maybe the
door hadn't broken Sam's fingers, but something had happened to the man. Carl linked his fingers beneath his head
and grinned at the dark ceiling and at the shadows that had
settled around him like contented cats.

*Damn, I wish I could astrally project myself like some
people can do. I'd love to float into Sam's room and watch
him right now.*

The thought made Carl smile. He could imagine Sam
sitting on his bed, cradling his wounded hand, debating on
whether to go downstairs to call for an ambulance or try
to splint it himself. Sam would be wondering, did Carl
have anything to do with this since I got mad at him this
afternoon?

*Oh yeah, buddy, I sure did. My power is growing. No-
body better get in my way, fuck with me, or make me mad.
No-siree-bob.*

The floor trembled slightly beneath Carl and his bag.
Carl lay still, waiting for it to stop. It did. But then the ceiling rattled, causing the light globe to creak in its metal
holder. Carl pulled himself up on his elbow and looked
around. There was no discernible wind outside battering
the house.

What's this?

Something behind the stairwell thumped, and the metal
stairs could be heard scraping and grating against the bolts
that held it in place. There was something else, too. The
sound of scratching. Digging.

The pit of Carl's stomach rolled. His mouth went dry. It
didn't sound like mice. It sounded much bigger. Rats?
Maybe. Charles Manson, escaped from prison and hiding
in the stairwell? Or maybe Leatherface with his chainsaw?

Oh, shit!

Carl scrambled from his sleeping bag, scraping his knee
on the rough floor and tearing up a big hunk of splinter, took
the alarm stick from the main door and slammed it up
against the door to the stairwell. Leatherface was a hell of a
lot scarier than Sam. Then Carl sat on the floor, the sleeping
bag around him like a shawl, staring at the stairwell door and
the wood, picking at the splinter, and praying for daylight.

SIXTEEN

APRIL 1978

Saturday morning, Sam was still feeling "poorly" as his mother would have called it, and his first inclination was to stay in bed the whole day. His throat was raw, and he felt like he'd been run through his grandmother's wringer washer. But he'd told Jeanette Harris he would meet her for lunch, and he didn't have her phone number (she wasn't listed in the directory, the library wasn't allowed to give it out, and he hadn't asked her for it . . . gee, wasn't that thinking ahead?) and the last thing he wanted to do was have her sit at Salty Eddie's and wonder why she'd been stood up.

He lay beneath his covers, savoring as best he could the warmth from the radiator and the warmth from the sun through the windows. He could see the tops of several trees across Columbia Avenue and was surprised that they were budding; tiny, mint-green tips twirled at the ends of the branches. Branches of another tree bore small white clusters. In a week or two, these would open into flowers. Spring was on its way, after all. That realization came as a small yet surprising relief.

Sam listened to the sounds within the great inn, none of which were odd or suspect at the moment. Carl running water in the bathroom sink, then running downstairs. Rebecca's shrill voice in the first-floor reception room, laughing at something someone on the telephone had just said, and then her voice suddenly shifting to an unhappy cry, "Carl, what on earth did you do to your hair?" Mitchell in the front yard, talking to someone who'd stopped by. A man with a gravelly voice, a golf cronie or a workman.

Sam wasn't as bad off as he'd been last night, thank

God. He'd had the runs throughout the evening, giving him cause to make countless frantic trips to the bathroom, and he'd gone from feverish to chilled to feverish, but now he was just wrung out. He couldn't remember being that sick in a long time, so bad that everything around him had been unreal and terrifying. But now, he was on the mend. His hand stung where he'd slammed it in the bathroom door the night before. He'd wound a small bandage about the bruises and cut, but it, too, was easing a bit.

Sam would have been happy to keep his eyes closed and not move for a year.

He turned his head on the pillow and watched as the digital clock ticked off one minute at a time. He would get up at eleven. That would give him enough time to shower, dress, and wander down to the seashore to meet Jeanette at noon. It was five 'til. Through the window the day looked to be perfect, warm, even. A good day to start over. No more weird shit; it had all been the stress, and the sickness brought on by the stress. Sam would take the weekend to recover fully. He would arrange a meeting tomorrow with the whole of the Morrison family, to tell them how it would be with their son if they wanted him to stay. Carl could kick and scream and swear Sam had hit him all he wanted, but Sam would be back in charge like he had been at Jefferson Junior High.

Well, until Joy Spradlin had reared her ugly, lying head.

I'll go to the hardware store this afternoon after lunch, Sam thought. *I'll get a replacement doorknob and dead bolt for my bedroom.* He'd also buy a padlock, hell, two of them, the new round kind that couldn't be picked or snipped off even with bolt cutters. One for the outside of the bedroom door, the other for the closet door. When Sam had caught Carl sitting on his bed yesterday, opening his carpetbag, he'd nearly had a heart attack. Inside the bag was the evidence of Sam's self-imposed banishment. There was the letter from Diana Spradlin, typed on school notebook paper with a faded ribbon, accusing Sam of molesting her daughter. "You put your hands on her," the letter read. "You stuck your fat black fingers down her panties and into her cunnie. She tole me this and my girl wouldn't not make this up. You always wanted her pussy you think she's hot and so you took what you wanted." It went on to describe more vivid and more bizarre things Joy had accused Sam of doing to her, and Diana's final line, "I will tell your principel and the police what you done. Maybe your principel won't believe us, but the sheriff and deputies will and the judge will no matter what pussy-whip lawyer you hire. Your going to jail, boy. For a long time." Sam's first instinct was to burn the letter, but then he thought best to hang on to it. Who knew what might transpire, and this was evidence. But then a second letter came that said, "You give me $10,000 and me and Joy will let this go. It won't mean your innocent but we can turn the other cheek for that much money and besides we won't have to pay taxes to house and feed you in the big house." This letter, too, was inside the carpetbag. Sam had thought he could use them, but he had quickly decided that the cousin sheriff and the cousin deputies and the cousin judge wouldn't see them as anything but corroboration and cold, hard facts. Yet, he kept them. As proof of the ill one person can inflict upon another. And, in part, because he still couldn't believe it had really happened. He would keep the letters, and he would keep them in the carpetbag. And he would keep his room locked up, safe and sound.

The clock ticked over to 10:59. Sixty more seconds to lie in the warm bed. Sam pushed up on his elbow and reached for the glass of water he'd brought back with him after his last major stomach cramp. He took a slow sip, easing the dryness in his throat. A pigeon landed on the windowsill and peered in through the glass. It made a pretty, fluttery shadow on Sam's bedroom door. Sam smiled at the shadow, at the cartoonish bird rendered there in filmy gray. The bird did a little turn, as if knowing it was being appreciated.

Then Sam saw something on the floor.

At first he thought it was dark heel marks, scuff marks. Sam squinted. The marks were not black but dark red streaks.

Sam sat up all the way and looked at the marks. They started beneath the door and traveled along the bare floor to the foot of the bed.

April Fool.

He took another sip from the glass, only this time the water didn't cut the dryness in his mouth. He eased his legs over the side of the bed and put his feet on the rumpled bedside rug.

Maybe a wounded mouse crawled in here to die.

Maybe Carl hurt it and then stuffed it under my door as an April Fool joke.

"I wouldn't put it past him," Sam said aloud. "He was really pissed at me yesterday afternoon."

Sam stood, a bit wobbly then gaining his balance. The bird on the windowsill flew away. The marks did, indeed, travel all the way beneath the bed. Sam went to the door and knelt. Gingerly, he touched one of the marks with the index finger of his good hand. It was damp and sticky, with small hard flakes embedded in the wet. He smelled his finger. There was a copper scent of blood and the bitter bite of old iron. He crawled on his knees to the end of the bed. The bedspread hung down nearly to the floor, preventing him from seeing underneath.

A dead mouse. A dying mouse. That's what's under there. Carl, you're one sick, sad kid. If it's mangled and dead, that's bad enough. If it's mangled and dying, I'll have to put it out of its misery. I hate that kind of shit. And you, child, will need more help than I can offer.

Sam lifted the bedspread and peeked under the bed. All he could see was his carpetbag, his suitcases, and a couple socks he'd kicked off and forgotten. The marks meandered around the socks, the carpetbag, and behind the suitcases against the wall.

Moving around the side of the bed, Sam tossed the edge of the spread up and over the mattress. He lay down, his cheek nearly on the floor, little dust bunnies flying up beneath his nostrils. He pulled the socks out and threw them aside. Then he took out the carpetbag, hoping against hope that it wasn't stained with dying-mouse blood. It wasn't. He put it on top of the bed.

There were two suitcases. Blue Samsonite Touristers, dented, given to him by his parents on his college graduation. He lifted the small suitcase and eased it out, hoping not to accidentally squish the dying mouse before he might really have to do so. There was no mouse. The bloody red dribbles had trailed off behind the larger suitcase. And then he heard it. Faint, but close, from up against the wall, from behind the large blue suitcase. Not a mouse squeak. But a metallic *clink*. And another.

Clink.

Sam pulled the big suitcase out and shoved it across the floor. It was too dark to see what lay beside the wall, but the dark silhouette showed it was too big to be a mouse. Sam fumbled for the flashlight in his nightstand drawer. He trained it under the bed and flicked the switch. The batteries were dead.

"Fuck it," he said.

He snatched a yardstick from the closet and dropped back down by the bed. Fishing with the stick, he snagged the thing and hauled it, clinking and clanking, out into the daylight.

"Oh . . . my god."

It was a pair of rusted leg irons.

Sam released the yardstick and stared.

He'd seen this type of restraint in museums. They were used in the early nineteenth century for felons and lunatics. And primarily for slaves. The cuffs fit snuggly around the ankles, and a heavy chain from each cuff ended in a ring that was secured about the wearer's waist. Stamped into the iron on one of the cuffs was the manufacturer's brand: "Bolton & Co., Baltimore." Stamped into the iron on the other cuff was a dreadful motto: "Obedience is Freedom."

And caught up in the nicks of the cuffs and the links of the chains were bits of human flesh and tacky blood. A mouse had not crawled up beneath Sam's bed. This had.

Sam took a towel and bundled it around the irons, afraid for his hands to come in direct contact with the ghastly restraints. He tossed them into the closet and put his large suitcase on top, in case they . . .

In case they what?

. . . in case they tried to crawl back out again.

He slammed the door shut. His wounded hand throbbed mightily. He held it to his chest and felt the rapid rise and fall of his ribs as he looked at the closed closet door.

It was a long fifteen minutes before he was able to unlock his legs enough to take a shower. He found no trail of blood or rust in the hallway, so he did not know from which direction the leg irons had crawled.

But leg irons can't crawl, Sam!

He dressed with effort, fumbling with his aching hand, and when he finally got to Salty Eddie's, he was almost a half hour late.

SEVENTEEN

"So, what happened to your hand?"

Sam turned his hand palm up on the booth, studying the fresh bandage he'd slapped on after his shower, as if it was as much a surprise to him as to Jeanette.

"Oh, I was coming out of the bathroom," he said. "There was a puddle on the floor. I didn't see it, and I slipped, grabbed onto the doorsill. The jostling caused the door to swing shut. Harder than I would have guessed it could, and it whacked me something fierce. At first I thought I might have broken a knuckle, but it's only bruised and cut, with a couple blood blisters on the nails. That's why I was late." Okay, a small lie, big deal. "I'm sorry. I'm usually on time, going places."

"Oh, I don't mind," said Jeanette, and he saw she really didn't. How different from Dani, who was frequently tardy herself but couldn't tolerate that flaw in others.

"Do you want to get it checked out?" Jeanette put her water glass down and touched the bandaged hand gently. He liked the feel of her fingers, feather-soft even through the wrapping. "My physician's office is open Saturdays. Dr. Heatwole. You can't take your hands for granted, and she's really good, and a friend. I could get you in because she owes me. I baby-sat her two-year-old twins last Sunday. All day. That's *all* day." Jeanette made a face.

I have no insurance anymore, Jeanette. "No, I'm fine." He wiggled his fingers beneath the bandage. It hurt a little, but he didn't let on.

"Sure?"

"Sure."

Jeanette said, "Okay, then," and put her hand back around her water glass.

Sam really did feel better than he had an hour ago, wrung out in his room with that damn . . . thing . . . under his bed. Sitting in a sunlit booth at Salty Eddie's having a hot crab cake sandwich with Jeanette was working wonders. Even though he had little appetite, it was good to be with her. It made the world feel right, safe, and nearly normal. Jeanette had not mentioned his lateness to lunch. She had met him just inside the door, dressed in her blue pea coat and blue jeans, hands on hips, a big smile on her face. She had touched his arm and asked, "Have you eaten here before?"

"Yes, the second day I was here. Good pecan pie." They'd moved through the café to a booth, and for a brief moment Sam thought it would be nice to take her hand except that one of his was bandaged, and the other clutched the bone handle to his carpetbag. He wasn't going to leave the bag in his room until he had the padlocks in place.

Jeanette plopped down onto the cushioned seat. "As a native, let me vouch for the crab cakes. Maryland may claim they are the crab-cake capital of the world, but they're deluded. New Jersey holds that crabby crown, proudly though quietly."

He'd followed her lead. Two crab-cake sandwiches, two side salads—Sam's with oil and vinegar and Jeanette's dry—and coffee.

They talked about familiar things at first—funny stories about kids in the library, funny stories about kids in the classroom, bantered back and forth across the table and accompanied by light laughter and knowing nods. Jeanette showed him on the little place-mat map where she'd been born and where they had moved when she was six. Sam flipped his place mat over and drew a rough outline of Virginia, and showed her where he had been born and had lived until the first of March. They compared birthdays— Sam was a 1946 Leo; Jeanette, a 1948 Virgo. They argued the merits of their particular favorite childhood toys— Jeanette's best memories were of the Circus Boy Adventure Game she got for Christmas when she was ten, and the

Silly Putty that showed up several years in a row in her stocking. Sam had loved his Lincoln Logs and Collier's Junior Classics books. Once their respective families had broken down and bought television sets, Jeanette discovered the thrills of *The Twilight Zone* and Sam found *The Untouchables*. They both hated *Sing Along with Mitch*, which their parents tuned in to sing along with every week. Sam had tried to go to the March on Washington in 1963; Jeanette had actually been there on the grounds of the Lincoln Memorial with her family on that day in August, listening to Dr. King proclaim his dream to all who would listen.

Then Jeanette put her fork on her plate and said, "We could talk about ourselves all day, but I know you wanted to learn about old Cape May from an old Cape Mayer."

"Yes, you have to tell me the entire history," said Sam with a wink, "starting from the era of the giant ground sloth. Don't leave out a thing. I'll know if you're skipping."

"Sorry, but you've got the wrong section of the country. The ground sloth was in the Midwest and West, we were the woolly mammoth and the eohippus."

Sam hesitated. "No kidding?"

"Good Lord, I have no idea, Sam."

"You told me librarians knew everything."

"Did I really?"

Sam laughed.

When Sam had spoken to Jeanette at the library on Thursday, she had promised him a show-and-tell Saturday, a walking tour if the weather was good and a trolley tour if it wasn't. As Sam ordered pecan pie and Jeanette ordered sherbet for dessert, he thought about how nice, how refreshing a leisurely stroll around the town would be. *Shake off dem Abbadon Inn blues, boy.* Geary would have said, *All right, then.*

"You read some Cape May history in the library," said Jeanette as she scooped up a spoonful of frozen lime. "Is there anything in particular you are looking for that you couldn't find?

"I want to learn about slavery in Cape May."

"Well, it was here, all right."

Sam cut a piece of pie. "I know all the colonies indulged in the practice. The southern colonies were no worse than the middle or northern colonies in the early years."

"No, and New Jersey was the last of the northern states to abolish the practice," said Jeanette. "White New Jerseyans loved their human property. In 1804, the Act for the Gradual Abolition of Slavery was passed. All black children born on or after July fourth, 1804, would be free after serving an 'apprenticeship.' Twenty-one years for females and twenty-five years for males. Slavery wasn't formally outlawed until 1846. This got rid of the apprenticeships for black children born after 1804, but those slaves who had been born prior to 1804 still had to remain 'apprentices for life.' It was still slavery, just another name for it. It wasn't until the thirteenth amendment was passed in 1865 that the 'apprentice for life' bullshit was crushed for good."

"That's horrible."

"Yes."

"What was the general attitude of the white population toward slavery in Cape May in the mid-1800s?"

"Pretty much what you'd expect—seriously differing viewpoints. There was a strong Quaker influence, and many of the whites were pro-abolition. But others were anti. Some held slaves until 1846, and after that some maintained their 'lifetime apprentices.' After the Fugitive Slave Act was passed by Congress in 1850, no one could be seen as helping runaways. What, and be arrested or fined?"

Sam shook his head.

"There were quite a few all-black communities such as Springtown and Marshalltown that welcomed fugitive slaves. There are recorded cases of slave catchers being run out of town when they were discovered. And although the nearest documented Underground Railroad community in New Jersey was Greenwich, there was another clandestine route that passed through Cape May."

"Really?"

Jeanette nodded.

"People escaped all the way across the bay?"

"By way of Quaker fishing boats from Delaware to New

Jersey. Several Cape May citizens took it upon themselves to hide runaways in their attics or crawlspaces, in their sheds, or even under their beds in trunks bored through with holes."

"Incredible."

"All told, about fifty-some fugitive slaves made it safely from here to Canada."

Sam bit into his pie and rolled a chunk of pecan around his molars. He thought about the leg irons in his closet. A chill scraped at the inside of his skin, as cold and rough as rusted metal. Why were they in his room? How did they get there?

Who wore them?

"Harriet Tubman lived here during the summers between 1849 and 1852," said Jeanette, "working in the new hotels and clubs as a cook, laundress, and scrubwoman. She used the money she earned to finance her trips back to Maryland to guide other fugitive slaves to freedom. God, what courage she had, to go time and time again to bring people out of their bondage. I don't know if I could have done it. I don't think most people could have been that courageous."

"The responsibility and dangers she faced were tremendous."

"I've often wondered if any of my ancestors were runaways." Jeanette looked pensively out the window, then back at Sam. "But my parents had such sketchy information about their parent's parents and on back. I wish I knew more. It's odd, isn't it, that some families, most families, don't have whole stories of their pasts? If only I could wake them out of their eternal sleep and get some anwers."

Sam reached out for Jeanette. Her hand was trembling slightly, which surprised yet pleased him. "It's not odd at all," he said. "Many people didn't want to talk about their sufferings, but to get on with life. My family has lived in the same place for a long time. I say my family, but in truth there is only me now. My brother died in Vietnam, and my parents have both died."

"I see. I'm sorry."

"My house is the same one my grandparents built in

1910. But there are still many things I don't know and will never know. I can trace back only so far. I do know my great grandfather Cicero was born into slavery sometime between 1857 and 1860. But that's about all I know. That's as far back as I can take it."

"We can search all we want, but there will always be details we can't fill in, not with certainty anyway. As historian and librarian, we both know that."

"Even though librarians know everything."

"Even though." She smiled. Sam took it as his clue to let go of her hand.

"So," said Jeanette. "You still interested in stuff about the Abbadon Inn, as well?"

"Yes. In particular, I was wondering if Nicholas Abbadon owned any slaves?"

"I don't know anything about him except that he built the inn. As you can imagine, it's not been a subject in which I've been all that interested."

Sam smiled, nodded.

"Maybe the folks at the Preservation Society would have more information. You should contact Margie Rothman. She's one of the head honchos of the Cape May Preservation Society. They're in the phone book."

"Thanks."

Could those leg irons have belonged to one of Nicholas Abbadon's slaves? No, think. He couldn't have owned any. Slavery had been outlawed by the 1850s. But perhaps he had a claim on some of the so-called lifetime apprentices?

Jeanette patted a spot of spilled sugar on the tabletop with her thumb. "I have a collection of old photos at my apartment, pictures taken by my grandparents, my parents, and myself throughout the years. I looked through some of them again last night. Many are just goofy pictures, you know, ones of my sisters and me acting like idiots on the beach and in the backyard. But others are of the town, some as far back as the twenties, showing other people, other places. I even have a few photos of the Abbadon Inn, if you'd like to stop by my place and see them."

"I would." Sam put an elbow on the table. "But why'd

you hang onto the pictures? You said the inn scared you as a kid, that even today you don't like the place."

"I *don't* like it," said Jeanette. "And I didn't. But that didn't stop my dad from clicking a picture of me holding a stray kitten one Sunday when we were walking past that place on the way to church. And I know there are a couple others in there, too, one when Sally and Renee stopped to pet the trolley mules in front of the Abbadon Inn, another when my high school band performed in a Fourth of July parade. Dad was across the street with Mom, clicking away, calling 'Jeannie! Over here!' My dad was never without his camera. As a family we rarely sneezed, laughed, or took a step that he wasn't capturing for posterity. And there wasn't a building in town that he didn't find interesting within a certain casting of light, a certain shadow, something worth snapping and developing."

"He was an artist."

Jeanette smiled. "He was that. He worked on a fishing boat from the time he was fifteen, but he fancied himself a photographer. He talked about someday joining up with National Geographic and touring the world behind his shutter."

The waitress stopped by, and after both Jeanette and Sam declined coffee refills, she slipped the check beneath the edge of Sam's pie plate and moved on.

"Are your parents still living?" asked Sam.

"Dad was killed when their boat capsized in a storm back in 'seventy-three. Fishing is such a hard way to make a living. Mom moved in with my Aunt Karen in St. Louis when Dad died."

"How about your sisters?"

"Sally's in Baltimore, a legal secretary. Renee's in New York, a part-time actress and a full-time adult education teacher. I'm the only New Jersey hold-out."

"Few people stay in the same place they grew up in, the same place their parents and grandparents grew up in. I did, until I moved here."

"Had to shake that Virginia soil off your feet?"

Sam wiped his mouth with his napkin and flipped over

the check the waitress had just laid on the table. "Something like that. It was time for a change."

"Speaking of change, what's the damage on my end?" Jeanette nodded at the check.

"I'll get it."

"This isn't a date. We met so I could show you some of the historical spots around town."

"It's my small thank-you for your time."

"You often have to pay people to spend time with you?" Jeanette grinned.

Sam smiled back and shook his head. "Sad, but true." The waitress stopped by and took Sam's twenty. "Thanks," he said, and the two left the café.

They took a circle route, northeast up Beach Avenue, north along Queen Street, then down Madison to Lafayette, and on to Franklin. In spite of Sam's lack of energy, the walk was just what he needed. He savored the air, the sun, and the company. Jeanette didn't give a rambling and sterile account of what they were seeing, but instead offered interesting facts and personal recollections of what she knew of the homes and the inns, the churches and the museums.

On Lafayette she noted a plain yet pleasant two-story house with a gray shingled roof. "That's where I grew up," she said simply. "Most of my extended family lived near us. Many are still in town." She pointed out the Allen AME Church on Franklin Street, the church she and her family attended for "Oh, generations. I can't think of a time we were here that we weren't members of the congregation. We walked here every Sunday, every Wednesday night. We walked everywhere we went, in fact. My uncle had a car; we all shared it, but you couldn't fit eleven into that old thing. So only the oldest of the old folks rode to prayer meetings. How many kids in your family?"

"Just my older brother and me."

"Oh, that's right, you told me. Killed in Vietnam."

"It was hard. Nearly destroyed my mother, and it took a lot of wind out of my father, though he never gave up his work. I often thought I should have tried harder to talk him out of enlisting, but I didn't. Robbie was hardheaded."

"So sad he died."

"Yes. But my memories of Robbie are good ones. He was a wonderful asshole, always knew how to pull my chain."

At each art gallery and gift shop, Sam slowed to peer in the windows, wondering if he might spy a familiar painting, but he didn't recognize any of the work.

How're you doing, Dani? Are you still in town?

When Sam stopped in front of the fifth or sixth gallery and cupped his free hand to the window glass, Jeanette said, "Well, you going to tell me why you're hauling around a carpetbag, or are you just hoping I'd guess?"

Sam was ready for the question. He had planned on telling her he had thought about buying something arty for his room at the inn, and that it was a good, sturdy bag to carry something around in, but when he opened his mouth, he said only, "The boy I'm tutoring is a chronic sneak. I caught him in my room, going through my things. Until I get a genuine, no-can-pick lock for my door, I'll haul my few important things with me."

"Oh. That kid sounds like—"

"Everything you're probably thinking. And then some."

"And yet you stay on to teach him. You're a better man than I am, Gunga Din."

On Perry Street, they passed shops, small eateries, more Victorian homes, and assorted contemporary businesses and houses. Maples, sycamores, and oaks proudly displayed their brand-new buds, dipping with the breezes and shaking themselves off as if having just finished a pleasant seaside dip. Jeanette explained that Perry Street was one of the first two public roads laid out on the cape. Sam wondered how many feet had pounded the ground beneath it, going to and from, for so many years. How many slaveholders and slaves? How many runaways heading for freedom?

They reached Jeanette's apartment on Elmira. Sam had expected a modern apartment complex, but it was yet another Victorian house, less ornate than many, converted into several units. Jeanette's was on the first floor in the back, reached by a set of wobbly rear steps and a short, narrow hallway. Jeanette unlocked the door, and they stepped inside her room.

"I think this room was once a library, what with the bookshelves," she said, nodding toward one wall that was nothing but shelving, floor to ceiling. She drew open the curtains, letting in a wash of afternoon light. "Some doofus painted them baby blue; that's how they were when I moved in six years ago. I didn't ask the landlady if I could strip them and refinish them but I did, anyway. I mean, baby blue? Not to mention the flakes it left on the edges of my books."

The shelves were indeed filled with books, with not an inch of space vacant. There were novels by Edgar Rice Burroughs, Toni Morrison, Earnest Gaines, and a couple by the new horror phenomenon, Stephen King. An entire shelf was devoted to the works of W. E. B. DuBois and Booker T. Washington. On another sat several sets of encyclopedias, Betty Crocker cookbooks, books on Egyptian art and American airships, the music of Scott Joplin and John Phillip Sousa, poetry by Robert Penn Warren and Langston Hughes, and paperbacks on gardening and furniture repair.

Sam said, "Huh."

"I have varied interests."

Sam scanned at the rest of the room. There was a sofa, a floor lamp, a small television on a cloth-draped board atop cinder blocks, a magazine rack stuffed to the gills, a dresser and mirror, a square dinette table, and two matching red chairs. A short sideboard held a hotplate and cans of food. On the floor beside the sideboard was a dorm-sized refrigerator. The bathroom was a cubby between the sofa and the television stand, separated from the main room by a batik sheet. There was a closet with a coatrack tacked to the door. A clock shaped like a strawberry hummed on the wall.

"I don't entertain much," said Jeanette, without a trace of embarrassment. Sam liked that. "I've always been used to things being simple."

"Simple is good."

Jeanette opened the bottom drawer of her dresser and

pulled out a cardboard box tied with a string. Before she shoved the drawer closed again, Sam caught a glimpse of some of her intimate apparel—red, blue, black, pink, and striped bras and panties, with sheer pantyhose rolled in tight bundles. He pretended not to have seen, though he found it pleasant and curious that she was into bright colors for underwear.

"I'll show you what I found," said Jeanette, dropping down on the sofa, kicking off her loafers, and tucking her feet beneath her. Sam sat by her, putting the carpetbag on the floor by the magazine rack. "As I said, I was just going through these last night and found some that might round out the tour, or at least give you a look at the town prior to all the renovations. And then I found those of the Abbadon Inn. They're here. She took the top off the box and lifted a white envelope from the pile. She passed the envelope to Sam. "I sorted these out."

There were five photos. Sam laid them on the seat between himself and Jeanette. Jeanette folded her hands in her lap.

The first photo was the one of Jeanette as a little girl holding the kitten. An ink date on the back of the picture put it as September 6, 1953. There was a blur beside her, one of her sisters swinging her Sunday purse above her head. Jeanette's round face was buried in the kitten's gray fur, only her eyes rising above the little body, the crinkles at the corners indicating a smile.

"You were cute."

"Oh, thanks." There was no lilt to Jeanette's voice; she was watching Sam intently to see his reaction to the rest of the picture.

Behind the girls, across the street along which a very round Chevrolet was parked, and behind an iron fence that looked as if it was bowing toward the camera, was the Abbadon Inn. The entire façade of the building was not visible, just the first two floors of the left side, including the porte cochere and the oak trees. The photo was taken in bright morning daylight; Jeanette and her sister cast pointed shadows into the street, and the Chevy cast a round one up into the yard of the inn. But the inn itself sat in a dark shadow. There was no reflection of light on any of the windowpanes; no bright glints off the metal lattice trim work on the edge of the porch. It looked as though no sunlight could pierce through to the building.

"The place looks so cold," said Sam.

"Always did. And you know what struck me even as a child? The color of the place. It was always painted white as far as I know. But it never really looked white to me. It seemed bluish."

"To me, too."

"You know why that has bothered me since studying art in college?"

Sam shook his head.

"Blue is the color of the devil."

This was hardly what Sam expected. His heart kicked an irregular beat. "I thought the devil's color was red."

"There was a period of time when artists contended that because Satan was so far removed from the warmth of God's love, that he could only be cold and desolate. So they painted him in shades of blue."

"Curious." *Geary said the devil was on your tail.*
Enough of that, Sam.

The second photo showed Jeanette's sisters, twins he could see now, in sundresses and matching hats, tentatively reaching out for the velvety noses of two mules pulling the Victorian Village Transit Company's trolley. The driver, a smiling man in vest, bow tie, and cap, stood beside the girls, holding the reins of one mule.

"My dad let the driver think he was with a newspaper, or magazine, snapping a photo to use in some sort of article or review," said Jeanette. "He didn't actually tell the man that, but somehow that's how it all came about. This was the day my Aunt Karen got married. The wedding was over, and we were walking to the beach to have a look at the water. Dad loved the ocean, taking photos of it. Mom and I had walked ahead with a couple cousins. I was jealous later when I found out they got to pet the mules. I loved animals. Still do. I'd have a pet if the landlady wasn't such a hardnose."

In this picture, the inn was a bit closer. The photo

showed the front entrance, the edge of the wraparound porch on the right, and a slice of the second story and windows. The day was cloudy, so the inn didn't appear to be any darker than the rest of the scene, but at each window there appeared to be a figure peering out. Dark, featureless, but pressed to the windows beneath the partially drawn shades. Sam flipped the photo over. In fading ballpoint it was inscribed, "Saturday, June 7, 1958. Sally and Renee on the way home from Karen and Robert's wedding."

"1958," said Sam. "Who ran the Abbadon Inn then?" He guessed his question would be rhetorical, and Jeanette answered as he'd suspected, "I don't know."

"Do you have a magnifying glass?"

"No. How come?"

"Those people in the windows. They look more like dark cutouts than real people. It reminds me of something, something I've . . ." Sam touched one of the figures. Where had he seen this before?

His dream.

"Something you've what?"

Shit.

He'd seen these figures in the distant Abbadon Inn in his dream. He had come up over the hill, barefoot, wearing only ragged pants, and had found the chained, dead man held by a hooded gang. And beyond them, looming against the dark night like a tsunami, the sickly moon above it. The figures never moved, they held in place like frozen corpses, but he could hear their terrified, whispered cries.

There he is!

He's coming here!

GO AWAY!

"What on earth is wrong, Sam?" It was Jeanette. He only then realized she'd leaned over and was clutching his arm.

Nothing, nothing Jeanette, I'm fine, I'm just going a little crazy that's all.

"Sam?"

"I've seen this before, those people in the windows, posed just that way."

"When?"

This is going to sound so insane. "In a dream."

"Really. When?"

"A couple nights ago. It was really unsettling."

"Want to tell me about it?"

"There's not much to tell . . . me, in the woods, a dead slave with a chain around his neck. The inn in the distance with figures, those figures, looking out of the windows. A man came up beside me. He had a custard-white face and dark beard. He claimed to be Nicholas. I'm guessing Nicholas Abbadon. He told me to come on to the inn with him. But the figures in the windows were yelling 'stay away!'" Sam realized his voice had risen, and he'd nearly yelled the last two words. His hands had drawn into fists. He forced his voice to soften. "They were yelling 'stay away,'" he said again.

"Yelling for who to stay away?"

"Me? Nicholas? I don't know for sure. It was just a dream."

Sam picked up the other three photos. These showed the Fourth of July parade, dated Sunday, July 4, 1965. Daddy Harris had moved from black-and-white to color. A high school band marched in fairly straight lines up Columbia Avenue, heading northeast. The photo captured clarinets, trombones, and tubas, fluffy tall hats and sharp elbows.

"The summer between my junior and senior year," offered Jeanette. "I was clarinet, second chair." She pointed to herself on the far side of the line, just visible behind a portly tuba player. "My hair looked awful that day, I remember that. It was the only time I can think of that I was thankful for those god-awful band hats."

Each photo was pretty much the same; high school kids marching up the street, with the camera snapping from the same vantage point on the sidewalk, sweeping its angle along with the parade. Again, in each one, the Abbadon Inn was across the street behind its iron fencing, with only the first two floors visible. Only a few people were watching the parade from the inn's yard, and even they looked a little uncomfortable. Maybe it was only because the sun was in their eyes. The inn's siding hung off in spots, and several of the windows were broken. Porch balustrades looked like piano keys blown from an angry keyboard.

"That was probably the lowest point for the inn," said
Jeanette. "It was abandoned. Cape May hadn't yet burst
into its new flurry of restorations. Quite a few places built
in the last century were in disrepair. The Preservation Society had started their efforts to save the old buildings, but it
had a rough time with some of them, trying to block sales
and demolitions."

Sam studied the windows in the photos, searching for
even a faint outline of the figures he'd seen in the trolley
picture. These photos were not as crisp as the others,
slightly smudgy with the movement of the camera as it followed the band. The shadows beneath the tattered shades
could have been figures but could just as well have been
torn screens making human-shaped patterns.

"The inn became a hangout in the 'sixties," Jeanette continued. "A popular place for South Jersey hippies. Locks
and windows were broken so kids could easily get in."

Sam angled the third photo toward the window in an attempt to see more clearly. There was a man on the top step
of the entrance porch, back against the double doors, not
looking at the band but straight at the camera. Sam's bandaged hand, which had eased, began to throb anew.

"Some people died in the Abbadon during those years,"
Jeanette continued. "Mysterious deaths they called it in the
paper but then, the people who died were listed as bums,
nobody anybody would care much about or miss. Once my
parents realized how bad things were there, they stopped
walking by on the way to the shore after church. But by
then, I was already a freshman in college."

The man was hard to see, with the blurring and the
shadows and the distance. His clothing was a nondescript
white shirt and dark pants, with dark vertical slashes indicating suspenders. He wore a dark beard on his very pale
face. The man was turned straight toward Jeanette's father
as the shutter had clicked, and even though the eyes were
impossible to make out except for a hair-thin line beneath
the dark hair, Sam suddenly thought that if he could see
them they would be bright, silver chips.

"What, Sam?"

"Nothing."

"You've already shared your dream, and I didn't call the nut house. What's the matter?"

"That man on the porch looks like Nicholas Abbadon."

"He does?"

"Of course, I only saw him in my dream. I really don't know what Abbadon looked like in real life." *That's him, the man I dreamed about!*

Jeanette sat back on the sofa.

"He had that very white skin, that dark beard."

Sam looked at the first two pictures, taken only seconds before the last one. No man on the porch. No man on the porch. Then, a man on the porch. Could he have climbed up there so quickly from the viewing crowd? Did he come out of the inn in those few seconds and close the door to stand there and watch the parade?

Maybe.

But why wasn't he watching the parade, then? Why was he looking at the camera? Who was he?

"Sam?"

"What?"

"Do you believe in ghosts?"

"No."

"Really?"

"No."

"Do you believe in things you can't see?"

"Like what? God? The Devil? Angels? Demons?"

A shrug. "Anything."

"I was taught to believe in all that. My dad was a minister, remember?"

"But now?"

"This has nothing to do with ghosts. Ghosts are wishful thinking on the part of the living, or projections of fear on the part of the uncertain."

"A bit of undigested beef, a bit of cheese," Jeanette said in a low, throaty voice, and then made an apologetic face. "I was trying to do Scrooge. Bringing a little levity to the moment."

"Oh. Thanks." Sam tried to smile. It felt like he did but he wasn't sure how it looked. "But no, I don't believe in ghosts. Do you?"

"I can't say I do, and I won't say I don't. I've talked to people who claim to have encountered them, and they are as sure as the noses on their faces that they weren't imagining things. They tell me that ghosts don't haunt places constantly, but that the spirits remain in a state of sleep or unconsciousness until something disturbs them, something specific awakens them."

"I see."

"I can't discount something just because I've never encountered it." Jeanette put one arm on the back of the sofa. "Do you think your dream was trying to tell you something about the Abbadon Inn?"

I'm afraid it was. That, and the spinning bottle and the dead-smell and Rebecca and her horrible red eyes and . . . "I don't know." *And the bloody, rusty leg irons.*

"You aren't tied there. You can leave whenever you want. I would."

"I know. I'm just not ready to throw in the towel with Carl. He needs someone. He certainly doesn't have his parents."

"Even if you're having nightmares? Even if there are ghosts?"

"I can't accept the idea of ghosts. My mother was superstitious. So was my grandmother and some cousins. It was infuriating, the way they fretted about ladders, broken mirrors, spilling salt, and the devil always looking for a chance to climb inside your soul. I'm not going to carry on that family tradition."

"Okay."

"Okay."

"Do you want a beer?"

"That would be good." Sam just then realized how tired he was; his stomach was still fluttery from the night before, his muscles taut and tense.

They sat and sipped their beers without speaking. Sam kept the photos on the sofa, and Jeanette did not let her gaze come in contact with them, though every so often she would reach across them and gently touch his shoulder. His heart beat erratically, and his breathing was shallow as he looked at them again, over and over again. Then he stuffed

them back into the envelope and put the envelope back in
the box. He put his beer bottle on the coffee table with a
decided click. The clock on Jeanette's wall read 4:11.

"You ready to go?" Jeanette asked.

"I should. I need to get to a hardware store. Get those
padlocks before it closes."

"You want to take those pictures with you?"

"No, that's okay." Sam stood and picked up his carpetbag.

"We're done with the walking tour," said Jeanette.
"Why don't I drive you to the store and then home."

At first Sam said, "No, thanks." He wanted to be alone
with his thoughts and didn't want to put Jeanette out. He really liked her. He didn't want to overdo anything, certainly
not his welcome.

But it was going to be dark soon, he didn't feel all that
great and, well, fuck . . . it was going to be dark soon.

EIGHTEEN

Well, this is a miracle, thought Sam as he looked at the faces of all three Morrisons together in the same room at the same time. He had caught Rebecca fixing a cup of evening tea in the kitchen and Mitchell sitting on one of Rebecca's new chairs in the reception room, brooding over *The Life and Heroic Deeds of Admiral Dewey* from the collection brought down to the bookshelves from the second-floor suite. Carl was in the backyard, doing something he wouldn't talk about, and when he came into the kitchen to grab some cookies, smelling vaguely of smoke, he was not happy to find both his parents and his tutor standing there, waiting for him.

"What?" he snarled.

"I see you went with the Mohawk," said Sam.

Carl touched his hair defiantly. "I see you got your hand messed up. Slammed in the door, was it?"

How'd he know that?

"Come with us, Carl," said Mitchell.

Carl dumped the bag of cookies onto the counter. Three rolled off onto the floor. He snatched two from the countertop and jammed them into his mouth. "Where to?" he gurgled around the cookies.

Mitchell said no more, but led the way into the restaurant. He pulled out a chair for Rebecca, who sat with her tea and then Carl, who swallowed his cookie, drew his mouth up into an angry bunch, but then sat, jamming his elbows on the table loud enough to make a crack. Mitchell remained standing. He lit a cigar, shook out the match, and dropped it into a ceramic ashtray on one of the empty tables.

"All right," Mitchell said, in a tone of voice Sam could imagine him using with a client or a witness. "You've got the floor, Mr. Ford. Say what you need to say."

Sam looked at Carl and the bushy stripe down the center of his head. He looked at Rebecca, sipping her tea in her paisley jumper. He looked at Mitchell, cigar smoke rising above his head and an expression that said, *I may have pulled everyone together but by God, this better be important.*

Sam remembered parent-teacher conferences back at Jefferson. Anxious parents, sitting in desks waiting for Sam to tell them how good, bad, or average their children were in the classroom. Angry parents, refusing to sit, arms crossed, heads tossed back, refusing to believe Sam that their children had truly earned the C/D/F on their report cards. Beaming parents, hands folded, all smiles and wide eyes, knowing the glowing report to come word by word (as they'd heard it every conference, every year) but there just to bask.

And here were Carl Morrison's parents. They fit in none of the categories of conference-attending parents. People like the Morrisons never showed up at all. They were just happy to have their child gone seven hours of the day, and preferred to know nothing more about it. Ignorance was bliss.

Sam said, "We need to talk."

Carl squirmed in his chair and rolled his tongue in and out of his mouth. Rebecca wrapped her hands around her teacup. Mitchell squinted his eyes and drew on the cigar. A filmy coil of smoke rose to the ceiling and bounced along the rafters.

"I've been here a couple weeks now. I've found Carl to be an incredibly smart and intuitive student. He has a lot of ability and a great deal of potential."

Sam expected Mitchell and Rebecca to at least smile at this point, but their expressions didn't change. Carl picked cookie globs from his teeth with a little folding knife he'd taken out of his pocket.

"Carl and I have come to an understanding on some things. He's come to accept his lessons and has amazed me with his grasp of subjects he's not had much experience with, math especially. He completes his work without a great deal of complaining."

Mitchell picked a crumb of tobacco from his lip.

"Aren't you proud?"

Rebecca said, "Oh, yes, of course we're proud."

Mitchell said nothing.

Sam sighed audibly. "But it's other issues that are bothering me. Things you need to know about, Rebecca and Mitchell, things I can't tolerate if I'm to stay."

"Oh, you have to stay," said Rebecca, putting her cup down and casting an urgent glance at Mitchell. "Mitchell, he has to stay!"

"First things first. I spoke to you, Mitchell, about the problems with the temperatures in this place. I was ill last night, and I'm sure a lot of it had to do with the constant fluctuations from hot to cold. I'll be moving to the room next door tonight and hopefully, it will be better there."

"You can't do that," said Carl.

"But if it isn't better, then we've got a big problem."

"You didn't remind me to call the heating man," said Mitchell.

Shit, man, you can't remember something as simple as that? "Then I'm reminding you now."

Mitchell's chin twitched. Sam could tell that pissed him off, but at the moment it didn't matter. "And speaking of my room," he said. "I had to buy several padlocks this afternoon. Carl doesn't seem to understand the meaning of privacy."

"Do, too," the boy muttered. He'd put his knife away and was dragging one set of fingers through his top notch.

Sam looked directly at Mitchell, and Mitchell looked directly at Sam. There was a small chill of tension between the two men, a squaring off, a silent posturing for who was in charge in the household, who was in charge of Carl. "He was going through my things yesterday. My door was not locked, but I didn't really think that was necessary. And not only has he been in my room and through my things uninvited, he's shoved some items under my door just to harass me."

Carl stopped pulling at his hair. He looked genuinely confused. No matter, Sam had concluded that the only way the leg irons had come into his room was that Carl had shoved them under. They had skittered across the floor, dragging their chains and whatever blood Carl had doused them with—his own, some dead mouse's—and had ended up beneath the bed against the wall.

"At this moment in time, Carl can't be trusted. I hope that will change, that he will want to regain my confidence, but it will only happen if you two support me one hundred percent." Sam looked at Rebecca, and then at Mitchell. "I will not have my space violated. I won't work under those circumstances. It must change."

"You violate my space all the time," said Carl. "This is my home. You violate my time. I don't give a shit about learning anything from you!"

"Carl," said Rebecca. "We don't go through your things, and you shouldn't go through other people's. That's not right, and it's not nice. All right?"

Carl bugged his eyes.

"Okay, so that's done," said Rebecca. She stood up.

"No, it's not done," said Sam. "Where are my guarantees? I need something from you two, to know this won't happen again."

"Where in life are guarantees?" asked Mitchell. "Carl has heard you out, and we have heard you out. Carl will stay out of your things and your room. He may not be saying anything, but he's hearing me."

Sam looked at Carl, who had his knife back out and was cleaning wax from his ears. A good sudden tremor shaking the house, and he wouldn't be hearing his dad or much else out of that ear.

Sam almost said more, but there was nothing more to say. He'd made his demand, and the parents would either take it upon themselves to have something to do with Carl's behavior or they wouldn't. Sam left the restaurant and went upstairs. He would move to the room next door to his. He would install the padlocks and wait to see if they gave him the security he needed. Short of an ax or explosives, Carl wouldn't be able to get them off.

"I should just leave," he said to himself as he flung clothes from the dresser onto the bed. "Dani and Jeanette were both right. What the fuck am I doing here? Is this really something I have to prove to myself, to anybody else?" He straightened out a tangle of T-shirts and sweatshirts, folded them into lopsided bundles, and then went for more. "Maybe I should just find myself a job driving a mule trolley, or cleaning up behind the mule trolley. That doesn't require references. Do I need any of this shit, truly?"

"Hey."

Sam stopped in mid-toss, a pair of jeans in hand. Carl stood in the doorway.

"You said 'shit.' I heard you."

"Yeah, okay, Carl, you caught me cussing. You want to drag it out, really?"

Carl put his hands on his hips. He looked like a little red-haired skunk with that strip of hair. "You can't move to the other room."

"Why not?"

"I moved in there this afternoon."

"No, you didn't."

"Yeah-huh. Go see. My sleeping bag's in there."

"Why on earth did you move? Can't you get settled anywhere?"

"I dunno."

"Well, I claim that room." Oh, God, but did that sound juvenile. "I need it. This one isn't healthy. I'm sure your parents will back me up on it. Get your sleeping bag and go back down the hall."

"This whole place isn't healthy."

What an odd thing for Carl to say. Sam tossed the jeans on the bed and grabbed for a handful of socks from the drawer. "What do you mean?"

"Nothing."

"Carl . . ."

"I don't want to stay in that other room. I don't like it there."

"What don't you like about it?"

Carl sniffed, trying to regain his cool. "I just don't,

that's all. That's good enough reason for me. This is my house, so I get dibs."

"No, Carl. I'm the adult, so I get dibs." *Good Lord, Sam, listen to yourself.*

"Nuh-uh!"

"I . . ." began Sam, but a brief grimace flickered over the boy's face, an expression that revealed genuine worry. Had Carl moved into the room next to his tutor because Sam, and no one else, actually—cared—about him?

Sam said, "Carl, hear me out. I can't stay in this room. I think I like it about as much as you like the one you just left."

"How about the one on the other side of the one I'm in? That might be better because—" he was grabbing at straws, "—the room's bigger and its got wall-to-wall carpeting, even though it's crusted with dog pee or cat pee or something. Yeah?"

"Carl, I . . ."

"Okay, here's the deal." Carl held up his hands as if bidding in an auction, one he really wanted to win. "I'll move here, and you move in where I am now."

But can I let him in stay in here? Is it safe?

"Okay?"

Why wouldn't it be? You just got sick and dreamed things, imagined things. So if he's up to those temperature fluctuations . . .

. . . and creeping flowers and crawling leg irons.

There are no creeping flowers and crawling leg irons. There are no such things as . . .

Carl stomped his foot. "Sam!"

. . . ghosts.

"Yeah, okay, fine, Carl, we'll switch rooms. But promise me. If anything seems strange or if you don't like it in here, you get out. Knock on my door and wake me up. I won't care."

But then Carl tossed back his head and frowned. "What would wake me up and scare me, huh? I'm not some pissy-pants baby that's gonna come crying to you."

"I don't think that."

Then Carl was gone from the door, and Sam finished

packing his clothes for the trade. He was going to ask how Carl knew he'd slammed his hand in the door, but why pop another blister at this point in the game?

Sam lay awake on the bed, worn out, waiting for sleep. It was smaller, this room, though as of two A.M. the temperature remained steady and comfortable. There was a good, sturdy deadbolt lock on the door, inside, and Sam was more than happy to latch it before he crashed for the night.

It had taken him some wrangling to get the mattress, bed frame, dresser, and the large area rug he'd bought for himself out one door and in through the next. Mitchell surely heard him dragging and thumping but didn't come upstairs to help. Rebecca usually retired by ten-thirty in the evenings, so she offered no assistance. Carl, of course, was nowhere to be found, probably out in the backyard again, doing whatever he'd been doing before the oh-so-successful family meeting. Funny how a room spooked him but being out in the yard near or even in that shed amid the tangle of dark, thorny bushes at night didn't seem to be a problem.

Moving the items from one closet to the next came last. Sam had opened the closet door, quietly picked up the suitcase, and then the bundle holding the leg irons. They didn't move in his grip, they didn't scream or struggle or bleed. They remained hard and inanimate and just a little bit jingly, like leg irons were supposed to be. He didn't peel back the towel to look at them again—he knew what they looked like—and he debated putting them back into the closet and just letting them stay there.

Then he thought, *I can't leave them in here with Carl, even if I padlock the door.* But he immediately countered with, *I swear, Sam, you are starting to sound like your grandmother. Carl shoved them from beneath the door and they slid in, dragging the rust and blood with them. They did not get in here on their own.*

Yes, they did.

Shut up, Sam.

Sam took the irons downstairs to the bar, where

Mitchell was drinking and back into the story of Admiral Dewey.

"I found these," Sam said simply, unrolling the towel and letting the irons and chains clatter onto the table. "They seem to be genuine antiques. I don't know where they came from—the cellar maybe, or the shed out back? You might want to do something with them. Display them over the bar, perhaps, or hang them in the reception room. Whatever, they're yours. Just don't let Carl get hold of them again, if you will."

Mitchell blinked at the leg irons. Sam went back upstairs.

It took twenty minutes to get the lock installed on the outside of his new door. The doorframe had lots of holes in it already (had others felt the need to put on locks at some other points in time?) but Sam at last found a solid section of wood and secured the hasp and padlock. He wouldn't need it while he was in the room, but he would certainly lock that sucker up when he was out and about. The dead-bolt and the padlock on the closet door took another half hour. *Time well spent*, Sam told himself. At last, he felt as if he were able to exhale.

The shadows in this room were different. With only one window, there was no play upon the floor of streetlight glow from two sources, no crossing of patterns or layerings of grays and blacks. Sam lay on his side and looked at the wall and the dresser. He thought about Jeanette's dresser and her colorful panties and bras. He wondered what she would look like in the red set. He wondered what she'd feel like, pressed against him wearing only those. Nice, he knew. Jeanette was shorter and rounder than Dani, and her demeanor was less challenging, more thoughtful, more . . . patient. He liked her. He thought she liked him. Maybe he would call her tomorrow night, or go by the library with Carl Monday. Carl wasn't finished with his illustrated report yet, and Sam could do a bit more research on the town, the inn. He'd see what there was on the mysterious runaway passage to and then through Cape May, and try to find out if Nicholas Abbadon did indeed own slaves or life-time servants. Sam would then ask Jeanette to dinner, something a little nicer than lunch at the café. Maybe go to

the Merion Inn, which Jeanette had pointed out on their little walkabout.

Sam crooked his arm up over his head and closed his
eyes. His bad hand tingled but no longer ached in spite of
having used it so much. Tomorrow he'd take the bandage
off, maybe just slap Band-Aids over the cut for good
measure.

This room was better. No scratching noises. No smells.

His mind began to drift and spin the way it did in the
moments before sleep took him under. He thought of
Jeanette and how she sat on her sofa with her feet tucked
under her. He thought of Dani and how she looked across
the table at their New Year's dinner at his house, beautiful,
confident, talented, bold, sexy. He thought of Geary and
wondered if the house was being taken care of; of course it
was, Geary was a good guy; Sam could count on him. He
saw in his mind the photos laid out on the sofa seat, pictures
capturing a 1965 Fourth of July parade, the high school
students hunched over their respective instruments, puffing
and huffing into mouthpieces while staring ahead so as not
to run into the kids in front of them. He saw the porch of
the Abbadon Inn, dilapidated porch, shattered porch railing, loose siding. He saw the man on the porch, standing
back against the double doors, staring at the camera.

Staring at Sam . . .

The man winked both eyes at Sam. Sam put his hands
over his face because he did not want to see those silvery,
winking eyes.

And then someone said, "What the hell you doin', boy?
Holding still like some 'possum, thinkin' I can't see you if
you don't move?" There was a blazing sharp blow between
Sam's shoulders, and he cried out and opened his eyes.

He was in a large, rolling field. The sun was hot on his
head and on his naked shoulders. He wore only a pair of
ripped trousers. His bare toes clutched the rocky, tilled
soil. All across the field, likewise barebacked, bareheaded,
and barefoot black men, and black women in long skirts,
plain blouses, and colorful kerchiefs wielded picks and
shovels against the earth. Some were digging up rocks and
tossing them into cloth sacks on their backs. Others

cleared narrow pits with their shovels and dropped in seeds from bags across their shoulders. They moved almost in unison, as if they had done this work their whole lives and knew the best rhythm, the best speed, to get the jobs done.

Sam reached around to his back and felt a hot, sticky slash there. What the fuck? He spun on his bare feet and came face-to-face with a white man in a broad, dirty hat, and a grim mouth. In one hairy-knuckled hand he clutched a leather crop. "Don't give me that look, boy, I gotta give you the lash," he said. "You don't think I should go 'round playing fav'rites, now do ya? How would that look to the others, huh?" The man winked, then let go with several phlegmy coughs, spraying Sam with his filthy breath. "Now get back to work afore I have to smack you again."

"Who do you think I am?" Sam demanded.

"Why," blew the man through crooked teeth, "you ain't fuckin' President Buchanan, now are you? Look in the mirror lately, or the pond? See your tar-black self in there? Enough talkin'! Go!" He waved his crop and jerked his head in the direction of the field. Sam, not knowing what else to do, stumbled over the dirt toward the nearest man.

That man is a slave, Sam. Jesus, these are enslaved people. Where the hell am I?

The man was old, in his seventies perhaps, his hair white and his teeth mostly gone. He had one shriveled arm that hung by his side like a dried vine. But with his other he swung a pick up and over with the steadiness of a machine, driving the tip into the soil, popping out large chunks of sparkling quartz and dull clots of granite. Behind him stood a teenaged boy—

Robbie! It's Robbie.

—who snatched up the rocks and tossed them into his sack.

No, it's not Robbie. It just looks a little like him.

"Gotta get these rocks out," the man muttered to himself. "Up and out and down to tha' road. Gotta fill it in where the river washed it out las' week."

"Yes, Grandpa," said the boy.

"Gotta get these rocks out afore them seeders get over

here with them sacks. Can't have rocks in the way of the cotton. Can't have stones chokin' up the crops."

"No, Grandpa," said the boy. The boy gave Sam a sideways, disinterested glance, and went back to clawing up the rocks.

"What's your name?" Sam asked the boy, but the boy just shook his head.

"Don't play no games with me. Massa Josiah's on his horse behind you, over with Bernard, watchin' and just hopin' we do somethin' wrong."

Sam turned. The white man with the crop was at the edge of the field beneath a stand of maple trees, talking to another man, dressed in tailored coat, trousers, and well-polished black boots, sitting on a dapple gray mare. Both men stopped their talking and stared in Sam's direction. Sam said, "Let me help you with those rocks," and he stepped toward the boy but his foot twisted in the soil. He went down on his face.

He came up, coughing, and he was no longer in the field but in a small, damp, cabin. It was night. Beyond the walls and the open door he could hear the shrill chirping of tree frogs and cicadas, and the pop-crackle of a fire. Orange and yellow danced on the wall just inside the door. There was someone else in the cabin with him, sitting cross-legged next to him on a straw-filled pallet. It was a young girl, beautiful, with dark skin and huge eyes. She reached out for Sam's hand and held it tightly.

"I don't wanna listen," she whispered, her breathing heavy, her hand cold. "I don't wanna hear it! Sing to me so I don' gotta hear it!"

Sam began to say, *Listen to what?* when he heard what she meant. The shout of an enraged man—"You get there, ol' Roger, and let Bernard hitch you up. Got to show everyone what they can expect when a Negro goes a-wandering where he shouldn't be, sticking his big ol' nose where it ought'n be. Now, put your arms—put your damned arms out. Roger, you fight, and I'll shoot you through the head."

The girl's face squished up, and she let go of Sam's hand. She drove her palms over her ears. "No, no, no, no, no!" she cried.

Severe shadows cut through the firelight on the wall, rapid, fluttery movements, and then there was a sound of scuffling and grunting. A woman came to the door and held on to the sill. She glanced in at the young girl and at Sam. Her eyes were ablaze with horror and fury.

Sam stood up but the woman held her hand, urging him to stay where he was. The only window in the cabin was on the far side of the room, so Sam could not see what was transpiring outdoors. The girl grabbed his calf and said, "Don't go away!"

Outside, there was panting, wheezing. The woman in the doorway took a deep, noisy breath and tipped her head sideways, still watching out the door. Then, suddenly, there was the sound of something flying through the air; a second later, the sound of flesh being flayed apart. There was a gutteral groan, a growling hiss, and laughter.

"Sing to me, please!" begged the girl on the floor.

The air was split again with the shrill whistle, and then Sam could hear the whip cutting into the body of the victim. The man grunted and choked, a single agonized sound that made Sam's own flesh freeze.

"Sing to me, Roger," said a man outside.

Sam pulled free of the girl and went to the door. Out in the night beside the fire, a naked black man was tied to a cross beam that was planted in the ground, his buttocks cut open. Bernard, the white man who had spoken to him in the field, held a bullwhip in one hand and a stout quince branch in the other. There were eyes in the dark doorways of other cabins. Massa Josiah stood back a few yards, arms crossed over his fancy vest, holding a pistol and nodding slowly as the braided leather looped down and up like an elaborate question mark . . .

Why? Why is he being beaten?

. . . and then unfurled with a snap and crashed into Roger's shoulders, ripping out a chunk of flesh and bearing through nearly to the bone. The man's bare back arched, making a near perfect *C*.

"Why?" screamed the woman next to Sam.

"Sing to me," said Bernard. With a powerful thrust he

brought the thorny quince branch down into the bound man's shoulders, then yanked it back.

Roger fought the pole, twisting his head back and forth violently, his lips stretched open so far it seemed as if his entire skull would be revealed. The whip flicked up— *crack!*—and down and into his back. The branch followed quickly, slamming into the same gaping wound, the thorns catching the flesh and tearing out bits.

"Sing to me," said Bernard.

The black man snarled in pain but did not cry out.

"You're gonna sing to me, boy."

Crack!

The woman beside Sam put her head on his shoulder and screamed into him.

"Sing to me," said the man with the whip.

Crack!

"Heavenly Jesus, stop them!" The woman dropped to her knees, her hooked fingers trailing down Sam's thigh as if she were drowning and he was her only lifeline.

Crack!

Roger's back, buttocks, and shoulders were blistered open in gaping, red mouths. Blood as black as his skin poured down his legs and pooled around his feet. Each blow cut another deep valley. His body spasmed and heaved, but still he did not cry out. Bernard bore the branch down across Roger's hip and the branch broke. Bernard tossed the end away. "Don't matter, I can make you sing so pretty with just this." He flicked the whip against Roger's legs.

Crack!

"Sing to me."

Crack!

"Sing to me."

"Jesus God Holy Spirit, help my husband!" cried the woman on the floor.

Crack!

"Sing . . ."

Crack!

". . . to . . ."

Crack!

". . . me."

And then the bound man's head fell back as if his neck were broken, his knees collapsed, and he issued an unholy shriek that split God's black night and locked Sam's heart in midbeat. The woman on the ground clutched her head and wailed.

For good measure, the man flicked the lash out one more time, driving it home across the man's waist.

The whip fell to the dust and lay there like a dead snake. Bernard chuckled. The eyes at the other cabin doors were brighter now, rimmed with enraged tears. Bernard wound the whip back up into his hand, looked at Massa Josiah, and winked. "Pretty tune there, weren't it, sir, like a little black angel? Send that music clear up to heaven."

"Leave him there," said Massa Josiah. "Let him regain his strength. I have one more treat for him tonight, one more reminder to stay where he needs to stay." Massa Josiah turned on his heel, disappearing into the darkness.

Sam pulled back into the cabin, his breath coming in loud, painful gasps. His heart raced. Sweat coursed down his face and chest. Tears boiled at the backs of his eyes. "Jesus God fucking shit, this is wrong, wrong, wrong!"

Outside, he could hear the other slaves offering up prayers and encouragement to their mangled brother. Roger was weeping in great whoops, unable to hold it back any longer.

The little girl crawled over from the pallet and tugged on Sam's pant leg. Her face turned up to his, her eyes pinched, her mouth twitching in anguish. "I don' wanna hear it, sing to me!"

Sam knelt beside the girl and held her. He wanted to sing but the only tune that he could remember was something from another life outside this place of hell.

He began in a tremulous, fear-shredded voice, " 'Counting flowers on the wall, that don't bother me at all . . .' "

There was pounding then, somewhere outside the cabin, somewhere beyond this place, a pounding like gigantic drums. A tidal wave of sound it was, rushing from far away toward the slave quarters like elephants crashing through the trees.

" '. . . smoking cigarettes and watching . . .' "

The pounding grew louder, thundering down, closing in.

Boom Boom Boom!

Oh, God, what is that sound?

" '. . . Captain Kangaroo . . .' "

The little girl lifted her face to Sam. It was no longer the slave child but his little cousin Rose, dead a week, her face bloated, her eyes milky white.

"No!"

The pounding engulfed the cabin and shook it like a furious parent shaking a child. Sam lost his balance and fell on his back.

Boom Boom Boom!

The girl leaned over him. Her eyes were gone now; in their place were hollowed out black holes.

"Sing to me!"

Help me!

The pounding kicked the cabin like a giant's foot. The cabin fell apart around him, blew apart, the beams flying upward into the sky, the dirt floor bucking and splitting.

BOOM BOOM BOOM

Jesus God Holy Spirit, help me!

His sticky lids popped open.

He was in his room. His new room, the small one with the good heat and the deadbolt lock and the single window.

The room was bright with daylight. Beneath him, the sheet was damp, and he hoped it was only sweat.

Sam pushed his hand against his ribs and his thundering heart, and stared at the window. His throat was dry and raw.

Fucking, fucked-up dream!

There was pounding somewhere outside his room. He tried to focus, to understand what the sounds were. And then he remembered. It was Sunday morning. Rebecca had hired a couple carpenters to come in, at time and a half, to reconstruct and erect the bar down in the Letters Lounge. They were doing it off the books, she'd mentioned in passing a few days back, and she was taking care of it the way Mitchell took care of Sam's salary.

Sam sat up and scratched his knees. It was 9:10. He'd overslept again. The damp beneath him was sweat and not urine, one small consolation. He wiped the crust from his eyes. The dream still clung to him like a nasty film, one he wanted to wash away in a good, hot shower.

He'd had bad dreams before, nightmares, but never recurring. Why did he dream about slaves again? Was it the memory of those damned leg irons Carl had slid under his door—*You know the irons could not have slid all the way to the wall, quit ignoring that fact, Sam*—the night before? Was he experiencing a profound empathy for the faceless many who had been enslaved in Cape May prior to the Civil War, or for those who had come through the town in an escape from the ravages of field and whip?

Or were the dreams fueled by spirits from the past? Spirits that, according to Jeanette, had been disturbed out of their slumber by something. Someone.

"There are no spirits," he said.

And if there were spirits, why were they trying to get his attention?

"There are no spirits!"

Sam stood and stretched, his neck popping. He felt like such an old man. He needed to take more walks, like yesterday. Good, brisk strolls to open his lungs and his mind. He was feeling so out of shape. Back in Virginia it was part of his daily regimen to walk or jog or spend a half hour with his barbells. He needed to clear out the physical and mental junk that had accumulated while being between these many walls.

I suppose Carl made it through the night okay. Sam dragged the bedspread off the bed and let it fall on the floor. He needed to change his sheets, and hell, do a whole load of laundry while he was at it. The washer and dryer were in the cellar, an unpleasant stone-walled dungeon that smelled of seawater and old biscuits. He *could* haul his plastic basket three blocks to the Wash 'n' Go, but he never thought about washing clothes or linens until the last minute. It had been the same way back in Virginia; it was when he had somewhere to go in an hour that he realized he had nothing clean to wear. It was when he'd stripped the bedding from his mattress that he saw he had no clean sheets to take their place.

He yanked the top sheet off, balled it up, and threw it on the floor. He reached for a fitted one. As he tugged, he heard a soft clinking sound.

No.

He looked at the door. The deadbolt was still turned. He looked at the space beneath the door. This one was much more narrow than the one beneath the door in the other bedroom. Nothing could have been slid beneath this door, save a piece of paper or two.

He tugged the sheet again.

Clink.

He dropped the edge of the sheet and rubbed his arms. The sound came from beneath the pillow.

It's just some change that slid up under there from my jeans pocket when I remade the bed last night.

A bit of undigested beef, a bit of cheese, Jeanette had said.

Something hard and cold turned in his gut.

Only that, and nothing more.

He picked up the pillow. There, in a tidy coil, were the rusted, bloody leg irons.

NINETEEN

He couldn't get Margie Rothman on the phone in the reception room, and no one answered so he could leave a message for her. He slammed down the receiver. Jeanette was not home, either. He let her phone ring twenty times before he accepted the fact that he could not talk to her.

And so he cornered Mitchell Morrison. The man was supervising the reconstruction of the bar in the Letters Lounge, his hands on his hips, his gaze following every move of the flustered carpenters. Wrapped in a bedspread on the floor, Carl was watching cartoons on the bar's new color television that was bolted to the wall near the ceiling. Misshapen characters danced across the screen to irritating, high-pitched music.

"Mitchell, I need you to tell me everything you know about the Abbadon Inn's history," said Sam. "I mean everything."

Mitchell turned and, clearly still feeling challenged from the family meeting last night, shook his head. "I'm sure you can see I've got my hands full. If you're around when this is done, maybe we can talk."

"Now. I need some answers. If I'm going to stay here and tutor your son, I need to know what the hell kind of place this is. If I can't find out to my satisfaction, I'm out of here. And you might want to consider the same." *You sound like a maniac, Sam, but what the hell, at this point.*

Mitchell held up his hands. "Whoa, whoa, whoa. Don't throw threats at me."

"It isn't a threat, it's a fact."

"That we need to leave our home? This beautiful inn we

have spent so much time and money on? It sounds like a threat to me."

"It's an observation. I'm not sure this place is . . . safe."

Mitchell's cheeks pulsed. "Don't bullshit me."

Carl's attention had moved from the cartoons, and his eyes were trained on his tutor.

"Tell me what you know about the Abbadon Inn."

"Crazy," muttered Mitchell, shaking his head in the direction of Carl and the workers, who were staring silently and wide-eyed. He blew out a breath and said, "I don't know what you want to know about this place, but like I told you earlier, this whole thing was Rebecca's idea. She liked it, we bought it. Simple as that. I know virtually nothing about the Abbadon."

Sam said, "Where's Rebecca?"

"What's the exigency?"

"Where's Rebecca?"

"Jesus, I don't know. Wait—outside in the backyard. She decided to plant some kind of flowers out there. Flowers, and we don't even have a finished restaurant!" He turned back to the men. "I don't think you have that flush, there, measure that again," he said to one, and Sam could hear the man's silent groan. It sounded as if Carl snickered.

Sam went outside through the kitchen. Rebecca was next to the bulkhead to the cellar in a red-and-black cloak, jeans, green gardening gloves, and knee-high rubber boots. Her hair was in two stubby braids, making her look like a pink-nosed child. She glanced back at Sam and smiled. "I'm putting in anemones, glads, and lilies," she said. "What a nice day for this, all this sun? I'm going to go around the inn, starting here at the back, weave these in among the bushes I had planted a couple weeks ago. Well, I'm not planting the exact same flowers all the way around, but something so there is 'uninterrupted space.' That's what the garden-center lady told me. 'The best plots have uninterrupted spaces filled with all sizes, shapes, and colors of blooms.' I wonder if anyone else ever cared enough to landscape this place? I would think so, maybe fifty years ago, but . . ."

"I need to talk to you, Rebecca. It's urgent."

"Oh?" She looked at the bulb in her hands. "Is Carl all right?"

"It's not about Carl." He glanced up at the windows above him, feeling for a moment that he would see the dark figures pressed there, staring down at him. He glanced over at the shrub-enshrouded shed. A small crawl hole had been cut through the brush to the door—Carl's newest hideaway, certainly—but he saw nothing moving there. Yet the feeling of being watched didn't leave.

"How can I help you, Sam?"

"Tell me what you know about the Abbadon Inn. From its beginning. Back in the 1800s. Surely you didn't buy this place without the sellers giving you some idea of its history?"

"I . . . I know Nicholas Abbadon moved to Cape May and built the place. I know he had a woman, a wife, named Lillith. I told you that before."

"You did. What else?"

Rebecca took off her gloves. "Ah, it survived the great Cape May fire in, um, 1878, I think they said it was. Why do you look like that?"

"Like what?"

"So angry?"

Because I fucking am angry! Fear is an angry emotion! "Tell me what you know about Nicholas Abbadon."

"He built this place in 1856 . . ."

"I want to know if he owned slaves."

"Slaves?"

"You know, black people who worked and died for no pay? Remember them from your social studies lessons back in school?" Damn, but he did sound angry. But something was fucking with him. He did not like being fucked with.

Rebecca put her bulb down and ran a glove under her nose. She looked a bit angry herself, now. That was okay. She said, "Why don't you come with me?" Then she stood, pulled off her gloves, and went around the side of the house to the door beneath the porte cochere. Sam walked with her.

The porte cochere doors opened on the inn's office. It

contained metal filing boxes, a metal desk, an electric typewriter, and a disconnected telephone. Yet, of course, new, crisp, rainbow-colored curtains hung on each of the two back windows.

Rebecca went into the reception room and took the antique register from under the counter. She placed it carefully on the top and put her hand on the cover, as if afraid it might pop open on its own and start screaming.

I wouldn't be surprised at anything anymore, Sam thought.

"I really don't know much about this place," said Rebecca. "I admit I haven't researched like someone else might have, someone more into that kind of thing, but I do know what is in this book, and why it is in this book. I didn't want to let you look the day you signed in. I felt it might upset you. I thought you might be offended."

Sam slid the register away from Rebecca.

"At the marker," Rebecca said simply.

Sam flipped the book open to the yellowed strip of cloth near the back. There, filling the last few pages was a whole other list of signatures. These were not beautifully scripted as the ones in the front had been, but scratched out in a hard, labored hand. They were all single names—first names. Each was followed by a date and then an uneven "X." But although each name was different—"Willie, April 1857," "Hanna Mae, April 1857," "Rosa," "Callie," and "Zeus," all signed in June 1857—they seemed to have been penned by the same person. Ink blots and grime covered the paper, as if the one wielding the pen had just come in from the field.

"You thought I would be offended?" Sam asked, and Rebecca drew her arms up around herself protectively. "Do you mean you thought I would be ashamed?"

"Call it what you will. Those are slave names."

He had known it before she had said it. They were slaves' names. Single names with no surname. English names given to African people.

"Why should I be ashamed?"

"Well," said Rebecca, her face drawing up at bit, her pigtails bounding. "Not ashamed, I guess. I just didn't want to embarrass you."

"I'm not ashamed, and I'm not embarrassed. My family suffered through slavery, as did thousands and thousands of other families. It's a lash under which they suffered and under which they bore up."

"I'm sorry. I though I was being nice."

Sam shook his head, knowing in some strange way she did think she was being considerate but that she had no idea how loaded the subject was, how painful, how heated even after more than a century's time. "Nicholas Abbadon owned blacks," he said, more to himself than Rebecca. "It *is* what I thought. And with some sense of faux magnanimity, he put their names into his registry and had them validate the names with an X. In the back, of course."

Are there ghosts, then? Ghosts of black men and women who suffered under Nicholas Abbadon's roof? Are they trying to get my attention so I can help them in some way? Did I awaken them, and they recognize a sympathetic soul?

"No, it isn't what you thought." Mitchell was at the door to the reception room. He'd obviously heard the discussion across the hall and was allowing the carpenters a moment of autonomous activity. Carl stood beside him, hands in his pockets.

"Nicholas Abbadon didn't own slaves," said Mitchell. "Slavery was not allowed in New Jersey in 1856."

"I know that. But there were blacks in this state who were considered 'lifetime apprentices,'" said Sam. "It's the same thing, just legal semantics."

"Abbadon didn't own lifetime apprentices, either," said Mitchell.

Sam stared at the man. "You told me point-blank that you knew nothing about the inn's history."

Mitchell crossed his arms. "Maybe not the inn, but I've heard a little about Nicholas Abbadon. He was a known abolitionist."

"What? Abbadon? No . . ."

"He never owned human beings. Quite the contrary. This inn was a safe house."

"I don't think so." *Is that true, or is this just Mitchell Morrison bullshit?*

Mitchell pulled a glass cigar tube from his shirt pocket

and pulled off the cap. "When we bought this place the Preservation Society was all over us, all chatty and happy that one of their historic babies was going to live and breathe again." Mitchell pulled out the cigar and stuck it between his teeth. "One of the women told us that even though very little is known about Nicholas Abbadon, he was, in fact, a dedicated abolitionist. He secretly opened the inn to those who came at night, to those who had been guided here, running for and from their lives. He gave them a spot in his guest register." Mitchell struck a match on the door frame and lit the cigar. He took a satisfied draw, his head tilted back slightly.

Sam looked at the registry again, and touched some of the names and the Xs that followed them. They grew instantly warm, and then hot, at his touch. He lifted his fingers. Was that his imagination, his rage?

"Nicholas Abbadon must have asked their names and written for them," Sam said. "Southern blacks were forbidden to read and write. After Nicholas put their names in the book, each slave then added his or her own X to make it real. To make it official."

"Looks like," said Mitchell.

"Abbadon might have been anti-slavery, but it speaks to the man's character that he would not let the runaways sign in the front of his book like the other guests."

"You can think less of him for that," said Mitchell. "But what if some of the guests who came to this inn were pro-slavery? What if they had seen that list of runaways' names and figured out what was going on? They might have done something about it; they might have reported the names of the runaways to slave catchers in the South. There might not have been telephones and televisions, but word could spread quickly even then. Seems to me fugitives were safer with their names in the back."

Of course. Mitchell was right on that. Abbadon was indeed being careful to protect the identities of the former slaves.

Sam took a breath and looked at the names again. He was amazed that so many passed through the Abbadon's doors on their way to new lives.

"Silas, Levi, April 1857."

"Tillie and Mingo, July 1857."

"Livey, Matilda, Roger, September 1857."

"Jane and Stonie, March 1858."

Wait a minute. Roger? Is this the man I saw savagely beaten in my dream?

Sam touched the name, the X beside it. It blazed, and he jerked his finger away. He wanted to ask Rebecca and Mitchell to touch it, to see if they felt it, too, but he knew they wouldn't.

Then he looked at the signature that was directly below Roger's. He gasped. It was clear the Morrisons had looked at the slave names in the registry but had not studied them closely. If they had, they would have seen what Sam was now seeing.

This has to be wrong. I have to be seeing something that isn't there.

The name was "Sam Ford." Dated, "September 1857."

He scanned down the list, coming upon the signature of "Sam Ford" several more times throughout 1858, 1859, 1860, and 1861.

"What's the matter?" asked Carl.

Who was he? Oh my God, was this one of my relatives? Did my ancestor come through here on his way to freedom? Why does his name appear so often?

"Nothing," said Sam. He closed the register and wiped his forehead. He couldn't answer the boy; he couldn't tell the Morrisons that his name was there amid the others. They'd find it easily enough on their own if they looked, though it was a secret he wished he could keep. "The names just carry a lot of emotion, that's all."

"Hmm," said Mitchell.

"I said I didn't want to upset you," said Rebecca defensively.

But not only is it my name, Sam thought as he placed his hand on the thick leather cover of the book. *The signature isn't Abbadon's. In fact, it's very much like my own handwriting.*

It was at that moment that he realized that in some bizarre and disturbing way, he was linked to the Abbadon

Inn. And even if he'd had moments thinking he should leave, that it wasn't worth his while, that his sense of responsibility to Carl or to his word or to whatever drove him through life wasn't enough to make him stay, those reasons now melted in face of a dreadful and unreal reality.

He had a connection to the Abbadon Inn.

Sam Ford, who are you?

This was why his hand had burned the moment he signed his name in the register. His signature had been recognized. And now, for some reason, the inn or something inside it was trying to make itself known to him.

TWENTY

Margie Rothman of the Cape May Preservation Society was an accommodating woman in her late fifties with graying brown hair and lopsided reading glasses. She didn't seem upset that Sam had come to her home without an appointment, and welcomed him into her living room after he explained who he was and the area of his interest.

Sam had never been one to drop by someone's home unannounced, well, except for Geary's. It wasn't polite; it wasn't done. It was part of his home training as a PK; respect one's home as you respect one's person. But he had not been able to get Margie on the phone, and so had taken a cab and, surprisingly, found her home with the radio on and her Pomeranian running free in the front yard.

"Mrs. Rothman?" he asked when her face appeared behind the screen door. The dog sniffed his shoe. "My name is Sam Ford. Jeanette Harris at the library gave me your name as a member of the Preservation Society. I tried to get you on the phone but wasn't able, and I need to talk to you if you have any free time."

"Well, Mr. Ford, I was doing some spring cleaning, but you said Jeanette gave you my name?"

"Yes, she said you might be able to help me with some historic research I'm doing on Cape May."

"On a Sunday afternoon?"

"Yes, I'm afraid so."

"All right, then," said Margie. "Do come in. I always love to talk to a fellow history-lover. If I can help in any way, I'm happy to do it."

Her living room was small, with a matching plaid sofa and love seat and a small fireplace with a few freshly stacked logs inside. Her walls were covered with framed family photos. She sat on the love seat. Sam sat on the sofa.

"You sound in need of information right away," said Margie, holding her knees. "Are you working on a thesis?"

"No." *I wish it was that simple.* "I'm living at the Abbadon Inn as a tutor. I am researching its background for my own interest and for the education of the family with whom I'm living."

"I see," said Margie. "And this . . . is urgent?"

"It's hard to explain,"—*no shit*—"but if you'll just indulge me? I appreciate it more than you can know."

Margie brought out box after box of her own private collection of Cape May history. She said a bit sheepishly, "I've given quite a bit of materials to the Society. I am all for them having as complete a collection as possible. But, well, I shouldn't say this, but the current president of the Society, whose name I won't say but whose initials are Turner Little, is not as careful a leader as we thought he'd be when we elected him last December. The Society has a building, not quite a museum, but our plans are that it become one, and Turner has up and lost several important boxes filled with donated items. It was then that I decided there were some things I could offer to the public and take a chance, and other things I needed to hold on to myself. Turner's term is up in just a few months, and I'm running for office. Maybe then I'll feel comfortable enough to turn these items over to the care of others."

"I understand that completely," said Sam.

And Margie's collection was impressive, comprised of not only old souvenir glassware and trinkets from the turn-of-the-century resort town, but a hefty selection of old registers, magazines, newspapers, and diaries, all tidily collected and cataloged in thick notebooks. These works were spread out on the floor, and Sam climbed down with them. Margie sat on the edge of the love seat and picked up the notebooks one at a time.

"I don't have a specific subset of things that deal with the Abbadon," said Margie. "I don't know if anyone in the society does. There are so many historic places in our town, sometimes, I think, too many!" She winked. "I'm kidding. But I've learned bits and pieces here and there. I know that the Abbadon Inn was not one of the more expensive hotels. It suited folks who couldn't or didn't want to pay the higher prices."

"I see."

"Yet the inn did cater to specific tastes."

"What kinds of tastes?"

"Oh, you know. Ladies. They entertained by the hour or by the night. The Abbadon had its own bar and gentlemen's club, which featured gambling and what my mother used to call 'undercover sports.'"

A gentleman's club, certainly. Women with expensive bodies and cheap perfumes. I smelled perfume and sex in the Abbadon Inn.

"But that wasn't unusual at the time," Sam said. "Brothels were everywhere, from the Civil War battlefields to the streets of the nation's capital."

Margie nodded. "No more unusual than today, and it was disguised in much the same way places today disguise their more intimate offerings. I can't imagine there is a Fortune Five Hundred company that doesn't, somewhere, in some secret hideaway, have all sorts of perks for those who want them. People don't really change over time. And yes, there were other gentlemen's clubs in town, but they were more upscale and, for lack of a better word, more refined and proper for the time. The Abbadon Inn, however, was situated away from the oceanfront and on what was at the time an often passed-by side street, was not expensive, and did not cater to the most posh of customers. It seems it appealed only to certain people of specific tastes. Some of the clientele came summer after summer. Others went once and never stepped foot in there again."

"Why not?"

"No one knows for certain, though there is speculation by our own historians that the Abbadon offered sexual favors that were a bit out of the norm."

Margie didn't elaborate. Sam was left with only his imagination. Gay trysts? More than one woman to a customer at a time? Bondage?

Sam flipped through a notebook containing an 1866 periodical entitled *Cape May Inns and Hotels*. Partway through he found mention of the Abbadon, but it was brief, stating merely that the building remained under the management of Nicholas Abbadon and that "as it had throughout the dreadful war, the inn continues to offer services and comforts to patrons." The periodical was filled with notices, articles, and advertisements, though it seemed Nicholas Abbadon was not one to advertise but rather to let others write about his place as they would.

"Nicholas Abbadon didn't promote his inn like so many public places," Sam noted, leaning back against the sofa.

"From all accounts," said Margie, "he was very private, to the point of aloofness. I've read reports that he was a businessman first and foremost. I took that to mean he did not care to waste his time on making friends in town, that his clients were more important than his standing in the community. Yet he was successful, it seems, as he ran his inn into the 1930s. He left Cape May at that time. I heard he and his longtime companion Lillith went abroad, to somewhere in Europe."

"Into the thirties? Amazing. He must have been at least one hundred by then."

"I suppose so."

"Was he a hated man?"

"Not that I know of. I think he was more of a mysterious man."

Sam and Margie perused the notebooks for a long and silent forty minutes. Then Sam came upon a personal notice from a May 1862 tourism booklet.

He read aloud, " 'Nicholas Abbadon is traveling abroad again on business, and is not expected to return until autumn. His inn, however, still welcomes roomers and other guests.' That was during the Civil War. I wonder what business he had elsewhere during such a difficult time?"

"The man traveled quite a bit, before, during, and after the war. But other people got around, too. The country didn't freeze in place during the Civil War. Even though the number of vacationers went down, there were still

Northerners and a few wealthy Southerners who were determined to continue as they had, spending time in Cape May at their favorite hotels."

Thirty minutes later, Sam came upon another article in an 1872 edition of the *Cape May Star and Wave*:

> Nicholas Abbadon has declined recognition by the former members of the Southern New Jersey Abolition Society for his work in the movement before and during the dreadful war. As financer of the small but powerful abolitionist newspaper *Freedom's Voice*, Abbadon made his views and the views of all justice-minded people heard. Abbadon, who did not care to be interviewed or rewarded at the anniversary gathering of the Abolition Society this year, sent a short note to the group. It read, "It was always my hope that the dastardly practice of one man owning another be ended. The goal has been accomplished."

Sam put the notebook down. "Do you have any copies of *Freedom's Voice*?"

Margie shook her head. "No, unfortunately. The Society had a few, but they were among the items Turner lost. Don't get me started on that man."

Sam rubbed his eyes. *So it's true. Mitchell Morrison was not lying to me. Nicholas Abbadon assisted runaway slaves. He did not own blacks himself. He was a good man, then.*

The front door opened and two little blonde girls tumbled in, dressed in matching jeans, red jackets, and sneakers. A man of Margie's age came in behind them and closed the door. The girls smiled shyly at Sam on the floor. Margie hopped up and gave the girls a hug and the man a peck on the cheek.

"This is Sam Ford," she said. "A fellow historian new to our town. Sam, this is my husband, Duane, and my granddaughters Erin and Elizabeth."

"Nice to meet you," said Sam, standing and extending his hand to Duane.

"Same to you," said Duane. The girls ran off down the

hallway, one calling, "Come on, Granddad! You said you'd order pizza as soon as we got here!"

Sam thanked Margie for her time, phoned for a cab in the front hall, and stood out on the walk to await its arrival. It was nearly dark, with the moon appearing like a vague yet harmless specter in the cloudy night sky. Sam didn't want to go back to the inn. He didn't know what he would find beneath his pillow or under his bed, running in the yard or spinning on a tabletop. The whole thing made his blood slow in his veins and the hairs on his arms bristle.

But there is something trying to contact me. I have to be there. Jeanette said that ghosts stay put, stay still, until something jostles them into awareness. That something was me. I know it now. As much as it scares the shit out of me, I know it.

Margie's dog trotted over to Sam and barked at him through the chain-link fence. Behind Sam, Margie opened the door and called for the dog. It trotted off.

I do believe in spooks, I do I do I do I do I do believe in spooks.

"Here's your son, Dad," he said to the moon. "The cowardly lion, going after Dorothy and battling the wicked witch."

At last the cab arrived, and Sam rode in silence to the great inn. When he got out and looked at it from the walk, looming against the navy sky, the moon impaled atop the cupola's copper weathervane, he sensed it shift like a huge and lumbering creature, moving ever so slightly to watch him with its many window-eyes. He knew it was waiting for him. He knew it had something to say.

And he wondered if was strong enough to handle the message he was going to receive.

TWENTY-ONE

There was a knock on Sam's bedroom door. Sam put down the notebook in which he was writing and looked at the clock. 11:52 P.M. "Who is it?" he called.

A pause. Then, "Carl."

I knew that. "What do you want?"

"Can I come in?"

"You should be asleep."

"I'm not."

"Are you sick?"

"Are you hiding something in there?"

"Wouldn't matter if I was, Carl, it's my room."

"I know. Let me in." Another pause, and then the rare, "Please?"

Sam glanced around for whatever he didn't want the boy to see. No dirty underwear on the floor or bed. The carpetbag was in the closet. The leg irons in the cellar. *We'll see how much good that will do.* Candles burned on the nightstand, in the window, and on the seat of the straight-backed chair, lopsided tapers Sam had scavenged from the pantry in the kitchen and stuck into jar lids he'd made sticky with melted wax. Glowing candles felt right; they felt comforting. They felt almost . . . holy, protective.

"Okay?" pressed Carl.

Sam slid his notebook beneath his pillow and unlatched the door. Carl stood in the dim light of the few working sconces, dressed in a T-shirt and pair of sweatpants. His remaining hair was spiked in all directions. His arms were crossed, and his chin tipped back.

"Talk to me, Carl," said Sam. "Don't just stand there."

"In your room. Or don't you trust me in there?"

"Come on." Sam stepped back.

Carl sat on the foot of the bed. He looked at the candles. "Somebody die?"

Still standing, Sam asked, "What did you want, Carl?"

"Nothing. I just wanted to see if you'd let me in."

"Is that right? Well, I did. Happy to have passed the test of friendship. Now go back to bed. Tomorrow you have to finish your illustrated report, and you have a science fair project to begin."

"Science fair!" spit Carl. "You can't have a science fair with just one kid."

"Sure you can. And as I already told you, if you do a good job I'm going to submit it to the county science fair. See how you rate with the kids in the public schools."

"Whatever you say, boss." The boy's toes wriggled back like worms on a fishhook.

"Now go," said Sam. "I've got work to do."

"What kind of work?"

Sam opened the door and held out his arm.

Carl didn't get up but the toes wriggled faster. "Not yet."

"Why?"

"I just can't sleep. Okay? Big deal. I'd watch TV if there was something good on, but Sunday night? And we get just three channels. You want to go down and see what's on?"

Then Sam saw the truth. *The kid's scared, that's it. Something has him spooked. He doesn't want to be alone.*

"Well, you want to?"

"No, thanks," said Sam.

"Hmmm." Carl glanced around, looking for another stall. *He's really nervous. Has he been seeing and hearing things, too?*

"So what are you doing with those?" asked Carl as he nodded toward the candle in the window, "Having a séance?"

Sam opened his mouth then shut it. Actually, that was very close to what Sam had been doing. Or thinking of doing. "Uh, no."

"I know all about séances." Carl crossed his legs on the bed and clutched his knees. The wiggling toes were tucked out of sight.

Sam moved the candle from the chair and placed it on

the floor. He sat down and leaned forward. "Not that I was séancing, because why would I believe in that kind of thing? But I am curious. What do you think you know about them?"

"What I *know*, I know, not think I know," said Carl. "First of all, you got to have somebody who is psychic, somebody who is connected to stuff on the other side, somebody who has the power to link from regular stuff to supernatural stuff."

"I see."

"Then, you got to make sure you don't have any disbelievers in the group, because disbelievers can mess it up."

"Mess it up how?"

"Like making it go wrong. Though someone with enough power can make it happen, anyway, screw the disbelievers."

"Really?"

"Yep. And there doesn't have to be a group. One person can have a séance if they believe in it enough. It's good to have the lights low to keep from getting distracted. Sometimes people put flowers out but that's pussy. Candles are used to attract good spirits or to keep back bad ones."

"Why do you want to talk about séances, Carl?"

Carl frowned. "You asked me about them."

"And you brought it up."

"Look at all these candles? What am I supposed to think?"

How to put this. "Do you think I should have a séance? Do you think there is something in the inn that we should know about, something that should be contacted?"

"Ha!" said Carl, but his eyes flickered ever so slightly in alarm, or fear. "What are you talking about?"

Sam shrugged. "Supernatural stuff."

"Well," Carl's voice slowed down as if he didn't want to say what he was about to say, "there's some things that have happened."

You, too, Carl? Sam's heart picked up a faster pace. "Like what?"

Tell me, what are you afraid of? Why are you insisting on being in here instead of your own room? Are there pounding sounds? Whirling objects? Creeping wallpaper? Carl, are you seeing and hearing things, too?

"Stuff, okay? In that room over the porte cochere. And then in the room you used to be in."

"What kind of stuff?"

Carl looked away from Sam, toward the candle on the nightstand. He stared at the flame. "Noises. A smell like dead people, stinky and sweet at the same time. And the room started shaking one time, kinda like an earthquake." Then he looked back at Sam, his expression cool and unreadable.

There was a long silence between the two. Sam's thoughts flew back and forth—should he tell the boy he'd seen and heard the unexplainable, too? Should he keep it quiet so as not to frighten Carl more than he was? Would Carl feel comforted knowing his tutor was having the same experience, or would he feel safer thinking it was all in his mind?

"So, that's all, no biggie," said Carl, straightening up. He cleared his throat. "Noises, smells, and a shaky room, so what? Right?"

But they weren't all in Carl's mind. The question wasn't what would make the boy feel safer, but what would *make* the boy safer?

"Carl . . ." Sam began.

"I'm going down to check out the TV, anyway," said Carl, hopping from the bed and straightening out the legs of his sweatpants. "Better than sitting here trying to talk to you. Good luck with the séance. Be careful."

"Carl," said Sam as the boy went out the door, but then Sam said no more and let the boy go. Because Sam, alone, was the one who was responsible. It was Sam's name in the back of the register amid the names of the runaway slaves. It was Sam the spirits wanted to contact.

And so I'll have to take care of things myself.

He moved the candles to the floor, making a triangle of their points. He sat in the center.

My father would have clobbered me good for dabbling in something like this, something outside the preachings of the Bible. He would have said, "Sam! Get away from that! Fall on your knees and pray. The Lord will lift you up if you

*raise your arms to Him. Blow out those candles and ask
God for his help."*

Sam crossed his legs. He thought there was something
about crossing your legs during a séance, though he didn't
really know. He rested his arms on his thighs and turned his
palms face up. The breath he drew in was deep and ragged.

"I'm here. Sam. Roger. Matilda. Livey. Tell me what
you want me to know."

His gaze locked on a candle, and the flame sputtered
then steadied. The digital clock hummed quietly on the
nightstand. Three floors downstairs, Carl had found some
variety show on the television. The inaudible bass pulsed
against the floor.

"Come on. I don't have all night."

Yes, you do.

Sam stared into a candle. The red and orange filled his
sight and his mind. His eyes closed, but he forced them
open again. He didn't want to fall asleep. He was the
keeper of the fort. He was the man at the door. He was responsible.

Chanting seemed wrong. Instead he repeated the names
he remembered from the back of the antique registry, the
names he'd scribbled in his notebook before Carl showed
up at the door. Sam said the names slowly, in monotone,
giving none of them more emphasis than another. The
litany became a chant in itself.

"Silas, Levi, Tillie, Mingo, Livey, Matilda, Roger, Sam.
Silas, Levi, Tillie, Mingo, Livey, Matilda, Roger, Sam."

The front wall rattled a bit, and a low wail passed
through a gap in the window. Wind, nothing more. *I'm
scared.* Sam continued his list.

"Silas, Levi, Tillie, Mingo, Livey, Matilda, Roger, Sam.
Silas, Levi, Tillie, Mingo, Livey, Matilda, Roger . . ."

He remembered Roger's scream during his torture with
the whip and quince branch. This Roger and the one in the
registry had to be the same. Roger had clearly lived, in
spite of the dreadful beatings. The man had lived; had traveled the dangerous route to safety and had received welcome and rest at the Abbadon Inn.

". . . Sam."

*Sam, are you related to me? Or is it a coincidence that
we share the same name and handwriting?*

*And who are Silas, Levi, Tillie, and Mingo? Who are
Livey and Matilda?*

"Silas, Levi, Tillie, Mingo, Livey, Matilda, Roger, Sam.
I'm here, what are you waiting for?"

There was silence in the room.

"I know you suffered, and I want to tell your story. But
what is your story?"

The wind kicked up again, whistling through the window, rattling the glass. The pen with which Sam had been
scribbling fell off the nightstand and rolled across the floor
and into the triangle of candles. Sam stared at the pen, but
didn't pick it up.

"Help me out here. I'm new at this."

Something thumped the wall, hard, behind the bed.
Sam glanced around quickly and saw nothing. His mouth
went dry.

"Silas, Levi, Tillie, Mingo, Livey, Matilda, Roger, Sam."

A door slammed shut somewhere down the hall.

"I know you can do that," said Sam. "But I don't know
what it all means."

A frigid pocket of air blew by Sam and drew goose
bumps out all over his body. He shivered but kept his hands
in place on his legs. The dead-smell drifted down from the
ceiling and wrapped itself around his face. He heaved, and
then gasped through his mouth. The stench burned his
tongue.

"What does this mean?" he demanded. "Tell me."

The candle south of Sam began to rattle in its little metal
stand. The flame flared bright then went dull, and out.

"Tell me what it means! If not, shut the fuck up and
leave me alone!"

The smell faded. The wind outside died down. He
waited. Faint rock and roll drifted up through the floor
from the television in the Letters Lounge.

He waited.

"Is that all? Don't tell me you're done?"

He waited.

Then he blew out the remaining candles.

TWENTY-TWO

Carl didn't like his father's cigars, but he liked the idea that he was smoking them. His father's cigars were the most expensive someone could get short of illegal Cubans, made in Honduras or some Spanish kind of place. Carl couldn't remember what his father had said and didn't really care. Mitchell kept the glass-tubed cigars in a polished wooden box in a front bedroom on the second floor, a room he had designated as his home office. Mitchell didn't have any office furniture yet, though he was awaiting an entire roomful that he'd ordered weeks ago. And so, the cigar box was stashed in the top drawer of an oaken file box that had come with the family from Danbury.

Of course, by now, Mitchell would have guessed that Carl was stealing the cigars. Or maybe he thought Sam was doing it. That would be funny, to hear Mitchell get on Sam for lifting a few free smokes.

Carl sat on pink and blue throw pillows on the lumpy dirt floor of the shed, sucking on the brown wad of dried leaves and letting the smoke rise up and around him. There were mice out here, but he knew they were mice— he'd actually seen them scutter along the edge of the walls—so their little noises didn't disturb him. He'd left the television on inside the bar so Sam would think he was still there. The door to the shed was shut tight, which had taken a lot of heave-ho-ing on Carl's part. He'd shoved the wooden latching board across the door for good measure, to keep out trespassing cats or dogs. Someday, he thought, he'd buy one of those locks like Sam had put on his bedroom door and secure the shed with it. He'd keep the key to himself.

The shed was cold as witch's milk, but Carl had dragged his and his mother's coats off the coat tree in the front hall. He wore his; his mother's coat was wrapped around his bare feet. The shed had only one window, facing the inn, but it was so caked with dirt and grit, and laced over with branches that it might as well not be a window at all. There were two rooms in the shed, a big one in the front and a small closet with a missing door and broken wooden shelves. The building had been a kitchen at some point in time. There were moments when Carl though he could catch vague scents of frying meats and boiling potatoes. Old rusted kettles and pans sat deep in the dirt, draped in cobwebs and crusted over so much they looked as if they were either growing up out of the ground or melting down into it. Large iron cooking utensils hung on hooks inside the dilapidated brick fireplace. The walls were chinked with mud and wads of old papers. Carl had pulled one out once to have a look. It was a thin, crumbling newspaper, with the title *Freedom's Voice*. He'd crammed it back between the boards.

He liked the shed. For one thing, nobody could get to him when he was there. He'd cut a hole through the lower part of the shrubs with some brush trimmers, making an opening just big enough to crawl through without scalping himself on the thorns. For another thing, being in the shed meant being out of the inn. The inn had gotten kind of creepy recently. Weird things were happening that he didn't like too much.

Carl drew his knees up and tucked his mother's coat around his legs and feet more closely. He drew on the cigar and blew the smoke out along his tongue, trying to make a smoke ring. The smoke came out flat, like paper. He tried again, and accidentally inhaled. The burn down his windpipe made him cough.

He thought he might stay in the shed all night long. Smoke a few cigars, masturbate, snack on the Chips Ahoy he'd brought from the kitchen, share them with the mice. Maybe he could catch some mice and use them in his science experiment. Near the back of the science textbook Sam had given Carl, there was a chapter about animal be-

havior. One scientist put birds and rats in boxes and trained
them to push levers to get food or to keep from getting an
electric shock through the floor of the box. Another took
baby monkeys away from their mothers and gave them
hunks of cold wire with eyes and nipples as replacements,
or gave them soft, warm, but mean mechanical mothers
that blew cold air or water on the babies when the babies
held on to them. Some experimenters put other baby monkeys into solitary confinement and watched them go crazy.
What could Carl do with mice? There were plenty of the
little rodents. He'd have to make a trap that didn't kill them
and then come up with something cool to do. Maybe he
could teach them to smoke cigars. Okay, they had little
mouths. Cigarettes, then.

Carl put the cigar down on the dirt, balanced against a
small rock, and tugged a couple cookies from the bag. He
could catch mice with cookies. Mice loved shit like that,
and peanut butter, too. How could he make the trap? Maybe
in the morning Sam would help him figure something . . .

There was a low, guttural growl outside the door of the
shed. Carl dropped the cookie he had poised at his mouth.
He stared at the door. *Oh fuck oh fuck what is that?*

"Who is that?" he asked.

There was no sound for several beats, and then the
growl came again. It didn't sound like an animal growl, it
sounded like a person growl.

*Who could have made it through the crawl hole? Fuck
fuck fuck!*

Carl didn't want to know. He looked around, frantic,
and grabbed for one of the rusted iron pots. The handle
snapped off in his grasp. "Shit!" he hissed. He scrambled
on his knees across the damp floor to the fireplace and
tugged on one of the dangling iron hooks. It would not
give way.

"No!"

The growl came again, followed by raspy breaths.
Something struck the door. The latching board began to
rattle in place. Dust and wood bits flew. Carl's knees were
soaked with the damp of the floor, and now the insides of
his legs were warm and wet with urine.

"Who is that? Go away! I have a gun!" *Go away go away!*

Carl snatched up a brick and held it like a club. His lips curled back, exposing chattering teeth.

The board rattled harder, causing the latch in which it sat to creak on its nails. A cold rush of air, more frigid than the night, passed by—*through*—Carl, and clutched his bones and guts like ghoulish, taunting fingers. He screamed, waving the brick. "Stop it! Go away! I'm armed, I'll kill you!"

The board went suddenly still. Carl stared at it, at the door, his fingers tightened around the brick. Then, slowly, the board lifted from the latch and drew back. The door opened inward, squealing on its antique hinges.

There was nothing behind the door but the dark and twisted branches of the shrubs and the shadowed hollow that was the crawl hole.

Carl blinked, stared.

The branches shivered. The thorns clicked together like gleeful claws.

"Go away," Carl whimpered. Tears blurred his vision.

Then, it came into the shed. A black translucent shape, three feet high and four feet wide, shimmering like oil and smelling like death. Carl scrabbled on his hands and knees to the back shed wall and slammed himself against it, clutching the brick.

"What are . . . ?" he choked.

The shape wobbled and bobbed and panted in place. The top turned downward for a moment, as if studying the boy, and then, faster than anything Carl had ever seen, streaked across the floor and disappeared in the fireplace.

Carl screamed.

TWENTY-THREE

There had been no sleep for Sam the entire night. He had gone to bed but had stayed awake until morning, watching and waiting, unable to do anything else, wondering if he would be able to summon the distraught spirits or if contact would always be on their terms. Afraid they would come to him, afraid they wouldn't. At times he thought he heard his name whispered in the hallway. But there was nothing else.

Questions flew through his mind like caged bats, making it hard to focus on any one in particular. Yet he spent the hours trying to untangle them, to look at them to answer them. He felt like Jacob wrestling with the angel, every bit of his mind and body focused and strained, fighting for something he did not know exactly and for something he did not really want. But unlike Jacob, who prevailed over the angel and was strengthened, Sam just felt like shit when the room at last began to grow light with early morning.

He stumbled across the hall to the bathroom, brushed his teeth, and then stared at his reddened eyes in the mirror. *You look like you've been on one hell of a bender*, he thought. He rubbed his eyes, and it made them worse. He put a clean blade into his razor and dragged it over his cheeks, chin, and neck. It was a piss-poor job, and he nicked his chin, but he didn't care. Maybe he'd grow a beard, starting tomorrow. Might be easier.

What am I supposed to do now? Just go on with life as usual?

Back in his room he found a pair of fresh jeans in the

dresser and put them on along with the black turtleneck sweater Dani had given him for Christmas.

There isn't a life as usual now, Sam.

He put the candles in the dresser, happy at least that the leg irons had not returned, and then went downstairs to face whatever the day had to offer.

It was not quite seven, too early for Mitchell and Rebecca to be up. But Carl was in the bar on the floor, wrapped in his mother's coat, asleep in front of the blaring television set. A televangelist stomped back and forth on a dais, gesturing wildly and shouting, "I said Amen! Amen!" The congregation echoed, "Amen! Amen!"

Sam switched off the set and gently tapped Carl on the back. "Carl, wake up."

The boy mumbled something and, his eyes still closed, flipped over toward the wall and pulled the coat with him.

"Carl, get up. It's got to be miserable on the floor there."

There was a sigh, then, "Leave me alone."

"Are you sick?"

"No."

"I'm going to make pancakes. Want some?"

The boy looked over his shoulder, one eye closed, one open. "You can cook?"

"You'd be amazed."

Carl struggled to his feet, and they walked through the restaurant and into the kitchen, Sam leading the way, Carl still wrapped in his mother's coat. Sam pulled out a frying pan, spatula, and mixing bowl. From one of the refrigerators he collected eggs, milk, and butter. He turned to the set of canisters on the counter and bumped into Carl, who was already handing him the one marked "flour."

"Thanks," said Sam.

"Yeah."

Carl sat at the windowside table, chin on folded arms, studying Sam as he went through the steps of creating homemade pancakes. It was as if the boy had never really watched someone cook before. Sam said nothing as he cracked the eggs, beat them into the flour and sugar and baking powder, then ladled a large glop into the buttered pan.

"That smell's going to wake up Rebecca and Mitchell," said Carl. "I can't think of the last time Mom cooked anything for breakfast. She's always getting those bran muffins at the store, and cereal, and other shit. Stuff."

"You prefer they stay asleep?"

"Well, yeah, wouldn't you?"

Sam created four pan-sized pancakes, served with honey he found in the cabinet. "Honey's as good as syrup," he said as he brought the plates and forks to the table. "Even better. My grandparents raised bees, and we always had fresh honey at home."

Carl unfolded himself, picked up his fork, and looked at the pancakes. Sam sat across from him. The boy didn't move.

"Did I cook up a fly in yours?" Sam asked.

"I want to talk about my science fair project."

"Really? I'm impressed, Carl. Have you picked a topic?"

"At first I wanted to build a hovercraft, but I don't think we can get the stuff."

"No."

"Last night I thought about training mice. There are a bunch of them, and I'm sure I could catch them without hurting them."

"But . . . ?"

"But now I think I have a better idea."

"You think?" Sam cut a bite of pancake and put it in his mouth. The warmth and sweetness made him, for a moment, feel better. Better was good.

"I want to do my experiment on magic."

Sam swallowed. "Magic? What do you mean?"

"To prove magic is real. I can do it."

Sam knew he made a slight face, and Carl picked up on it immediately.

"Don't you like my idea? You haven't even heard what I want to do."

"Magic isn't a science project, Carl, sorry. The point is to come up with a question and then make a hypothesis . . ."

"I remember." The boy was exasperated. "You think I

never listen? You make a hypothesis and then test it to see if you were right. I can prove that magic is real."

"Where is this coming from, Carl? Because you thought you saw me having a séance last night? If so, I'm sorry to have steered you off in the wrong direction."

Carl put his fork down and narrowed his eyes. "You have no idea, do you? You have no idea what is really going on in this place."

"I thought I smelled something cooking!" Rebecca breezed into the kitchen, her pink terry robe tied at her waist, fluffy slippers *whoof-whoofing* on the vinyl flooring. "I woke up, nudged Mitchell, and said, 'Am I dreaming or are those pancakes downstairs?' He just turned over, the old gruff, but I suddenly felt hungry." Rebecca came to the table and leaned on it. "Those are huge!"

Carl rolled his eyes. His mother didn't see.

"Would you like one?" asked Sam.

"Oh, no, I don't think I should." Her face said she should. Sam thought of offering her one of his, but then Carl shoved his plate in her direction.

"Have mine. I haven't poured any honey on them, so they aren't messed up yet."

"Carl, aren't you hungry?"

"Not now," said the boy. He got up and stalked out of the kitchen.

"Lessons start at nine!" Sam called after him. Rebecca smiled at Sam. Sam looked at his pancakes. The last thing he felt like doing was dining with the woman as she chatted about whatever-the-fuck she would chat about. But there was no graceful way around it.

And yammer on, she did.

"Carl?" Sam rapped on the boy's door.

"Go away."

"Let's talk."

"Why? You think I'm an idiot. You think my ideas suck. Well, you'll wish you knew everything. You just wait."

It sounded as if Carl drew in a sharp breath of air. Sam said, "Carl, are you okay?"

"Couldn't be better."

"Did you hurt yourself?"

"No. Go away. Don't worry, I'll be downstairs in time for your stupid little lessons. I'll be there nine o'clock sharp. I can tell time, even if you don't think I can."

Sam put his ear to the wood. Again, he heard Carl gasp softly. Maybe he was hurt; maybe he was just jacking off. Sam pushed away and went back downstairs, passing Rebecca on her way back up. She said as she went by him, "I've got shopping to do this morning. New light fixtures for the third-floor hallway. I'll bet you'll be glad!"

"That's just super, Rebecca," Sam replied.

As he stepped down into the first-floor foyer, he thought he heard the cellar door rattle, but then it was silent. He walked down the hall to have a look, but it was secure and still. He put his hand on the wood. It was neither hot nor unusually cold. He reached out for the knob, held it, then let it go.

He felt a bit dizzy from lack of sleep. The inn was soft beneath his feet, a little unsteady. But he knew the uneven feeling was more than weariness, that the inn and the spirits within were just biding their time. There was a charge to the air, a ragged energy that coursed through the rooms. Whatever it was, it was well aware of Sam.

Returning to the kitchen, he cleaned his cooking mess. He could hear the mistress of the inn upstairs, singing some tune he didn't recognize. *Rebecca,* he thought, *it must be easy being you.*

"There you go, try this one on for size," said Carl. He pulled the straight edge razor across the inside of his elbow. The skin parted; hot blood ran red and free. Hot became cool, pain became power.

"Thinking I'm some stupid kid. Fuck you."

He nicked the skin again. More blood. It dripped down to his wrist and pattered onto the sleeping bag.

"You're gonna hurt, just you wait."

Nnnnnnnn.

Carl nicked his arm again.

"You didn't get hurt enough with that slamming bathroom door, well, this is going to make up for it!"

Nick. Nick. The tracks of small slices moved up his arm.

Carl directed his magical anger downstairs to wherever Sam was at this very moment. He was too mad to focus, but hurled his power through the floor. "Hurt him, I don't care how, just hurt him!"

Carl pressed the cuts to make the blood flow faster.

Nnnnnnnnn!

He glanced up at the window. A spider the size of a mouse lumbered across the screen. It stopped and looked at Carl.

Die you stupid, worthless creature!

"Nnnnnnn!"

The spider's many black eyes glared at Carl, and it did not fall, it did not die. Carl picked up his *You Shall* book and hurled it at the window. The spider fell away, backward, down into the yard.

Carl made another nick. He hummed, the sound burring against the enamel.

"Nnnnnnnnnn!"

Nick.

Carl laughed and squeezed his arm and watched the blood plip onto his sleeping bag.

TWENTY-FOUR

Carl was true to his word. He was downstairs with his books at nine, looking as if he'd actually taken a shower and washed the boot brush atop his head. He wore clothes Sam hadn't seen before, a fresh blue shirt and brand-new khaki pants. He walked quietly into the kitchen, where Sam was rinsing out his teacup, and said, "Where are we studying this morning? Here, or in the bar?"

"Here," said Sam. "Your mother has workers coming in around ten to paper both the restaurant and the bar. We can close the door."

"Fine." Carl walked to the table, sat, and stacked his science, literature, history, and math books neatly on top of each other. He opened his spiral notebook, folded back the cover, and uncapped a ballpoint pen. Then he looked at Sam. His face bore no discernible expression.

This isn't normal Carl, Sam thought.

"New clothes?"

"Nope."

"You look . . . nice." *More weird than nice, actually.*

The comment didn't seem to register. Then Carl said, "How are *you* feeling? Are you hurt? Yet?" The question wasn't taunting or sarcastic. It sounded hollow.

"Hurt? What do you mean?"

"You look like you're hurt."

"No, I'm not hurt." *What is the kid talking about?* "But I am very tired. I had a long night. What about you?"

"I'm just fine."

Sam sat across from Carl and looked at the boy. Carl returned the gaze without grinning or otherwise changing his expression.

"Are you sure?"

"I'm sure."

Sam said, "You look . . ."

"What?"

He looked like a kid Sam taught during his second year. Adelmo, from Mexico. Adelmo's mother came to Albemarle County to work as a domestic on one of the large horse farms. Adelmo was smart and funny. He wanted to be liked, but he was different. Other kids targeted him, picked on him, and one weekend when he was riding his bike, he was jumped and severely beaten. Adelmo was hospitalized, and when he came back to school several weeks later, he had that same hollow look in his eyes. The look of rage that had congealed into volatile resignation.

"What?" repeated Carl.

Fury pushed down, yet ready to spring back up at the drop of a hat. A month after the beating, Adelmo nearly killed another student after a football game. Adelmo spent a year in jail, even as a juvenile.

Carl is furious.

"Nothing," said Sam. "Let's start with literature this morning. We finished the O. Henry stories. Let's pick up on eighty-nine with Edgar Allan Poe."

Carl opened his book to the assigned page. He read "The Raven" aloud and then answered the questions that followed in the textbook. Sam pretended to review the upcoming history lesson in his teacher text but he only stared at the page. His nerves were on edge. He felt like his own breathing, his own movements, were in slow motion. Everything felt askew, off-kilter. Even Carl's oral reading sounded muffled and sluggish as if the air was too thick.

I'm waiting for the other shoe to drop, he thought.

He'd felt this way before; watching the teenaged boys get out of their trucks on the isolated road as Sam clutched Rose's thin hand and whispered "it'll be okay," holding the letter in his hand that would announce the death of his brother overseas, staring up the street in Richmond at the line of police just prior to the students' protest, waiting day after day while his father lay dying in his bed. Trying to act normal through a span of time, be it a moment, a

minute, or a week. Believing that to act normal would prevent the inevitable. At least Rebecca and Mitchell seemed
oblivious to the strange occurrences. Carl had sensed some
himself, and Sam thought that would have something to do
with his youth and sensitivities. But what shoe would fall
next, and when? He believed now that daylight was not the
enemy of ghosts. They had no concern for dark or light.
Unlike the horror movies he'd seen at the drive-in theater
and on television, spirits didn't have to wait until the sun
went down.

When Carl was finished with the questions, Sam and
Carl discussed them. Carl's voice remained cool and
steady. He didn't joke, he didn't complain. Sam felt his
skin crawl and needed to break the tension.

"I see you cut a hole in the brush to the shed outside."
Sam tipped his head toward the window. Carl glanced out.
"Yep."

"Anything of interest in there?"

"Like what?"

"Antiques?"

Carl shrugged. Then, "Are we through with literature?"

Sam counted to five. Then, "Are you angry with me,
Carl?"

"Why would I be angry?"

"About your science fair project? About me saying no to
magic?"

"You can't say no to magic, Sam." Carl smiled then,
suddenly, his mouth opening in a hideously wide smile.
Then it snapped shut.

Sam caught his breath. Then he said, "What do you
mean by that, Carl?"

"If you don't know yet, you'll find out soon enough."

There was a knock on the open kitchen door. Two men
stood there in overalls and boots. Sam was surprised he
had not heard them come through the restaurant. "Hello
there. We're from Randall's Floor and Wall Company. We
are here to put up the wallpaper in these two rooms. We
just want to check first to make sure the paper we brought
is what was ordered. And it only goes down to the chair
rails, right? And the same pattern for both rooms?"

"Rebecca Morrison should tell you that," said Sam. "Didn't she let you in?"

"Yeah," said one of the men. "She did, but then she went into that little front room on the left there and started all this stretching and stuff. She is still in there, moving her arms and legs around with her eyes closed. I thought maybe she was, you know, limited upstairs? I thought someone else here would be able to tell us exactly what is needed."

"You'll just have to wait until she's done." He almost made mention of the drinks in the box behind the bar, and suggested the men help themselves, but then he didn't need grief from Mitchell.

"We don't have all day," grumbled the worker. The two disappeared from the doorway.

Sam looked back at Carl. "Carl, talk to me. I know your parents don't listen. They don't listen to me most of the time, and I'm an adult. They don't listen to each other, either. But I'll listen to you."

Carl sighed, looked out the window. Then he looked back. "It's too late for that."

"Too late for . . . ?"

At first Sam thought the men in the lounge had turned on a saw or sander, but the noise was too close. He spun about in his chair and saw it there, trembling on the counter at the end of its cord like a mad dog on a leash. Rebecca's electric knife, the blade vibrating back and forth, revving in place.

"Look at that," Carl said calmly.

Sam's first and only rational thought was, *Did she leave the switch on when she was down here earlier? Was she cutting something?* But then the knife flew off the counter and hurtled toward the table, its silver fang slashing the air.

"Shit!" Sam cried out, and he lifted his hands to protect himself and Carl and thought in that second, *We're going to die!*

The knife flipped as it flew, like some haunted Asian dagger, wailing as if it were alive. Sam struck out and the knife drilled through the palm of his right hand. He screamed, and he stared in horror as the thing embedded itself clean through. Then the knife went still and silent. It dropped from his hand and clattered to the floor, taking chunks of flesh with it. Sam fell to his knees beside the knife, holding his hand to his chest, blood pouring from the wound, waiting for the terrible rush of pain that did not come immediately . . .

"Sam?" This was Carl, his voice giving a little as if the trance was ended.

. . . but then came on like a blowtorch.

"Jesus!" Sam growled. "Oh, my God!"

Carl came to him and watched him with furrowed brows. "Wow," he said.

"Carl, I need . . . to call . . ." Sam began, but the pain sucked away his words. Blood and sweat poured from his body.

Carl got a dish towel from the wall rack and handed it to Sam. Sam wrapped it around the wound and pulled it tight. *Direct pressure, direct pressure will keep me from bleeding to death.* The room wobbled and swayed.

The workers were at the kitchen door then, one of them asking something like, "What happened in here?" and the other one saying, "That guy's really cut." Rebecca pushed past them and trotted in. When she saw the knife and the blood and Sam holding his hand, she said, "It's not my fault! You have to be careful with those things!"

"I need to get some help," gasped Sam.

"Call an ambulance," said one of the men to Rebecca. She touched her lips, then vanished.

The men came to Sam, helped him to his feet and back to his chair.

"You want ice on that?" asked one, moving toward the refrigerator. Sam almost laughed because it sounded funny—*You want ice on that?*—like a waiter offering ground pepper to a freshly delivered meal, but it really wasn't that funny, and Sam didn't laugh because he felt sick and dizzy, and he felt like he'd been crucified.

For what? What was the reason for the attack? What had he done wrong?

He wished he were anywhere else at that point besides the Abbadon Inn. He fainted then and got his wish.

TWENTY-FIVE

Mitchell picked Sam up from the hospital emergency room in his new beige Oldsmobile Omega. He had put a bath towel on the passenger seat, something that Sam found offensive, though intellectually he knew the man was afraid Sam would bleed, pee, or throw up on the expensive leather seat.

Sam's hand was bandaged tightly and secured in a sling. The flesh had been cleaned, stitched, and dressed, and he'd been given a prescription for Demerol which, at the moment, was cutting the worst of the pain pretty well and putting cotton in his brain. *Amazingly enough,* the doctor had mused, *the blade went between the bones.* Then he'd said, *Now, how exactly did this happen?*

"That was quite an accident," said Mitchell, not looking over. He was jockeying his legal position. He and Rebecca weren't going to let a tutor sue them for shit. Sam wasn't planning on suing them. It wasn't their fault.

But it was no accident.

Mitchell slowed at a stop sign, flicked on his blinker, and turned left onto a main thoroughfare. "You sure seem to have trouble with your hands. You did something—paper cut was it?—to one hand the day you signed the guest book. You slammed your hand in the bathroom door not long ago. And now you cut the hell out of one with an electric knife. That some kind of subconscious thing?"

"Mitchell," said Sam.

"What?"

"Let's drop it."

Mitchell shrugged.

At the Abbadon, Mitchell parked along Columbia. He

opened the door for Sam, though he didn't move to help him from the car. Sam worked his way free and stood on the sidewalk, breathing heavily. Part of his mind, blurred with drugs, fought going in again.

You don't want to go back there. You don't know what is waiting for you there.

But another part of his mind pushed back with equal determination.

You have to find the answer. It's your responsibility. They are depending on you.

"You coming?" asked Mitchell from halfway up the stone walk.

Sam swallowed hard, then made it to the iron gate. He stopped, clutched the gate, and looked up at the new bushes, the stone walkway. He looked at the wraparound porch with its wicker rockers side-by-side and the green-cushioned porch swing at the far end. He looked up at the repaired shingles and the yet-to-be-replaced third-floor windows. He saw Carl's silhouette standing in one, and Rebecca's in the one next to it.

He began to raise his hand to wave.

No.

It wasn't Carl. It wasn't Rebecca. They were standing on the front porch.

Sam looked back up at the windows. The figures were still there, featureless and dark, hands pressed to the glass. Watching Sam.

The sun went behind a cloud, and the Abbadon Inn was thrown into a deep shadow. The oaks and lilacs in the side yard groaned in a breeze. Sam watched Mitchell climb the porch steps and stand with his family, he saw Rebecca motion for him and mouth, "Come on, Sam," but he could not hear her. He could hear only the trees, the wind, and a whispered name.

"Saaaam."

On the third floor more figures appeared, four and five to a window now, hands pressed to the glass, motionless, yet Sam could read their tormented, pleading thoughts.

Go away.

Go away.

They're warning me, Sam thought.

Go away . . . !

But the warnings were too late. He would not abandon this place, these souls. Sam felt suddenly empowered with righteous anger, felt himself rise out of the drugs and the pain and the fear. *I won't go away. I'll take their part, whatever that will mean. I'll try to make it right, for Roger and Silas, Matilda and Livey. In memory of Rose and Robbie and those who I did not and could not help. I'll do it for Carl, to rid his home of the tangled and dangerous energy. I'll do it for the mysterious Sam Ford who signed his name in the back of the registry.*

I'll do it for myself.

The cloud shifted, and the Abbadon was again in the sunlight. The figures in the windows faded and were gone. From the porch Rebecca called, "Did you hear me, Sam? I've made supper for you, no need to fix your own or eat out tonight."

Sam stepped inside the iron gate, then he bent over and heaved liquid pancakes into the grass.

"Nasty," Carl said.

Sam wiped his mouth, stood straight, and went inside.

TWENTY-SIX

"A Jeanette Harris called while you were gone," said Rebecca. She lifted her cloth napkin and patted both sides of her face. "I took her number. It's in the reception room, on the desk under the paperweight."

"Did she leave a message?" asked Sam.

"I would have said she did if she did," said Rebecca. It was clear she was still on edge over the knife incident.

The four sat at a table in the Orchid Restaurant, eating baked chicken, wild rice, and salad. The table bore a new red cloth, as did all the other restaurant tables. Rebecca bought them to match the red-and-gold wallpaper that had just gone up. In truth only the family was eating. Sam had no appetite, which was just as well because he had a hard time managing fork and knife with his left hand. Rebecca offered to cut the chicken, and Sam let her have her magnanimity, though when she was done he ate only one bite. His stomach would have none of it.

Sam's first inclination had been to decline the dinner offer. He wanted to rest, and maybe read. But then he had acquiesced, not minding a short period of company when he knew that ahead of him were hours and hours of being alone in this place.

Though not quite alone.

"Who's Jeanette?" asked Carl. It was the first thing the boy had said through the whole dinner, although his parents had kept up a lively conversation about the final choice of windows for the third floor and the fact that the matchbooks Rebecca had ordered for the restaurant had misspelled it as the "Orchard Restaurant."

"She's a librarian."

"Oh, yeah, I remember. You like her?" asked Carl.

"She's very nice."

"You like her more than Dani?"

"Your chicken's getting cold."

Rebecca then reminded Mitchell that he needed to get her car inspected that week, and Mitchell told her he wouldn't be home the next three nights for dinner, and Carl went back to flipping rice over with his spoon.

After another five minutes Sam excused himself. Rebecca had gone into the kitchen to retrieve a pie she'd unfrozen, and when she came back out he was pushing his chair in with his foot.

"No pie? But I thought you liked cherry."

"I do. But I'm not feeling very well."

"No. Well," she said.

"Thanks for supper."

"Yes. Well."

He found Jeanette's note—nothing more than her name, number, and time of call—in the reception room, tucked under a glass duck. The pendulum clock on the wall, a brand new addition, read 7:16. He wanted to return Jeanette's call but didn't want to while the family was across the hall within listening distance. There was a phone in Rebecca and Mitchell's room, but he didn't want to go in there again. He would insist a line be put into his room. He'd pay for it.

The floor and Sam's gut began to roll slightly, and Sam pushed the heel of his hand against his eyes until the sensation faded. He wouldn't wait until the family was through dinner, he would just call Jeanette in the morning. He tucked the note in his jeans pocket, readjusted his sling with the utmost care, and climbed the stairs to the third floor. On the landing, he flicked the hall light but none came on. He flipped it up and down several times, and at last the three connected sconces lit up. Sam leaned against the wall to slow his breathing, then went into the bathroom.

Standing at the mirror, he splashed cool water on his cheeks, eyes, forehead. He looked at his face, which seemed a good ten years older than it did in January. Then he studied the soft cast and sling. There were crusts of

blood on his exposed fingertips, and he wondered how he
was supposed to shower with his right hand like that.
Maybe cover it in a plastic bag? Or just resign himself to
baths for a while?

Sam turned off the light and went into the hall. Carl
stood there, hands on his hips, the irregular streaks of darkness in the hall hiding his eyes.

"Whoa, Carl, you startled me."

"I know."

"What is it?"

Carl shrugged. That careful, calculated attitude. Nothing had changed since morning. Not sleet nor snow nor
dark of night nor a near-amputation by a flying knife.

"I want to tell you something," said the boy.

"Then tell me."

"It's more a show-you than tell-you. Really, it's both.
Come with me." Carl stepped across the hall to his door
and pushed it open. He flicked on the overhead globe,
sending pallid light onto the floor and into the corners. Sam
stood in the doorway, looking at the painted flowers and
peace symbols on the walls. Carl sat down on his sleeping
bag and looked up at Sam.

"What is it, Carl?"

"I figured it's time you knew. It's all me."

"What's all you?"

"All of it." He turned his hands palms-up like a suppli-
cant. "I've done it. I've mastered it. 'Do what you will shall
be the whole of the law.' I did what I would, and I've made
it the law around here."

"I have no idea what you're talking about."

"Don't you want to come in my room?" Sam didn't like
the boy's voice. It didn't carry normal, teenage snideness.
It was hard, cold. "You might not want me in your room,
but you're welcome in mine."

Sam stepped in through the door.

"Good," said Carl. "Now shut it."

"No. Carl, what is this?"

Carl put his hands on his hips and said, "I'm the one who
has made everything happen here in the Abbadon Inn."

"What?"

"It's been me. I have been studying magic for nine months now. I've learned how to move things with my mind. I made the door slam on your hand. I made Dani's neck and arms and legs hurt so she would leave." He jabbed his index finger at points along his own face, neck, and body. "There, there, there, and there!" He grinned. "Surprised?"

Sam was stunned. "No, Carl, you didn't. You couldn't possibly have done that."

"Oh, yeah, I did." He reached into a cloth laundry bag beside him on the floor and pulled out some old books, a handful of little metal pendants, and a crude doll made from a pillow that bore staples up and down it.

"A voodoo doll." Carl picked up the pillow doll and rubbed the marker-drawn breasts with his thumb. "See? Looks just like her!"

"Dani left on her own."

"It's easier to think that, isn't it?"

Does he really think he's responsible for the haunting of the Abbadon? "Carl, listen to yourself."

"No, you listen to me! I've read a lot. I know about how to sit and what to chant and what to think while I'm chanting. I've tried it out on Dani, you, my mom and dad. I killed our dog back in Danbury just by thinking about it! I made my dad have a car wreck! Dani left, and your hand got slammed in the bathroom door. And today, that knife flew off the counter and stabbed you. That was me!"

"Stop it, Carl."

"There's a lot of power floating around here, and it's coming from me." The boy smiled then, that awful, stretch-mouthed smile Sam had seen that morning in the kitchen.

Sam walked to Carl, his fist clenched. He wanted to grab the boy and shake him back to his senses, but Carl scooted back on his butt and laughed.

"Touch me, and I'll tell my parents on you!"

"Carl," said Sam, trying to keep his voice even. "You don't know what you're talking about. I know that . . ."

"No, you don't know what *you're* talking about!" said Carl, his voice rising, and his body going with it. He clambered to his feet and pointed a finger at Sam. "I have made

lots of things happen since we've moved here. Some I
didn't even mean to happen, but it did, and I'm going to
take control over it. I saw you with your little candles in
your room, trying to chase away the evil. You can't chase it
away. You can't chase *me* away."

"Carl, listen to me!"

"If you don't believe me, I'll just make it worse for you,
just wait and see! But if you do believe me, then I can teach
you some really good stuff. We can do it together!"

He's delusional, thought Sam. His hand had begun to
throb dreadfully, sending barbs of pain up through his
spine. *I'm in no shape. Tomorrow, we'll talk. Tomorrow . . .*

He clamped his teeth as he felt the bile flutter in his
stomach. Turning, he grabbed for the door frame and then
pulled himself out into the hall. He could hear Carl snick-
ering behind him.

Sam took several steps down the hall toward his room.
He dragged his left hand along the wall to steady himself.
Ahead, the electric sconces began to sputter and hiss. He
squeezed his eyes shut against the pain, the nausea. He
opened them, and the sconces were gone. In their places
were glass hurricane lamps clamped to the wall in tin
stands. Candles blazed against the sooty glass. The floor
was covered in a tattered blue runner, and a wicker linen
cart sat beside one of the far doors. From behind closed
doors came the shrill giggles of women and the grunting of
men. Headboards banged rhythmically against walls.
Boom, boom, boom, boom, boom. Someone screamed in
pain or orgasm. At the far end of the hall, the door to the
porte cochere room slowly opened, revealing a coal-black
emptiness. Sam could not move; he clutched the wall and
stared at the dark, distant room. Then there was a rush of
air, a wind, hurtling from the room, bearing with it tendrils
of smoke and ash. The wind slammed into the walls, back
and forth and back, as it hurtled toward Sam. The candles
on the walls blew out in its passing. In the oncoming wind
Sam heard his name, stretched out long and low,
"Saaaaaaam!"

The wind struck him on both sides, raking his cheeks
and engulfing him in the putrid, overwhelming dead-smell.

Sam stumbled but remained on his feet. He looked behind him to watch where the wind was going, what it would do next—is it after Carl, too?—but there was no wind, no smoke or soot. When he turned back, the iron sconces sputtered on the wall. The distant door of the porte cochere room was closed.

Quit fucking with me! he thought, *just tell me your story, your truth . . .* but then pain roiled again from his hand through his arm and chest and head, and he could think no more. He made it to his room, to his bed, dry-swallowed two painkillers, and fell into a dreamless sleep.

TWENTY-SEVEN

He awoke with cotton in his mouth and agony on his right side. *More pills*, he thought, easing up and fishing in his jeans pocket for the little amber bottle they'd given him from the ER pharmacy. He took two, hoping it would cut the pain enough but still allow him some sort of clear thought. Today he was going to begin his search, to go over every inch of the inn. Surely, Rebecca and Mitchell wouldn't expect him to jump back into tutoring the day after his impalement. Surely, they would let him wander at will as he tried to adjust to life with one hand.

There was a knock on his door. He expected Rebecca with a halfhearted peace offering of toast on a tray. "Yes?"

There was no reply. Carl? Sam repeated, "Yes?" Silence. "Fine, then, whoever you are."

Roger? Sam?

He'd slept in his clothes, and it was hell stripping from his jeans, shirt, and underwear and tugging on clean ones. After securing the padlock outside his door, he went to the bathroom and clumsily brushed his teeth and combed his hair. Then he studied the graze marks on both cheeks. They were tender and raw, as if he'd gone face down on a strip of sandpaper.

They're making a show for me. But when will it become clear to me what I'm to know? Surely they sense that I'm confused. They're as confused as I am. Their energy is tangled and unfocused. That's how I got hurt. It has to be revealed soon. It has to. I can't suffer any more wounds.

Sam went out to the sitting area, grabbed the stair railing in his left hand, and swung around and down the steps.

Carl was waiting halfway down the stairs, in the center

of the step, arms crossed. Sam drew up short but hoped the surprise didn't show on his face.

"Morning, Carl. I hope you're feeling better than you were last night."

"I wasn't feeling bad last night."

Sam came down, expecting Carl to step out of the way. He didn't.

"Move, Carl."

Carl slowly turned aside, and Sam continued to the second-floor hallway. Carl said, "Turn about's fair play, you know."

Sam looked back. "You have to be more specific if you want people to listen."

"Okay, specifically, then. It's my turn. I want reciprocation."

"Hey, you remembered your vocabulary word." Sam tried to sound lighthearted. It sounded forced.

"I opened my room to you to tell you my truth. Now show me your truth."

"What truth, Carl?' Sam was angry. "What truth? You claim to be some sort of Houdini . . ."

"Crowley."

"Whatever, whoever."

"I let you in my room. I told you about my secret power. Now it's time for you to share your secret with me."

"What secret, Carl?"

"Whatever it is you hide in your room. Whatever you freaked out about when I was there, looking in your cases."

"There's nothing you want or need to see. There is nothing you want or need to know. Yes, I'll admit it, there are things going on in this place that are out of the ordinary. They seem supernatural, magical. But you had nothing to do with it. I'm going to find out what it is, but rest assured it isn't you."

Carl's face twisted. "You don't know shit!"

"I know you should trust me. Stop trying to be such a tough guy. You're lonely, frustrated, even scared. That's okay. I'm a bit scared, too. You saw what happened to me yesterday. But don't try to make it your own. I don't want anything to happen to you."

"Shut up!" the boy cried, and ran up the stairs.

Maybe that's better, Sam thought. *His anger is out in the open again.*

Then he called up the steps, "I care about you, Carl. Remember that!"

He heard the boy's door slam shut.

Jeanette answered the library desk phone. "Cape May Public Library."

"Jeanette. It's Sam."

"Sam! Hey, I called you yesterday."

"I got your message."

"The lady who answered said you'd be out for a while but didn't say how long. Out shopping?"

"She didn't tell you where I was?"

"No. Should she have?"

Sam looked across the hall from the reception room to the open doors of the Letters Lounge. No one was there. Mitchell was gone for the morning. Rebecca was upstairs somewhere, wandering the inn with one of her Bed-and-Breakfast Brigade buddies, carrying curtain swatches on big metal rings. "I was in the hospital."

"Really? What happened? Are you okay?"

"My hand was run through with an electric knife."

"Oh, my God! That's terrible! How did that accident happen?"

"It wasn't an accident."

A moment of silence. Then, "What then? Did the owners try to . . . kill you? And you went *back?*"

"No, no." He almost laughed. "Not the owners."

"Who then? Intruders?"

"In a way, yes." He looked again across the hall, then walked around behind the desk and leaned on his good elbow. He could hear the women upstairs in the room over the porte cochere, clomping around. Rebecca's friend said, "A spiral staircase, how charming!" Upstairs in the guest wing carpenters hammered and sawed—new baseboards, chair rails, whatever else Rebecca had put them to doing.

Sam lowered his voice, "You remember saying you weren't sure if you believed in ghosts or not?"

"Ah," Jeanette lowered her voice, too. He could see her, her hand cupped to her mouth to keep out the prying ears of library-goers. "Yes. Why?"

"First of all, Nicholas Abbadon didn't own blacks. He was an abolitionist. The inn was a stop on the road to freedom for more than fifty runaways. Yet, some of them are," okay, just say it, "still here."

There was total silence. Then, "Just a minute." The phone clunked, and he could hear her muffled voice say something to someone about a reserved book. Then she was back. "You're saying some of the runaways are still there? Like their . . ." her voice lowered, ". . . spirits?"

"Seems that way."

"Why do you think so?"

"There are names of runaway slaves in the back of the old guest registry here, signed in by Nicholas Abbadon and finished off with each slave's mark. My name is there, Jeanette. Sam Ford. Right there in the book, in handwriting that looks so much like my own. I think one of my relatives might have been a runaway who came through Cape May on the way to freedom, and hid here in the Abbadon for a while. He might be trying to get my attention. Him, and others, too."

"That's incredible."

"I know. But there have been so many strange things. The dreams I told you about, and other occurrences. Pockets of cold air, smells of old perfume and decay, things no one else seems to notice except me, and sometimes Carl. I've heard whispers and laughing when there is no one around. I've seen things at the corner of my eye, things moving. A bottle from which I was drinking shattered in front of me. And I found," *Oh, Jesus, here it comes*, "I found a pair of leg irons in my room, still covered in bits of flesh and blood. I think they crawled in, and then later just *appeared*. There was no way anyone could have planted them in my room."

A pause. "You're not making this up, are you?"

He realized how desperately he needed her to believe him. "God, Jeanette, I wish I was. And yesterday, and this sounds insane so you don't have to say it does, the knife in the kitchen jumped off the counter and cut through my palm. I'm lucky it wasn't any worse than it is and that Carl didn't get hurt."

"This is insane."

"I said you didn't have to say that."

"It sounds like something there wants you out. That something is really angry at you."

"No. Not angry, but confused, unsure of how to get my attention. Sam Ford, or Roger, or Tillie, or one of the others or all of them; they are desperate to show me something. I don't know what it is, but I have to find out. I'm needed here."

"You're needed gone, Sam. It isn't safe. And you're putting the child in danger, staying there, and the rest of the family, too."

"I've thought about that. So far, though, the energy has been focused on me. Carl's only seen and smelled a few things. If I can find the answer to this mess, if I can exorcise the torment somehow, then it will be over and done with. The Morrisons will have their home, the spirits will have their peace."

"And what will you have?"

Sam didn't know what to say. The knowledge that he'd at last done a good thing, a strong thing? That instead of being a worthless piece of shit as he was when Rose was dragged away into the truck and killed, as he was when Robbie asked Sam for a good reason not to go to war and Sam had nothing to say, as he was when his father had lay dying in extreme pain and Sam found himself unable to pray with the old man even though that was all his father had asked for in his last moment, he would do what had to be done for once? Like his waiter uncles, he would endure for his family, for the Sam Ford he had never known, and for the greater family of suffering souls whose names graced the back of the registry. Sam clutched the receiver and wished Jeanette were there to hold instead of the cold, hard plastic.

"I can't believe you're still in that hell house," said Jeanette at last. "Sam, meet me tonight. Let's have dinner and talk." She sounded almost desperate. "Say yes, please."

"That might be good."

There was a soft sound of air through lips. "All right. I can pick you up after work if you want. I'm done at eight tonight."

"But I have to tell you now that I won't move out of the inn. Not yet. I have work to do. Just know that."

"What? Sam, oh, never mind. We'll talk. Be watching for me. Don't expect me to come in there to find you. I won't do it."

TWENTY-EIGHT

He decided to search the whole inn. How many square feet would that be, four thousand? Five? Sam didn't know, yet consciously exploring—stepping slowly over every available inch while keeping his mind open to psychic input—was the only thing he could think of doing. He would not just sit by and wait. There was danger in too much time passing. He had to push for answers; there had to be clues there, on the property.

God helps those who help themselves, his mother used to say. He hoped the same was true with tormented spirits.

The pills began to kick in—he could feel the easing warmth in his hand and the buzzing in his mind. Artificial peace pumped his veins. Yet he trembled as he opened the cellar door and went down the creaking steps.

The cellar was a cold, damp, low-ceilinged hole with an irregular floor of hard-packed, sandy earth. Several naked lightbulbs in steel fixtures were nailed along a center ceiling beam, each dangling its own string. A single washer and drier stood toe to toe at the bottom of the steps. Sam couldn't imagine Rebecca would let the cellar stay like this for long. Once guests started coming to the inn, they'd want some sort of laundry service, and Rebecca would have to hire a person to spend a great deal of his or her time down here in the hole. That person would not tolerate these conditions.

Sam brailled the walls with his hand, trying to catch a sense of anything down here that might tie in to the ghostly agitations. He moved with intent, sliding his feet along the floor, his head angled to the wall, listening, feeling. He walked the entire perimeter of the room, across racks of rotting wood shelves and old boards standing on end, past rusty-banded barrels and an old table used for folding the laundry. He felt nothing other than the cold of the stone, the damp of the air. Then he reached the carved-out space beneath the slanted, bolted bulkhead that opened to the backyard.

From upstairs, he heard Rebecca call, "Carl! I'm going out for a bit. Carl? Did you hear me? Carl?" Then the cellar door opened. "Sam! I'm going out for a bit."

"Yep."

The door closed.

There were no stairs leading to the bulkhead. They had likely rotted away years ago and had not been replaced. Old scraps of wood had been tossed under the door like a giant game of Pick-Up-Sticks. Sam kicked away some and squeezed in to stand beneath the doors. He reached up and touched the splintered wood. It rippled as though it was filled with worms or termites. The wood grew warm, then hot. Sam took his fingers away. The doors shuddered against their latches then went still.

They came through here, didn't they? The runaways? In the dark of night they sneaked through the trees and were accepted into the cellar by way of the bulkhead.

And then what?

A narrow corridor led off the main room of the cellar, sealed by a door that was in the process of returning to the earth from whence it came. It was behind this door that Sam had put the leg irons. The door was still closed; he knew Rebecca and Mitchell had not been back there, and he was certain Carl did not have the physical strength to open the door over the hard lumps of flooring. Sam pressed his face against the splintered wood and listened. There was silence in the corridor. He grasped the steel latch with his left hand and jerked it as hard as he could. The door wobbled but held. He yanked again, bearing back with all his weight. The door refused, then scraped open a few inches. Sam pulled again, and the door opened far enough to let him enter, sideways.

He peered into the darkness. The leg irons, which he had tossed inside the door were still there, snagged on a ragged stone at the base of the wall.

All right, he thought. *That's good.* His heart hammered with exertion and uncertainty.

The walls here were also stone and slick with mildew. The floor was irregular, tipping slightly from right to left. Sam stepped around the leg irons and moved into the hallway, bending down so as not to scrape his head on the ragged ceiling. With the small slice of light from the cellar's main room, he walked to the tiny room at the hall's end. In the faint light he could see that this room was likewise walled with stone, and there was a section of pipe protruding from the wall. Sam felt along to the pipe, reached inside. It was empty. It seemed to head out in the direction of the sea. Perhaps it had been used for waste at some time? Yet Sam felt no supernatural stirrings, smelled nothing foul.

He turned back.

The leg irons lay just outside the door, blocking Sam's clear path through the corridor to the main room beyond.

Sam's heart lurched. He drew up, his fists clenching. No one could have sneaked in to move these. It had been only a few moments that he'd been inside the small room.

God help me.

The irons and chains lay coiled like a steel serpent. Sam would have to step over them to get out. What would they do? What could they do?

Anything.

Who did this? What are you trying to tell me?

The irons lay still.

Were slaves hidden down here? Was someone hurt down here? Was someone lost or did someone die here?

There were no whispers, no sounds.

Tell me.

Nothing.

Sam touched the leg irons with his foot. They flopped over and lay still.

Tell me!

Nothing.

Sam held his breath. He lifted one foot and carried it over the leg irons. He planted his foot, looked back and brought his other leg over. The leg irons did not move. Sam's gut clenched. Keeping his eye on the iron restraints, he backed slowly down the length of the corridor. Once out, he braced his shoulder against the door to heave it shut. When he looked back into the hall, the leg irons were gone.

Fuck.

Where are they?

As quickly as he could, Sam shoved the door shut. His breath came out in long, jagged blasts.

He waited, his cheek against the wood, and listened.

There was nothing.

Don't play with my head! Show me what they mean!

Nothing.

Sam made his way upstairs. In spite of the drug, his right hand had begun to ache.

He stood in the hall, his head back slightly, listening, waiting. Nothing. He put his good hand on the wall and traced from back to front, beneath the hanging portraits, across the French doors to the foyer. The wall vibrated slightly beneath his touch, as if charged with static. Out in the foyer and on the front porch, there was nothing. Nicholas Abbadon welcomed men and women through this portal, but not escaped slaves. Slaves would not have passed here. They would have come in through the cellar.

And they would have stayed in the cellar until it was time to move on.

Right? There was no reason they would have gone any-where else at risk of discovery.

But there were disturbances all over the inn.

Sam moved into the reception room, where he'd been so many times. This time he focused his mind into emptiness. Unlike the hero in *Village of the Damned*, who envisioned a brick wall to keep the nightmare children's thoughts from breaking through, he saw in his mind a cloudless sky with no intrusive ground line. Walking the perimeter, trailing his hand, he saw the empty sky, waiting for something to fill it. A sound, sensation, smell.

He caught a whiff of the dead-smell as he reached the

door to the office, so he moved in and continued dragging his hand along the wall. Over and around the file boxes, past the door to the porte cochere where he hesitated but received no sensation, around to the two windows that overlooked the cellar's bulkhead and the backyard. The glass in the windows rippled to his touch, like water. He stared at it, then his focus shifted to the yard. The stand of briary bushes. The shed within the tangle.

A dark, shadowy figure appeared in the hole in the brush, a small dark shape hunched over yet seeming to float in place. This was the form he'd seen before, in the backyard. Sam's palm pressed against the window glass; he squinted, his heart pausing in midbeat as he gazed at the specter. He could see now, could make it out. A head, shoulders, a torso. But no features, just darkness, just a negative space where something had once been but no longer existed.

The shape spun and disappeared through the hole.

What was that?

Who was that?

There was a sudden loud crash upstairs. A distant, muffled voice cried, "Fire!"

Sam spun from the window. "What? No!" He stumbled from the office and out to the front hall, then darted up the staircase, two steps at a time. He heard men shouting and heavy, frantic footsteps. He reached the third-floor landing and nearly ran into one worker hurrying through the open door from the guest wing, carrying a paint-stained tarp. The man flung it across the hall in the direction of Sam's bedroom. "Smother it!" he shouted.

"No, wait, Andy's got it, we're okay, water's got it," said another man inside Sam's room.

Smoke crawled out of Sam's room through the top of the door and clung to the hall ceiling. The door itself was shattered and lying in chunks inside the room. The deadbolt lock dangled from a single loose nail. A third worker stood outside Sam's bedroom with a dripping bucket in his hand.

"Got it, it's out," said the man with the bucket. He looked back at Sam and shrugged. A thick puddle of water trailed from him, across the hall, to the bathroom.

Oh, shit, my stuff's burned up!

"This your room, buddy?" said the man who'd thrown the tarp.

"Yes. It is. Was."

The man in Sam's room shoved the bedroom window open and waved his hand, trying to chase the smoke outside. Sam went into the room. In the center of the floor was his rug, burned in half and soaking wet.

Damn.

The bedspread was scorched along the edge, but the bed itself looked to have suffered no major damage. Neither had the walls, the floor beyond the rug, the dresser, the nightstand. They were only streaked with soot.

"How'd you catch the fire?"

The man with the bucket said, "Oh, Ralph was takin' a dump in the bathroom down where we're working. He was takin' his sweet time, too. I had to go, said, 'Ralph, pinch it off and get outta there,' but he didn't. So I came on up here to this bathroom, and that's when I smelled smoke. I saw a little curlin' out from under the door. But there was that damned deadbolt lock! I keep a hatchet with me, for tappin' off stubborn bits of wood, so I got it, came back here with it and a bucket, and whacked at it hard. Danny and me pushed through the rest of the way. Seen the rug on fire. I was pretty rattled. But Danny doused it with water from the bathroom. Three bucketfuls did it. Then ole Ralph comes out of the bathroom and drags his tarp down here. But we had it put out."

"Yep," said Danny. "Had it put out."

"You're lucky we was up here," said the bucket-man. "Old as this place is, it could have been a goner in just a couple minutes."

The smoke continued to roll out the window. Sam said, "You guys take the rest of the day off."

"Nah, we can't. We're supposed to get all the windows in the third-floor guest wing today. Mrs. Morrison was adamant."

"Go. I'll have her call you when it's safe to come back to work."

"It was just a little fire, but it's over. And we can't go without Mrs. Morrison's permission."

"I'm in charge while she's gone. I'm telling you to go and wait until you get called again."

The men looked at each other uncertainly, corners of mouths hitched. "I don't know . . ." said Danny.

"I'll pay you for today," Sam said. "Cash."

"That's three hundred dollars."

"Each," chimed in Ralph.

Sam got his wallet from his dresser and counted out nine hundred dollars. With that gone, he had just under one hundred left to his name. It didn't matter. What mattered was getting these men out and away.

They collected their coats and were gone in five minutes.

Sam knocked on Carl's door. He was surprised when the boy answered, "What?"

"Come out here."

Carl opened the door but did not come out.

"Did you hear the men shout 'Fire'?"

Carl nodded.

"But you stayed in your room."

"Yep."

"Didn't you know the whole place could have gone up?"

"I knew someone would put it out. If they didn't, I would have. I'm not stupid enough to let the inn burn down. I live here, in case you forgot."

"You had something to do with it?"

Carl grinned. "I said you better believe me, or I'd show you what I could make happen."

Sam grabbed Carl by the shoulder. The boy twisted but Sam held on, his fingers digging into the flesh. He brought his face close to Carl's and could smell cookies on the boy's breath. "You're not responsible for what's going on here! It's something much more powerful than you can imagine. It's after me, no one else. I want you to leave the inn for a while. Go to the library. Don't come back until late this afternoon. You hear me?"

"I'm not going anywhere!" Carl squirmed under Sam's grasp. "I started that fire, not some stupid spirits! I'm the one you should be scared of!"

"Just shut up and get out!"

"No!"

Sam yanked the boy out into the hallway. Carl jerked free and punched Sam on his right hand, a solid blow that cut through Sam's wound like a laser. He cried out and went down. Carl clutched his hands together into a single fist and drove them down on the back of Sam's head. Sam bit the rough wood floor.

"Don't ever touch me!" Carl snarled. He slammed the door.

Sam pulled himself to his knees, his teeth clenched, his head spinning, and his hand screaming. He bit the inside of his cheek so he would not pass out. *God, oh, my God . . .* Slowly, he made it into his bedroom, through the puddled water, over the splintered door chunks and charred rug. Pills, he needed his pills. They were on the dresser. He reached up for them. His fingertips scraped at the bottle but could not catch it. He inched closer. His hand slid around the bottle but then pain and the smell of smoke grabbed him by the back of the neck and dragged him under.

TWENTY-NINE

Carl sat on his sleeping bag in a cross-legged position. He listened as Sam moved into his bedroom next door. Then, there was silence. His shoulder hurt where the man had squeezed him. *How dare he!* Carl would tell on him when his mother or father got home.

Inside the sleeping bag was the instrument of magic Carl had used to set the fire. Carl had tried humming, had tried visualizing the man's room and his prized possessions burning up, but it hadn't worked. Carl had to resort to another source of power.

He took the frayed extension cord out from the bag and whirled the ragged end around like a cowboy's rope. The 30-foot cord had been stolen from the workmen's supplies. Carl had used his folding knife to cut off the plug and strip the insulation back a couple of inches. He'd plugged the cord into an outlet in his room, then had run the cord out and down to Sam's door. Threading the cord through, he stopped when he felt it strike the soft fabric of the rug. Then he waited. He smelled the smoke before he saw it, then escaped to his room and listened to see if anyone would notice. If they hadn't, he would have gone to find Sam, to tell him of his latest magic stint, in time to save the rest of the third floor.

But the workers had been there, and it had been perfect.

Except that Sam still didn't believe Carl about the magic.

Except that Carl hadn't been able to do this magic on his own and had to use a damned extension cord. That sucked the most.

THIRTY

Sam was in a chilly field at night. Tall crops waved in the night breeze; cotton plants heavy with cotton balls. Overhead, stars saw him and shut their eyes. Sam was alone, but he could hear voices beyond the field, in the woods, down a dirt road. He rubbed his face, to awaken himself, but it did not work. Dressed in a cotton vest and dirty trousers, he took the dirt road in the direction of the voices. On both sides of the path, in the trees, early-autumn insects chirred.

He came to a slave quarter, the one he had dreamed of before. Fires had burned out. Heavy pots sat empty in the coals. The sounds of sleep rumbled from inside each cabin, drifting through the open windows. Sam lowered himself onto a rough-hewn bench outside a cabin door. He made a move to rub the wound in his right hand, but it was no longer cut. Raising the hand, he looked at it in wonder. It was healthy and whole.

"Sam?" came a hushed voice from inside the cabin.

He looked to see a thin woman in the threshold, beckoning him. He'd seen her before, weeping as her husband's back was flayed apart. Sam stood and went inside.

Roger lay on a straw mattress against the wall. He was curled up, facing away, his exposed back covered with thick, raised welts. Roger turned his head and looked at Sam, but he said nothing.

"Are you ready?" asked the woman softly.

Ready for what?

The little girl from his earlier dream appeared suddenly at his side and took hold of Sam's hand. Her beautiful face turned up to him. "Sam," she whispered. "Is it clear?"

Sam didn't know what she meant, but then he heard himself say, "Yes, Livey, dear. It is clear." And with his words he did know what was clear, and he was afraid.

The girl sighed. The woman put her hand over her face and wept silent tears. Roger sat up with great care and drew on his jacket and his worn shoes. Sam saw that his left hand was missing, cleaved away from his wrist, the stump tied with strips of cloth and held against his chest in a makeshift sling.

Roger, what happened to you?

Outside the cabin, sounds of night-creatures grew louder now, probing and prowling at the edges of the quarters. The woman and girl slipped their shawls about their shoulders. Roger stood, his eyes cold with determination. *It is up to me*, Sam thought. *That's what I'm here for, to lead them away to safety. To guide them to freedom.*

But where do I go? I don't know where that is!

Yet his feet seemed to know more than his mind.

"It's time," he said. "It's time to run."

And then they were, indeed, running. Sam in the lead, pounding over hilly rises, through knots of close-pressed trees, across stones in rushing streams, as the near-full moon shed its light on the scene.

I am Sam Ford, he thought in amazement as he tracked forward, northward, never once losing his footing on soft soil or beneath tangled roots. *I am my ancestor. I am a guide. I am leading these people to freedom. This is what he did, as Harriet Tubman did, and I never knew! He did the right thing at his own peril.* His heart swelled.

Sam glanced over his shoulder at the three fugitives struggling behind him. He slowed so they could catch up. The girl wheezed and coughed. The woman, holding the child's hand, was drenched in sweat. Roger remained upright, his head held proudly, his scarred chest pumping in and out, the stump at the end of his arm leaking orange through the bandage. Sam said quietly, "There are homes along the way, and barns, and churches. I know where they are. Just an hour to the first one, and we will sleep there."

Roger said, "Thank you for saving our lives."

"Thank you," said the girl.

"Thank you," said the woman.

Thank you, whispered the moon. Sam looked up. Creases in the moon had formed an ugly smile; spots winked like evil eyes. Sam's stomach lurched.

Thank you!

The moon's windy words taunted the people on the craggy woodland path. And then the moon laughed, howled loud and long, causing Sam to press his hands to his ears to hold back the sound. The moon ballooned and swelled like a yellow blister, swallowing the stars and the night until the sky was blindingly white. Sam heard Roger and the woman suddenly scream, but he could not see them in the light. He felt out into the whiteness, and they were not there.

Sam sat bolt upright.

He was in his room, on the floor. His heart pounded; his heart swam with fear, anger, and bitterness. Had Sam Ford not saved the young family along the way? Was this the agony he was supposed to understand? But, no, their names were in the guest book. They had made it to Cape May.

What, then, was the screaming?

Sam wiped his eyes; his hand came away with tears and sweat. He forced himself to his feet, though it took several minutes before his legs were steady beneath him. Blood hissed in the vessels behind his ears.

Then he saw the note on the floor. It was notebook paper, folded over and tucked in itself. The handwriting on the outside was Carl's. It read, simply, "Sam."

Snatching the note from the floor, Sam pulled it open. The message, in craggy black scribble, read, "I'll go to the library. I don't want to be here when you're being such a stupid asshole. I'll give you until five o'clock. And don't ever touch me again."

Carl was gone. Sam had the place to himself.

"Good," Sam breathed. "Good."

All around him, he felt the inn turn its attention to him. Entirely. Sam nodded. "All right, then," he said. A charge crawled through the walls and the floor. The hairs on Sam's arms stood at attention. He went into the guest wing to find the workman's hatchet. Then he went downstairs.

THIRTY-ONE

The air was riddled with mist, a salty, briny fog that had crept into the yard like a huge and ornery dog. It patted Sam's face and caressed the hatchet handle, leaving it slippery and damp. Sam stood before the spiny clot of brush in front of the shed, wrapped his fingers around the handle of the hatchet, and planted his feet apart slightly. The hatchet wobbled unsteadily but Sam forced his thoughts to keeping it secure.

Do it quickly and stay alert. You can't afford any more whacks to the head with a quince branch.

He gritted his teeth, took a breath, and then swung the hatchet as hard as he could against the branches. The impact jarred his body, and he grimaced. But the branch gave partway. Again, again he slammed the blade into the brush. Left right left right. He grunted with each effort and found added strength in the sound of his own voice. Many limbs bent with the blows then snapped back into their original positions. Others gave way with several hard chops to the joints. Sam moved in, snagging his shoulders, scraping his face, and continued to beat the barrier down and away. Several larger branches, though broken, would not give. Sam twisted them with his hand and snapped them off. Thorns gouged the fleshy meat on his palm. Slowly, the crawl space was opened.

With one bloodied hand and one worthless one, Sam forced his way through to the shed. He lifted the door's latch; the door swung inward.

His first impression was one of disappointment. He didn't know exactly what he'd expected, but it was more than a few busted antique pots, mouse dung, a crumbling fireplace, and stogie butts that Carl had stubbed out in the dirt and left scattered about. The dark shape, perhaps, ready to lunge at him? Or the leg irons waiting to slap themselves around his ankles?

Oh, God, no, not that.

But something of a revelation.

The slippery hatchet dropped from his hand to the floor with a soft thud. Sam stood, panting from his efforts.

Well?

Overhead, mud daubers had fashioned crude clay pipes along the shed's center beam. Cobwebs waved in the drafts from ill-sealed walls. Bent, rusted utensils hung from hooks inside the fireplace. Yes, it had been a detached kitchen, and amazingly had not been torn down nor renovated in perhaps one hundred twenty-five years. If this had been another reality, Sam would have brought with him a sketchbook, to take in the details of the carpentry, the masonry. If he'd had his class of students with him, they would have made their own rough blueprints by measuring the floors, pinpointing the location of the doors, the fireplace. They would have written creative stories based on who might have worked in this place, what they might have cooked, who might have partaken of the food prepared here.

But reality was no longer what it had been.

Sam stood, carefully rubbing the fingers of his bandaged hand.

And then the dead-smell came.

THIRTY-TWO

From behind the oak tree beside the porte cochere, Carl heard Sam go into the backyard and start whacking on the brush by the shed. He had waited until he knew the man was okay, had heard him stirring in his room, before going outside to hide. Sam needed to believe he was alone before he would feel free to go about whatever ghost-scouting expedition he had in mind. And so after Carl knew his tutor was awake, he'd gone out to the tree and had counted to six hundred. Ten minutes.

Then he sneaked back inside and went up to Sam's room, where the door had been blown open by the workmen when they put out the fire.

Carl expected Sam to rummage around on another floor, but the fact that he'd come outside was even better. He was back there, chopping brush with his left hand, a job that could take a long time.

Excellent! He's going to share with me whether he wants to or not! Ha!

Carl had his choice of weapons. The workers had gone with their money but had left their tools in the guest wing, as if expecting, perhaps, to come back to work later in the day if Rebecca gave them a call. Carl selected the small circular saw.

He plugged it in the outlet beside Sam's closet door. If he did it just right, it would look like something the workers did in their enthusiasm to check for stray sparks. Like they'd chopped this door, too.

Carl hurried across the hall to look out a back bedroom window first, to make sure Sam was still occupied. He was.

Down there, heaving and ho-ing, pausing to catch his breath, then going at the bushes with the hatchet again.

Then, Carl took out a chunk of the closet door with the saw.

There was nothing in the suitcases of any interest. Some condoms tucked into a little elastic side pocket, a spare toothbrush, and several quarters. But the rug-covered bag had intrigued him the most. Carl sat on Sam's bed with the bag in his lap and unlatched the clasp.

There was a wrinkled manila envelope in the bag. *Is that it?* Carl wondered. He'd hoped drugs, or a great stash of money, or maybe photos of Dani, naked. Carl took the envelope from the bag and opened it. Letters.

Boring.

And then he read the first few lines of the top letter.

He swallowed, hard. He looked up, around, and then back at the paper in his hands. His heart began to race.

Oh, my God . . .

THIRTY-THREE

Sam held the back of his hand to his nose and drew breath through his mouth. The dead-smell was stronger here than it had been anywhere else in the inn. The air shifted from cold to frigid. His breath was suddenly visible in filmy clouds. His nose began to run.

I'm here. I'm here for you.

The walls of the shed began to creak as if battered by a strong wind. In the old fireplace, dangling iron hooks swayed back and forth. Several mud-dauber nests cracked and dropped to the floor at Sam's feet.

I'm here.

Through the chinks in the walls, he heard the whisper. "Saaaaam."

Don't hurt me anymore. I'm Sam Ford. You know my name. I'm here to help.

"Saaaaaam!"

On the dirt, the hatchet began to dance in place, shivering back and forth like a water drop on a hotplate. *Shit!* Sam stomped on it with his foot, but it continued to struggle. He felt a rush of cold air and twisted his head around in time to see a dark form, small and hunched over, dash from the door into the fireplace. It had been fast, so fast, but he knew what it was. This time, he recognized it.

Jesus.

It was the silhouette of a young girl, bent down, terrified, and running for her life. Running from whom? Running to what?

"Livey? Is that you? What's wrong? Where are you going?

The inside of the fireplace began to bleed. Bright fresh

blood oozed from between the ancient soot-coated bricks and dribbled down along the creases in the mortar. The blood hissed, as if alive, as if daring him to stay back.

Sam lifted his foot and snatched up the hatchet. It squirmed in his hand.

"Stop it!" he shouted.

He shrugged from his sling and grabbed the handle with both hands. His right hand resisted, but he forced it to clamp as tightly around the hatchet as his left. He felt several stitches give way. The center of the soft cast went instantly red.

Sam walked toward the hearth, fighting the hatchet. His wounded hand screamed with the effort, and sweat stung his eyes.

With a roar, Sam forced the head of the hatchet against the brittle brick. Chips of brick and flecks of blood flew. He struck a second time, a third; more bits sprayed the air. Another blow. Another. Another. Larger chunks of masonry flew away, dropping to the blackened hearth.

The iron hooks in the fireplace shook where they hung, shivering as if trying to get free to fly at him. More bits of fireplace brick fell free and shattered on the floor.

Don't you know me? I'm Sam Ford!

And then Sam saw the edge of something behind a crumbled brick, something out of place. Something dreadful. The hatchet stopped squirming.

What is that? he thought, though he knew what he was seeing.

And he whispered, *"Who* is that?"

THIRTY-FOUR

The Oldsmobile engine's rumble was familiar, and Carl's ears picked it up a half-block away. The boy scrambled to the window in Sam's bedroom and clutched the sill, looking out.

Mitchell was home.

Good!

Carl bounded down the steps with the manila envelope and met his father at the front door.

"Carl?" inquired the man as he slipped off his coat and dropped it onto the coat tree. "You look like the cat that swallowed the canary." The man went into the Letters Lounge. Carl followed. Mitchell took a bottle of whiskey from behind the bar, tugged a glass from the rack, and then stared at his son.

"Aren't you in class?"

"Sam's got that hurt hand, so he can't teach me today."

"Well, can't he spend time with you? Where is he, anyway?"

"Cutting down the brush outside the shed in the backyard."

"He's good enough to cut brush but not to work on your lessons?"

Carl shrugged. Excitement thrummed his chest.

Mitchell poured a half-glass of drink. "I'm just home for a few minutes," he said, more to himself than his son. "I've got to pick up those forms Jack asked for. Didn't know he'd want them this soon, but it's his . . ."

Carl held out the folder to his father. "I found this."

"What? Is that mine? Were you in my office?"

"No. It's Sam's. It's something he didn't want you or me or Mom to see."

"Oh?" This clearly piqued Mitchell's interest, though he said, "Didn't we just have a family meeting about that kind of thing?"

"Yeah, but you need to see this, anyway."

Mitchell let out a breath. Then, "Let me have a look."

Carl passed the folder over and crossed his arms as his father put down his drink, pulled out the letters, and put them on the bar.

Mitchell picked up the first letter and leaned on his elbow on the bar. From his father's changing expression as he read, Carl knew that it didn't matter whether Sam believed Carl had power or not. This was going to change all that.

In a single sheet of paper, Carl possessed the power to make all sorts of changes.

THIRTY-FIVE

The hatchet went quiet and still in Sam's grasp, but he did not loosen his hold. The memory and the pain from the kitchen knife were far too fresh, and he had no idea what it might try to do. With the dulled blade he picked around the gray protuberance, knocking the sooty crumbs away. It was a small human shoulder bone.

Oh, Jesus.

As carefully as an archaeologist on a dig, Sam scraped at the brick, tearing clumps from the bone. His right hand cried out for him to stop, but he continued to chip. A knot formed in his throat, hard as a stone. His heart clenched.

"Is this you, Livey? How did this happen, sweet child?"

He chipped and picked, knocking more brick to the floor and revealing more bones—ribs, a smashed skull, vertebrae, another skull, larger than the first . . .

Another!

Sam looked down at the hearth, where the blood had run and was vanishing between the stones. He knelt and chipped at the stone, loosening one. He pulled it up and back. From the hard-packed earth there was the outline of broken hipbones and several scattered finger bones.

People who were loved and respected were buried in cemeteries. Those who were hated and despised—or murdered—were buried where no one would find them.

Runaway slaves, rescued by an abolitionist. Then, why despised? Why dead?

Sam stood again and looked at the bones in the wall behind the brick. Then he pulled at the shoulder bone, loosening it. It cracked in half; one part coming free in his grip, the other remaining embedded. He dropped the hatchet between his feet.

Sam clutched the bone to his chest. His vision began to swim, to flutter, and then blur, and he saw an image overlaying that of the fireplace before him.

It was of a barren room, empty of all furniture and carpeting, its windows shuttered tightly; a dim room at night, the sole light emanating from a lantern in the center of the floor. It painted the walls with a sickish, curdled glow. The room was familiar, though Sam's mind couldn't reason out where it was as other things quickly filtered into the picture. People against the walls. Chained there.

A man, a woman, and a girl. Naked, their hands bound by chains over their heads, their feet secured in leg irons and chains run through heavy iron rings in the floor.

Roger. His wife, Matilda. His daughter, Livey. The people Sam Ford had safely escorted to the Abbadon Inn.

Matilda and Livey wept, their shoulders and chests heaving mightily yet their voices almost inaudible. The woman's tears cut silvery paths down her breasts and stomach. The child's urine had collected in a puddle between her feet. They stared at each other as if the other was a lifeline to sanity, a protection against what was happening and what was to come. Roger stared at Sam, his eyes reflecting the dancing lantern glow, watching and waiting, defiant even in his vulnerable position.

Sam tried to move forward to the chained people, to find a lock, to set them free, but his legs would not move. He tried to speak, to tell them, "Wait, wait, I'm here for you! I don't know how this happened, but I will make it right!" but he had no voice.

To Sam's right, a deep voice hissed, "Now, what did you expect, really, you naïve creatures?"

Sam could not turn his head to see who stood beside him, to see who had spoken. Yet he could smell the man—the bourbon, the clove, the odor of rain-dampened wool. He had heard the voice before.

Roger lunged against his restraints, snarling, "We didn't 'spect this! No, by God, not this, you devil!"

The man next to Sam began to laugh. Low chuckles at first, then rising to a thundering belly laugh. On Sam's left, a woman began to giggle. He could smell her peppermint breath and strong perfume.

"Saaaaaaaaaam!" He heard the call from beyond this room of torment.

Who is calling me?

The vision broke and fell away like fragments of a fragile mirror, taking Roger and his family with it. The fireplace was before Sam again, its inner wall chopped to pieces. The bones in the wall and floor were there, stripped of their century-old disguise of brick, mortar, and stone. The iron hooks hung, suspended and motionless. Sam slipped the bone into his jacket pocket, then he heard the call from somewhere near the door.

"Saaaaam!"

Sam drew his wounded hand to his chest and pressed it hard, hoping to squeeze out the pain. He glanced down at the hatchet; it lay still as if waiting further instructions. Sam licked his lip and looked back at the shed door.

"Saaam!"

This voice was familiar, too.

"Sam!"

It was Mitchell Morrison, calling from the inn.

What the fuck does he want?

Sam rubbed his eyes free of the sweat and—tears?— and left the shed. He pushed through the ragged opening to the yard, tipping his head down to keep from snagging it on the thorns. Mitchell was at the open office window above the cellar bulkhead, leaning forward with his head pressed into the screen. It looked as though the man was frowning, though it was hard to tell with Mitchell, given his less than ebullient personality when not drinking.

"What is it?" Sam called back. Was the man pissed because he wasn't tutoring Carl? Well, he had an excuse, a good one, what with his crucified right hand. He should be granted at least a single sick day. And if Sam was able to understand the ghosts of the Abbadon Inn, and quell their fears and their anger and rid them from the place, Mitchell should not only give him some days off but a damn big bonus, too.

Not that Mitchell would ever know or even understand what was happening beneath his very feet and above his very head.

"We need to talk," said Mitchell.

Argh. Sam hated that expression. His father used to use it when he found out Sam had done something he shouldn't have. *We need to talk.* It left Sam instantly defensive, instantly on guard, without his own stick with which to protect himself.

Sam went into the inn through the porte cochere. Mitchell was no longer in the office. Sam walked through the reception room and into the front hall. Carl and Mitchell were seated at a table in the lounge. Carl had a shit-eating grin on his face.

"So your hand's better, is it?" asked Mitchell, noting Sam's missing sling. "Good enough to do some yard work?"

There was no explanation that would work. Sam said nothing.

"Good enough for yard work but not good enough to work with Carl on his science project?"

"Mitchell, you have no idea . . ." Sam began, but Mitchell held up his hand and said, "Oh, but I do!"

Carl put his hands over his mouth, clearly pleased.

"I do have an idea. I have more than an idea. I have the truth, and the truth wears an ugly, ugly face."

"What are you talking about?"

What Mitchell held up from behind his back made Sam's gut lurch.

Sweet Jesus, no . . .

"I won't even entertain the idea of a conversation about privacy, Sam. I won't listen to some pathetic attempt to put the blame on my son for looking through your papers, when there is a much greater ill at hand."

Fuck fuck fuck. Carl, I thought under all those layers of crap there was some hope for you! I'm screwed. I'm so fucking screwed.

"I have not had time to think about my next step," said Mitchell, putting the envelope on the table and steepling his hands over top it. "I've hired a pedophile to teach my son. So, in part, I suppose, there is some blame on my part. On Rebecca's part. But even if we might be seen as unsuspecting accessories before the fact, you, my friend, are the truly guilty party.

"Mitchell," began Sam, "at least hear me out. That letter is a bald-faced lie. The woman fabricated it all so I would leave the school and pay her money. I . . ."

"The guilty pay people off, Sam, not the innocent. You had legal recourses if you were taken advantage of, but here you are in Cape May, having left an abhorrent situation behind. Sounds like a guilt-driven exodus to me."

"There is more to it than you know, Mitchell . . ."

"I know enough!" Mitchell jumped to his feet, his chair flying backward, his face suddenly red and swollen in rage. He raised his fists, and Sam knew he would have struck him if the space between them had been smaller. "Enough! Get the hell out of my house! Get your fucking shit out of your room and get the hell out of my house! I don't know what I'll do next, but the first step is to have my son far from your filthy clutches, you goddamned son of a bitch! If I can find a reason to have you arrested, rest assured I will. But for now, you have exactly ten minutes to get your trash and your fucking, trashy self gone!"

Sam went upstairs, packed his things, and left the Abbadon Inn.

THIRTY-SIX

He walked to the library, feeling like a bum, hauling his
suitcases and carpetbag. His bad hand complained mightily beneath the weight of the small case, but what choice
did he have? Kick it up the walk? He tried to formulate
what he would say to Jeanette, but nothing came to mind.
His thoughts were too knotted to sort them out, too furious
to create a complete and coherent explanation.

I'm not finished at the inn.

Carl had been at the foot of the steps as Sam had come
down, suitcases and carpetbag in hand. He'd crammed
some of his books in the carpetbag but had left the rest so he
could carry it all in one trip. Fuck the books. He could get
more. Carl smiled at Sam, and handed him the envelope.

"Are my letters in there?" Sam had demanded.

"Yep. Mitchell doesn't know I'm giving them to you. I
think he wants to keep them."

The only thing Sam could think of to say was, "That
would be stealing." It sounded stupid and pointless, but he
said it anyway.

A new wind had kicked up, cold and fierce, batting
early spring buds and leaves about at the end of their
branches, tossing birds from tree to tree like feathered
beanbags, forcing Sam along the street at a quick clip.

The shoulder bone bounced and jabbed Sam's hip with
each step. It went hot to cold to hot. Sam didn't reach in to
touch it. He was afraid.

*I can't leave the inn like this. They need me. There is no
one else.*

A jogger passed by Sam on the sidewalk, trailing a
golden retriever on a leash. The dog's head snapped up and

back as she went by Sam, as if sensing what was in his pocket. The owner said, "Sandy!" and the dog's attention turned back to her owner and she picked up her pace.

A mother and two children were coming out of the library as Sam went in. They had to dodge Sam's luggage, and they gave him a quick but curious look. Inside, a clump of teenagers were gathered by the magazines, two old men were chatting quietly near the shelf of encyclopedias, and Jeanette was helping a middle-aged woman open a stuck card catalog drawer.

Sam put his cases beside the checkout desk and waited. Jeanette jiggled the drawer, gave it a tug, and it came free. She pulled a couple crumpled cards from deep inside. Shaking her head, she said to the woman, "Kids get in here, rip the cards out, and cause all kinds of trouble." Jeanette turned back toward the desk.

The expression on her face when she saw Sam was not what he'd expected. It was guarded and cool. She walked past him to the other side of the desk and folded her hands on the top. "What are you doing here?"

"I . . ." Sam began. "What's the matter? What's happened?"

She knows. How the hell does she know?

"I got a phone call from Carl Morrison a few minutes ago. He told me about his discovery and how his father has just . . ." her voice lowered as a patron came to the desk with a stack of books. "His father has just fired you for, well, you know. I didn't believe it, didn't want to believe it. But here you are. I see you have all your things with you."

Jeanette turned to the patron and stamped the books. Then she looked back at Sam. Her eyes were accusatory, her face tight with disgust and disappointment.

"Jeanette, it's all a huge mistake, a misunderstanding. Please, let's talk. Is there somewhere we can talk?"

"I don't want to talk you, Sam. I want you to leave."

"But you know me, you can't believe the lies."

"I don't know you, not really. We've spent, what, a day together?"

"Somewhere else, please? Give me the benefit of five minutes?"

Jeanette clenched her jaw but came out from the desk. Sam went outside. Jeanette followed.

She stood on the sidewalk with her arms crossed, the wind playing with her mid-length skirt. "Go ahead," she prompted.

"People react to things in their lives in many different ways. There are so many things I could have done differently."

Jeanette was not moved; her eyes remained cold.

So standing there in the frosty April wind, Sam told Jeanette the truth about Joy Spradlin and Jefferson Junior High School. It was the first time he had spoken the words aloud, and they were dreadful hanging on the air. He found himself breathing harder and faster as the rage came to the surface yet again. Jeanette listened, seeming not to even blink, and when Sam was done, said nothing.

"Do you believe me?"

"Why should I?"

Sam groaned, looked away, and shook his head. Why should she, indeed? Paying off Mama Spradlin seemed a sure sign of guilt, in spite of the racist bastard cousins and uncle who waited at the end of the legal line had he decided to fight the accusation.

"Fine," Sam said then. "Fine, Jeanette. You don't believe me. You don't have to. I was hoping you would understand, but you don't, so there we are." He stalked into the library, collected his cases, and walked back out again. Jeanette hadn't moved, though her face was not as hard. Maybe she was truly giving it some thought.

Sam paused, "I've made some bad mistakes in my life. I've been weak, and I've been stupid. But I've never, ever taken advantage of a child. I've never, ever been inappropriate with a student, or an adult for that matter. I know that. I wish you did. But you don't."

He tightened his hands—both good and bad—around the grips of the suitcases and carpetbag. The Surf 'n' Sand Motor Hotel was a good twelve blocks away. He had some walking to do.

THIRTY-SEVEN

Carl paced the floors of the inn, alternately clasping his hands in victory and pausing nervously to listen to the faint, unnerving sounds around him. Within the last hour, since Sam had been banished from the Abbadon, something had been growing, brewing, within the building. The windows rattled, then went still. The floor rippled beneath his feet, then lay flat. He thought he could hear furious voices, whispering, growling, somewhere deep in the walls.

It was as if the place was enraged that Sam was gone.

"That's impossible," Carl said to himself. He stood at the bottom of the stairs to the third floor, looking down the hall toward the room over the porte cochere. The door to the room was closed, but a soft pounding came from inside. "Sam has nothing to do with it. It's all my doing. My power is coming to full force. I created all this." The hairs on Carl's arms prickled. The skin on his knees jumped up and down.

"I'm home!" It was Rebecca in the front hall, home from her shopping. Carl went to the head of the stairs. He watched his mother, the lower half of her body, actually, as she took off her coat and scarf then dragged them away into the Letters Lounge. "Mitchell? Where are you? Carl?"

Mitchell was in the kitchen. He'd had a drink in the bar, then had gone off to find a snack. The man had debated calling the police on Sam, then admitted to his son there was nothing he could have Sam arrested for. "But he'll get his, oh, he'll get his."

As Mitchell had fumbled back and forth in the kitchen, slamming cabinets and drawers, Carl had wandered the inn, savoring his newly found freedom and the power he had exerted over his teacher.

And feeling uncomfortable, uneasy.

Carl tiptoed down the main stairs and into the Letters Lounge to listen to his parents' conversation. Most of the words between them were too soft to decipher, but Rebecca did say loudly, "Oh, no!" and "Oh, dear!" Mitchell's voice was deep and dark; Rebecca's high-pitched, pinched. They continued to talk until Rebecca cried she was too upset and needed to lie down, to think. On hearing this, Carl spun about and raced up to the third floor. He hid in the bathroom and waited. His mother came all the way to the top floor, calling, "Carl?" There was a pause, then, "What in heaven's name happened? Carl? Are you up here?" Then, to herself, "Did Sam set his room on fire when Mitchell fired him? Fire for fire?" It sounded as if she were starting to cry.

Carl eased into the tub and pulled the shower curtain around on the rings, quietly, hoping his mother would not decide to come in to find him.

The door to the guest wing opened with a clunk. Rebecca called, "Hello?" Then, "Damn it, where are my workers?" Rebecca rarely if ever cussed, and when she did it was "hell's bells." She was upset, and in a big way. "It's not time for them to be off! Carl? Carl!" She stomped back downstairs. Carl let out the breath he'd been holding.

He suddenly was aware that his sneakers were wet. Looking down, he expected to find puddles collected from Sam's morning bath.

But his feet were bathed in blood.

Carl leapt from the tub, clasping the curtain, his foot catching on the tub's lipped edge. He tumbled forward and struck the tiled floor with his shoulder. "Shit shit shit shit!" he wailed. He smacked at his feet as if they were aliens there to chew him alive.

But he saw that his feet were only wet. They were not red, not slicked in blood. Carl peered in over the rim of the tub. There were puddles in the tub, stained light brown with the dirt from the bottom of his shoes.

"Damn," Carl said, breathing hard, "I'm so stupid." He

rubbed snot from his nose and wiggled his shoulder. It didn't hurt too much.

In Sam's uncleaned room, Carl sat on the bed, legs crossed. His mother had collected the burned rug, he guessed, because it was gone, dragged away out the door, trailing sodden ash. Carl lay down on Sam's pillow. He wondered where Sam was going to sleep that night. Maybe he'd get a hotel. Maybe he'd catch a bus back to Virginia.

Ha.

Carl had shown him. The place was all his now.

He rubbed his fingers across the strip of hair on his head. Maybe he'd shave it down to nothing, make himself bald like a genie. Genies had lots of power, too.

No more lessons, no more books, no more teacher's dirty looks.

No more chess in the afternoon. No more trips to see stuff. No more joking with Sam, making him irritated, making him smile.

Carl looked at the ceiling. There was a shadow there, looking like an enormous spider. When Carl blinked, the shadow had moved a foot across the ceiling. *What?* He squinted, hard, and looked up again. The shadow was now in the corner between the wall and the ceiling, the dark extensions that resembled legs probing as if looking for the best path down to the floor. Carl abruptly sat up and stared at the spider-shadow. He glanced at the window, to see if something on the glass was casting such an eerie shape. There was nothing on the glass. He looked back. The spider-shadow was larger now, and halfway down the wall.

Jumping from the bed, Carl cried out, "Get away from me!" He inched from the bed toward the doorway, and the spider-shadow slid easily to the floor and felt its way up and over the boards of Sam's shattered door.

Carl raced through the door, imagining the spider tossing a dragline at him and pulling him down. To kill. To devour him.

No!

He reached the top of the steps and looked back. There was no length of silk flying out toward him, no spider-shadow in the doorway. Carl's heart rammed against his ribs, his breath hot over his tongue. He waited. He waited.

Nothing came out of the room.

"Okay," he said. "That's enough of this. I'm going to put it all back where it came from. It's coming back into me." Carl caught his lips between his teeth, closed his eyes, and leaned his head back.

Nnnnnnnnnn. Pull it together. Bring the energy back into me. I'm in charge, I'm in control. Man power. Blood power. Indian power. Yang power. Focus on the task at hand, focus on bringing it all back into me to use later when I choose.

"Nnnnnnnnnnn."

The floor beneath Carl shifted, like an elephant moving its weight from one foot to another. Carl opened his eyes slightly and put his hand out on the banister. "Nnnnnnnnn!" he hummed angrily.

The floor rippled again, and Carl nearly lost his footing. He grabbed the banister with both hands.

"I said stop it!" he screeched.

From the second floor Rebecca called, "Carl, is that you?"

The floor went still. Carl held the railing, waiting. *I'm in charge, I can make this stop!*

"Carl?"

"Yeah." He tried to make his voice sound even, calm. It didn't work very well. "It's me."

"What happened up in Sam's room?" It sounded like his mother was down in her bedroom, in her doorway.

"I think he was smoking. The workers put it out."

"Oh, well. Another good reason he's gone. Where are the workers?"

"Sam sent them home after the fire."

"He had no right!"

"I know."

"A third good reason he's gone!"

"Yeah."

"I'm going to take a nap. The day's been too much. Tell your father I'm napping."

"Okay."

The bedroom door clicked shut.

Carl stood still for a moment. The floor did not move.

"There you go, you know who's in charge," Carl said, making himself smile, though he didn't feel it. Then he started down the stairs.

Halfway down there was an airy whistle, and something lashed up between the balusters, slamming his left leg and winding itself around his ankle like a cold, ragged snake. It happened so fast Carl could not make out what it was; he gasped, stumbled, and fell down the remaining steps. Crashing to his side, he groaned, then screeched and scrambled into a sitting position. *What was that? Oh, God!*

He stared. Around his ankle, looped like the ropes of a bolo, was a pair of leg irons and chains. There was flesh embedded in the chain links, and the manacles were greasy with blood.

"Aah!" Carl cried, and shook his foot as hard as he could. The chains loosened and fell away. Carl jumped up and ran down the remaining flight of stairs. He heard his mother calling, "Carl, keep quiet! I need to rest!"

THIRTY-EIGHT

Twenty-two dollars. That was the cost for a single at the Surf 'n' Sand. Sam tugged his large suitcase and carpetbag into the room and threw them onto the bed. He'd ditched the small suitcase into a Dumpster along some alley; his right hand had refused to cooperate any longer. It didn't matter. There were only clothes in it. Thank God he'd brought his pills. He sat on the chair by the window and downed three of them. He had just enough money left for a dinner and a bus ticket to somewhere. But where? Sam's body was cold, colder inside than out.

He pulled back the sticky curtain and watched cars pass by on Lafayette, their headlights cutting the early-evening gloom. A family pulled up to the parking slot next to Sam's empty slot, and piled out of their station wagon. A father, mother, two little boys. They went into the room beside Sam, and he heard them laughing and talking. Their television went on. News, by the sound of it, then it changed quickly to something with a laugh track. Sam flexed his fists, then reached into his jacket pocket and touched the bone. The room began to waver around him, and he pulled his hand back out.

There was a phone on the nightstand. Sam dialed Geary's number. It rang twelve times. Thirteen. Fourteen. Fifteen. *Geary, be home! I need to talk to somebody!* Geary wasn't home. Sam slammed the receiver down then paced back and forth from bed to window.

I can't leave the business unfinished. I can't leave those tormented spirits in hell.

Next door, through the wall, "Stop bouncing on the bed, honey."

I have to go back.

Sam thought of calling Mitchell Morrison, and trying to explain what he'd learned about the inn, about the spirits, the murders of the runaways. But Mitchell would hang up. There was no way he'd give Sam even a minute's time.

I can't go back.

He dialed the library. Jeanette answered. He hung up.

"Goddamn it all!" Sam snatched the lamp from the nightstand and hurled it at the wall. It shattered and crashed to the floor. A kid next door said, "Mom, what was that?"

"Shhh, Vincent. Probably just an accident."

THIRTY-NINE

In the reception room, Mitchell was smoking and reading a newspaper, kicking back in one of the easy chairs. A floor lamp offered cool yellow light to the pages. Carl stood in the doorway, looking at his father. *Look at me*, he thought. His father didn't look. *Nnnnnnnn, look at me!* His father didn't look.

"Hey," said Carl. Mitchell looked up.

Trying to keep his voice steady, Carl said, "Did you feel something a couple minutes ago? Like the inn was shaking kind of? I dunno, like an earthquake?"

Mitchell frowned, blew out a long coil of smoke. "I don't think so. Why?"

"Nothing."

Mitchell went back to his reading.

"I tripped on the steps. Something got me around the ankle and tripped me."

Mitchell didn't look up. "Oh? You all right?"

"I think my leg's gonna have a bruise."

"Be careful from now on."

"It could of broke."

"Those steps can be slick."

Carl stood until Mitchell turned the page. Clenching his jaws, he crossed the hall to the lounge, clicked the TV on and clicked it off. He sat at one of the tables but drew his feet up into the chair. He didn't want anything else snatching at him. His ankle hurt; his shoulder hurt. His stomach was tight. Why did those chains come after him? How did that happen?

Because you sent the power out and haven't brought it

back. It's running wild like a bunch of fucking dogs without a trainer.

The thought clawed at Carl's mind. The hairs on his legs and arms stood straight out against his shirt and jeans like little, useless sentinels, like the fur on the back of a frightened kitten. Carl hated it and tried to rub it down.

He put his forehead on the tabletop and briefly thought how it might have been cool after all to do the science project Sam had assigned. It didn't have to be magic. It could have been training mice to smoke cigars. Whatever, it would have been better than those public-school kids' projects. Sam would have made sure Carl did it right. Maybe Carl would have gotten a prize at the fair. Carl had never won a prize before.

And Sam never molested anyone before.

"I know he didn't," Carl said into the table.

The minute he'd read the letters in the rug-bag he'd doubted it was true, though the discovery was too good not to use as revenge. The minute Sam denied it in front of Carl and Mitchell, Carl knew Sam was telling the truth. The woman who'd written the letters blackmailed Sam out of money. People did that kind of stuff sometimes, making innocent people look guilty. Carl had seen enough TV shows to know how that happened.

And because of Carl, Sam had been banished from the Abbadon Inn. His parents would never let him come back again. Mitchell said he was going to tell his friends that there was a pedophile in town and to beware and not to hire him for anything.

Sam wasn't such a bad guy.

But he didn't believe you. He didn't trust you.

He wanted to, though. And he knew about the weird stuff here. He was one person who knew.

Carl put his feet up on the chair on the other side of the table and gave it a shove. It scooted back several feet and fell over. From across the hall, Mitchell said, "Don't be breaking your mother's furniture, Carl."

Carl tucked his legs back up and shook his foot. Faster, faster. It felt good, like shaking off the scary feeling. But then the chair was shaking beneath him. He stopped his foot. The chair kept on. Carl hopped from the chair. The room, itself, had begun to tremble. The glasses hanging in the ceiling rack clinked in place.

Stop it, stop it! I'm the master! I'm the magic man! Stop it now! Nnnnnnnnnn! Nnnnnnnnnnnn!

The room shook another few seconds, then went still.

"Did you feel that?" Carl called to his father.

There was a pause, and to Carl's surprise his father said, "Yes. That was odd. Maybe Cape May is on a small fault line."

Carl went into the hall and swung on the reception room doorsill. "You really did feel that?" *That was me, Mitchell, that was my power! Look at me! I'm strong!*

"Yes," said Mitchell. "But I'm sure it's nothing. Don't go Nervous Nelly on me. I've got enough to think about with liquor licenses, your current lack of schooling, and your mother bouncing checks."

Carl looked at his father. He looked up the stairs. He thought he heard a clinking of iron up there, but then it was silent.

"Go do something. Read a book, why don't you?" said Mitchell.

Carl bristled. He strode to the fireplace, grabbed the poker, and went back to the front hallway.

"What on earth is that for?" asked Mitchell.

"Mice," said Carl, and as he cautiously yet defiantly crept up toward the second floor, he heard his father chuckle.

FORTY

"I am the one in charge," Carl said to the candles on the floor. "I have called out the power, and I will bring it back again, back into myself, out of the inn. I wish it so. I will it so. It shall be done. Nnnnnnnnnn."

The candles were arranged in a triangle. Carl sat in the center, on the floor. Sam had tried this once, to get rid of Carl's scary power. Carl had found the candles in Sam's dresser drawer. Fire was power, as was chanting and humming and bleeding. He had taken off his shirt and had picked the scabs from his previous cuttings. He squeezed his forearms and the backs of his wrists. The red zigzagged down.

Yes, Carl was powerful. And his power had started to scare the shit out of him.

"I call you back into myself until I need you again. Obey me."

He paused and listened. He heard nothing in his room or outside. That was good. No rumbling, no booming, no chains clinking. He did not know where the leg irons had gone. Maybe his mother had picked them up and thrown them away.

Or maybe they were just outside his closed door, waiting for him.

New sweat broke out on his face and bare chest, and he squeezed his cuts harder. "Blood power. Man power. Back inside me, now!"

If I told Sam about the leg irons, I bet he would believe me. He wouldn't know why or how they attacked me, but he would believe it happened. I wish Sam was here.

Carl held still then, his hands upturned on his crossed

legs, waiting to feel it pour back into him like his blood poured out.

Waiting.

He heard a sound. He opened his eyes to see a shadow of a spider on the wall, feeling its way down to the floor. Its substanceless legs clicked audibly on the plaster.

The window began to rattle in its frame, then opened itself, held, and slammed back shut. It opened again and slammed shut.

Carl scrambled up. "Stop it! Obey me!" His heart beat so hard he could barely catch his breath. His legs shook as if trying to toss his body off. He fell toward the door, but the knob was slippery and would not turn in his grasp.

He heard a whisper from out in the hall. Close, quiet. "Saaaam."

"Sam?" Carl repeated, incredulous. "Why Sam?"

"Saaaaaaaaaaam." The hot voice poured under the closed door and wrapped itself around Carl in a foul and stinking blanket. Carl jerked the doorknob, but the door would not open. He glanced at the wall. The spider-shadow had reached the floor and was coming his way.

No no no no no no!

He shook the doorknob and kicked back with his foot. *Stay away from me! No!* The window opened and slammed shut, opened, slammed shut. The spider-shadow crawled closer, tapping its translucent legs, reaching for him.

Carl screamed. He yanked the doorknob, twisted, turned, pulled. The door gave way and opened. Carl nearly fell backward into the spider-shadow. He scrambled up and ran across the hall to the bathroom. He slammed the door shut and threw himself against the door, his lungs heaving like bellows. "Mom! Dad! Help me!"

The bathroom door began to rattle on its hinges. The bathroom window opened and slammed shut. A dead-smell seeped beneath the door and rose in an ashy cloud.

Carl spun toward the mirror and stared at himself. His face was like a melted clown's mask, his eyes huge and wet. This was how he would look at the moment of his death. His power was going to kill him. He had done this to himself.

The mirror began to bow back and forth, and suddenly it
flew apart in great and tiny shards. Carl ducked, and
chunks bit into his scalp. "Mom!" Pieces landed in the
sink, on the floor, in the tub.

Carl pounded his face with his fists. "Stupid stupid stupid!" he cried. He looked down at two large mirror shards
on the floor. His own fractured reflection did not look back
at him. There was another face in the shards. A black man
with large eyes and scars on his cheeks and neck. In both
pieces, in unison, the black man opened his mouth to reveal yellowed teeth and a bloody tongue. He hissed,
"Saaaaaaaaaaaaaaaaaaam!"

"God help me! Mom!" Carl kicked the shards and sent
them sliding against the toilet. "No more magic! No more
no more no more!"

There was only one way to stop it.

Wiping mucus from his nose, Carl grit his chattering
teeth and pulled open the bathroom door. The spider-
shadow was not there, but the light fixtures on the walls rattled and sputtered. Carl hurried to his room and peeped in.
There was no spider, no leg irons. The windows were still,
though two of the candles had been blown out by the air the
windows had stirred. Carl scooped up his magic books and
the burning candle, then returned to the bathroom. Keeping
his eyes averted from the bits of broken mirror, he knelt
and dumped his books in the tub. He held the flame to the
edge of the *You Shall* book. The corner smoked and then
caught fire. Carl lit the others, and watched as they smol-
dered, then went up in a beautiful, roiling blaze.

*Yes, yes! Fire purifies. Fire will stop it! Fire will put it
down, make it go away.*

When only clumps of ash remained, Carl washed it
down the drain. It was done.

No more magic.

"No more magic," he panted.

The inn was safe once more.

FORTY-ONE

Rebecca lay on her bed, shoes off and slouch socks on, picking at dry skin on the back of her knuckles. She had let a child molester in her home. She'd called only one reference and had believed the man on the other end of the line. Sam had come waltzing into her home and had taken her son under his wing. Had he done something to Carl? According to Mitchell, no, but Carl was such a careful, calculating liar. Would Carl try to protect Sam, even after revealing the letters that condemned him?

The day had started out fine and had gone quickly downhill. She hadn't found any rugs she'd liked for the guest-wing rooms. She'd bounced a couple checks, and Mitchell had caught the notices in the mail before she had.

Sam was found to be a child molester. And the inn had shaken a little while ago as if it was sitting on some kind of sinkhole.

Wouldn't that just be the icing on the cake? she thought. *All my dreams sitting on a sinkhole?*

She wiped moisture from the corners of her eyes.

I should be fixing dinner. It's nearly seven-thirty. But I can't think about cooking.

Rebecca dragged herself from her bed and opened the door. She listened. She'd thought she'd heard Carl call her, but now there was no sound other than the ticking of the clock on the bedroom wall behind her. She shut the door and went back to the bed.

They'll have to fix something on their own. There are leftovers from last night. They'll be all right.

She lay down and ran her fingers through her hair.

You need to pull it together, Rebecca. Practice what

you've been learning. Meditation. Relaxation. Concentration.

Rebecca rolled onto her back and put her arms up so that her palms were flat against the engraved metal plate on the headboard. Then she stretched her legs out, toes pointing. The mattress was a good one, firm, and it helped her back and bones. Mitchell didn't like it, though. He said it felt like sleeping on an old park bench.

Rebecca closed her eyes and visualized her body floating peacefully on a still-yet-solid sea. She focused her thoughts on clouds and sun and a soft sound of waves. Everything was all right, everything was fine. She just had to let it go and let it flow.

Her feet reached farther down the mattress, feeling for the footboard. She'd not been able to extend her body that far yet, but elongating her spine felt great. If she could just touch her toe to one of the slats there, she believed she would have reached perfect position, perfect posture for her tiring body.

One toe brushed a wooden slat. Yes, okay, keep it there. She hunkered down her hips, and reached out with her toes again. Her big toe on her left foot connected with a wooden slat and stayed. Now the other foot. *Reach, reach!*

Her left toes touched one of the iron slats. *Yes, that's* . . .

A powerful electric current surged from the metal headboard, through Rebecca's instantly rigid body, and out through the iron slat. She did not even have time to wonder what was happening before her finger tips went black, her back arched, her jaw locked, her curly and clipped hair started to smoke, and her dead eyes were forced from their sockets with an ozone-charged pop.

FORTY-TWO

〰️⤙⟡⤚〰️

"Hey," said Carl. He'd found his father in the kitchen, making something that might have been supper. A slab of meat on bread, sprinkled with Parmesan cheese and surrounded by Fritos and raisins. A bottle of beer, dripping sweat, sat by the plate. Mitchell obviously didn't have a get-together that night, for some reason or other.

"It's supposed to sleet tonight," Mitchell said, glancing up at his son as if he'd read the question in Carl's mind. He opened the utensil drawer and rattled around, then brought out a small knife to cut the sandwich. "Some of the guys didn't think we should get together for poker." *So that's what you do at night,* thought Carl. *I really didn't know.* "Old farts, afraid to drive in the ice. They need to move up to Danbury for a while, see what hazardous driving conditions really are. Huh."

Mitchell slapped the knife through the sandwich. "Your mother still napping?"

"I guess."

"What do you want for supper?"

"Pancakes."

"Don't be silly. What do you want?"

"I'm not hungry."

"Are you sure? We're on our own tonight. I don't want to bother your mother. I think she needs space right now." Mitchell sat at the table by the window. Carl went to the fridge for a can of Pepsi.

"What's that on your hands?" asked Mitchell. Carl turned his hands over. He'd not cleaned off all the soot from the burned books. "And what is that smell, smoke? Have you been into my cigars? I've been missing a few."

"Does this smell like expensive cigar smoke to you?"

"Don't get smart with me."

"I think Sam was taking them. I mean, he did set his rug on fire, remember?"

"Probably," said Mitchell. "But you do smell like smoke. Have you been burning something? Are you playing with fire again like you did back in Danbury?"

"I never *played* with fire. I just made it burn."

"Are you making something burn today?"

"No."

"Because this place would go up in a flash as old as it is."

"I'm not so stupid to burn my own house down."

Mitchell considered this. He took a bite of his sandwich. Carl popped the tab on his can and leaned against the fridge. He took a long swig. Overhead, the ceiling light flickered, hummed, and then returned to normal. Carl flinched and looked up.

"Wonder what that was?" asked Mitchell. "We paid the electricians enough to have state-of-the-art wiring, I can tell you that much."

Carl said, "Well, it wasn't me." *No, it's just wiring that isn't state-of-the-art.*

"What do you mean it wasn't you?"

Carl's lip hitched in a sour smile. "I mean what I say. It's not me and won't be until I get it figured out better, when I get it under control better. And when I do, you'll be the first to know, believe me."

"What are you talking about?"

"It doesn't matter, now," said Carl. He took another long sip. *It won't matter again until I'm ready. But I will be. I'll take my time and make sure I know what the hell I'm doing.*

Mitchell finished his meal in silence while Carl finished his Pepsi. Mitchell took his plate to the sink and rinsed it off and stuck it in the dishwasher. "I think I'll go see how your mom's feeling," he said. "Then I'm going to do some work in my office up there. You need anything?"

"You want to play chess before you go up? A quick game?

"Chess is never quick, Carl. Anything else?"

"I'll watch TV."

The man nodded and left the kitchen.

Carl looked for a bag of cookies, but there were none. His mother hadn't grocery-shopped today. That would be tomorrow. He took the bag of Fritos into the lounge and turned on the TV set. He sat at one of the tables, wishing they had a sofa here like they did at their house in Connecticut. It was more fun to lie down and watch television.

He listened as his father walked the hall upstairs, first flushing the communal toilet—probably so as not to wake Rebecca in their room—then into his office at the front of the inn. Carl punched the remote control and the stations clicked three to six to twelve then back to three. Faces blurred by; clips of voices and song, a couple holding hands, cowboys on horses, a commercial for soup.

Carl was still on edge. Yes, the books were gone, their influence changed to carbon and washed away. He had chanted his last chant for a long time. But as he watched the people and the horses and the soup click one to another, around and around and around he thought of the leg irons catching his ankle. He thought of the spider-shadow crawling after him. The slamming windows. The black man's face in the mirror shards. If he'd not stopped it then, what would have happened? What could have happened?

Why were they calling for Sam?

Carl stopped scrolling on the soup commercial, which ended and went to Sammy Davis, Jr., singing about Alka Seltzer. *Oh, what a relief it is . . .*

Upstairs, Mitchell continued to prowl the second floor. Then at last Carl heard their bedroom door open and close.

Sammy Davis grinned at the camera. The commercial faded and a movie came on. Some comedy. It didn't look funny, but the music that blared forth insisted it was.

Carl picked up the remote again.

And then he heard his father upstairs, through the closed door.

"Oh, God no! God no no no! Please no!"

FORTY-THREE

Sam got a burger from the joint next-door to the motel, and he sat at one of the tables beneath the irritatingly bright lights and picked the seeds off the top of the bun. A pair of teenagers sat at the booth behind him, bouncing up and down on the seat, laughing, and tossing French fries.

He pulled a loose flap of beef from outside the bun and put it on his tongue. It was as though he'd forgotten how to chew. The meat just sat there. He spit it out.

Now what do I do?

He'd been asking himself that question the past two hours. He would stop himself, tell himself to get a grip, get something to eat, get a good night's sleep, and *then* ask it again. But the question wouldn't let him be.

I have no money. No job. No reputation beyond that of a criminal, both in Virginia and New Jersey.

The teenaged girl bounced again, causing Sam's seat to likewise bounce, and said, "Get me a milk shake, Michael. I'm still hungry."

"I don't have any more money, Tina. Get your own milk shake."

"I thought this was a date," Tina whined. "I'm still hungry."

"Well, I have to get gas and that's going to take the rest of what I got. Don't you have a couple dollars with you?"

"Yeah, but this is a date," said Tina. "And I'm still hungry."

Sam got up from his booth, gathered his uneaten burger in its little paper wrap, and slapped it down on the tabletop between Tina and her boyfriend. "Here," he said. "It's not a milk shake, but it's free. Enjoy." He stalked out of the restaurant, with shouts from the boyfriend. "Hey, who do you think you are? What's this all about? Get back here and get this off our table!"

It was sleeting. Cold, hard pellets bounced off Sam's head, shoulders, and the sidewalk. The ground was slick, and most of the cars on the road were taking it easy. Their headlights cut through the icy rain; their tires crunched along the tarmac. Some squealed as they came to abrupt stops at the light up the way. Sam shoved his right hand into his pocket. Yet again, he'd left his hat at the motel.

Slowly he lowered his left hand into his pocket, and his fingers grazed the bone. He felt the electric spark and yanked his hand out again. He turned his face to the sleet and let it cut his cheeks.

It had just started to rain when the boys came up in the trucks. It was a warm rain, though, a summer rain, and Sam and Rose had laughed about who would carry a soggy bag of groceries back home. The truck tires didn't squeal because the damp road was dirt, and tires didn't squeal on dirt. Rose squealed, though, in terror, after the boys had knocked Sam down with a bat and snatched her up in their arms. The only thing he saw of her after that was her decomposing body in the river. He'd heard a body had been found, and he'd gotten there soon after the police. Her head and shoulders were submerged in the river, the meat chewed away by fish, crayfish, turtles. He remembered how white the bones of a black girl were. Bones, he thought, should be the same color as the skin. Black, brown, tan, yellow, white.

He hadn't helped Rose.

He had been left with just bones. Bones and dreadful, unanswered questions.

Not this time, he thought. He wiped sleet from his face and turned southeast. Screw the hat, he didn't need it. Anger would keep him warm, determination would stop the cold. *Not Mitchell nor rednecks nor Carl nor baseball bats nor vengeful spirits are going to stop me this time. Fuck 'em all.*

"Fuck 'em all!" he shouted to the traffic and the sleet as he picked up the pace on the slippery, glistening concrete.

FORTY-FOUR

Mitchell had gone insane. He'd been angry before, and drunk, but he was now insane. Carl sat against the papered wall as his father banged up and down the Oriental runner in the second-floor hallway, tearing at his hair and swearing.

Carl had peeked in at his mother, once. Once was enough. She looked like a mannequin, her arms up over her head, her legs stretched out long, the fingers and toes charred like hotdogs dropped in a campfire, her nose, ears, and elbows blistered and torn. Her eyes resting on her cheekbones.

He'd stared, not certain at first if he was even seeing his mother, then knowing he was and dry-heaving in the doorway. Carl had turned back away, and had slid to the floor, his hands clutching his head.

"They're going to pay, God, yes, they're going to pay!" Mitchell stormed past Carl to the end of the hall, his lips rolled back and exposing his old man's teeth, his eyes wide and wild. He wasn't talking to Carl, he was just talking. Summing it up as if giving a closing statement in front of a judge. "One can't do this and think it will be ignored or forgotten. No! These electricians put in faulty wiring, they carelessly, with forethought and malice, chose cheap, shoddy wires and fixtures, with desire only for profit and expediency, they not only put the lives of my family in danger, they killed my wife! What will I do without Rebecca?"

Carl couldn't blink. His eyes were stretched open, fused almost as if he, too, had been electrocuted. Rebecca was dead. Rebecca was gone.

I didn't stop the power. It is still running wild.
I killed my mother!

"They will pay, they must pay." Mitchell stopped to wipe his nose. Was he crying? It was hard to tell, his red face was squished and puffy. He started talking again. "A life, of course, cannot be measured in money, but there must be justice. There has to be a balancing out in some manner or other."

Carl thought they should call somebody. Who came for dead people? He didn't want his mother lying in there forever. Or even for a couple more hours. He'd tried to say something to his father, but his father brushed him off, almost slapped him, and said, "Carl, I have to think! Leave me alone!"

And so Carl did. He stayed on the floor beside his parents' bedroom door and thought, *This is my fault. My mother is dead.*

Mitchell's footsteps were heavy in the hall, and the floor bounced as he walked back and forth. It hammered Carl's teeth and shook his bones. *Thump thump thump thump.* Carl shoved his fingertips into his mouth and bit them so he would not scream.

Stop it, Mitchell! You're making me sick!

Mitchell reached the end of the hall, then stormed back again, his head swiveling side to side, repeating, "Yes, they'll pay. I'll squeeze every drop of value from their goddamned company, and they'll pay!" Mitchell reached the bedroom. He stopped to stare in at his dead wife.

But the hall continued to shake. *Thump thump thump.*

"Oh, God," sobbed Mitchell.

"Stop it!" cried Carl. He struggled upward, made it to the staircase, and ran down and away from the nightmare and from his dead mother.

But the front hall downstairs was also vibrating like a dog in the cold. The portraits Rebecca had hung on the wall clacked back and forth on their nails. In the Letters Lounge, glasses tinkled in the ceiling rack. Carl heard the television give way and fall from its brackets.

He grappled for the phone and phone book on the reception room desk. The pages would not turn in his clumsy, fumbling hands. "Damn it!" he shouted. He gritted his teeth and willed his fingers to work. He caught the page, the next page, the next, until he reached the *C* listings. Cape May, Public Library. According to the pendulum clock it was eight forty-five. The library closed at eight.

"Be there, be there." Carl forced his index finger into cooperation, placing it with effort on each button, and he dialed the number.

On the wall, the pendulum clock began to run backward.

Deep in the receiver, Carl clung to the sound of the ring. The sound of impending help. *Please please please please answer!*

"Hello?" An exasperated voice. But a voice.

"Is Jeanette Harris there?"

"I'm sorry. She's on her way out. You can call back tomorrow."

Carl grabbed the phone with both hands. His lips scraped the mouthpiece. "Please, please, put her on! I need to talk to her!"

"Is this a prank?"

"No, please, it's important." His voice was quivering. Maybe that was what convinced the woman on the phone.

"Just a minute, then." The phone clacked down, crunching, a distant voice, "Jeanette, there's a kid on the phone who says he needs to talk to you right away."

Something cold brushed the back of Carl's neck. He gasped and looked around. There was nothing.

Then, "Hello? This is Miss Harris."

"Miss Harris," Carl's teeth were chattering, "this is Carl Morrison. We talked before . . ."

"Carl," she interrupted, "if this has anything to do with what Sam might have done to you, I really recommend you call the police and a counselor."

"He didn't do anything, Miss Harris. I swear to God."

"Carl, you can't backtrack. You called me this afternoon. You told me about the letters. Sam came by and confirmed the letters."

"And he told you he was innocent."

"Of course he did."

"He didn't do it. I know it. I believe him. Okay?"

The walls in the reception room began to whisper,

"Saaaaaaaaaaaaaaaaaam!" On the shelf beneath the desk, the guest registry thumped up and down as if trying to get out.

"Shit!"

"Carl, what's wrong?"

"You've got to tell me where he is!"

"I don't know where he is."

Carl could hear Mitchell's footsteps coming down the stairs. *Thump thump.*

"I need to know, quick! He has to come back here and help! I'm . . . I'm scared."

"Of what, Carl? Of the . . ." and the woman's voice changed, ". . . ghosts?"

Carl's heart leapt. "You know about the ghosts?"

"Where are you, Carl?" It was Mitchell at the top of the stairs, his voice crazy and echoing loud like God's. Carl stared at the reception room door.

"Carl," said Jeanette, "what's happening?"

"They killed my mom," Carl managed.

Then the phone went dead in Carl's hands.

Mitchell was in the doorway, his brows a huge line across his blazing eyes, his mustache bristling outward, his fingers strumming the air. "Who're you talking to? I said no police, no coroner, not yet! You didn't listen to me! I'm in charge here!"

"I didn't call them."

"Who did you call?"

The register banged harder on the shelf, up and down, *wham wham wham wham wham.* Mitchell didn't seem to notice it, or the backward clock, or the whispering walls.

"I was trying to find Sam," Carl sputtered.

"Sam?" Mitchell's face registered nothing at first, then, "That pervert? Why?"

"We need him back!"

"For what? I've got my case now, boy!" Mitchell held up his hands and smiled. It was hideous. "I'm making my plan, don't you worry. Those electricians will never work again; I'm going to charge them with manslaughter. But God, if I could make it murder! God, she's gone!" He sobbed, twice, and grabbed for his chest.

The window beside Mitchell's favorite easy chair

opened, then slammed shut. It opened again, slammed shut. Carl clutched the desk, wanting to clutch his father.

"See that? We got to get out of this place!"

Mitchell looked at the window, and for a moment his expression became that of Carl's retired, curmudgeonly father. But that expression drained away, and the crazy man was back. "What, you're afraid of a window? After what your mother has been through, you're scared of a god-damned *window*?"

Carl saw there was nothing he could say to his father. The man was beyond sense. And there was no way he could get Sam back in time to stop the enraged spirit of the inn from tearing things apart. Carl's own power was nothing compared to whatever was raging throughout the Abbadon. He could hum all he wanted and chant all he wanted and cut all he wanted, but the spirit in the Abbadon wanted Sam for some reason, and Sam was the only one who could stop it. Everything else was just in its way.

"We have to leave!" Carl said to his father. He pushed past Mitchell to the front hall and tugged open the door to the foyer. "It's going to kill us like it did Mom!"

With a roar, Mitchell grabbed his son and jerked him back. Carl's teeth snapped down on his tongue, and he screamed. "No!" shouted Mitchell. "You're going nowhere!"

"The place is haunted!" Carl cried around the blood in his mouth. "We'll die!"

Mitchell drew Carl up close to his reddened, maddened, agonized face. "If that's true, then let it have us! I'd rather you and I die here with Rebecca, to be put out of our misery! Carl, I don't want to live without her! I won't let you leave me like she did!"

"No, please, no!"

Mitchell threw Carl back against the staircase and locked the front door.

FORTY-FIVE

~~~~~~~

Sam felt the current before he reached the corner of Columbia and Ocean. It blew around him like a static wind, setting his skin on edge. As the Abbadon Inn came into view, he saw immediately the trouble. Wiping sleet from his eyes, he stared.

Lights flickered off and on in random windows, some of which rode up and down on their sashes. The building seemed to shimmer on its foundation.

"Oh, God," Sam moaned. He crossed the street and stopped at the iron gate. In the third-floor windows, he saw dark figures rise up, flail about, then disappear into the light behind them.

I'm back, he thought. His heart pounded in his gut; his mouth was bitter. *I'm here.*

He reached for the gate. It did not shock him. He went through and up to the front door. He turned the bell key. He heard it chime inside, but no one came. He tested the knob. The door was locked. "Carl?" he called. "Carl!"

The windows along the wraparound porch opened and shut, like anxious mouths waiting for a treat.

"God help me, God help me." Sam went around the left side of the inn, through the lilacs and oaks, and under the porte cochere. He tried the door. It, too, was locked. "Damn!" He shoved his hands into his jacket pockets. His fingers came down onto the bone and instinctively locked around it. It burned him, and he cried out, and he tried to shake it free, but it clung to him, seared to the flesh.

And a vision came.

FORTY-SIX

Mitchell was stronger in his rage and insanity than Carl would have ever imagined. With his gnarly fingers clamped around Carl's arm, he dragged the boy up the stairs. Carl shook and bit at his father, but the man did not let go. He only said, "Carl, enough of this. I need you to calm down so we can make our plan."

At the top of the stairs, Mitchell slapped his son across the face. "Stop being such a baby! We've got important matters to take care of. I need your help." He hauled Carl, kicking and twisting, down to the room where Rebecca lay dead. Mitchell threw Carl into the room. Carl skittered across the floor and thumped against the bed. His mother bounced on the mattress, once.

"Don't leave me—" screamed Carl, but Mitchell slammed the door shut. Carl raced against it, grasping the knob and bearing down with all his weight, but his father was on the other side holding it closed. "Don't leave me in here with her!"

"I'm going after the electricians and the dry-wall men," said Mitchell matter-of-factly through the door. "I think I might be able to hang something on both of them."

"Mitchell!" Carl wailed. He looked back over his shoulder, afraid his mother might be coming up out of her death to stare at him, to come for him, to choke him. But she lay there, eyes out, still uncovered by Mitchell, her blackened hands over her head, her blackened feet drawn up and pointing to the ceiling.

"Mitchell!"

"You won't run away?"

"No, just let me out!" *I'll run away, he can't stop me!*

The windows in the bedroom began to slid open and slam shut. Blood began to ooze from the walls; it ran in rivulets down along the irregularities of the plaster, forming slanting, red letters. They spelled: *Sam. Ford.*

"Mitchell!"

Mitchell let go of the door; Carl twisted the knob and the door flew open. He swung around on it and slammed into the wall. Behind him, he felt the wall coming up around his shoulders, feeling him, as if ready to pull him back into itself. Carl shoved up and away and dashed into the hall.

His father stood there, his eyes wide in horror, staring at something Carl could not see. The man's mouth was closed, but his lips and cheeks worked around and around as if he were trying to open it, trying to speak. Then, suddenly, he was slammed to his side onto the floor with a grunt. Invisible hands snatched him by the ankles and dragged him down the hall toward the room over the porte cochere. Mitchell's eyes bugged, his fingers grappled at the Oriental runner. He screamed from behind sealed lips, begging his son for help, the squashed plea coming out "Kwaw!!!! Kwaw!!!!"

The door to the room swung open. It was pitch black inside.

Carl put his hand over his mouth. *No, God God God God God!*

And before he could turn and run away, something strong and unseen bashed him in the back, driving his breath out and knocking him to the floor. It snatched his feet and pulled him down the hall after his father.

FORTY-SEVEN

Sam was not at the Abbadon Inn. He was in an open field, the same one he'd stood in before. It was late afternoon; the sun sat atop the trees to the west. Slaves were parceled out across the spread, their hunched backs visible over the cotton-heavy plants, picking the clumps of white and putting them into large shoulder bags.

"Old Sam!" called someone from behind. Sam turned to see Massa Josiah on his horse, ambling along the rim of the field, waving his crop. "You bring me Stonie and Jane!"

Sam did not know Stonie and Jane, but he heard himself say, "Yessuh!" He moved through the prickling brush toward a young couple. They heard him coming and glanced up nervously. "What?" asked Stonie. "Jane and me didn' do nothin' wrong, Sam! What you want with us?"

"Massa Josiah's told me to get you two. He's at the edge of the field. Wants you now."

Jane stood straight, her eyes blazing. "We didn' do nothin', Sam, can you tell him that for us? You's an overseer, he trust you, he might listen to you!"

"I'll do what I can, Jane." The young couple put their bags down between the rows and followed Sam out of the field.

I'm an overseer? I'm Sam? Old Sam? Sam Ford?

They reached the master on his horse. The man studied the young couple from beneath the wide brim of his hat, then he said, "Follow me."

The man rode off into the trees, the three slaves followed. Sam thought, *I know this place, the slope of land.*

Massa Josiah spoke without turning around as his horse

clomped down the winding path. "Jane, I understand you've taken to coming around my smokehouse at night."

"I . . ." began Jane. She turned terrified eyes to Sam. "I don' know what you mean, massa."

"And you, Stonie, you've taken to goin' with her on occasion, case she was caught in the act."

Stonie grabbed his wife by the elbow and grimaced. "Massa, I don' know what you talkin' about." Both Stonie and Jane looked at Sam. *Please!* Stonie mouthed. *Please help us!*

"Massa Josiah," said Sam. "I don't know if you heard right 'bout Jane and Stonie. Was there something gone missing?"

"Why," said the man on the horse. He flicked his crop; the horse picked up its pace. "There was at that. A ham. I'd twelve of them, and now one's gone. A reliable source told me Jane was hanging about several nights, trying to get in without notice, but she was noticed all right."

"You sure they seen right? Whoever tole you?" asked Sam. "I been spendin' time at they's cabin most nights. They just staying home, cookin' and cleanin' and mendin'."

The path dipped down and came to a river. *I know this river! I know that boulder, that crooked ash tree. It was old and crooked then and is old and crooked now! This is the land near my house in Albemarle County.*

Josiah dismounted and tethered his horse to the elbow of the crooked ash.

This is the land, this is the plantation that was later divided up and sold. This is the land upon which my grandparents will build their house in 1910. Sam Ford, my ancestor, was an overseer on this very farm.

"Go stand in the river," said Josiah.

Jane and Stonie clutched each other, but they went down and stood in the shallow edge of the water.

He was an overseer. And a secret guide to freedom.

Josiah handed Stonie the crop. He said, "Beat your wife's hands until I tell you to stop."

Stonie looked at the crop as if it were a snake.

Josiah said, "Do it, or I will have you lashed tonight, Stonie, with the whip and with the branch."

Jane's head fell to her chest, and she held her hands out. She sobbed, "Do it, Stonie."

And so Stonie beat the palms of his wife's hands. Beat them as she cried, until they bled, and until her knees buckled in pain, and she went down in the water as if going for baptism. Sam opened his mouth but could not protest, even when Stonie cast him horrified glances.

Then Josiah said, "Enough. That's good. She's learned her lesson. Now, wash the wounds in the river and get back to picking my cotton."

The owner of the plantation took his crop back, mounted his horse, and rode off across the river.

"I'm so sorry," Sam managed.

Stonie rinsed his wife's shredded hands in the rushing water. She sobbed softly. "I know you couldn't say nothin'," Stonie said. "You's overseer, you can't be testin' the massa or it'd be bad for you, too. But we know you's a good man."

"And someday," whispered Sam, "I'll do even better for you. I promise." He recalled their names, Jane and Stonie, from the Abbadon Inn register. After he'd led Roger, Livey, and Matilda to freedom, he'd done the same for this young couple.

Sam rubbed grit from his eyes, tears, perhaps, and when he focused again he was in the slave quarters, in a cabin, alone. He was at the door, looking out. Sam could hear snoring and the sleep-thrashings from the tiny log houses.

In the cabin across the center path, Sam saw two figures, holding each other side-by-side at the door. It was Livey and her mother, Matilda. They were awake while the rest of the quarters slept, staring to the left toward a cross beam planted in the ground next to the glowing embers of a dying fire, and the man . . .

I remember that man. Roger.

. . . tied to it. Beside him, Bernard sat on the ground, smoking a pipe, there to keep the wife and daughter from taking Roger down and spiriting him away.

Massa Josiah had said he would face a final punishment. *I don't want to see!*

But then there were the sounds of a horse's hoofbeats and into the gloomy quarters rode the master, dressed as if going to the best of parties. He sat on his horse and flicked his crop at Bernard, who immediately tapped out his pipe and stood. Then he shouted, "Come out, you sleeping blackies! It's time for Roger's last lesson. Come look at what happens to those who go where they are not to go and see what they are not to see."

Livey screamed and fell into her mother. Her mother held her daughter close.

Roger, who until that moment had been a motionless figure on the crossbeam, came awake, his head snapping up, and his eyes opening. Inside the dark cabins came grunts and cries and muffled curses that the master did not seem to hear, or if he did, found them entertaining. A few looked from their doorways, the rest chose to stay back.

"The slave Roger has been found guilty of the worst of sins," said Massa Josiah, rocking back in his stirrups. "He was seen scuttling about the Big House like a rat several nights ago, and was witnessed climbing the trellis to peer in to the window as my wife, Mistress Della Ford, was in a state of undress in her preparations for bed. A nasty, nasty beast is Roger, fouling my wife's soul with his dirty eyes! Using hands that belong to me, hands that are meant to plant and harvest my crops, to climb the wall to drool over the flesh of my delicate and pure Della!"

Ford? The owner of the plantation was named Ford? My ancestor Sam Ford took his last name from this terrible, cruel man? Why would he do that?

"He didn't do it!" cried Livey. "Somebody tole a lie on him!"

"Child," said Massa Josiah. "You keep quiet, or your father will suffer even the worst for it."

Livey began to weep in great, heaving whoops.

Massa Josiah drew a sword from his side and passed it down to Bernard, who with very little ceremony, raised it and brought it down against the right, bound wrist of Roger. The hand was cleaved from the arm. The arm dropped down, spewing blood, as the hand stayed in place. Roger shrieked and passed out.

"Cauterize it," said the man on the horse.

Bernard grasped the cool end of a log from the fire and held the red-hot tip to the bleeding stump. It sizzled and smoked. Bernard dropped the log and nodded. There was no more blood, only charred flesh and bone.

"There," said Massa Josiah Ford. "He will no longer be able to skillfully climb the trellis at my house. But he should still be able to pick and plant and hoe." The man spun his horse about and vanished, the echo of the hoof beats lingering long. Bernard picked up his pipe, stuffed it in his pocket, and followed after on foot.

Matilda and Livey, with the help several young men, untied Roger and carried him into Malilda's cabin. Sam followed them inside.

The slaves eased Roger onto a pallet and covered him with a blanket. Roger had awakened from his torture, and held his stump to his chest, but though his cheeks pulsed in and out with the pain, he did not make a sound.

"A bandage for that, and a sling," said Sam. "Here." He took off his shirt and ripped it into several strips. He helped Roger to sit and carefully wrapped and pinned the cloth about the stump, then fashioned a sling over Roger's shoulder. Into Sam's ear, Roger whispered, "Thank you."

Matilda lay by her husband. Livey sat beside him. The other slaves quietly left the cabin.

"I know how to get you out of here," Sam heard himself say in a low voice. "Massa Josiah thinks he owns us, but nobody truly owns us but God. I know the way to go. I know safe places to hide. Massa Josiah has a bad taste for you, Roger, and so has it for your wife and daughter, too. Who can say what he might have in mind for them, up at the Big House, if he takes a shinin'? Follow me, and I'll guide you safely to freedom."

Roger, teeth gritted tightly, managed, "Yes. We'll go with you."

"I'll check to see if the way is clear from the quarters," said Sam.

Matilda nodded.

"Thank you," said Roger.

Sam felt his gut clench in joy and in fear, but then he heard someone scream . . .

A boy screamed.

. . . and he didn't know who it was and where it was, but the floor of the cabin shivered, shimmied, and disappeared. Sam was standing, alone in the cold, beneath the porte cochere at the Abbadon Inn.

The scream he'd heard was Carl's.

Sam shoved the bone into his pocket and yanked on the door. It would not open. He snatched a large stone from the ground and threw it through the glass, then reached in to unlock the latch. Sharp glass raked his hand, his jacket sleeve. The door popped open.

"Sam!"

The caller was not Carl or ghosts but Jeanette, standing outside the porte cochere in the sleet, her hands to her mouth, her eyes large and unblinking, her uncovered hair speckled with water.

"Jeanette, get back, go away!"

"Carl called! I came right away. I think he's in danger! He said his mother is dead!"

"Jeanette, get away! It's not safe!"

"Do you think it's . . . ghosts?"

"Yes! But they want me, not him!"

Sam pushed through the door, into the office. Jeanette ran after him, her shoes crushing the broken glass. "Let me help!"

"Why?" Sam spun about and stared. "You think I'm a pervert. You think I'm a child molester! Get out of here!" Clenching his right hand in his left, he passed through the reception room to the foot of the main staircase. Jeanette did not follow.

He took the steps three at a time, reached the second floor and spun into the hall. He blinked, not believing what he was seeing. Carl and Mitchell on their backs, sliding down the hall toward the open door at the end. Both clawed at the floor, at the runner, but something unseen and powerful had them by the ankles and dragged them, bumping and yelling. The sconces on the wall had turned their brass heads toward the scene, following it like spectators watching a passing Fourth of July parade.

Sam ran for them, but the floor turned to mud beneath his feet, and he sank ankle-deep in the mire. "Carl!" he shouted. Carl looked back over his head and cried, "Sam!"

And then before Sam could even blink, Mitchell and Carl were yanked, one after the other, into the sunroom, and the door slammed shut.

Leaning forward, Sam worked against the suction of the mire. The sconces spread brass teeth and laughed tiny, tinny laughs. They let out long, cold breaths, filled with the dead-smell. Metal tongues lapped the air. Sam reached the door, twisted the knob, but it was locked. "Fuck!" He slammed into it with his shoulder, and it rattled but held. He rammed it again and felt the bone pop out of the joint and back in again. Bright pain exploded behind his eyes. Again, he threw himself into the door, feeling the dislocation and a faint snap. Jagged stars cut through his side to the base of his skull. The door blew inward with a *thwak!*

Sam stumbled through the barren room to the open door of a small closet in the corner. His shoulder bone grated in place; the shoulder bone in his pocket burned his hip.

Inside the closet was a steel spiral staircase, rattly and rusty, the center pole pulling loose from its bolts at the bottom. Grasping the metal railing, Sam bolted up the steps, around and around the tight, dizzying circles. The dead-smell oozed from the walls in the narrow shaft. Overhead, beyond the walls, the pounding began.

Boom Boom Boom Boom Boom!

A hammer into soft flesh.

"Carl!" Sam called.

"Sam!" screamed Carl.

The steps began to crack beneath Sam's weight. The length of the staircase seemed to stretch out above him, but he closed his eyes and took the last stairs with a burst of determination. He ran headlong into the closed door at the top. The stairs wobbled mightily beneath him, threatening to fold and collapse. He grabbed for the door latch. His shoulder and hand screamed at the abuse.

"Hang on, Carl!"

Boom Boom Boom!

Sam came through the door, his feet skidding on loose dirt. He stopped, panting. The stench in the low-ceilinged room was strong and hot, the air frigid.

Mitchell was up against a wall, his face twisted and bloodied, his mustache standing out like legs on a dead centipede. One arm was pinned over his head; his feet were flush against the baseboards. He struggled, and Sam could hear the clinking of invisible leg irons. With each boom, Mitchell's body shook, and he made a pinched, *whelping* sound. His raised left hand jiggled in place, and blood spurted from his palm in myriad spots. He was being nailed to the wall. Then his right hand was slapped up over his head and pressed to the plaster.

Mitchell burst into helpless, agonized tears.

Carl cowered on the floor. Large dark spiders clung to the ceiling and the corners, watching with their bright eye-clusters.

"What do you want?" cried Sam to the ceiling.

Boom Boom Boom!

Mitchell sobbed, squealed, and twisted against the invisible nails.

"I've tried to listen to you!" Sam said, "I've tried to hear you, but I don't understand what is happening. I know you are angry with me, but what did I do?"

Carl pleaded, "Sam, help us!"

Sam raised his arms and spread his fingers, demanding, pleading. His chest heaved. His heart ached. "Tell me what you want!"

The room went suddenly still, terrifyingly silent as if something huge had taken a breath and was holding it. The only sound was that of Carl, softly whimpering.

"What do you want?" Sam repeated.

And the voice came, bellowing but distorted, as if speaking through century-old lips, across one hundred years' time.

"I want you, Old Sam, punished and dead!"

"But I . . . he, Old Sam . . . only tried to help!"

"You, Old Sam," continued the voice, "and those of the Abbadon Inn!"

Mitchell's head rolled, twisted back and forth against the wall.

Then Carl was lifted and slammed against the wall opposite his father. With a clinking of unseen chains, his feet were secured. He wrapped his arms around his waist and balled his fists to try to prevent what had happened to his father from happening to him. Terror sucked his voice away, and he could not scream. Instead, his red-panicked eyes turned to Sam.

"I am not Old Sam Ford!" Sam cried. "These are not the Abbadons! Look what I found in the shed! I want to help!"

He removed the shoulder bone and held it up, but he was suddenly grasped around the neck by forces unseen and was dragged toward a third wall.

"Wait, damn it, look!"

As he clutched the bone, the room rippled, faded, and was gone. The earlier vision continued . . .

He was Old Sam, and he stood at night in the backyard of the Abbadon Inn beside a travel-weary Roger, Livey, and Matilda. Light from the moon puddled on the grass, crickets and cicadas chirring curiously. Lights glowed in various windows of the inn. From downstairs there came the sound of a piano, singing, and drunken laughter. Through upstairs windows floated giggles and grunts.

Sam kicked the closed bulkhead four times, then another four times. He smiled at the fugitives. All three were scratched and filthy. Roger was especially gaunt and worn. They had been on the run for three weeks, moving at night, hiding during the day. Roger's stump had pained the man greatly, and he had occasionally cried out in his sleep. But when they were awake and moving, he kept his agony to himself.

There was a voice within the cellar, and then the bulkhead doors were pushed up and open. Sam led the family down the steps into the dank and musty room.

A woman stood with a lantern. Clearly she was not a maid or servant. She was dressed in a fine, blue dress with velvet trim and wide skirt. At her neck were a string of pearls. She was dark of feature but was not Negro. Her hair was midnight-black, and drawn up beneath a lace cap, but her eyes were an almost colorless gray.

"Welcome, Old Sam. We are happy you have made it to Cape May."

"Evenin', Lillith," said Sam, bending in a slight bow. *So this is Lillith of the infamous bed. She is truly beautiful, but her eyes are empty.* "We got here Roger, his wife, Matilda, and daughter, Livey."

How does Lillith know me? Yes, wait, I've been here before. My name is in the register several times.

Lillith stepped forward, holding the lantern out to better see their faces. "Lovely, lovely." Her vaguely pink lips spread in a wide, thin smile. She smelled of sweet perfume and whiskey. "I am happy you've made it from the sin of slavery to our nest of safety. You will stay here until I can arrange for all our guests to be out of the way. We shall spirit you upstairs to our secret room as soon as possible. There, you can bathe and rest. And we will have a warm meal for you."

Matilda said, "Thank you, ma'am."

Livey said, "Thank 'um."

Roger nodded his head gratefully. Lillith turned and with a rustling of skirts, took the lantern up the wooden stairs and into the body of the inn. The light trailed her, and when she closed the door behind her, the four were in darkness.

"I don't like it here," said Livey.

"Shhh," said Matilda.

They waited for a long time. Roger stood with his arms crossed while Matilda and Livey huddled together on a bundle of rags. Sam sat on the bottom step. Every so often, Livey would say, "Mama, there's another spider!" And indeed, there were spiders in the cellar, strange, huge spiders the color of coal, scuttling across the floor in search of water and food. Sam drew his legs up so the spiders would not cross his feet.

At long last the door at the top of the stairs opened, and Lillith called, "Come."

The guests were in the casino off the main hall behind

the French doors. The doors were closed and the curtains on the doors drawn. There was no one in the reception room. Lillith directed them to wait there, saying, "I shall go for the proprietor."

Beeswax candles glowed in reflective wall stands, and a pleasant fire crackled in the hearth. Framed paintings on the wall showed exotic locations—waterfalls, colorful cafés, snowy and ragged mountain peaks. On the low mahogany desk sat an inkwell and pen, and a large, leather-bound register.

That is the book. That is where we sign.

Then the man came in. He looked as he did in Sam's dream and in Jeanette's photo, his hair dark and his skin light, his eyes set deep and shining as if with a light of their own. Sam's heart clenched. *He scares me still, though I don't know why. He offers his home, his food, to enslaved peoples who have come with nothing to offer in return.*

Nicholas Abbadon shook Sam's hand—a cool and firm grasp—and smiled at the newcomers. "I welcome you to the Abbadon Inn. Please, sign in to mark your arrival and the first true day of freedom."

Nicholas flipped the book open to the back and picked up the pen. He looked at Roger. "Your names, please?"

Roger put his arm on his wife's shoulder, though he retained his reserved demeanor. It was clear he was not totally comfortable in this man's elegant establishment. "This is Matilda. My girl's Livey. I'm Roger."

"Roger. Matilda. Livey," said Nicholas. He wrote them in the book with a steady hand, dated them, then spun the book around. "Put your mark here." He handed the pen to Roger, who looked at it uncertainly. Then he scanned the names that came before and followed suit, forming an *X* beside his name. Matilda and Livey did the same. Sam then took the pen and wrote confidently beneath them, "Sam Ford." When he looked up at Nicholas, the man gave him a slow and cunning wink, which made Sam's blood chill.

Nicholas led them to the third floor. Lillith was there to meet them, her hands folded properly at her waist. Her near-white eyes reflected light from the cheap, coal oil lamps that smoked and sputtered in tin wall holders. Behind closed doors were sounds of women entertaining men. The air smelled of sex, verbena, and an underlying drift of decay.

"Roger," Lillith said with a nod, "Your bath is there, and clean clothes. Please bathe, change, and join us in the room at the end of the hall. It is where you will reside until it is time to leave. Matilda, Livey, your room is across from Roger's. Likewise there is a bath and nice clothing. Bathe, and come down quietly to the little room."

Obediently the family parted ways and entered the assigned rooms. Sam stood in the hall with Nicholas and Lillith. No one spoke, but two of the other bedroom doors opened, and smiling, painted whore faces appeared there, and with them, the men they were entertaining.

Nicholas waved them back. "Soon," he said calmly. "Soon."

Soon?

Twenty minutes later, Roger appeared in the hall in simple yet clean shirt and trousers. Matilda and Livey were five minutes after, both in fresh and simple dresses. Nicholas and Lillith nodded. They went to the end of the hall, opened the door to the room over the porte cochere, and ushered everyone in.

Lillith shut the door. Nicholas pulled out his pistol.

"You did well, Old Sam," said Nicholas. "They never suspected a thing, did they? Had we theater for Negroes here in Cape May, I don't doubt your ability at playacting would have you a fine career."

"Thank you, Mr. Abbadon, sir," said Sam, bowing slightly.

"Put them up."

"Yessir."

There were leg irons on the floor, bolted to the wall. Sam grabbed Roger by the arm and pulled him, but the man, suddenly aware of the trap into which he'd fallen, spun about and slammed Sam on the side of the head. Sam growled and struck back, catching Roger against the chin, and the man, weak from his wounds and the journey, stumbled and dropped to his knees. Nicholas fired a shot beside the man's feet. "Sam, pull him up and put him up."

Sam shoved Roger against the wall. As Nicholas trained the muzzle of the gun up and down the man's body, Sam snapped the chains about Roger's ankles. Sam saw the engraving on the irons. "Obedience is Freedom."

Matilda and Livey cried but did not fight when it was each their turn. Lillith went to them, pulling sewing shears from her skirt pocket, and began to snip the clothing from their bodies.

"I've enjoyed my trips south," Nicholas said to Sam. "I do love Southern hospitality. I shall continue to travel there, meeting and dining with plantation owners. Offering them a fine bit of money to 'encourage,' shall we say, some of their slaves to run away, to escape and head north, more money than they would have gotten for the very same blackbirds on the fair market. Of course, these runaways need reliable guides, such as yourself, to make sure they don't take Moses' path but our own, across Delaware Bay, to the comforts of the Abbadon Inn." He smiled. Sam smiled, too, and was sickened by the feeling of that smile.

Then he was aware of the bone in his hand. He did not want to see more of the past. He hurled it away and heard it clatter on the floor. But still he was being forced against the wall, still he could feel the ghostly leg irons clamped about his ankles. He struggled and dug at his eyes with the heel of his hand. He could see Carl near him, his feet against the wall, but thankfully not yet crucified, as the spirit was concentrating on Sam. But then, like a transparency laid over reality, Sam could see the continuing story from 1857. Roger, Matilda, and Livey, naked on the wall. Roger's only hand nailed to the wall above his head. Matilda's hands likewise nailed. Livey's hands over her face, blocking out the horror. Nicholas to one side of Sam, nodding in satisfaction. Lillith to Sam's other side, slipping her arm through his, whispering seductively, "I like your hands, Sam. Strong hands, guiding your people to us. Trustworthy hands, doing what we ask without a moment's hestitation. Big hands, large enough to cup my breasts and probe my body. Bring those hands to my room before you leave, Sam. I have a new bed. Come, try the bed with me."

Lillith let go of Sam and opened the door. Six men in

boots, trousers, and unbuttoned shirts came in, rubbing
their hands and looking longingly at the figures on the
wall. Nicholas said simply, "These slaves are ready for
you, positioned as you requested. You've paid ahead of
time, in full. Do what you will with them. I only ask that
when you are done, do not leave the bodies on the wall. We
have the backstairs," he nodded at the spiral staircase
closet. "When you are finished, the remains will be taken
down to the kitchen out back."

Lillith left the room. Nicholas took a money pouch
from his jacket pocket and pressed ten gold coins into
Sam's hand. "Well done," Nicholas said. "We shall see you
in another few months, then?"

Sam nodded. He pointed to Roger, who glared back.
With a wink Sam said, "Don't be climbin' no more trellises, boy! You know the end can't be nothin' but trouble."
And then the Abbadon guests swarmed the chained runaways, engulfed them. Sam and Nicholas turned away. The
screams began.

FORTY-EIGHT

The vision was done. Sam knew the truth. It was in this inn, in this room, where Roger, his family, and other slaves were given to the Abbadon Inn guests who had made the highest bids. Slaves who had died at their hands and were buried unceremoniously in the walls and floor of the backyard shed. Slaves led to Cape May by Old Sam Ford. An overseer who pretended to be caring, but who was only out to make himself some money and buy himself some comforts. Who had even given himself the last name of the cruel and conspiratorial master who let him pretend to take business trips in order to guide runaways to the clutches of Nicholas Abbadon.

Against the cold wall, Sam felt the leg irons click in place. He felt the powerful spirit hand snatch his left wrist and force it up and over his head.

"Sam!" wailed Carl.

"Stop! Listen!" Sam shouted.

"I will do to you what you did to my family!" bellowed the voice. The walls reverberated. "What you did to me!"

"I'm not Old Sam! You thought I was when you saw my signature in the book! You thought I was he, but I am not! I am his descendent!"

"Listen to him!" screamed Carl, his head whipping back and forth, his eyes searching the room for the source of the dreadful voice. "Listen to Sam!"

"I am a good man," Sam insisted, "grown on the twisted branch of my family tree. Though Old Sam's blood runs in my veins, I have never done a cruel thing to another person. I want to make this right!"

He felt sharp pressure in the center of his palm. *God no no no!* "Hear me! Roger, hear me out! You thought I was

Old Sam. You wanted revenge. And when Mitchell threw me out of the inn, you could no longer reach me. Your rage blew wide open, taking Mitchell and Carl with it. Your rage has made you blind!"

There was a whoosh of air and an explosion of pain in the center of Sam's hand. The back of his head whacked the wall, and he bore down with his teeth so he would not cry out. Sweat beaded on his forehead and his upper lip. "Roger," he panted. "I'm not Old Sam, the betraying overseer. I'm Sam Ford, a teacher who has tried his best to live a good life. Your spirit is chained here. And from this place of torment, from this dark land between the living and the dead, you can still see many things, you can still feel many things. See this now, Roger. Look into my mind and see who I am and what I have been. I've been careless many times, and I have been weak. Forgive me that, if you can. But look, see, who I truly am."

The invisible hand grabbed his right arm and forced it up against the wall. Sam gritted his teeth in expectation of the second blow of the nail into the already butchered flesh. But it did not come. The ghost had stopped to listen.

Sam pressed on. "While you were living, you were a fair, godly man, a good man! I understand the need for justice and resolution. I am a good man, too. Look, Roger. Look and see."

He held his breath then, and waited. He closed his eyes, offering the anguished ghost the chance to look into him.

Help us. Help Roger.

Then he felt it. At first it was a strangely pleasant sensation, like warm water pouring over his scalp into his pores. But the feeling shifted as the warmth moved into his brain and began to explore. He felt suddenly sick. He took deep breaths through his mouth to counter the nausea. Behind his closed lids, in the swirling darkness, he caught bright, brief glimpses of the memories Roger probed. Sam as a baby, at home in the little house his grandparents had built on the remnants of the Ford plantation. Geary and Sam on the elementary school playground on a warm April afternoon, swinging side by side, talking about Curtis Roberts batting for the Pittsburgh Pirates for the first time. Sam rescuing a dog from a raccoon trap and nursing it to health. Sam pounding away on his father's typewriter, composing a cordial but firm letter to the editor about the poor condition of the county's schools for black children. Fighting with Robbie over the merits of the Vietnam War. Struggling with the teens who had stopped their truck on the side of the road; Sam fighting back with all his might— swinging, slashing out, holding Rose behind him until one boy caught Sam over the ear with a baseball bat, and he went down in the road.

I don't remember fighting them. But now I do. I did fight for Rose! I didn't just stand there and let them hurt me and take her. I tried. I forgot that. I did try!

The cool and ghostly fingers continued to dig through Sam's life. His sophomore class at the university when Sam virulently debated DuBois over Washington. Comforting his father at his mother's graveside, his arm around the large man as he wept. Holding his father's hand as the old man died in his sweat-soaked bed, trembling and praying God forgiveness for his sins, Sam assuring his father that God's great arms held no condemnation. Sam's first class at the high school, filled with myriad white and black faces, and Sam vowing to himself that first day to see each student as something beyond their color, their family, their fears. Sam, caught up in his own fear, paying off Diana Spradlin and packing his Nova in haste and rage. Sam taking Carl up the steps to the top of the Cape May Lighthouse, standing with the boy in the salty wind, hoping the cold air might clear Carl's mind so he could learn and grow; hoping that the same wind would wash away the nagging doubts Sam had about himself and his bungled life.

And then Sam felt the fingers move down his throat to his heart. The fingers pressed against the beating organ and held there, curious. Sam felt himself rise beneath the touch. Tears welled. Roger knew. Roger knew the truth that was Sam Ford.

"Roger," Sam whispered. "I've tried to do right. You did, too. You were good, strong, and just your whole life. It should have been a longer life. It should have been a life lived in freedom with your wife and your daughter. But the evil that rose up was strong. Evil that lived in this inn."

The fingers released Sam's heart. It sounded as if the spirit took a breath and held it.

"But you've already killed one innocent person," Sam said. "Rebecca Morrison was not Lillith. Rebecca was not guilty."

The floor of the room began to shudder. Carl shrieked. Mitchell groaned.

"Mitchell is not guilty. Carl is not guilty. I am not guilty."

Window glass burst inward and chunks of plaster from the ceiling fell loose in dusty shards.

"You didn't know what you were doing, Roger. But now you do! What can I do to put you at peace?"

As the vibrations increased, Sam struggled to keep upright, so he would not pitch forward and break his legs. The walls to the spiral staircase closet fell loose and crashed to the floor.

"Roger, how can I put you at rest?"

More ceiling pieces rained down. And then the booming, ancient voice said, "Take my bones and those of my family. Return them to the plantation. Bury them on that land. We were slaves there, but it is there that my aunts, uncles, and friends lay at rest. I want to join them and be free of the Abbadon Inn."

"I will!" shouted Sam around the noise of the collapsing room. But then, more gently, "Roger, God help me, I will."

He felt the leg irons vanish from around him. He toppled forward, catching himself on his bloodied hands. He glanced up to see both Carl and Mitchell tumble forward, too, toward the center of the room.

And at that moment, the entire room fell away from the Abbadon Inn, crushing the sunroom and the porte cochere beneath it.

FORTY-NINE

He wasn't dead, and it had stopped sleeting, those were his first realizations. He was bruised and banged up and sore. He'd bitten the inside of his cheek, and it was bleeding and raw. His wrenched shoulder was now certainly broken. His right hand bore a wide, gaping hole once more, all the stitches stripped. But he was alive. Somewhere nearby he could hear the whine of sirens. They seemed to be coming closer.

Sam sat up in the rubble, carefully, favoring his left side. Clouds of debris rose from the ruins like spirits ascending to heaven. The torture room had been pruned from the inn.

"Carl? Mitchell?" he called.

"I'm here, Sam." It was Carl. He scrambled from beneath a chunk of drywall, and stumbled over the boards and glass to Sam. His Mohawk was flattened, his face streaked in dirt and blood.

"I'm here," he said. He fell into his tutor's arms, and Sam held him closely. The boy smelled of cookies.

Then Carl said, "I think Mitchell is dead."

They searched for Carl's father and found him tossed free of the wreckage, crumpled on his side in the wet grass next to one of the inn's great oaks. Carl chewed his nails as Sam knelt with effort by the man, leaned down, and listened. Mitchell was breathing. Sam smiled faintly and nodded at the boy. "He's alive."

"I went across the street and called the police." Sam looked up. Beside a tangled, barren lilac, her arms tight across her chest, stood Jeanette. She was shivering with cold and adrenalin. "And the rescue squad, too. They're on their way. What Carl said on the phone, about his mother, the danger. Then, then there was the noise up there," she nodded toward the brutal scar on the inn where the rooms over the porte cochere had sat. "I don't know what happened, but my God. I heard the screams! I saw it fall!"

"Thanks for calling," said Sam.

"I'm . . ." she seemed at a loss for words, choking over the reality before her. "I'm sorry. So sorry. Will you forgive me?"

Seven times seven.

"Jeanette, there's nothing to forgive."

Sam turned back to Carl, who was staring at his father. Mitchell made a sound and stirred, then reached out his hand. Carl took it.

"He's going to be okay," Sam said again.

The boy burst into tears.

FIFTY

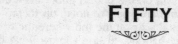

The bus rattled along Route 29 in the late afternoon sun, heading south from Washington D.C., taking a more straightforward route to Virginia than Sam had taken from it. White rail fences caught the light and tossed it back toward the road. Horses in fields flicked their tails and chewed at the early spring grass. A train on a roadside track struggled to keep up with the bus and then vanished along a curve into a strip of trees.

Sam sat near the front, across the aisle from a pair of high school girls who were going home from a shopping trip in the Capital City. They looked in and out of their shopping bags, comparing their new clothes, planning the party to which they would wear them. The middle-aged man in front of the girls cast disparaging glances their way, and then over at Sam, seeking someone simpatico. But Sam only smiled and shrugged. He didn't mind the loud chatter and laughter. These were kids, good kids, having a good time. Sure, they'd clearly skipped school, but sometimes you just had to take a little time off, go somewhere different, and find something new.

The large suitcase had been checked beneath the bus. The carpetbag he held in his lap. Inside were letters, damning letters that he would show Geary and then burn. The Joy Spradlin episode in his life was over. She and her mother were finished hurting him. He was strong. He would start over.

Perhaps he would apply for a position at Jefferson in the fall if there were an opening in the social studies department. He'd not left on a bad note; he had only left. Or he might tutor out of his home. Either way, he would continue teaching. He would continue studying history, maybe find out something more about his mysterious and merciless ancestor, Old Sam. What he would do with the knowledge, he couldn't know. But it was always better to know than not. And he would care for his little house on his small plot of land.

He would be home.

So, too, would the bones in the carpetbag.

Sam had known by touch which of the bones belonged to Roger, Matilda, and Livey. They weren't warmer, or cooler, but had a bristling energy he recognized, that Roger let him recognize. Sam had worked them free with a chisel and hammer, had wrapped them in a towel from the Surf 'n' Sand, and stowed them in the bag. Carl would have been fascinated with the excavation, but he had not been there. He was spending his time at Burdette Tomlin Memorial Hospital with his father, who was recovering, and who had promised his son they would move back to Danbury as soon as he was able. According to preliminary investigations by Cape May authorities, the death of Rebecca Morrison had been due to faulty electrical wiring, and the collapse of the rooms over the porte cochere the result of years of neglect and water damage causing rotted floorboards and weakened walls. These reports were not enough to convince the Morrisons to stay. They knew better.

Carl was spending his days at the hospital and his nights with Jeanette. Sam had the librarian's address and phone number on a little piece of paper in his pocket, though he didn't know if he would contact her. At the moment it didn't seem right. Later, perhaps.

Sam drew the carpetbag closer. He hoped he had collected all the bones, but couldn't be sure. He wondered, too, about the other bones buried in the old kitchen in the backyard of the Abbadon Inn. Where did they belong? Would they ever go home? Would they ever have peace?

He tilted his seat back and looked out the window at the setting sun. He wondered if anyone would buy the Abbadon Inn from Mitchell Morrison. He wondered what else might be lingering in the dreadful hallways, the barren

bedrooms, and the eerie cellar, waiting for acknowledge-
ment, waiting to be discovered.

He wondered, but did not wonder long. It didn't matter.
He had other things to think of, other things to consider.

All right, then, he thought.

All right.

New York Times bestselling author

MICHAEL MARSHALL

THE STRAW MEN

0-515-13427-9

Three seemingly unrelated events are the
first signs of an unimaginable network of fear that will
lead one unlikely hero to a chilling confrontation with
The Straw Men. No one knows what they want—or
why they kill. But they must be stopped.

THE UPRIGHT MAN

0-515-13638-7

Ward Hopkins is afraid. He's seen something dreadful
in the high plains of the Columbia River. It's sent him
fleeing cross country, forever running. And in his wake,
one by one, people are dying.
Something's following Ward Hopkins.

Coming September 2005
BLOOD OF ANGELS

0-515-14008-2

The thrilling conclusion to the *Straw Men* trilogy.

Available wherever books are sold or at penguin.com

J006